L.G. BURBANK

PRESENTS

LORDS OF DARKNESS

VOL. 1

THE SOULLESS

Dedication,
For Ed and Leland who have taught me much about love,
souls and courage against all odds. And for Mary, Wendy,
Connie and Ali, women I'm proud to call my friends.

October 2004
Published by Medallion Press, Inc.
225 Seabreeze Ave.
Palm Beach, FL 33480

Printed in the United States of America

Library of Congress Cataloging-in-Publication Data

Burbank, L. G.
  The soulless / by L.G. Burbank.
      p. cm. -- (Lords of darkness series ; v. 1)
   ISBN 0-9743639-9-5 (pbk.)
   1. Vampires--Fiction. 2. Highlands (Scotland)--Fiction. 3. Egypt--Fiction. I. Title
PS3602.U727S68 2004
813'.6--dc22

                                2004019297

For more great books visit www.medallionpress.com.

Acknowledgments

I am grateful for the fans who have waited so long for this. Many thanks for your patience and support.

A big shout to my Soul Sister, Helen. Thanks for making your wicked red pen bleed on this manuscript. You took the story and molded into the book it was meant to be and I am blessed for it.

Thanks go to Pam for her part in the 'bleeding pen' routine.

And to Terri for listening to my many woes along the way.

My thanks to Kelli for her unending support of this project in its many forms.

A huge thanks to Jamie, the one who works miracles with manuscripts, bringing them to this final form. She never gets any credit for the amazing job she does. . .well this time you did!

And last, but most certainly not least, I humbly extend my gratitude to Adam for so many things. Your knowledge, faith, and passion for life gave Soulless its soul. And the cover and illustrations are awesome! Thank you for believing.

L.G. BURBANK

PRESENTS
LORDS OF DARKNESS

VOL. 1

THE SOULLESS

GOLD IMPRINT
MEDALLION PRESS, INC.
FLORDIA, USA

The Black Sea

BYZANTIUM

Constantinople

Dorylaeum

BYZANTIUM

The
Mediterranean
Sea

HarMeggido

Jerusalem

The
Dead
Sea

EGYPT

Tanis

Petra

Giza

The River Nile

The Red Sea

1147 AD

THE JOURNEY OF
MORDRED SOULIS
FROM BYZANTIUM
TO EGYPT

CHAPTER ONE

Death mocked him, as surely as the mirage of a beautiful oasis wavered in front of him. It goaded him into believing paradise was just beyond the next golden dune. It whispered to Mordred of a quiet darkness where his pain and misery would slip away.

This was now a battle of wills, though Mordred's was fast waning. The savage heat rested upon his burned shoulders. It burdened him as if he were carrying a thousand men. He was familiar with war and the consequences if one wasn't fast enough with a blade. Fighting was instinctual within Mordred. It was what made him the highest paid of mercenary knights. But now, he fought an unseen enemy that toyed with him at every turn.

"I will not die!"

The roar of his words was quickly carried away by the rising wind. Howling, it twisted and wrapped itself around him, hampering his progress. Mordred dragged the remains of his tattered hauberk across the barely healed scars of his most recent conflict. He groaned at the searing pain.

The sand threatened to choke the life from him. The granules of gold left a metallic taste in his mouth that no amount of coughing or gagging could jar loose. And he didn't want to spit for fear he would lose what little water was left in his body.

The gritty particles blew into his eyes, ears, and nose as well as his throat. His lungs had to be completely full of it, he thought. His breathing was now labored. His chest rose and fell slowly, heavily, struggling under the thick air and dust.

No, damn it! This was not how he was going to die. He was not going to lose to death. He had vengeance in his heart, and he would live to see the day he carried it out. He would live to see his enemy pay.

Yet, even as those thoughts drifted through the haze that filled his mind, another voice told him this was the end. This was the way he would die. It was the furthest thing from how he had imagined his death would be. Mordred had always seen his demise as the last great act of a man long misunderstood. Wearing his polished plate armor, riding a finely decorated destrier, he would advance against insurmountable odds. With his final breath would come the sweet taste of victory.

His name would live on. He would be a hero. Even though he had never pledged fealty to any king or country, Mordred was sure there would be, in the end, someone who would recognize the man he had been. Though a mercenary, he would be revered as the kind of man kings dream of.

But, that wasn't the way of things now. Here he

was, lost, alone, and starving. His flesh was raw where the ragged mail shirt, its rings broken and torn away, touched him. The hot metal branded him in countless places beneath the sweat soaked aketon. He had long since divested himself of his plate armor. He'd learned early on it was a hindrance in this inhospitable land. Most of those men who gave up their armor quickly felt the deadly sting of arrows from the infidels. Mordred had determined he would rather take his chances with the weapons of the *Faris,* than find himself scorched alive by the molten metal pieces. He had removed the coverings on his chest and arms.

The muscles in his legs ached from the absence of water. It felt as though they were columns of dust. They seemed barely able to sustain his weight. Mordred tore the remaining pieces of the mail cuisses from his thighs. He pulled the scales of the metal greaves from the lower part of his legs.

It did no good. He felt he could strip himself naked. He could expose to the sun what flesh wasn't already marred by blisters. Still his body would simply turn to ash. And he marveled, in his stupor, that he was still alive and enduring this hell.

Thousands of men had fallen beneath the accurate aim of the desert people. They would ride out from seemingly nowhere on small horses, at incredible speeds. They would loose their arrows upon the knights and soldiers. Sometimes countless metal barbs found a home in one man alone. The horsemen would then disappear in the dust and haze created by the heat, long before the troops could rally a modicum of response.

It had been this way ever since the slaughter at Dorylaeum.

He winced at the thought. He tried to wipe away the horrors of that fateful day. Mordred reflected upon the devastation and destruction. It had come from the bowels of hell itself. If ever he had questioned the existence of a god, it had been that bloody day.

† † †

"We'll rest here," the King said

"We should not stop," Mordred Soulis said, keeping his voice low so only King Conrad could hear him. The King prided himself on his position. He did not like anyone to openly contradict or undermine his authority. Mordred hated playing these games. It wasted precious time. "Sire?"

"Soulis, look at the men, they're dead on their feet. They need water and rest. What on earth could be the harm in stopping for an hour or two? We've seen no sign of trouble."

Glancing around him, Mordred searched the rocky slopes and scrub brush. He could not shake the overwhelming feeling that they were being watched. Something was stalking them. Something unseen.

The King did speak truthfully, however. The men were in desperate need of relief, and the horses needed water as well.

"I still feel we should push on and get through this canyon before we stop. Let us get to someplace more open so we can defend ourselves properly. Here, we are

4

like caged animals if the enemy should come upon us. We cannot even draw our swords without striking one another, and our horses will be in the way."

The King gazed at Mordred disapprovingly. There was no love lost between the two. Mordred's only solace was in knowing the King was wise enough to hire the most lethal mercenary money could afford. That alone had saved his royal ass several times. Mordred watched as the King tried to come up with a reason to debate his logic.

"Sire, I mean no disrespect, but look at the way the walls of this canyon rise. If we are attacked from behind, there is only one way forward, and we know not where that lies. I think we should press on."

A crashing sound came to their ears, causing both men to turn and look behind them. One of the foot soldiers lay in a pile of dented armor. Another soldier gazed up at the king. "Sire, he's fainted from the heat and lack of water. We must stop."

King Conrad shifted in his saddle. His long flowing robes did little to conceal his own discomfort. He looked ahead and saw the greenery, more greenery than he'd seen in the weeks since they had left Byzantium. His men needed to rest, and he'd be damned if he'd let one overly cautious mercenary contradict his authority. After all, better to have the troops happy and rested than angry and dropping like flies in the sand.

Grimacing, the King looked at Mordred. "You go on ahead and scout. We'll stop here until you come back and tell us if there's something better ahead." The King turned to the waiting soldier and told him,

5

"Get those men out of the damned armor."

Mordred clenched his jaw. God, how he hated this land, hated this King, and hated this crusade. Without another word, Mordred urged his horse forward. Despite the large number of men, he felt entirely too vulnerable.

Slowly, he picked his way among the rocks, forging ahead. The sound of the army behind him was swept away by the hot, unceasing wind. It roared in his ears. Swirling columns of dust and dirt blew through the canyon in huge spirals.

The heat was so intense that its waves were visible to the eye. The white rocks reflected the sun, forcing Mordred to keep his eyes narrowed. He felt as though he were being cooked alive.

With his thoughts focused on the King and the crusade, it took Mordred a moment to realize the wind had stopped. Everything along the floor of the canyon stilled for barely a heartbeat; then the ground, as well as the sheer walls, seemed to vibrate. Mordred's horse threw his head up and down, prancing nervously beneath the rider.

Then came the sound of thunder. He thought the noise might be the harbinger of an unexpected storm, but the sky was the same blue it had been when they had started out in the morning. There were no clouds.

No, the noise could only mean one thing . . . the *Faris* had returned. As soon as the thought took shape in his mind, the earth opened up around him in a flurry of horses' hooves, crashing armor, bloodcurdling war cries, and the screams of the dying. The macabre chorus echoed off the stones. Mordred likened the sound to the wailing of banshees, the spirit beings who predicted death.

Gathering his wits, Mordred kicked his mount into a gallop. He kept himself low to his horse's neck for protection. The remaining mail on his chest and the armor on his legs chaffed him. They irritated the open, blistering sores on his cracked skin.

Man and beast raced through the canyon. The scene that spread before him would have made a grown man want to retch, and for Mordred it did nothing less. He quickly fought the urge to release the contents of his stomach and smoothly dismounted his galloping horse. He struggled to compensate for the pieces of plate armor he no longer wore.

Landing on his feet with the grace of a man born to war, Mordred took no time to survey his immediate surroundings. He launched himself directly into the storm of steel and arrows. With his heavy sword he began great, sweeping motions, arcing toward the riders on their small, swift steeds. He was a man possessed. Whirling forward and back he sought the enemy, wielding his blade with dead accuracy. Using it as an extension of his arm, Mordred struck over and over. Even with the dust, the noise, and the blinding light of the sun, Mordred moved right to left methodically. He slashed at the phantoms that came and went like wraiths carried on the wind.

The enemy, with only their eyes visible from within the light colored wraps that wound around their heads, came at him on their compact horses. These were the

Faris, the famed horse warriors and dreaded infidels. Having expended their arrows, they now rode him down with bloody lances and razor-sharp, wickedly curved swords. The air was filled with their chilling war whoops.

Mordred had advised the King earlier that the canyon would be a poor place to encounter the enemy. It was too narrow and would inhibit a quick escape for the army. He and his men were as good as dead. The deep gorge had come alive. It surrounded them. It attacked from behind first, then came from the direction Mordred had just ridden. The army was effectively cut off. They would simply be cut down.

A blade sliced the links of mail on Mordred's shoulder, but the blow glanced away before doing further damage. A lance came at his unprotected head, and Mordred had to duck to prevent the weapon from piercing his throat. With the speed of a great cat, Mordred turned his body around in mid air, struck out with his sword, and caught the rider in the spine.

Mordred kept going. He kept swinging. He kept wiping the spattering blood from his eyes and the trickling sweat from his lips. The entire army was being killed like animals in a cage. It wasn't a battle, it was a slaughter. Then, as quickly as the enemy had come, they disappeared, swallowed up by the howling wind. They left behind carnage, both horses and men, in their wake.

With his chest heaving and his muscles burning, Mordred searched for King Conrad. Perhaps he, too, lay beneath the pile of bodies. A few hours ago these same men represented one of the largest sections of the Second Crusade. He had no love for the King, but he also knew his job was to protect this man above all others.

An odd relief spread through him. He saw the familiar banner behind a large wall of stone. A robed figure waved a fist in the air. Mordred returned the motion but remained where he had fallen against a rock. A lone arrow had struck his thigh. It had burrowed past his mail tights like an insidious worm. Digging deep between the pieces of his leg armor, the barb tore into his flesh.

The dead and dying were everywhere. Many men had been reduced to body parts. Arms, with hands still connected to their weapons, lay motionless amid the gruesome scene. Heads torn from knights by the force of enemy lances lay strewn about. They stared grotesquely with open eyes and mouths. To Mordred it seemed as though they were condemning him for his failure to persuade the King to press on. He could not help feeling the dying men would haunt him for leaving them behind. And, for once in his life, he had a very real fear that he might break down. Never, in all his years at war, had he ever witnessed a slaughter on such a massive scale. It left him stunned.

His head lowered, the King approached Mordred, apparently acknowledging the mistake he had made. "We must press on. We cannot remain here. Those bloody heathens might come back to finish what they started."

Focusing on the arrow in his leg, Mordred gripped

the shaft and broke it. He made no sound or groan of pain. "Yes, Sire, we must."

"We need to determine who can still go forward and leave the rest behind."

"As you wish, Sire." This was said with such bitterness, Mordred had to keep his head down to prevent the King from seeing his anger. It would mean that men who had been wounded, but were unable to move, would be left to die. It could take hours, or days before all those injured would find peace in death. In the meantime they would wallow in their suffering with no help from those they had fought beside. It had been a mistake. It had all been a tragic mistake.

"Soulis, it will be your job to determine who goes with us and who shall stay behind. Does that sit with you?"

Mordred growled. Blood smeared across his face when he wiped it with his gloved hand. He couldn't tell if it was his blood, or the enemy's. He cared not. In his mind, he saw himself wrapping his hands around the King's neck and strangling the life out of him. An eye for an eye.

Now, because of Conrad's failure to listen, hundreds of men were either dead or dying. The damn fool thought to make Mordred the villain. Damn the King, he thought as he gritted his teeth. He pulled the remainder of the arrow cleanly from his leg, hiding his pain.

Tossing the barb away, he narrowly missed the King. Mordred queried with unmasked irritation, "Why should you care if it 'sits' with me, Your Grace? And why, Your Grace, should I care what you think? You and I, and a handful of men, are all that are left of a once vast army. Who here would stop me from venting my anger upon your royal hide?"

The King took a step back. His eyes opened wide. "Soulis, you go too far!"

"Nay, I think perhaps I haven't gone far enough. Look around you! Look at what your arrogant kingship has wrought," Mordred demanded. He still reeled from the burning pain running through his leg. Could the arrow be poisoned? Only time would tell.

"You are still a hired man, hired by me, and until I release you from your duty you will do as I say," the King threw back at Mordred. He was careful, however, to keep his distance.

Like a wounded beast, Mordred snarled. He moved to stand up. "Let me make this very clear. I am removing myself from your command. As a hired hand, I choose who I fight for, and you, Sire, are not one I wish to risk my life for any further. You should have listened to me. None of this would have happened if you had listened!"

Mordred stalked off. He tried not to limp from the stabbing pain of his wound. He knew he should remain still and not lose more blood, but to stay in the presence of a false king would do nothing to tamp down his rage.

On foot, he waded through bodies sometimes piled three and four deep where they had fallen on top of each other. Mordred was surrounded by the endless groans of those who could not get up. Several soldiers who had come through the attack unscathed administered to

11

those still lying on the ground. There were so many fallen it was impossible to tell who was still breathing and who had mercifully passed on. Mordred thought the lucky ones were those who had died.

"Sir, please, sir, help me . . . please," came a soft, barely heard whisper from a man just in front of Mordred's feet. His throat was slashed. He should have already been dead, Mordred thought. He was a fool for still breathing.

Mordred knelt down to hear the man.

"Please sir, please finish it. Please, I don't want them to come back. I want to die. Please."

The man's dying request hit Mordred in the gut. This was all so senseless. He looked at the soldier and gently wiped the blood from his face. He appeared to be a boy, no older than thirteen. Hell, he didn't even look old enough to be a squire, let alone be on crusade.

The boy coughed so hard it wracked his entire body. Blood spilled from his mouth and from the open wound at his neck. A strangled sob broke through his lips, "Please."

Mordred stood. He pulled his sword from its sheath and swore softly under his breath. Closing his eyes, he plunged the blade into the boy's chest. There was a moment when the boy's piercing blue eyes looked at him. Alert, as if he had somehow recovered from his wounds, he gazed up at Mordred. Then he was gone. The boy was dead. Despite the pain wracking his own body, Mordred bent down and brought his gloved hand to the boy's face and closed his eyes.

Mordred straightened his back. He started to move

on and heard another plea for release, and then another. Soon the air was filled with the begging. The hoarse voices of men and boys all pleaded for him to end their misery. Mordred could do nothing but honor their dying wishes. A part of him died with each life he ended.

He'd willingly killed hundreds, if not thousands of men in his lifetime, and yet he'd never heard a man plead for him to bring his death. There was no goodness in his actions. No satisfaction. Nothing that would let him feel the peace he gave them. Nothing but boiling anger and an intense fury at the necessity.

† † †

As if the heat and the endless sea of sand and dust weren't enough to break the wills of the men desperately searching for a way back to safety, the rain came. At first those who had survived the slaughter regarded it as a blessing from God. A sign that in the end they would indeed prevail. It gave them hope. They stripped themselves of their dirty, torn, and stinking clothing and danced under the pelting water.

Mordred, too, let himself bathe in the downpour.

"It's tears from heaven," claimed Radoc, a wiry, older knight who had befriended Mordred in Constantinople.

Mordred glanced at the gray haired man and shook his head. Untying the leather thong holding back his long black hair, he ran his hands over his head. The rain washed away the dirt and grime. Unlike the other men, he had not stripped down to his skin. Instead he remained clothed in his armor.

"Surely an old devil like you hasn't fallen under the spell of the crusade and now believes there is a godly redemption for all of us?"

Radoc let out a hearty laugh. He, too, remained clothed. "Nay, I haven't seen the light, if that's what you're after, but 'tis the word going through the troops that this rain is a sign that the angels weep for the fallen."

Mordred frowned and looked around. It had only begun raining. Already, with the dying light of the sun, he could foresee trouble ahead.

Sensing his mood, Radoc offered, "I see you, too, aren't blind to the problems we'll be dealing with if this storm continues."

"The ground isn't stable enough to hold all this water. We need to move to higher ground, away from the danger of a flood, or a mud or sand slide," Mordred replied. Droplets of warm rain poured down his face, making it nearly impossible to keep his eyes fully open.

"Aye, but I've seen no sign of Conrad. More likely than not, he's busy having his own private bath somewhere near the stream. Shall we pay him a visit, friend?"

"You know how well he takes our advice. I am almost ready to let him learn a lesson on his own."

Radoc glanced at Mordred, the rain streaming through his own hair. "Aye, but should the men here have to learn another lesson due to the ignorance of a King?"

Irritated at the mere thought of having a conversation

with a man he didn't respect, Mordred retied the leather thong around his hair, and nodded.

"You are the wiser of the two of us, Radoc."

"Nay, Mordred, not wiser, just less willing to die so easily."

Laughing, they walked down the slope to the streambed. They passed dozens of men engaged in the act of bathing while standing. There were no longer any horses. Those that hadn't been killed or run off during the countless episodes of heavy fighting had been slaughtered.

Every other animal they happened to come across—goats, donkeys, even dogs—became fodder for the starving troops. There had even been some men, who in their desperation to survive, had roasted pieces of the bodies of their slain enemies. Mordred shuddered.

Radoc interrupted his bleak mood. "Those fools won't be able to get their boots back on 'til tomorrow at best," he stated. "Me? I don't even want to see my feet until I'm back on English soil."

"I'm in agreement with you. I feel as if I'm walking on stubs of what used to be my feet. The bottoms of my boots have so many holes I'd be tempted to toss them out if I knew where we were."

"So, you don't think we are headed back to Constantinople?"

"Maybe, but I can't be sure. This area doesn't look familiar, and even though we're headed west, I can't shake the feeling we're heading too far north."

"Think you should tell the King?"

"Not until I'm sure."

The rain continued to fall in torrents. Sheets of life-giving liquid cascaded to the ground. Several times both Radoc and Mordred had to steady themselves to avoid slipping. Already the ground was moving. A thin layer of mud was beginning to inch its way down the slope.

A hastily erected and curtained canopy alerted them to the King's whereabouts. Two armed guards stood outside the entrance. Recognizing Mordred, they nodded.

"His Majesty is taking a bath. He has asked not to be disturbed," said one of the soldiers.

Before the soldiers could react, Mordred and Radoc barged past them and strode into the tented enclosure.

"Damn you, I told you I did not wish to be disturbed by anyone and that means . . ." King Conrad's voice trailed off as he recognized his intruder. "Oh, it's you."

The disdain in the King's voice was evident.

"What do you want now? Or are you here to lecture me on my failings as a leader again? Really Mordred, if not for your military prowess, I'd have had you drawn and quartered ages ago." The King laughed, but it didn't conceal his fear.

"I am not one of your subjects. I don't owe allegiance to you. Let me remind you, once again, you'd never be able to take me on."

Sputtering, the King sat up quickly in the tub. A shower of water splashed across the space between him and the two men. "Again, you go too far!"

With obvious contempt, Mordred wiped the water off his chest.

"I'm here to inform you of the situation outside. Once again you've somehow managed to pick the worst place to set up camp."

"Really? And why is that?"

Folding his arms across his chest, Mordred chewed the inside of his cheek. It was Radoc who spoke.

"Your Highness, we are situated at the bottom of a ravine, and with this steady downpour, Mordred and I feel there is a real danger of flooding. We should move the men to higher ground within the hour."

Exasperated, the King flung his hands in the air and slid further into the tub. Only his head was above the water.

"Well then, if that's the way of things, I suppose we should indeed break camp. So, since you brought this to my attention, why don't you both go tell the men they must move. I'm sure they will be thrilled to hear the news."

Mordred knew the maneuver was deliberate. The King hated that the remaining soldiers looked to Mordred as their leader. Many times they followed his orders over the King's commands, and the King was fast losing control of his own army.

The men would not be pleased to have to break camp and move. It would take them some time just to get everyone packed, and it would once again be a thankless job.

Without another word, Mordred removed himself from the tent. He listened as Radoc made his apologies to the King for their hasty intrusion and departure.

The rain still sluiced down the hillsides, creating

17

great streams across the ground. In the few short moments they spent with the King, the earth had loosened even more. Mordred watched as his feet sank into the now swirling mud.

"Right, well then, let's spread the good cheer, shall we?" Radoc said, as he came to stand beside Mordred.

Some of the men did indeed grumble and groan. The majority had already begun to notice the streambed overflowing its banks. It was now a torrent of rushing brown water. They knew moving to higher ground was the right thing to do.

Though it was the right thing to do, it was certainly not the easiest. It took the better part of the night to get everyone up the rain-soaked hillsides. Constantly sliding, falling, and slipping, men landed on top of one another at the bottom of the hill, only to try again with the same result.

The remaining gear had to be moved as well, and this proved as disastrous as moving the men. Over and over their burdens fell back down the slopes, forcing the men to pick their way back down to the streambed below, only to climb up the slippery slope again. And the more men that reached the top, the more treacherous the narrow paths became. The few sparse bushes and shrubs that clung precariously to the hillsides were yanked out easily by the men. It was slow, muddy going.

Finally, after spending the better part of the night getting the army resituated, the men settled in. Even the King had been moved. Mordred left the hammered gold tub behind. It was ridiculous to have brought it this far. The King would simply have to bathe like the rest of the men.

In the end there was only one injury, and that proved to be relatively minor. But the troops were exhausted. Unfortunately, they would lose valuable time allowing the army a much needed rest. Not knowing what lay beyond the next rise, Mordred remained tense and ever watchful. The others bedded down as best they could. Their dented and battered kite shields provided scant protection from the unending rain. What had been viewed as a blessing only hours earlier, was now regarded as a curse.

† † †

"Soulis, have you any idea where we are or where we're headed?" King Conrad asked several days later.

Mordred looked into the eyes of the man he loathed. King Conrad was a fool, a man who had joined the crusade to further himself and his own causes. Like many kings and the rulers of many countries, he thought he would find riches to make him a more powerful ruler. Instead, he proved himself to be an ineffectual leader and sorely out of his element when it came to military strategy.

"I say, Soulis, are you not over the episode back in the canyon yet? Good God, man, you really must get beyond it. You can't let it haunt you. You've seen men die before."

Mordred wanted to rail at the King. He wanted to unleash the dark thoughts that had been plaguing him

19

since the slaughter. Instead, he clenched his jaw and looked away.

"I have no idea where we are." He spoke the truth. He actually had a feeling they were simply wandering in circles. He also feared they had survived the massacre in the canyon for naught.

The rain had ceased. The ground gave way to a bleak landscape of nothing but eerily shaped dunes and blistering waves of heat. The rocky slopes and sparse greenery, which at times led the way to small watering holes, had disappeared. Only an endless sea of sand stretched out before them now. There wasn't a single tree or outcropping of stone in sight. Nothing would provide shade from the merciless rays of the sun. Nothing that suggested they would find the water they needed.

"So, what do you propose we do, Soulis?" the King asked, his voice cracking from thirst and heat.

Mordred turned and looked straight at Conrad. Narrowing his eyes, he could not prevent his lip from curling. He had no need to pretend if he was going to rot in the desert. The King couldn't threaten him if he'd never make it back to civilization.

Nervously, the King waited for Mordred's reply.

"You would ask me now, when it matters not what I think?"

"Surely you have a plan? You wily mercenaries always have a plan."

"I had a plan back in Constantinople, which included waiting for the French. I had a plan before we set out for Dorylaeum. I had a plan back in the canyon, but you didn't listen to me. Back then, when it would have mattered most, you didn't listen to me. Now you want my advice? Now we will all die."

Startled, the King snapped his head up to look around. The wind was rising again. Great clouds of golden dust blew toward them.

Mordred had the good grace to warn the King of the coming sand storm. Then he moved off to be alone.

The howling would go on for hours. There was nothing Mordred could do but lie down, back against the wind, eyes, mouth, and nose covered, and wait for the storm to pass.

The great gusts of warm air robbed the night of any other noises. To Mordred it sounded like the moans of thousands of departed soldiers. The ones who had died in the canyon. The ones whose souls would never find peace.

When morning dawned, the wind on the desert stilled. The life-giving night dew evaporated into the hot, dry air. Mordred discovered the King had taken a few men and left without so much as a warning. Where he went was a mystery, but he was gone. It didn't surprise Mordred a bit. That the gutless man had slipped away secretly, abandoning his troops to the merciless elements, was surely proof he was an inept ruler.

† † †

Mordred was left with what amounted to less than a hundred men in this strange and deadly land. They tried to find their way back to Constantinople. The endless sea of sand and jagged rock surrounded them. In the end they became hopelessly lost.

Men were dying by the day. They simply fell. One moment they were alive and moving; the next, they became one of the hundreds of dead on this failed crusade.

They saw no sign of their known enemy, the *Faris*. They saw no sign of any living thing. No birds. No beasts. No insects or snakes. Nothing at all to remind them they were still alive while traversing this godforsaken land. And yet there were unseen enemies around them every moment they remained in this bleak place. The oppressive heat and the scarcity of water were silent but deadly. The rays of the blindingly bright sun and the ferocity of the dust storms were Mordred's new enemies. And these foes could not be fought with sword and brute strength. They could not be battled at all.

In the desolate landscape of endless mountains of sand, the dunes shifted and moved with each step. A man could sink up to his knees. It was easy to tax oneself by simply walking a few paces. More men fell from exhaustion. They closed their eyes, and when Mordred looked back, Radoc shook his head. This told him without words that the fallen soldiers, wrapped in the golden blanket of sand, would not rise again.

Day after endless day, men died. Every morning Mordred knew their group would be smaller. There was nothing he could do. There was no end in sight. And still that wasn't the worst.

The haunting pleas came again. The words he never

wanted to hear. Yet, hear them he did. Over and over they begged him for the mercy of his blade. Each time a piece of him died with their deaths. He unsheathed his sword and killed his own men. Soon, the sight of the blood, and the strangled sounds of their death rattles, caused not a single feeling within him.

Until there were only two.

"Mordred, I cannot go on any longer. I think it is time I end this." Radoc's voice was a hoarse whisper.

Mordred whirled around to face the older man. He wanted to scream. He wanted to deny that the last soldier was dying. His only remaining companion was now giving up. He saw the burns on the man's aged face. The flesh of his arms and legs was blistered from the heat. He saw the dried blood on the man's mouth. His lips were cracked and split from lack of water. The skin color on one of his legs was a strange mixture of purple and yellow. A thick green liquid oozed from a wound Mordred was sure was now infected.

"No. Not you, Radoc. You are strong like a warhorse, you will not die."

"Mordred, even I can't fight this heat and thirst. I cannot make it much farther, and there is no safe haven in sight. What good does it do me to go on?"

Turning, Mordred searched the hostile landscape for any signs of trees or rock outcroppings. A place where he could shelter the man and return with water, or help. There was nothing.

"Damn you, you old fool, then I will carry you."

When Radoc laughed, it sounded to Mordred's ears like the rasping of a dead man. "Then we will both die.

Listen to me, you have a chance here. Put me to the sword and take my blood."

Confused, Mordred stopped. When his friend did not reach his side, he looked back. Radoc had fallen to his knees in the sand.

"I don't understand your words, Radoc. How will your dying help me, except to leave me alone out here?"

"My blood, Mordred. It won't sustain you for long, but it is something, and mayhap it will give you the strength you need to find help for yourself."

"Are you asking me to drink your blood?" Mordred's face contorted in horror. He'd done much in his life, but never had he resorted to this.

"It may be the only thing that saves you."

"No."

"Mordred, think. You must survive, for all of us who did not. Now, please, without further ceremony or sentiment, I wish to die."

"No."

Radoc sighed wearily, the effort taking most of his strength. "Where is the warrior I know? The man that is never defeated. Where has he gone? He would do this for another warrior. Let me die with honor. Don't leave me here for the vultures to claim."

Sick with emotion, Mordred fell to his knees. "Don't make me do this."

"You have to. It is the only chance you have. The only hope. Let me give you this gift."

"I don't want your life, or your blood."

"Take it, Mordred. Take it and live a few more hours or days. Take it to find your way out of this hell."

Mordred stared into the eyes of the man in front of him. He knew he had no choice. Like all the others before Radoc, he must have mercy. Yet, for a few moments Mordred hesitated, weighing the insurmountable odds of a rescue against the terrible act he knew he had to commit. Full of grief and desolation, Mordred unsheathed his great sword.

And then, only Mordred remained . . .

CHAPTER TWO

A pained mind left Mordred questioning his sanity. He wandered aimlessly in the bleak landscape. Alone, he felt as if he had been left behind. Abandoned, like an old man who had long since lost his usefulness, he drifted across the desolate terrain.

In this godforsaken desert, under the scorching rays of the sun that melded armor to flesh in a matter of seconds, this was the end of his days. Yet, he continued to move forward in spite of all the madness he had endured. One foot moved forward and then the other, over and over. Painfully, he trudged. He thought of all the men he had seen fall victim to this unforgiving climate. He cursed the enemy that moved with stealth and surprise. Anger surged within him. He found the strength to walk the last few steps, to look once more at the wavering visions before him.

Dust devils whirled up and around in great spirals. The wind whipped the sand in all directions. Dunes shifted beneath his feet, slithering menacingly like a waking beast. A hungry beast. One that had devoured his soldiers. Thousands of his men. Young boys with the dream of knighthood now lay dead beneath the golden grains. Young men with the dream of returning to their sweethearts had given their lives to the blades of the infidels. Veteran warriors, who had seen the worst kind of battle, had fallen like waves of grain before the sickle. None had ever seen this kind of carnage, or had endured so much pain.

Mordred tried desperately to keep his mind still. But, his thoughts always returned to those he had been forced to kill. It was an act of mercy, so he had been told. He had bloodied his hands with the deaths of hundreds of men, men who should never have come to the desert. Men who should have stayed in their villages and plied their trades and married young women and raised good children. His hands were stained with the knowledge that he had put them to the sword.

Their faces haunted him. At first it was only when he drifted off into a restless sleep. And then even while awake the images swept across the sands. They howled and cried out to him, shaming him. The visions plagued him mercilessly, causing him to weep with heavy sobs that wracked his body.

Yet there was no one to hear him. The sounds were stolen as quickly as they were cast out to the hot, hungry air, leaving nothing but silence.

There were no tears. The desert in its cruelty had stolen even this precious liquid from him. And so he was left with the madness of a man who had done far too much. A man whose soul was burdened by images and thoughts that would never cease. He was mortally wounded in spirit. And he was alone.

Each day when he was sure it would be his last, he cursed upon waking again. It appeared even death was in no hurry to take away his pain.

There was one memory that brought him closer to insanity than even the slaying of his own men. Radoc had told him what he must do to survive. The old warrior had begged him to stay alive, to give purpose to the thousands who had died on the crusade. And so Mordred had bled Radoc of his life.

† † †

"I can't do this!" Mordred screamed to the heavens. "God, if there is a god, please don't make me do this."

There was no answer. Only silence spilled across the dunes. Mordred rested on his knees beside the old soldier's body. He'd killed the man with his own blade before falling to the ground in grief. He remained frozen as the moon climbed higher. Silver light bathed the ever-changing hills of sand.

Again dry sobs shook his body. He prayed for death to take him.

"I cannot go on. Please, have mercy. Let me die. Take me to hell if that be your wish, but please do not make me do this!"

His voice sounded otherworldly. A strained, inhuman noise came from somewhere outside his body. Mordred closed his eyes and tried to still his breathing. He tried to return to himself and let the feelings of hopelessness pass.

Nothing changed. He was still alive. He didn't know for how much longer he would be alive. That thought brought another memory from long ago. After a particularly heated battle Mordred had stumbled across an old man not yet dead. He was a *Faris,* an enemy. He'd gazed at Mordred with such a peaceful expression. He was welcoming his demise, uttering prophetic words in his own tongue. "Death will not come to you in the way you will wish. You alone are destined for something greater than the rest."

It had taken days for Mordred to decipher what those final words had meant.

Now, Mordred heard the man's voice again.

Slowly, he lifted his head. Carefully, he took the small skin flask that once held water, and opened it. With no feeling, Mordred took a curved dagger from his belt. He pressed the point to the throat of the dead soldier. Pressing down, Mordred punctured a hole in the old soldier's neck. Immediately, the blood spurted out.

He held the flask, filling it with the thick, sticky fluid.

There was more than Mordred could take. What was left spilled over the sand beneath him. Mordred rose to his feet, closed the flask, and put it over his shoulder.

Then he moved again. The small skin sack weighed against him, as if it held a thousand stones. Guilt, remorse, and pain flooded him. He continued to walk, one step at a time, through the endless landscape of unfeeling sand, harsh wind, and deep night.

He would not drink the blood, he told himself. He would simply carry it. Drinking the blood would surely be damnation. Mordred was not a God-fearing man, but his time in the desert had taken its toll on his beliefs.

† † †

Unbelievably, the will to survive resurfaced. It warred with defeat, taking a stand within Mordred's lost soul. Self-preservation urged him on. It spoke to him in whispers, at times sounding very like the wind. It told him to drink the blood he carried. It goaded him into action. When Mordred could no longer stand the thirst, he drank, greedily.

At first the salty liquid made him sick. His stomach spasmed, and he feared he would lose what he had swallowed. But he held on to it, desperately. The blood gave him life for one more day.

Each time he drank, the desire to vomit the blood lessened. He convinced himself it made no difference at all. Hell had surely marked him.

But, in that hell he would find a way to inflict the worst kind of torment on those who had brought him there. One man in particular whose orders had visited death on thousands. Mordred determined that in this death, he would become the specter of evil. He would release his murderous need for revenge, and it would feed his hollow soul.

In his thirst-starved, blood-soaked mind, Mordred assured himself that he would succeed in his gruesome quest. From beyond the mortal realm he would return and make vengeance his.

Unable to form another coherent thought, Mordred

fell to his knees. His body was cushioned by the damnable sand. Greedily, the desert waited to feed on his corpse. It sucked the very life from him.

The hot wind stirred again, this time touching him gently, oddly devoid of the usual sting. Like a lover's stroke it held him in thrall. It lifted him to a standing position.

"What would you give to have your wish fulfilled?" questioned the sand and the air.

Mordred glanced around. He saw nothing. He was nearly blinded by the sun and the sand.

His mind was playing tricks on him again, teasing him. Taunting him to believe he was not dying.

Again, the voice whispered along the wind. The words were very clear.

In his weakened state he fell back to the ground. He began to laugh, a low, maniacal sound. This was madness.

"Show yourself!" he commanded, with what strength was left in his body.

"First, you must tell me what you would give me to fulfill your fondest wish," the phantom voice purred.

Trying to concentrate, Mordred shielded his eyes against the brilliant rays of the sun. He squinted, trying to discern if the enemy was near. There was nothing but brilliant, blinding light.

"You are running out of time, my friend."

Delusional and near death, Mordred played the game with the voice.

"Fine. I would give my life to kill the man who brought us to this ruin. I would rip his heart from his miserable body."

"And drink of his blood?" came the seductive murmur of the desert.

"Yes, damn the man, I will rip out his heart and bathe in his blood."

There was irony in the exchange, Mordred thought miserably. His life would be over soon. Therefore, he was not really exchanging or bartering with anything. Madness!

In that last moment of awareness, before the final stages of death overtook him, Mordred's vision cleared. He watched as the whirling sand took shape. It morphed into the image of a man. A striking man with long black hair and full red lips, dressed in finery that befitted a king. A mocking smile was planted firmly on the man's haunting face. His silver eyes glowed brighter than the sun and pierced Mordred.

A hand stroked his face gently, as if Mordred were only a babe. It was a soft touch, but devoid of any warmth. When it released Mordred, it was as if all of his bones had turned to liquid. He fell forward into the sand in a puddle of burned flesh, bloodied hands, and broken soul. Forward he fell, into the blackness that was to become his rebirth.

† † †

Death was strange, Mordred thought. For days, months perhaps, it had existed beside him like a comrade. Silent. Invisible to the eye. Yet, its constant presence was felt.

He had fought against death and lost. The thought

irritated him. Mordred had known death would indeed find him. As a warrior he was lucky to have lived this long. Still, he hadn't thought he would die alone on a field of battle so hostile. No one would know of his passing. These thoughts came to rest and then, like leaves in a breeze, they fluttered away. Other grim thoughts took their place.

He heard a ragged breathing sound and a constant moaning. When he stopped for a moment, he realized it was coming from him. His world was dark, quiet, save for the noise his body made.

He waited for the devil to present himself. His was no innocent soul bound for glory. After all he had done in his lifetime, he would pay the highest price. The gates of heaven would be locked to him.

There was no remorse in the thoughts of his destination. If there were a hell, then surely he would be sent there. God had never appeared in Mordred's life, and religion was for fools. Only faith in his sword and courage in battle had saved his skin until now. For Mordred it was hard to believe in any kind of god, given what he had witnessed in his life.

God could not have wished crusades against a people whose only crime was holding a code of beliefs that differed from the Roman Catholic Church.

God would not want the slaughter of innocent women and children in His name. And surely God would have come to the aid of His men, the faithful crusaders, when they were suffering their last breaths on the desert in His name.

Yet the faithful died just as easily as the faithless.

Nay, there was no God, but perhaps there was a devil?

Mordred had always wondered if the sins of man were just that. He had never been compelled to act for any other reason than his own greed. No one controlled him. Nay, he had been master of his destiny until this fatal crusade.

No God, no devil. Nothing.

He was left with only the steady sound of his own breathing and the very faint beating of his heart.

His mind drifted from dream to dream. Screaming men, howling winds, spilled blood. Over and over the faces of his victims flashed before him.

A deep, burning hatred uncoiled within. He had been sent to his death because the religious leaders had deemed it so. Mordred had signed on to the crusade with the promise of riches and great wealth. For a mercenary, living by his sword arm, it meant a vagabond life, being sent to whatever country or kingdom was in need of fighting men. Never putting down roots. No family, no wife or children. He was always on the move. Hack, slash, and continue on to the next battle.

He'd fought his own people in clan wars, fought the French against the English, fought the English against the Irish. Mordred had fought in battles between rival royal princes, emperors, and queens. He had laid waste with his sword for feuding families and against warring nations. He had fought for so many kings and countries that he'd lost track of all the skirmishes and conflicts. None of the fighting had brought him the life he'd hoped for.

Mordred hadn't even been duly knighted, though his men treated him with respect because of his reputation, and kings were quick to command that he lead their armies. Still, Mordred was left with nothing save his armor, sword, horse, a small fortune in gold and silver, and a decrepit castle in Scotland.

Goddamn God, and all who believe in Him.

His mind played with images of his childhood, his father, his family. Spinning pictures merged with macabre visions of death and destruction. Screams of the dying rang in his ears, covering the sounds of his breathing.

Blood poured from open mouths and eyes. It gushed into a mammoth river. In the center, as if anchored to an invisible island, was Mordred himself. He stood, clad in black, drinking from a goblet and laughing aloud.

He knew the liquid. He knew he bathed in it. He knew he was tainted by it. Condemned by the crimson fluid. And just as he would have screamed in abject misery and horror, the mocking visions ceased. There was nothing more but blackness. The faint beating of his heart coupled with his labored breathing slowly faded.

Mordred Soulis climbed an invisible stairway. Step after torturous step, he felt his body shift. It was fluid and constantly moving, drifting in the blackness around him. Like a hundred-year-old man, Mordred labored steadily toward some unknown destination. He felt himself awakening from what felt like an eternal slumber.

Stiffness caused him to feel as if his body were now a weight of solid stone. Something as cold as ice surged through his veins and then shattered. Thousands of tiny bone needles prickled beneath his skin. Flames surged from his core.

With a gasp, he felt his heart slam against his chest, nearly breaking his ribs with its force.

Was he dead?

Was this heaven . . . or hell?

The heaviness of his lids made it nearly impossible to open his eyes. After several failed attempts, he thought he forced them open. Mordred wasn't sure what to expect, just that he had expected to see something. Instead, his vision remained black. Opening his eyes wider to be sure he wasn't still dreaming, Mordred moved them left and right.

Pain shot through him, enough to make him groan and stop what he was doing. He closed his eyes.

His hearing was the next sense he engaged. A harsh sound filled his brain. If he had been able to lift his arms, he would have put his hands over his ears in an attempt to block out the deafening noise. But, he remained flat on his back, weak as a kitten, and unable to move.

He groaned again through clenched teeth.

"Shh, he wakes."

"Yes, he wakes. Be quiet. Bring the flask."

To Mordred the voices sounded impossibly loud, reverberating around him like the booming of thunder from a great storm. His brain tried to make sense of the words. They glided past him so slowly they became distorted. He could not fathom their meaning; he knew only that he was not alone.

His mouth opened. He fully intended to demand an answer to the many questions swimming in his throbbing brain. But when a stab of white heat ripped through his jaw, he closed his mouth again. Moaning, he wondered once more if this was death. And if so, why was he in such pain?

The voices quieted. It occurred to Mordred that they spoke in a language foreign to him. Yet, as time slid by he realized he could understand their words. How could that be?

Dimly, Mordred became aware that his entire body felt as if it were on fire. Hell? No, worse, it felt as though his bones were growing too big for his body. They stretched and tore beneath him, ripping his skin to shreds. It was agonizing. Mordred blacked out.

Once again he climbed back up the steps to consciousness, but this time he refrained from movement. Something touched his head and his lips.

Hands?

Liquid spilled across his mouth. Cool and sweet smelling.

"Drink," came a voice in the darkness, and Mordred found he could comply. He opened his mouth a small way, fearing the blinding pain would return.

Feeling a thick, soothing liquid melt down his throat, Mordred greedily swallowed. Again and again he drank in large gulps until the flood of drink became just droplets. Even then he licked at the mouth of the flask.

"It is enough for today. You must go slowly."

Mordred felt his head being lowered gently.

Suddenly he convulsed as his gut tightened with stabbing pain. Feeling as if someone were cutting him open from nose to toes with a rusty sword, he bellowed like an injured boar.

"What-is-happening?"

Words fell from Mordred's parched and cracked lips in a growl of agony. They echoed in his ears, buzzing like flies. He realized, somewhere in his mind, that he was speaking the language of the voices near him. How could he? How could he utter a single word of a language he didn't know?

Writhing, twisting in misery, he was barely able to breathe.

"He's in pain," a voice observed.

"Yes, and it is a good thing. It means he is still partly one of us. He can still feel. It will subside eventually as his body grows accustomed to the changes."

There was pressure placed on Mordred's chest. Someone was holding him down against the hard slab. As quickly as the debilitating pain had come, it disappeared.

"He drank too quickly. It will pass." A male voice had spoken.

A strange sensation flooded Mordred while he lay completely still. He feared any movement might bring on another bout of crippling pain. Why were the voices talking as if he could not hear them?

His mind began to allow him to form clearer thoughts. Still, many were mere shadows of something he couldn't quite comprehend. Wisps of things he had knowledge of dived and swept over him, then disappeared into nothingness. He half-feared that perhaps he had not died. Maybe he had been saved, only to be brought back to life with his mind destroyed.

"Where am I?" he asked in what he thought was a whisper. The sound of his voice boomed around him.

"You are safe," came the reply. Female, he thought.

"Am I dead?"

"No, not quite."

Not quite? What the hell did that mean? The thought was too much. It manifested itself into something physical and shot like the barb of a crossbow bolt through his skull.

"Rest. There will be time for questions later. Your sight will return, as will your other senses. The pain will eventually lessen, but you have a long road, my friend."

Friend? Was he back in—? What place did he call home?

Images of rolling green hills and snowcapped mountains, rivers of blue, and forests teeming with wildlife came into view in his mind's eye. An enormous castle loomed over him as if he were no more than a small boy. Home?

As quickly as the jumbled images came, they disappeared into a blurry haze.

A cacophony of sounds reached his ears. Mordred concentrated on his hearing, but the noises came at him from all directions in a deafening cloud, making it impossible to discern one from the next.

He ignored the sharp, stabbing pain that ripped

through the fabric of his mind as he tried to separate the noises. He heard a scratching and then the screeching of a . . . rodent? Many rodents. Water dripped incessantly, splashing into a puddle.

A flurry of beating, like the wings of a bird, yet, not so, overpowered the other sounds. More squealing. Something reminiscent of a heartbeat, no, more than one, and the sound of liquid pumping, flooded his ears.

His mind jammed with sounds. He winced. How could he hear so well? The scraping of a boot, the shifting of fabric, a breeze that filtered in from somewhere, he heard all of these.

And then there were the smells. Death reigned here. Rotting flesh, mixed with mold. Something tangy and metallic filled the place, nearly causing Mordred to vomit.

Visions of himself clad in armor, hands dripping with blood, hovered beneath his eyelids. Bodies ravaged by the desert filled his view. Fallen men littered the sand in a river of crimson. Faces contorted and frozen in pain stared at him, condemning him.

His life flooded back to him in one giant wave. For a moment Mordred feared he would drown from the intensity of the images.

Then nothing.

Had he blacked out again?

Conscious thought came to him, as he lay immobile on the cold slab of what felt like rock. He desperately tried to block the heavy scent of destruction that hovered close.

Death was no stranger to a mercenary soldier. In the

final days in the desert, Mordred had become much like the Reaper himself, ending the lives of many who could no longer stand the suffering. Death became his shroud. He wore it like a mantle on his shoulders.

The smells of corpses melting under the hot sun filled his nostrils, causing him to gag.

Mordred detected an acrid scent, something burning. A fire, or a torch.

He concentrated on a singular fragrance that was different from the horrid odors lying heavy upon the air. It was floral and exotic, something unfamiliar to Mordred. The smell was tantalizing and helped to clear his head of the foul stench that plagued his nose.

"Am I in hell?" he queried, quite sure the devil himself would confirm his question.

As though he'd been broken into thousands of pieces, Mordred could believe he had died and been sent to the netherworld where demons and monsters lurked, waiting for unwitting souls.

Even those without a religion were not immune to questioning what happened after death. Surely this was the explanation of the horror he sensed here.

A chuckle alerted him to a presence very near him. Something soft and cool glided across his forehead.

"Perhaps there will come a day when you wish you were in hell."

✝ ✝ ✝

Mordred Soulis slept. In the gloominess of dreams came strange figures, haunting him. A faceless man

41

clad in elegant black clothing drifted across the sands. He took on a shape as he floated above the dunes like a shimmering mirage.

With his arm extended he beckoned Mordred to follow, yet Mordred could not. His legs were lying in a puddle beneath him. They had melted like the molten steel used to forge his sword.

"Little pup, soon you will learn you are so much stronger than this world you live in," came the deep voice, touching Mordred. It stirred him; he felt as if he were merely a puppet on a string.

"My son, I have created you. You will live on through me."

Then the voice was gone, replaced by the howling wind that rose across the dunes. The golden grains shifted, undulating beneath him.

In a dream state, Mordred watched. His body, of its own volition, hovered above the ground.

A hand came from the swirling sand, pointing sky-ward. Mordred rose high into the air. Helpless and at this strange man's mercy, he could only do what he was bidden.

"You will know me."

It was whispered on the wind. A promise of some-thing unexplainable. A demand.

Completely powerless, Mordred drifted along on the currents. He could see the desert from the perspective of a hawk. The ground below was littered with bodies, tiny specks upon a bed of gold.

"Heal thyself."

Suddenly, Mordred plummeted toward the ground,

unable to stop. Just before he hit the earth, he saw himself lying upon the sand. Blood spilled from his neck, painting the grains a bright ruby color, changing the ground from dust to a river of red.

He wanted to help himself. He wanted to stop the bleeding. But all he could do was stare at his broken body. A low rumble of laughter filled the space around Mordred. It grew louder, becoming thunderous as it shook both earth and air.

Then, he heard another voice. Beneath the deafening sound of the man in black, something as soft as the cry of a night bird whispered. Though barely audible, Mordred heard it clearly.

"Fight, Mordred. You must resist."

Confused, Mordred continued to stare at himself lying upon the sand. The voice came again, stronger this time.

"Mordred, you must resist the temptation. Force him from your side and stand within the light."

"Who are you?"

The growl of an angry beast rent the air. It blasted away the softer speech. It was the masculine voice that replied, "I am your father."

Mordred wanted to close his eyes. The man in black was growing larger than his own vision could comprehend. Before him, over his broken body, came a brilliant golden light. Hues of the most beautiful dawn washed over him. Pinks, oranges, and purples merged with yellows and blues. The colors created a shiver that coursed through Mordred's body.

His corpse became animated and rose from the

desert floor. It stared back at him in condemnation, accusing Mordred of its demise.

This was impossible! He was staring at himself?

Pain ripped through his brain when he tried to focus on what was happening around him. Slowly, the vision wavered, then disappeared altogether.

Mordred awoke with a start, and his body paid the price. Searing heat undulated from his chest, through his limbs, and back to his head. He groaned aloud.

"Help me," he called out, praying someone would hear him.

The sounds of movement came to his ears. A cool hand touched his forehead.

"What is it you wish to do, Mordred? Do you wish to live or die?" It was the female.

Another voice sounded, harsh and angry. "You cannot ask him that. He must discover the answer himself."

"We are running out of time. Why can we not urge him along?"

"You know as well as I do that we cannot tamper with his fate."

The cool hand remained, but the voices stopped. Silence.

Mordred forced himself into a sitting position and opened his eyes. It took so much energy. Fear that he would topple back washed over him. He broke out in a cold sweat and forced himself to remain upright.

A dark cavern presented itself. Shades of black mixed with red. Mordred closed his eyes and opened them again, hoping to bring his sight back to normal.

It was no use, the images before him remained in shadow, except for the outlines of what appeared to be humans, standing near him.

This couldn't be happening. He blinked again. He was seeing right through the people. A thin glowing line of white outlined their bodies, but their hearts, and the blood pumping through their veins, were clearly visible. Mordred found this oddly seductive.

A pang of lust shot through him, and he found himself filled with an intense hunger. What was happening to him?

A form moved nearby.

"You awaken from your dreams." A statement, not a question.

"Where am I?"

"Safe," came the answer.

"Safe from what? Or whom?"

"Your father."

His father? What father? He had been told his father had been killed. It was Mordred's twenty-first birthday when he had received the news that his father was dead.

There was no remorse. He hadn't seen his father in years. He didn't even really know the man. What game was being played here?

"My father is dead."

The female voice spoke again. "In a manner of speaking."

His vision began to clear. He was able to see the physical features of the woman standing beside him. She still appeared transparent and fragile. It was as if he could reach right through her.

"Why do you speak in riddles?"

"In time, you will understand. We do not seek to hurt you, only to heal you," she responded, as if sensing his next question.

As his eyes continued to focus, he took in the clothing she was wearing. It was strange to him. As his vision blurred, and then cleared a final time, Mordred was relieved to have his sight back.

The woman was clad in an emerald colored robe, caught simply at the waist with a silver belt. Her feet were bare. She wore no jewelry and yet she was, in some way, incredibly beautiful in her plainness.

"Who are you?"

"My name is of no consequence to you. I do not matter in the wheel that is your life, or will my companions. We seek only to bring you back to life. The rest of the healing will be up to you."

"I don't understand."

"We are only here to see that you gain enough strength to move on. We cannot teach you what you must learn to survive."

Confusion settled on Mordred's mind like a thick, heavy blanket. Who were these people and what did they mean?

Weakness flooded him, and he lowered himself back down on the stone slab.

The woman placed a cool cloth on Mordred's forehead, soothing the fire that raged within him.

He could hear the sound of her heart and found himself immensely attracted.

She smiled then, a knowing smile, and moved away.

"You do not know the extent of your full powers, but one day you will understand what you feel now."

"Am I dead?" he queried again. The feelings were too powerful, too surreal.

"In a manner of speaking. We have brought you back to life, for better or for worse. It is the way. You must seek your destiny."

"My destiny died in the desert," Mordred spat angrily.

"Nay, your destiny was revealed to you in the desert, when you died."

Mordred watched a man clad in the same emerald robes come into view. The man stopped and stared at Mordred before glancing at the woman.

"Stop playing nursemaid to a soul stealer. You know they are dangerous when first awakened."

" 'Tis different with this one. He has anger and violence within him, but not toward us. There is hunger there too, but not for destruction."

A low laugh echoed off the stone walls. "Give him time. I'm sure he won't disappoint."

"Arad doesn't think he will. He thinks perhaps we have recovered the One at last."

"Arad still believes there is hope."

Mordred watched the woman face the man, her long braid swinging past her hips.

"You have given up hope, Judah?"

"Nay, not completely, but you forget I have seen this happen far too many times before. Only time will tell if he is to be the One, and we must remain vigilant, lest he turn to darkness."

Having remained silent long enough and annoyed that others were treating him as though he weren't present to debate his own fate, Mordred spoke. "I am confused," he said aloud, finally giving voice to his emotions. He pulled himself up to a sitting position again, though it took all his strength to do so.

Everything was stilled, quiet, as if waiting for his next breath.

"You are no longer human," came the male voice with an edge of bitterness.

Angry at their riddles, Mordred moved as if to take himself off the slab. "What?"

"Judah, no. It is too soon to bring him to this."

The man shook his head and shrugged. "You want to know for sure if he is the One. Then let us move things forward for him so we can be sure ourselves." He gazed at Mordred warily.

"You are no longer human. Your father, your creator, saw to that. You bargained with someone far worse then the devil, and he has given you back a life of sorts."

"Explain," Mordred demanded.

"There is much we cannot tell you. The Templars will help you get to your own kind, and hopefully, then the questions in your mind will be freed."

"Your name is Mordred Soulis, and your creator is Vlad. That is the only name you would know him by. His real name is a mystery," came the woman's soothing voice.

Shaking his head, Mordred refused the woman's claim. "No, my name is Mordred Soulis, and my father is Magnus Soulis."

The woman continued to speak, unafraid of Mordred's rising anger.

"No, your father is Vlad, and he will come for you. You must learn to defeat him. There is good in you still, hold to that, else you lose your soul. Listen to the wisdom of the Templars."

Denial rose high and hot within Mordred.

"No, this is untrue. Why do you tell me lies? I know who I am."

The woman moved away from Mordred. He heard the rippling fabric of her clothing as it ebbed and flowed with her movements.

"I speak the absolute truth. You have been given a new life. You would have, perhaps should have, died with your fallen troops, but Vlad walked among them searching for the next dark prophet. You are the Chosen One."

"What does this mean?" Mordred asked, infuriated.

"You, of all others, of thousands, have been chosen. You will become the savior of all mankind."

"No, I am—I am—Mordred—of the Soulis clan."

"The world that you knew is lost to you now. It will be easier if you accept this as the truth."

Mordred railed against the woman's claims. If he was not Mordred Soulis, of the clan Soulis, then who the hell was he? Could there be a shred of truth to the knowledge these people offered?

He glanced about the cave and saw another male form coming into the chamber, moving slowly in Mordred's direction.

"How does he fare?" the new arrival asked.

"He refuses to believe in the truth of his existence, and I am afraid. If he does not accept who he is from us, we will not be able to defeat Vlad."

"Trust in the good, Sister. He will accept his fate in due time."

Mordred listened to the conversation and became increasingly frustrated. Feeling the helplessness of a child that couldn't comprehend the words of adults, Mordred fought raising his arms to cover his ears.

"I am a mercenary soldier. I only know of swords, and steel, and killing. I am not the chosen one you claim me to be. I am just a man, nearly killed in this crusade. A simple man."

The new figure, wearing the same clothes as the others, smiled at Mordred, unafraid. It was the voice of the other man that spoke.

"Denial is only the beginning. It will not change the course of your fate. You will waste valuable time wishing otherwise, and there is no time to lose."

Silencing a protest from Mordred with the raising of a tanned and weathered hand, the man continued. "Vlad grows stronger each day. We found you almost too late, but there is still hope. It will take years, centuries even, for your darker side to become dominant, and during that time perhaps you will resist."

"If I am dead, but not dead, then I am not human, a mortal, and if I am not a mortal, then what the hell am I?" Mordred questioned. Clearly, his skull was shrinking as he spoke, giving him the sensation it would burst at any moment.

"You are a soul stealer. A vampyre."

Mordred shook his head, no longer caring if the movement resulted in more excruciating pain. He ran his hands through his hair, and in doing so brushed against something wrapped around his neck.

Peeling the fabric from his skin, Mordred touched his throat with his fingers. There he felt two distinct holes, punctures.

"No, this can't be . . . happening,"

Pushing off the slab, Mordred moved through the darkness deftly, unconcerned with the absence of light. He swayed back and forth with the effort of his movements. Mordred prayed he would not collapse, but the longer he remained upright the weaker he felt.

"No, let him go."

"But the light . . . he is not ready."

"Then, he will learn the hard way. Perhaps the only way his mind will accept his path is by this proof," one of the men replied.

Amazingly, Mordred was able to make his way through one hallway and into another. He used his heightened sense of smell to lead him to the source of the fresh air his nostrils detected.

By now Mordred could only slide himself against the walls of stone, fearing that without their support he would crumble. His skin scraped against the cold, jagged rock, but he cared not about the damage he inflicted upon himself.

He had to get out, get away from these crazy people. How dare they try to tell him he was a vampyre? A member of the undead? A soul stealer? Lies! They were telling him lies. But why?

L. G. BURBANK

Sliding through a narrow opening between two slabs of rock, Mordred pushed himself from the darkness of the tomb into the sunlight.

Breathing heavily, Mordred tried to slow his racing heartbeat. Every fiber in his being screamed with a blinding pain. He clenched his teeth and forced himself to stand unaided.

Where the hell was he?

Shielding his eyes from the white light of the sun, Mordred considered his options as he took in the scenery before him.

Nothing but sand. Endless mounds of golden sand.

Just as he was about to step forward and begin a journey to some unknown destination, his entire body began to burn. Mordred glanced down at his arms and watched, with growing horror, as his skin began to bubble.

"Agh!" he screamed in agony. He was literally burning alive. And then the brightness of day tilted, slanting at an unnatural angle, bringing a welcoming blanket of blackness. The darkness covered him, concealed him, and brought him back to safety.

CHAPTER THREE

"This man is to be the savior? He is a fool who will be easily killed by his creator." The man's voice came to Mordred's ears, and he realized he was back inside the cavern.

"Perhaps, but we must give him a chance to prove himself as we did those who came before him."

Mordred tried to sit up, but found he was wrapped so tightly in cloth he couldn't begin to do anything more than lie flat on his back.

"So, the light didn't kill you?"

With his eyes adjusting to the darkness, Mordred quickly scanned the area close to him and discovered the woman. She was holding pieces of cloth and rubbing them with a strange gray paste. The sharp fragrance of something Mordred could not place filled his nostrils.

"Why am I trussed up like an animal soon to be slaughtered?" he asked.

"Your body is badly burned, and while in time you will be able to withstand the light, now you are at your most weakened state. It is the time of your rebirth, and like a child, you must learn to go slowly during the transition."

"What do you mean?"

"Your body and all that will come to you must be achieved with patience," she replied while unwinding some of the bandages covering his right hand, revealing the blistered skin.

"You speak in riddles that I cannot understand. How is it that I know your language?"

The woman smiled, an expression that lit her face in the golden glow of the torchlight. She had long, ebony hair and deep set green eyes that, to Mordred, looked like large, oval gems. There was something mysterious about the woman that begged him to want to know more.

As if sensing his thoughts, the woman took a step back. Mordred watched her inhale deeply.

"Who are you?" he whispered, his throat suddenly dry.

Mordred had never been at a loss with women. With his dark, brooding looks and his prowess on the battlefield, the fairer sex was never far. He was never without the temptation of women, no matter where he traveled, no matter what strange culture he encountered. Yet, in time, Mordred found the simple act of fornicating with countless unknown women less than exciting. It was a physical release and nothing more.

Without fail the ladies always wanted more than one night with Mordred. He would never be able to give them what they desired. He was a drifter, a loner, a mercenary knight, and he had little need to marry. As a warrior for hire, he could not rise above his station by marrying a titled woman for he would never be considered a proper match. Like a barbarian, or a dangerous beast, it was better for Mordred to remain alone, always ready to move at a moment's notice. It did no good to put down roots. It did no good to feel anything other than the love of battle. Anything else would be deadly.

"Why do you move away from me?" Mordred asked, as he watched the woman remain just outside of his reach.

She took a piece of cloth and quickly coated it with the gray paste. Looking up, she met his gaze and his breath was taken from his body. She smiled again.

"You do not know your own powers. It is safer for me not to feel your touch, for even I would not be immune."

"What do you mean 'my' powers?"

There was a soft sigh. "You were always a sensual man, and now you are even more so. There is something that calls from deep within you, and there will be many who will respond to that call. You are not, however, ready to pursue the desires within your body, and I am no fool. Succumbing to your powers would leave me dead."

Shocked that she would think he might kill her, Mordred tried to deny her words. He attempted to rise from the slab, but her hand came quickly to his chest and he found himself as weak as a newborn babe. She stayed him with the brief touch of her hand.

"I do not think you would knowingly harm me, but you cannot control your change yet, and until then it is best we limit the number of times we make contact."

The woman brushed against his skin and then quickly began the task of wrapping cloth strips around his burned hand. When it was covered completely and securely, she did the same with his other hand.

"You never told me your name," Mordred said, fearing she would retreat and leave him to his own dark thoughts.

"I told you before it would not matter to you, and still it does not. We are only the first stop on your journey, and in time you will forget us. In a few days one of us will take you to those who wait, even now, for your arrival. They are the Templars and they will be able to give you the knowledge you search for. All of those you meet, that are preordained to assist you, are only the instruments of a greater purpose."

Suddenly his head ached. The woman spoke in riddles again, and Mordred was more confused than ever before.

She quietly picked up her bowl of paste and the extra cloth strips, and left the room. He was alone. The thing he feared most.

I'm a vampyre?

The thought made his stomach lurch, and he feared he'd vomit what little sustenance he'd been given. His skin itched. It gave him cause to believe what the stranger had told him. His body was now alien to him. His bones ached and his veins pulsed with renewed life.

His heartbeat pounded in his ears, reminding him of what he used to be.

Could he have a *heartbeat* if he were truly a vampyre? Would he have to drink blood to survive? Would he exist only in the shadows, never to feel the warmth of the sun? A thousand questions raced through his mind. A constant stream of anxious worry, like thousands of tiny, sharp arrows, jammed his senses. It paralyzed him with something he'd never known before.

Fear was foreign to Mordred. To feel fear as a mercenary would have been certain death. It was ironic now. He couldn't die. And he'd never been more afraid of his future.

Whether he was ready or not, the changes within him came. Days passed and he grew stronger, and more restless. The pain of his ordeal in the desert and the burning of his skin eventually subsided. He wondered at the quickness with which his body had seemingly healed. His injuries, including the strange melting of his skin, could easily have killed him or kept him convalescing for months. Even without a definitive measure of time, he knew his body had healed more quickly than ever before.

"You will bear the scars of your foolishness," came the silky voice of the woman, as she neared him with yet another foul smelling paste, this time the color of camel dung. As his acute sense of smell took over, he realized his guess was not far from the mark.

He wrinkled his nose and heard the woman laugh softly.

"There is truth that at times the cure is worse than the illness, eh?" she asked.

Wondering if she meant what she carried in the bowl, or his vampyrism, Mordred adjusted his position on the slab so he could focus fully on the mysterious being.

"So, I will always scar?"

"No. Even these will fade with time, but you are so very young in your vampyre state, and your body will take centuries to come into full being. You must go slowly. Be careful. Let your body catch up with your new role."

Mordred stuck on one word.

"Centuries?"

"Yes. Hundreds of years will pass before you grow into the full measure of your powers, and until then, even then, you will always have a weakness. You must be vigilant of your creator. The one called Vlad has been bestowed a greater power than you could ever hope to gain. The foolish actions of a few will affect the lives of thousands over time.

"Vlad will come for you, and once he discovers you will not turn to him, he will seek to destroy you. From him you will receive wounds that will not heal, and the scars will remain. You are vulnerable with him. Be warned."

"But I thought I was to be immortal?"

"You are, but there are things far more dangerous than the blades and arrows of men. There is dark magic and power stretching back to the beginning of time. Those are the things that will seek to harm you.

Vlad is not mortal, but he is of man's making. You must defeat him."

Bewilderment settled over Mordred as it always did whenever she spoke to him of things far beyond his understanding. Battles he could well imagine, but dark magic, sorcery, and the beginning of time left him stupefied. How could he even begin to think on what it would be like to survive longer than his mortal lifetime?

He also wondered at the people who had taken him in. The three were kind to him, in a distant way, and they always watched him with an undisguised wariness. It wasn't fear Mordred detected, but something deeper. A reservation, a hesitation to get closer, and perhaps some measure of respect.

"Do you fear me? Will others fear me?"

She smiled, and once again a strange warmth crept through his bones. She was like the sun, bringing light to his darkness. "I do not fear what is not evil. Others fear what they do not understand. And you now fear everything."

He watched her rub the paste on his burned skin after she removed the old strips of cloth. His skin barely showed any signs of the horrible damage of the sun's rays.

"I fear what my mind refuses to believe. How can I, a man, a mercenary warrior with nothing, be this great champion? How am I to believe I am now changed?"

"You must remove the veil from your eyes and see who you truly are. You cannot fear what has happened or he will rule you with it."

Mordred sat up. There was no pain. He turned his

hands over to gaze at his palms. He looked altogether normal to his eyes.

"No one rules me. No one ever has."

A movement at the back of the chamber alerted Mordred to the presence of one of the men. "You underestimate the power that is Vlad, and that will be your undoing, like all those before you."

Mordred watched the man as he approached. He appeared very old, with a long gray beard that hung to his waist. He wore the familiar loose fitting green robes with the strange emblem of a tree on the front sewn with silver thread.

Moving to stand, Mordred was pleased to discover his body was gaining strength. This was the first time since his gruesome duel with the sun that he was able to remain upright, without the support of walls or stone.

"There were others before me? But I thought I was the Chosen One."

Waving his hand dismissively, the man eyed Mordred with strange silver-blue orbs that danced and shone more brightly than the flames of the torches. "There were many before you. They were all Chosen Ones."

"And what happened to them?"

The man shrugged. "They all failed, and now, there is only you."

"Wouldn't you know which person would be the right one?" Mordred asked incredulously.

"It is not for us to determine. We only bring them back to life, and then take them to the Templars."

Mordred had heard them speak of the Templars

before but he had not concentrated on them. Instead he had preferred to understand more of his own plight. This time he queried about the mysterious organization shrouded in secrecy.

"The Knights Templar?" He had heard of the organization of warrior knights who allegedly protected the pilgrims searching for the Holy Land. "What have they to do with vampyres?"

There was a laugh. "That will be for them to tell you, if they choose."

"Why did you not leave me in the desert?"

"That is not your fate. You are the Chosen One," the man repeated, not showing any outward sign of annoyance at having to answer the same questions over and over. "And so were many others."

"You confuse me, old man."

"There is much that will confuse you on this journey, but know this: You determine the outcome of what happens to you."

The woman broke the strained silence between Mordred and the man. "It looks as though you are strong enough to walk about. Let us show you where you are. Let us show you the Lost City of the Dead."

† † †

The sun was setting, casting hues of purple and pink about the walls of the steep canyon. The sky appeared as a beautifully painted canvas in shades of blue such as Mordred had never seen. And then there were the stars, appearing at a breathtakingly rapid pace, creating a blaze of silver light in the heavens. A soft, shimmering light fell to the ground, illuminating the stones that rose high around them.

But, these were not the simple rocks shaped and molded by the strong desert winds. These were incredible monuments carved by men. Stunningly detailed works of what could only be called art, surrounded entrances into the walls of the canyon. It looked to be an entire city contained within the natural stone walls.

Blinking several times, Mordred realized he could see everything around him as though it were daylight. He could pick out the colors of the stone, somewhere between a deep brown and a rose. He saw the strange markings and symbols in place over the arched doorways. His eyes followed the straight lines and angles that decorated the walls of this ancient city.

There was magic here, Mordred thought. Even without his new self, he would have known this. Something special dwelled here among the rocks, and it tugged at Mordred's soul.

"Where am I?"

"You are in the Lost City of the Dead. This is a necropolis. The first of many you will see. Each door leads to a chamber, a tomb for one who has passed on."

While they continued to walk, Mordred watched the night creatures stirring in the crevices and cracks. Scorpions shifted soundlessly. Snakes undulated across the sand. The images within the carved doors came alive in the night to Mordred.

His eyes saw the colors of the stone reflected in the stars' gaze. The tiny tracks in the sand by a desert rodent.

And everywhere there was an indefinable air of something strange. Something dark and mysterious chanted softly, causing a ripple beneath his skin.

"You are feeling the ancients. The ones who have been here before you. Let them speak to you. Let them give you their wisdom."

Mordred turned to the old man. "How is it you know what I feel? What magic do you possess?"

"No magic. We only serve the Templars. We only know what they tell us. You are affected by the dead because you were once dead yourself. You will always be thus. And you can call on the dead for help, should you need them."

"What help can the dead bring to me?"

"Nothing that can be seen with mortal eyes. You will learn, young one, not to question what is put before you. Just remember you will be most at home amid the cities of the dead."

This last left Mordred feeling unsettled and angry. He didn't want to feel at home in what amounted to a graveyard. He wanted to feel at home in the sun. He didn't want to hide in shadow, but stroll among the hillsides of his homeland in the daylight. He didn't want to be immortal; he simply wanted to be a man.

Everything had changed according to this mysterious trio.

They stopped walking and listened to the sounds of the wind as it blew through the canyon. It sounded to Mordred like the voices of thousands of people all speaking at once. He was almost ready to cover his ears, but he knew that wouldn't lessen what he heard.

Beneath the voices, he could hear the night. Things moving, rocks shifting. Heartbeats and pulses. He could hear a grain of sand, sounding as loud to him as the scratching of a stick across hard ground. He could hear a rippling from somewhere under him, and he realized slowly that he was hearing water as it ran far below the sand.

"One day you will be able to hear each voice as it calls to you. You will know which ones are true and which ones lead you astray. For now it is all a jumble, but one day, if you trust in them, the dead will lead you home."

"Scotland?" he dared to ask. The images of rolling green hills, crumbling stone, and churning seas, filled his mind momentarily.

"Home," was all the woman offered.

"It is time," came the voice of the one man who walked beside Mordred. "Arad, the other, will take you as far as the Templar stronghold north of here. The rest of what happens will be up to you. Listen well to the Templars, for it is they who can help you."

† † †

The man called Arad moved quietly within the catacombs, packing materials. All items were loaded into several cloth sacks. He offered no words, leaving Mordred with a feeling of isolated dread.

He was leaving the only people who knew about his new self. The only people who could even remotely understand what he had become, and what he would become. While they had certainly kept their distance, Mordred was beginning to relax around them. He felt an odd measure of safety here, and now he was being told he had to leave.

The Templars. What would the Templars have to do with vampyres? They were a holy order of knights. Men who gave their lives to protect the pilgrims, who searched among ruins, and relics, for the word of God.

They had many castles across this strange land and seemed largely concerned with securing their own wealth. There were even rumors among the soldiers that the Templars had discovered and absconded with sacred relics, including the Holy Grail and the Ark of the Covenant, things Mordred knew nothing about.

It all came back to God. Something Mordred had no faith in. God wouldn't have sought to create such a monster as a vampyre. If this entity was almighty, then why on this earth would there ever be such a gruesome creature as a vampyre? Nay, a vampyre could surely only have come from the devil. Only evil could come from evil.

Once again, confusion surrounded him like a heavy cloak.

Sensing a presence near him, Mordred knew without turning that it was the woman.

"What am I to learn with the Templars that I cannot learn here?"

"All you need to know about being a vampyre. The Templars have spent hundreds of years studying and understanding what is to come. Only they have the information and the learning to teach you what you must know to survive."

Mordred frowned and brushed a lock of his hair from his eyes. Arad was still busy stuffing items into satchels. "The Templars haven't been around for centuries. They are a newly created order."

"The order, yes, it is newly created, but the people belonging to the order, their families, their blood, are all linked to their knowledge in a way even we do not understand. It is true however that they know nearly all there is to know about vampyres. They will even know about you."

"Me? I have never met a Templar."

"It wouldn't matter if you had. Everything is about timing. Now the time is right for you to make the journey and to begin the path your life will take. They knew you were coming long before you did."

Feeling as though he were caught in a bizarre dream, and that at any moment he would wake, Mordred sighed.

The woman reached out to touch his shoulder, and while she stopped just short of his body, he could feel the heat of the near contact. It rippled through him like a flame. "Do not lose heart, Mordred, for at times that will be the only thing that separates you from the others. That, and your soul."

He clenched his jaw as he watched her move away from him, her robes curling and flowing silently with her motion. "I thought I didn't have a soul anymore."

She stopped then, and turned back to him with something akin to a half smile on her face. He could still feel the warmth of her presence within him, like a golden light, cleansing him.

"You have a soul, Mordred. You will always have a soul, for as long as you will it."

The woman turned her back to him and moved past Arad making no sound. The man motioned to Mordred that he should follow. Wearily, Mordred pushed himself up from the rock. The black robes he had been given fluttered around him, sending a cooling breeze across his heated skin.

Mordred gave one backward glance at the place that had served as home to him for this part of his new life. Then he strode from the cramped room of the ancient underground tomb. The journey to the Templars was upon him.

† † †

A maze of tunnels led Mordred and his silent companion beneath the desert and its shifting sands. It was almost impossible to believe they were covering great distances under the earth, as the journey was slow going.

They stopped to rest only long enough for Mordred to drink a strange, bitter liquid from the flasks that had been packed.

At night, under the cover of darkness, the twosome came above ground and traveled through small towns and desert outposts, only to find another entrance to another cave. Always, before the sun crested the hills, they descended back into the endless catacombs.

Moving through the vast network of tunnels, Mordred feared that if his guide should suddenly slip away, he would rot in the catacombs. He could never possibly find his way to the surface on his own.

Beneath the sands and away from the wind, which at times howled through the narrow passageways they traversed, there were incredible sights to behold. Ruined temples and the remains of villages long forgotten lay undisturbed and unseen by those who walked above.

Treasures twinkled here and there, catching some tiny ray of light that filtered its way through a crack or a crevice. Other times gold glinted, and silver shone brightly beneath the flame of the torch Arad carried.

Occasionally, the smell of death, a smell with which Mordred was all too familiar, came to him. Now, however, he could determine without seeing whether the scent of decay was from an animal or a human.

They passed through what must have served as crypts for the dead, but unlike the walled necropolis Mordred had come from, there were no voices or sounds to be heard. It was silent. Nothing but the sounds of their movements, their breathing, and their hearts beating.

Once, Mordred caught sight of the skeletal remains of a warrior, sword still in hand, lying against the walls. The catacombs had become the man's eternal tomb.

Strange sights and even stranger smells came to him, and always Arad pushed on, both determined and silent. A thousand questions waged a mighty war within Mordred's mind. While outside himself there was silence, inside his head was the sound of endless truths and falsehoods, thoughts and feelings that crashed in a deafening roar within him.

Each time he thought he might grasp an answer and make some sense of the madness of his being, the thought disappeared. Each time one door closed, hundreds more opened within the confines of his consciousness.

Who was he? What was his destiny?

The realization that he was a vampyre was still slow in settling into his bones. Every now and again Mordred would open his eyes hoping to find himself waking from the nightmare. But it persisted.

The Mordred of the past had been a simple man. Raised by the might of the sword, he had earned his rank within the armies. He never took any sides in battle. He abstained from the political and religious debates that raged through the countries. He kept himself isolated from everyone else, serving only himself.

There was nothing for him to lose faith in, for he had no faith in anything but himself. He was a drifter, a wanderer. He hadn't been home in years. He had been a lost soul, but never in his past life had he ever felt the loneliness as he did now.

He had been in peak physical condition from the day he'd squired for a friend of his father's. He'd been sent away from home at the tender age of six, first to learn how to be a page, then to squire for a knight, and finally to become a knight himself, though it was unofficial, as the claim was not from a birthright.

His reputation and respect were things earned on the field of battle. Mordred felt this was the truer way to uphold the virtues of chivalry; the upper echelon of society disagreed. He was never welcome. Always the dark horse, the dangerous one, the mercenary.

His old life, Mordred realized, was small and in some ways safe. It was consistent. Unlike other men, Mordred had never questioned his existence or his mortality. There would be battles, and each time Mordred would fight on.

Whether he lived or died was never the issue. He simply existed in his world of blood and steel. Never afraid. He trusted in the strength of his body and the might of his sword.

A strange disquiet crept into Mordred's hidden places as the days wore on. It disturbed his thoughts like the prickling of a spear point, keeping him on the edge of something and creating a tension he'd never felt before.

His future and his life had been taken from him in that one instant in the desert. Stolen without his absolute consent. Taken in the madness of death and now he was expected to fight against something all-powerful. It was entirely too surreal.

The edges of his world were no longer clearly defined, but blurred as if by an artist's brush. An artist of the macabre.

In the dimness of a chamber somewhere along the journey, Mordred allowed himself to fully experience his range of emotions. His mind sifted through feelings as if they were grains of the sands above them.

One day during this process, Mordred suddenly came alive with the knowledge that the blackness settling within him, snuffing out all light, was indeed the beast of fear.

Fear had captured him and now held him in thrall. Unleashed, dread wreaked havoc inside, playing with his mind. It caused him to doubt the man he had been. It made him believe he was not the mighty warrior knight he had thought himself to be. Instead it coerced him into thinking he was only a man, easily dispatched. One that could not possibly survive this new quest.

As if sensing the change that had fallen over his charge and knowing its cause, Arad turned to Mordred while they squeezed between rocks and sand and spoke the only words he would utter on the journey. "Fear is the first step to awakening."

CHAPTER FOUR

Both Arad and Mordred came above ground, exiting yet another tomb. Mordred exhaled a sigh of relief. He was glad to be free of the noise that filled his head to bursting. Noise from the dead supposedly, yet he could make out no real words. It caused a great deal of pain to absorb the different sounds. He felt tired, lonely, and still the fear dogged him like a hound on the scent of a kill.

The night sky was filled with the glory of a thousand stars, each one twinkling like a precious jewel. Deep midnight blue brushed the sky and mingled with purple and black. The shining glow from above illuminated the area as if the sun still shone.

The air was cool and sweet. It was fresh and different from the air that had previously filled Mordred's lungs. He took great breaths, uncaring of how he might appear to the silent man beside him.

Cautiously, Arad motioned that Mordred should follow him. He raised a finger to his lips letting Mordred know there was danger close at hand should they be discovered. Mordred wondered what they needed to fear, as he was an immortal. A shudder shot through him at his silent question. No answer was forthcoming as they wound their way through large dunes and narrow passageways.

From seemingly nowhere, there appeared before Mordred a small building. It was unassuming and looked rather worn. The wooden beams of the structure were warped and bent from the powerful winds of the desert.

Mordred discerned a cross on the top of the building. It was a chapel.

Arad pointed to the dilapidated building and then back to Mordred.

Frowning, Mordred questioned the odd man. "I do not understand. What is it you wish me to do?"

Arad sighed and motioned again toward the building.

"No, I don't need to seek sanctuary and I'm not a believer in God, so let us move on."

The old man, smaller in stature than Mordred, drew himself up to his full height and, with a shove, sent Mordred in the direction of the church. The gesture was so quick Mordred barely saw his hands move.

Finally, realization dawned on Mordred.

"You want me to go to the church?"

This time the man nodded, a small smile crossing his face. Mordred thought it looked like a smile of relief rather than happiness.

Why couldn't the man simply tell him what he was supposed to do? Was he afraid that if he spoke more than a few words to Mordred, Mordred might simply eat him?

"Well then, come on. It's to church we go."

The sand, still retaining the heat of the sun, filled his sandals with warmth. He would give much to have his boots and surcoat back. He paused then, and looked over his shoulder. Arad hadn't moved.

"Well, what are you waiting for? Are you coming with me or not?"

He saw Arad shake his head and knew then that he would have to take the next step of his journey alone. He let out an audible sigh and turned to look at the unassuming building. What on earth was he doing in the middle of the desert entering a holy place? It was a little too late to save his soul, he thought wryly.

As he turned back to thank Arad, he saw that the man was already gone, having disappeared into the night like a shadow.

Mordred paused as he came before the old building. It looked as though it was losing the fight against the wind, and that someday very soon the desert would reclaim it. The dunes on both sides rose to such a great height that if he had not been led here, Mordred was sure he would never have seen the church.

This was supposed to be a place of great learning? The place where he would understand what it was like to be a soul stealer? This was where he was to walk the line between the living and the dead? The Knights Templar resided here?

If accepting his fears was his first lesson, perhaps his second was that appearances were deceiving, Mordred thought. This was the last place he would have pictured finding enlightenment.

He touched the intricate wrought iron that covered the door, but before he could reach for the handle, it was flung open. Several robed and masked figures appeared. Eight attackers came at him.

With an inhuman swiftness, they grabbed at him, pushing him forward. No weapons were drawn, but the strength of the assailants was great. Mordred had little time to think of his next course of action. Something else took hold of him.

Instinctively he reached for his sword. Then he remembered he'd lost it in the desert. Defenseless and wearing nothing but a robe and sandals, he had only two choices. He could stand and fight with his bare hands. Or he could run. He'd never run from a battle before. He certainly wasn't going to start now.

Mordred spun around and kicked out with his feet as the figures moved in. And then in the blink of an eye, he could no longer feel the blows, and his body was not registering his hits on the robed assailants. His punches appeared to hit only the air, yet he watched figures stumble and fall.

With a detached sense of self Mordred continued defending himself. Soon the figures began to fall away toward the walls of the chapel. He could scarcely believe it was his own power that sent them away from him. A strange energy flooded Mordred. It was like the battle instinct that had come over him in his former life. Everything became quiet, and in the midst of ultimate chaos, his mind was serene, his muscles fluid.

One by one, and then two or three at a time, the robed figures continued to charge him. Each time he thrust, kicked, and turned with the grace of a great predator. Slamming his fist into . . . no . . . through, a jaw. It was the same strange feeling as his knee found a home in the groin of an attacker. The force of the blows simply vanished into air. As if he weren't causing damage at all. Yet, the scene before him told him otherwise.

Sounds were slowed into a symphony of groans. Bones cracked with a sickening snap. Perhaps the most surreal thing of all was the vast amount of red that spilled across the white tile flooring of the holy place.

The bodies flew through the air, crashing into the walls and falling onto the wooden pews. Wood splintered with the force of Mordred's blows. Still they came at him as if he caused no damage. And still he fought on.

It felt good to fight. This was familiar. A part of his old life returned to him. He became the center of calm amidst the storm of attack, his movements so clean and precise the attackers had no hope but to perhaps wear him down. To Mordred it felt as if he could go on for hours; a renewed surge of strength flowed through him.

Catching one figure by the throat, he tried to lift the man. But his hand did not hold flesh. The figure slid to the floor and before Mordred's eyes, disappeared.

It left Mordred momentarily stunned. What kind of trick was this? He could hear the blood pounding through the attackers' veins and the beating of their hearts. He could smell the unique tang of blood. But they were not real?

Interrupting his dark thoughts, a voice sounded from

the shadows at the back of the chapel. Mordred whirled.

"Lesson number one . . . nothing will be as it appears. Always look for otherworldly interference before you begin your attack." came the deep voice from the shadows. "Welcome to the Templars. You are the Chosen One."

It was a statement of fact that did not demand an answer.

The language was French, though with a strange accent. Mordred spoke little French. However when he spoke his words were fluent, as if he'd spoken this language all his life.

"I am Mordred Soulis. I have been instructed to seek out the Knights Templar. Why were you just now attacking me?" This he said in a tone that did little to disguise his anger. His teeth remained clenched. His fists were tightly balled awaiting further attacks.

He turned to face the strangers only to realize they had all vanished.

"They are my protectors," the voice spoke, answering Mordred's question.

A man appeared from the shadows clad in a long gold robe emblazoned with a large red cross.

"They were real enough. Come closer so that I may have a good long look at you."

"Who are you?" Mordred demanded.

"I am Jakob, Master of the Templars, servant to all that is holy. And you are in HarMeggido. You will remain here for some time. I will be your teacher for this part of your journey."

Mordred cocked his head to one side. Who should he trust? The green robed people in the tombs had shown him nothing but kindness. They had led him to this place and told him this was where he would learn about his fate. Yet, despite the knowledge, Mordred was not at ease under the piercing silver-blue gaze of the man before him.

"You are wise not to trust so soon. It will help you in the future. Come, we pose no threat to you, and you and I have much time we must spend together so you can be prepared for what awaits you in the future. When you are ready, you will be shown the next leg of your journey."

When Mordred didn't move closer as instructed, the figure did. His long surcoat and cape flowed behind him like great golden angel's wings.

A beard of brightest white reached to his waist. Full and neatly groomed, it gave the impression Jakob was impossibly old. In his eyes, however, Mordred saw the glint of steel. This man was not to be trifled with. Whatever his profession proved to be, he was master of it.

The brilliant crimson cross undulated of its own accord, as if alive. It called Mordred's attention, and he found himself staring rather like a boy seeing a knight for the first time.

Beneath the surcoat of gold, exposed at the shoulders, Jakob wore a shirt of brilliantly polished silver mail. It glowed and sparkled under the many candles that filled the chapel. Its exquisite craftsmanship was revealed in the thousands of tiny shining rings. Beneath the mail,

Mordred could see the white cotton cloth of his gambeson.

There was more to the man than his appearance though that was impressive enough. Jakob was a tall man, nearer to Mordred's height than most, but he was graceful in his movements.

"Come, walk with me. Truly, I mean you no harm," the man said, and he extended an aged hand.

His skin was nearly transparent, and Mordred saw blue veins rippling and pulsing with life just beneath the surface. Mordred's nostrils flared as he picked up the scent of the stranger. It wasn't the scent of soap the man had used at last bath that held Mordred captive. And it wasn't the smell of the cooking fire, though these things existed in the scent. Nay, it was something far more intoxicating and seductive.

Licking his lips, Mordred moved forward only to have the man raise his hand and motion him to stop. His voice gave rise to a sound that echoed off the stone walls of the chapel, surrounding Mordred.

"This won't do at all. I am to be your teacher, not your next meal. You must learn to control yourself and your growing appetite."

Disgust rose immediately in Mordred, but it waged a fierce battle with an internal hunger that proved almost too painful to deny.

"I was not thinking to eat you," Mordred growled.

"Ah, you are so very young. Your actions, even tiny, nearly imperceptible ones, give you away. You will need to be far more careful and in control at all times if you are to succeed in this quest."

Mordred replied, incensed at the man's perceptions, "I am not exactly sure I want to go on this quest."

Jakob cast a hand to the air. "That, my boy, has been taken completely out of your control. Your fate was decided the day you should have died upon the sands. Nay, me thinks perhaps even before then. Now you have no choice but to accept the role of the Chosen One."

"Don't I?" Mordred dared the man to tell him otherwise. Anger surged through his veins, blocking out all else. His vision tilted, blurring for a split second before returning. Now, however, everything he saw was bathed in a dark shade of red.

"Control yourself!" came Jakob's thunderous voice. It was so demanding it shook the wooden timbers, causing dust to rain down upon them from the rafters.

When Mordred turned to look at the man, he could swear Jakob had somehow gained the power to fly. He appeared to be hovering above the ground, his large cape flowing around him. He looked very much the part of an avenging angel in the tiny chapel.

Jakob's eye glowed bright silver with warning. Flecks of blue dotted his irises.

"Make no mistake, Mordred Soulis, you will take this journey. There is no other choice, and until the time you leave our temple, you will obey."

He bowed his head, shaking loose the thong that held back the length of his black hair. It was the closest thing Mordred could summon to show his acceptance, and it worked. Immediately, everything returned to normal. Jakob now stood beside him with a kindly look in his now blue eyes.

"We will go below now."

"Below?"

Jakob snorted, "Surely you didn't think this was all there was to our existence, did you?"

The man's face lit up with a most disarming smile. Blue seeped into the silver of his eyes changing the color. To Mordred it appeared as though a light shone from within, creating a white glow around his pupils. He realized despite their short time together, he liked Jakob. The old man had a regalness about him. He exuded a quiet strength.

"Why do I get the feeling you could have handled me on your own?"

Jakob laughed as he held out his hand. "Me? I am but an old man. One who has lived far too long and seen too many things."

"Yes, perhaps, but I get the distinct impression your soul is older than your outward appearance. What secrets do you hide, old man?"

Leading Mordred past the wreckage of his earlier fight, Jakob moved soundlessly. "In time you will learn more. Now, however, it is time to show you your dwelling place, for the next step in your journey."

Following Jakob, Mordred surveyed the tiny chapel. The rows of wooden pews were completely destroyed. The wood paneling covering the stone walls bore evidence of the recent battle, leaving indentations where bodies had landed. It was difficult for Mordred to believe that the force of his blows caused such damage. Bearing witness to the havoc he had wreaked caused him to wonder at the truth of himself. But before he could ponder further, Jakob interrupted his thoughts.

"I can only guess what you are feeling now, but you must acknowledge your fears and the powers that come with this new self. To deny them causes weakness, and evil thrives on weakness."

Mordred remained silent. He continued to eye his surroundings.

At the back of the chapel hung a painting, part of a larger series that flanked each of the walls. Though the colors had long since faded, the images radiated a strange glow, making the figures easily discernible.

"The angel Lucifer, being cast out from heaven."

When Mordred remained silent, Jakob continued, "Ah, so you are not a religious man. Good. Then, the transition will be far easier for you."

"Easier?" Mordred ran a hand through his hair.

"It is always easier to teach a babe the first time than to undo years of training."

Turning to Jakob, Mordred asked, "So you are saying religion is a bad thing?"

"Not at all. What I am saying is that the *teaching* of religion is a bad thing."

"I don't understand."

"In time, as with all things, you will. For now, let me say that the concept of faith is not wrong, only how that concept is taught."

Confusion swept over Mordred. He narrowed his eyes. "Are you not the leader of the Knights Templar? Are you not a holy order based upon the principles of God? Is not the entire organization dedicated to religion?"

"That is what we tell the Church. All things are not what they seem. In order to exist in the shadow of the Church, we play a game. We have faith, do not misunderstand me. But we see far more clearly than any pope or king, because we know what is real."

As Mordred continued to survey the room, he noticed more images, strange figures, some not human, gazing down at him from the walls and ceiling. Silent watchers.

One face caught his attention. It stared at him as if mocking him. It was the Celtic symbol of the Green Man. A laughing face, peering through green leaves, its eyes strangely luminescent.

"Ah, so you recognize something familiar," came Jakob's voice, softly.

Mordred tilted his head to gain a better view of the artistically designed image carved in stone. "Yes, I know this symbol well, but why is it here, so far away from Celtic lands?"

"That, my friend, is one of the many hidden symbols you will come to recognize when searching for an ally among the enemies. The Green Man is the mark of a Templar church. The one place you will find sanctuary. Search for it in the future."

Jakob's hand moved quickly over the painted wall before them, faster than even Mordred's eyesight could detect. When he stopped, there was an eerie scraping sound, stone moving against stone.

The wall split in two. The opening gave way to a large stone staircase that spiraled downward into darkness.

"You will forgive my humanness?" Jakob turned to reach for the only burning torch within sight and lifted it from its holder. "I do not have your keen eyesight."

Mordred followed Jakob as they began their descent.

"I am confused," Mordred admitted.

"Already?"

"More than you could possibly imagine. Did you just say that I could find sanctuary in a church? But I am something unholy. How can that be?"

"Be warned. You will not be safe in just any church. Those not made by Templars could well spell your doom. Always look for the symbol of the Green Man, or another symbol which we will make you privy to soon. Sometimes they are well hidden within the design of the building and not readily seen by human eyes.

"We have existed with the Roman Catholic Church, but we are not well liked. They would not appreciate us putting our mark on something they feel belongs to them. Thus we do so in secret."

As they continued to spiral downward, Mordred could see nothing but an endless stairway and the stone walls closing in on them.

Jakob continued. "Remember that not all churches will be safe for you. There are those not of our making that could cause you greater harm."

"I did not imagine vampyres welcome in any religious building," Mordred replied, his sarcasm unmistakable.

"You would be correct in your thinking. You forget, however, that you are not a true vampyre."

"If I am immortal, why do I need a safe haven?"

There was a soft chuckle before Jakob responded. "It appears the order left a few things out. No matter. That is why they brought you to me."

The scraping of sandals on stone broke the sudden silence. Mordred stopped counting the number of stairs they had come down.

From somewhere far below, a cool breeze wafted upward. It carried the scent of water, fire, and a host of other familiar smells.

"What can kill me?"

"Only those who know your secret will try to kill you. They will wait until you determine the course of your destiny. They will bide their time in the hope that you show a weakness they can exploit. If they find you are not agreeable to their way of thinking, they will come for you and you will need protection."

"But I am a vampyre . . ."

"You are only partly a vampyre for now, which means you can still be killed. You could find immortality someday, but until then you are not indestructible. You must always be aware and alert to the dangers that will follow you. Sometimes they will be well disguised. It will take hundreds of years before you grow to become the man spoken of in legend."

"Man, or vampyre?" came the almost hostile reply. He felt Jakob's hand upon his shoulder.

"All in good time, Mordred. All in good time."

Jakob pulled Mordred to a halt when the floor became level.

It took Mordred a moment to realize Jakob knew his name. His head ached but he wasn't sure it was from this new place, or the hunger that rumbled through him.

"Come, I will show you to your quarters. I will have food brought to you."

"Food?" Mordred wondered if Jakob actually knew what sort of food he would require. The man was far too hospitable for one who understood Mordred to be a blood-sucking creature of the night.

He didn't want to think about the sweet liquid he had been given each day since he awoke. Now he found he craved the drink with a passion that was beginning to scare him. He counted the hours until he would be given the crimson fluid again. When it was given to him, he drank his fill, and still he hungered.

How could any of this be real? One minute he was a mercenary soldier fighting the infidels for the good of the Church, and now he was a vampyre, or a half-born vampyre, or something other than wholly human. How was he supposed to simply accept this?

It felt to Mordred as if he were sleepwalking through some horrible nightmare. Somewhere he knew it was a dream from which he would never awake.

Perhaps he really had died and this was Purgatory, the place he would suffer eternal penance. Perhaps his soul was not worthy of a final resting place. Perhaps he was destined to never find the peace in death he sought in life.

Mordred did not bow to religious ideals, but as he pondered the recent events the twists and turns his life had suddenly taken, he began to wonder if he shouldn't have taken the concept of faith more seriously.

Perhaps if he had existed as something more than a

man who killed for a living, his life would have ended better. How could he be considered the one to save the human race? He had never tried very hard to save anyone but himself.

There had to be a mistake. He was unworthy to be a savior of any kind. He had experienced the seven deadly sins and then some. He'd never thought much beyond the immediacy of each day. He had never been the one to care about anyone but himself. How then could he be deemed the Chosen One?

Jakob had ceased speaking after Mordred's comment on food and instead came to a halt beside an arched and intricately carved wooden door.

Mordred peered into the darkness of the endless hall. It ran for as far as the eye could see in either direction. The torches blazing in their holders lent the only warmth to the stone passageway.

There was, in the far distance to the right, a bright light. Mordred could make out shadows cast upon the far walls. They flickered and danced in twisted rhythm. Hearty but faint laughter came to his ears. Beneath the laughter was the note of strange music. Somewhere, there were other inhabitants.

"You must rest now. There will be time enough to introduce you to the men. I'll send someone in with your drink. When it is time to continue, I'll have you brought to me."

Feeling uncomfortable as a sudden weariness settled in his bones, Mordred nodded.

Jakob opened the door to reveal Mordred's accommodations, and he entered. When he turned to ask

Jakob a final question, it was to discover the old man had slipped away, as silently as he had first appeared. He was only a flicker of white in the distance, soundless save for the rippling of his surcoat.

†††

Mordred felt completely alone again, sitting in the near darkness of his strange surroundings. The chamber itself was large. Its curved ceiling and intricate carvings could almost have passed for a grand castle in his homeland.

Thoughts of Scotland brought even darker despair to Mordred as he sat on his soft bed. What would become of him?

Images of the men who had died in the desert still plagued him. In blackness that was night, their voices called out to him. Each time he closed his eyes, he feared seeing them. But he feared the haunting dreams even more.

Though he was not an educated man, he had done well learning the world around him. Mordred had sailed on ships and visited places few men had dared to go. In his duty as a mercenary fighter he had been summoned to the courts of kings and princes in far away lands. He'd been to isolated kingdoms perched precariously on snow-covered mountaintops. He'd bathed in the clear blue waters of a tropical paradise that one could only imagine in dreams.

Mordred had learned of politics and greed and the worst of human nature from those he had fought for.

He'd seen the ugly side of humanity that often left him wondering if all mankind wouldn't be better served simply destroying itself and starting over.

He reflected on the nature of things from what he saw before him. Through his life came his learning. Through his actions came his education. He had little use for philosophy and for current religious ponderings. Life was won and lost every day in a world that never slowed. What did it matter which god one believed in, if in the end everyone would die?

And what was death but an ending, absolute. There was nothing to believe in but the constant cycle of birth and death.

Placing his head in his hands, Mordred wondered about what he had heard from men he'd encountered in the camps before battles. Some prayed, some wept, some drank. Everyone pleaded to the heavens to spare their lives. Mordred had begged for death and had been denied. Where was God?

And if there was truth to the belief that God had created man in his own image, then what kind of God was there to believe in anyway? One that supported massacres and genocide and rape and plunder? One that encouraged hatred and violence? Mordred had never seen any other side of a supposed god save the one he had witnessed on the battlefield. And that was not a god he would pledge his life to serve.

So what then was the devil? Or could it be that God and the devil were one and the same?

A fierce pounding started just behind Mordred's eyes. He heard something slither in the air, something shifting.

A feeling of cold crept up his spine, and he raised his head. It felt to Mordred as if he wasn't alone and yet, even without his newfound keen eyesight, he could tell there was no one else in the chamber. At least not one he would consider human.

He raised himself from the bed and reached for his sword, only to remember once again that it had been lost in the desert. Could there be danger here? He had been told he would be safe. Why then did he feel something malicious hiding just outside his field of vision?

Like the sniffing of a beast outside his door, Mordred could barely make out the distinct sound of something searching, smelling, trying to locate him. His fists tightened, clenching with suppressed strength.

A shadow slipped past his door. Mordred saw the shifting of light and dark just beyond the wood frame. He crept closer and then in one swift move, yanked open the door. His fingers came in contact with cloth and something altogether human. Angrily he throttled the being and pulled it into his chambers.

A crashing sounded against the stones, metal hitting the ground. A voice called out, filled with fear. Mordred's nostrils inhaled the fragrance. He felt something stir to life within him. The beast that had lain dormant awoke.

His eyes burned and the words coming to his ears sounded altogether distorted and nonsensical.

It was a man. A young man, robed much like Jakob. His surcoat bore the crimson cross of the Templars. The man struggled to get his feet on the ground, while trying to get Mordred to release the grip on his neck.

His skin started to turn from white to red to blue. Gasping for breath the man rasped, "Please, sir, please. I mean you no harm. Please . . ."

Miraculously, for the young man, Mordred's hearing returned to normal and he immediately stopped throttling him. He turned away, unable to face that he had nearly killed the man. "Leave."

"Yes, yes, sir. I will have some more food brought. I'm sorry I dropped the tray."

"No, no more food. Go . . ."

The young man really didn't have to be told twice. He stepped backward out of the chamber and fled down the long hallway.

Mordred closed the door. The feeling of something else being in the room with him was now gone. But he couldn't shake the feeling that he was being mocked. It was as if the sounds of silence masked the laughter, but still he heard them.

Was this the madness of a soul lost?

91

CHAPTER FIVE

"He is here now?"

"Yes," Jakob replied softly and looked up from a stack of charts and decorated manuscripts, pages rustling with his movements. One of the papers rolled off the desk and fell to the floor. It came to a stop at the tip of the black boot belonging to the visitor.

Only Markus dared disturb the Master Templar without so much as a knock.

Smiling, Jakob watched as Markus in one smooth motion plucked the scroll up and returned it to Jakob. His heavy chain mail shirt tinkled musically.

It was only right that Markus should question, Jakob thought. He had trained him well, and it was expected that Markus would be concerned.

Both his strength and his understanding would serve him well in his new role. Though he knew it not, Markus would be Mordred's protector until he left the Templars. Even here he would not be safe for long.

Evil, like the very air one breathed, infiltrated everywhere. Every sacred temple and each bright spot could easily become tainted. Even in such a place of goodness and hope, it crept unseen along the very corridors of the Templar stronghold.

Jakob knew it was inevitable that one among his rank would betray the order. Such was the way of humankind. Such was the way of malevolence. Cleverly disguised, it tempted saints.

There was a noticeable difference in the air tonight. One that would certainly keep the Master Templar long awake. It wasn't that he had welcomed a vampyre into the stronghold, though that would surely keep a few of the men locked behind their doors. Nay, it was that something dark and wicked stalked this place, searching for the one man who would betray the order. Now was not the moment, but it was in the near future. Jakob feared it, and he feared the damage it would do to Mordred's soul.

Jakob prayed it would not be Markus. He had become his comrade on the quest to save mankind, and along the way he had also become Jakob's friend.

"Are you sure he is the One?"

"I am sure," Jakob replied. "Even if he, himself, refuses to believe it."

Markus's blue eyes met Jakob's. Thoughts needing no words passed between them.

Candlelight haloed Markus's blond hair. No, it would not be Markus. *Please, God, let it not be Markus*, Jakob prayed silently.

"If he refuses to believe, then we are in trouble. He must believe," Markus said, an angry edge creeping into his voice.

Nodding silently, Jakob rubbed his eyes. He was tired of late, as if the final chapter in the fate of the human race sapped the lifeblood from his veins.

"Are you unwell?" Markus approached the dais and placed a hand on Jakob's shoulder.

"Nay, no more so than yesterday and the day before that. I am just overtired," he lied, slightly ashamed by how easily he had done so.

At this juncture, like Mordred, he could trust no one completely, and it pained him to deceive Markus. None could know he weakened.

Jakob laid his hand on Markus's and gave him what he hoped was a convincing look.

"I am fine, friend, but I thank you as always for your concern. Now, tell me what troubles you."

Markus retrieved a wooden chair and pushed it in front of Jakob's desk. He noticed the elder still held the scroll.

Markus's eyes widened as he made out the words etched eons ago on the parchment. "Truly, he is the One? Without a doubt?"

Jakob brought his attention back to the paper he reviewed. He rubbed his balding head and sighed in weariness, "He is the One."

Not to be placated, Markus rested his mail-covered elbows on the table across from Jakob.

"What of all the others? The men who came before? How do we know this time we have the right one? Wouldn't we be better off finding another solution?"

Anger thrummed through Jakob. He fought quickly to control himself, the clenching of his jaw the only evidence of his annoyance.

It wasn't that Markus's question was out of line; it was the opposite. How could he tell if Mordred was the answer, the Chosen One? How would he know that Mordred would prove himself different from all the others? Beyond a simple feeling, Jakob had yet to see proof that Mordred was worthy of the huge investment of time it would take to teach him what he needed to know. What he must know in order to be the savior.

The others were just that, men who had been turned by the wickedness. The Templars had tried in vain to bring a vampyre out of the blackness of evil and into the light through education and training. Yet, each had eventually succumbed to Vlad's destructive force.

There were only two things that gave Jakob hope that this time he had the right vampyre. The first thing in their favor was that they had found him early enough in the transition to instill the light. The second was the lineage Mordred shared. Within his ancestry were many who had fallen prey to Vlad, in a strange and dangerous, pattern.

What was it about the Soulis clan that both the Church and Vlad sought them? What power did they wield that had caused them to befriend such great good and great evil through the centuries? What secrets could the bones of Mordred's elders reveal?

"Markus, I can well understand your concerns, and I respectfully note them. But we are talking about the end of the world here, not just the end of an insignificant war. This is indeed the truest crusade we have ever taken part in. The fate of us all will rest in his hands. You must not lose faith now."

Markus settled back in the chair. It was his turn to rub his temples. "I'm sorry, Master. I know you have the knowledge to bring an end to this threat. I should not question you."

"A good student always questions, and a good teacher is not offended by the inquiry."

Markus nodded.

As he instructed Markus, something alerted Jakob to the presence of another. Turning his head to the entrance of the chamber, he listened for the sound of footfalls.

Markus followed Jakob's attention.

"Mordred?"

From the shadows of the hallway, as if summoned, Mordred appeared.

Jakob watched him soundlessly approach. Like a great predator, he moved gracefully, carefully, and with intent.

Markus rose, standing to his full, impressive height, and blocked Mordred's path to Jakob. It did not stop him. Instead, Mordred walked right past the giant in chain mail.

Jakob remained seated. "Something disturbs you, Mordred?" he asked calmly. Mordred squinted, not really sure what day or time it was. "Should I not be awake? What time is it?"

"In time you will not feel the weariness the daylight brings, but yes, for now, you should be resting. It is noon. What troubles you?"

Jakob's voice was soothing, and Mordred found it calmed the constant thrumming in his head, an almost deafening cacophony. He flinched and twitched as if he were nothing more than a mouse beneath a predator's hungry gaze. With his senses overstimulated day and night, Mordred feared he would lose his mind long before he saved the universe.

A slight scraping sound and the beating of a heart reached his ears. Mordred turned to face the other man in the room. He could smell resentment oozing from the man's pores. That mixed with a measure of fear.

Jakob stood and swept his arm outward, gesturing to the man standing across from the desk. "This is Markus. Markus, this is Mordred Soulis."

Mordred stared at the abnormally large man. If he had met him on a field of battle, he would most certainly have given him a wide berth. It was more than his size, however, that urged caution. Something in his wide blue eyes spoke to Mordred. It warned him not to cross the man.

They were engaged in a standoff. The man stared back at Mordred, blinking only once as time passed in silence. In the dim glow of the torches, he saw the look of challenge cross Markus's face and welcomed the man's simmering animosity.

Mordred had discerned a sense of hope, from the moment he had first appeared in the chapel. It brought to the surface an undeniable fear. Jakob truly thought the incredible tale concerning the Chosen One was true. His unshakable faith caused Mordred to constantly fight the anxiety threatening to consume him. This one man believed in him, to the extent his entire being illuminated his faith. Truly, the weight of the world was resting upon Mordred's shoulders.

He was more comfortable with Markus's disdain.

He had never been loyal to anyone but himself in the past. Never a king or a country, and it had been a measure of safety. No one depended upon him, and his quests were his own. He could pass through the world as an unknown soldier of fortune, untainted and unstained by the deep emotions that propelled the crusades or other battles.

It was, of course, the plight of a coward to remain detached from everything and everyone. It protected Mordred, and it had served him well over the years.

He wished to shrink from the inevitable task that was slowly coming to life. But he knew the knight within would not allow him to turn from what would become his greatest challenge.

The sound of Jakob's cough brought Mordred out of his mental wanderings. Markus had remained standing, watching, assessing, as though Mordred were no more interesting than a block of carved stone.

"Markus is to be your guardian while you are here," Jakob explained when Mordred cast him a questioning glance.

"I will need a guardian?" he asked, suddenly curious.

"You will indeed for many years of your life. You see, as I have mentioned, you are in your infancy and it will be centuries before you will become an immortal, fully versed in your powers. You will need more than one protector on this journey."

"Centuries? This great battle, this end of the world, will not occur in your lifetime?"

Smiling, Jakob looked on Mordred with a fatherly expression. It made him uneasy.

"No." Jakob coughed again, a great hacking that shook his body. For the first time since Mordred had entered the room, Markus moved. Within a step he gently brought Jakob back to his chair.

Loyalty and love shone from the giant, while Jakob suddenly seemed but a ghost of his former self. And there was no question that Markus would protect the frail Jakob with his life.

A dark mood descended upon the chamber. It stole the very warmth from the stones. Icy air drifted through the cracks. Mordred shivered.

Jakob was dying. Mordred knew it. As he watched the Master Templar, he saw the look that Jakob sent him. He would not question Jakob's health aloud.

"Damn sand. I've spent far too long beneath the desert. I fear I've half the place in my lungs."

"You should rest, Jakob. I will bring Mordred to the others and watch over him."

Jakob nodded. "You may begin his teaching then. Tell him of the Templars. Tell him who we are and what we were meant to be."

"Yes, Master." Markus glanced at Mordred. "Come. We shall meet the rest of the men."

As the two left Jakob's presence, Mordred ventured to ask, "Will Jakob be all right? Perhaps you should stay with him."

Markus growled. He didn't look at Mordred but focused on the light spilling from a door far ahead. "Jakob is far stronger than any of us. Well, perhaps not you. He will rest, and when next you see him, it will be again as if he were the lion leading us to victory. It is the way with him, and what plagues him."

Dismissing any further discussion with the wave of a gauntlet clad arm, Markus led the way through the twisting, turning halls of the complex. They passed the place where the light shone, but did not stop. Onward they continued into the dark and dangerous bowels of the underground complex.

CHAPTER SIX

The noise of hundreds of men greeted Mordred's already sensitive ears. It was deafening. Markus cast him an odd look when he placed his hands on either side of his head.

They approached an archway carved gracefully of stone and ornamented with tiny faces of the Green Man. When they stepped through the doorway, Mordred gazed about the room. It was enormous. The ceiling rose to great, vaulted heights in numerous levels. Each section above them was beautifully painted with religious scenes, or what Mordred could only assume were scenes from the bible.

He recognized an image of Jesus and his disciples at their last supper. There was an image of the Crucifixion. At the highest part of the chamber, set in the very center of the room staring down upon the occupants, was a depiction of the Resurrection.

He may not have paid any attention to the religious teachings of his day, but he had learned of Jesus and his plight through the crusaders.

Supporting the ceiling were huge stone pillars, each column carved more intricately than the next. Some were made to look like great trees with their many branches both hiding and revealing unknown signs and symbols. Others were carved into beautiful images of men and women.

Mordred gazed up once more and noticed an abundance of five pointed stars winking from lofty heights.

At eye level, in various states of dress, the Templars sat at long wooden tables. The sound of their conversation caused a buzzing in Mordred's ears. He tried to catch bits and pieces, but it all came to him in a single sound. Suddenly, with the drop of several knives on metal platters, the hall stilled.

Every man seated brought his attention to the visitor. Many peered warily through hooded eyes, waiting. These were men loyal to God. These were the men who had pledged their lives to a higher power. Mordred couldn't have felt more insignificant standing before them.

"This is Mordred. He will be staying with us for a time. Each of you must pledge yourself to protect him, for if he falls then so do we."

It was stated simply enough by Markus, though Mordred believed there were many in the room who would rather he never have come.

After an imperceptible nod from Markus, there was the sound of movement as one by one, row upon row of men brought themselves from their seats to their knees upon the stone floor.

Their heads remained bowed in deference. Each

man in the impossibly large room pledged his fealty to Mordred as though he were a king and they his knights. It made his skin crawl.

He had never been treated with the kind of high regard reserved for men of royal birth. He was a bastard and would remain a bastard. All he had ever attained in life came from the might of his sword. He was reminded constantly by those who hired him that it was they who would be the conquerors in the end. To them Mordred was simply a means to an end. Nothing more.

He had been invited to feasts and ceremonies and extravagant balls only to be treated like a leper. No one wanted to know the man who killed hundreds without remorse. His reputation was prodigious, at times confusing even Mordred. Stories of his death dealing were told over campfires in hushed tones. Mothers used his name to strike fear into the hearts of misbehaving children. People crossed themselves when he came near. He was a pariah.

None of it mattered to him. It meant he never formed attachments, never cared about anyone. And no one cared about him. To be despised meant he would never be weakened. It was good to wear the invisible armor. He had convinced himself he was better for it.

Now, however, he stood before hundreds of men who pledged themselves to him. They were giving him their lives, and he was not sure he wanted that sacrifice.

Unsure, and uncomfortable, Mordred looked to Markus. But, the large Templar kept his gaze focused on the kneeling men. He whispered so Mordred alone could hear him.

"They are, by this gesture, swearing to protect you at the cost of their own lives. You cannot ask for more from these men."

Mordred would have made a rebuttal, but a low hiss from Markus told him his comments were not wanted.

"You will accept this fate you have been dealt. Not in front of any of these men will you reveal yourself as anything other than that which you have been called to do."

Swallowing against the knot growing in his throat, Mordred remained still. He wanted to scream that all of this was false. That he could no more be a great hero than he could fly. He wanted to rebel against the fates that had cast him this lot. He was false, an unbeliever, and he did not merit the lives of the men before him.

How could the world place its faith in him? He was not pure or holy and had never claimed to be. He had railed at God, questioned God, defamed God. He never sought enlightenment or a higher purpose. He was a warrior.

Mordred had sinned repeatedly, according to the holy book. And he knew evil intimately, for it dwelt within him. Worse still Mordred had never felt a pang of regret for his killings. He'd never felt remorse and he'd never asked for forgiveness. Only once when he had been forced to kill his own men did he think twice. A mere few among the hundreds he had bled in his lifetime.

How could someone who had never sought to be absolved of the sins of his creation become a savior?

Nay, he was worse than a man who had simply been misguided. Mordred had trained for death. He'd lived alongside it, welcomed it. He had never placed a value on life. Each day was lived to its fullest as if it might be his last. He had bedded whores and he drank excessively. He had easily fallen into step with the seven deadly sins. There had even been times in his bloody past when he relished the killing, as a victorious warrior might. Times when the flames and destruction and horrors of battle merely melted away into nothingness. He had not been haunted by his past . . . until now.

He was not a good man. He did not merit being the Chosen One. Still he stood in the pained silence as his supposed destiny was revealed. He felt as though he would explode from all the pent up feelings of frustration.

"Follow me," Markus ordered.

As Mordred walked behind him through the throng of men, no one moved. They remained on their knees, heads bowed. It wasn't until he was well past the hall that he heard the din of conversation return.

Markus brought Mordred to another chamber. It too had the same fanciful artwork of every other room. Surely this place had taken years to build. The attention to detail in the stone, even the furniture, was astounding.

Emotion washed over Mordred as his hand touched one of the stone columns. This place had been, and continued to be, a labor of love for these men. They had given their lives to this order, and it showed in every square inch of their stronghold.

"I will be your shadow in the days to come. You may not always see me, but rest assured I will be there."

Mordred took a seat offered by Markus at a vast stone table. The knight sank into a chair facing Mordred.

"You do not like me," Mordred ventured.

"True."

"Then why are you doing this?"

"I do not question Jakob's will. As for not liking you, through the years I have had much contact with your kind and not found any redeeming qualities in any of you."

Mordred narrowed his eyes. "I do not understand."

"You may be the Chosen One, but there have been others who came before you. Each one held the promise that you hold, and each one, in turn, failed us."

"But Jakob said this was not to be settled within his lifetime?"

"Yes, that is the truth of things, but the Templars have not been able to find one who is able to war against the evil within. Each vampyre before you has turned to darkness. Each failure has cost us precious time, while the thing called Vlad, and his army, grows stronger."

"So, you are already disappointed in me?"

"I do not have to like you to do my duty, if that is what is asked."

Mordred sat silent for a moment. "Even if protecting me means you must give up your life?" he continued finally.

"Even then. That is the way with us. We live and die by our word. But respect is earned."

For a moment Mordred thought Markus nothing more than a mindless drone, a soldier in a holy army who was only doing the bidding of his master. Nevertheless there was something altogether noble in the way Markus saw his duty and the Templars.

His loyalty to Jakob was unshakable.

"What will you teach me?" Mordred asked.

"What you will need to know about us, and them."

Mordred's head ached. There were too many unanswered questions, each one shouting to be heard. He put his head in his hands.

"There is so much I don't know. So much I don't understand."

Markus nodded. "Aye, there is truth to that, but there is a lot you do know. You are a warrior. In your past you were a knight, and that in and of itself will serve you well."

"I was never a true knight. I did not come from royal birth."

"In the ways of the Templars, you were perhaps the truest of knights. You fought great adversity. You were an unknown, a man who could have walked a thousand different paths, and yet you chose to fight. You created your own life. Some of the lowest born of us rise to the greatest challenges. As did you.

"Locked within you is a wealth of information. It will reveal itself when you find yourself in need. You will also begin your training, and this will afford enlightenment as well."

Mordred cocked his head. He brushed a stray lock of hair from his face. It was strange to feel like a child being schooled for the first time.

"When do I begin my training?"

"You have already begun. You must first accept your fate. To dispute it, even within yourself, allows a tiny space for Vlad to take hold. Men have just pledged their lives in the keeping of yours. You cannot be afraid. If doubts plague you, you must keep them silent. You cannot allow anyone to think for even a moment that you are unsure or unready."

† † †

Hours later, Markus was still with Mordred in a room that served as a library, housing scrolls, books, and ledgers. Archives and histories of nearly every race were stored in the vault. The knowledge of a time before man, languages none could now understand, and sheaves of papyrus with ancient symbols lay strewn over stone tables.

Some looked as though they were being artfully and carefully translated. Some looked as though they would dissolve into dust at the touch of a human hand.

Mordred had been allowed to stroll about the room. He could touch whatever he wished, and though there were moments when the images on the papers before him made no sense, he couldn't help feeling he knew their meaning.

Legends of the past blurred with the histories of kings and gods. Creatures spoken of in fables were confirmed alive and well in documents scattered about the room. To Mordred it was surreal.

He had been told by Markus that he needed to open his mind. He needed to allow belief in the impossible, that he, himself, would defy any previous notions of who he was and what he was about to embark on.

And when he had sat in his chair for the thousandth

time, Markus began new teachings.

Mordred looked up from a paper he was reading to find Markus watching him in silence.

"What of the vampyres? I was told there are more."

Reaching behind himself, Markus pulled an enormous book from the shelf. It was covered in dust and gave the appearance of having been undisturbed for eons. He handed the book to Mordred.

With reverence, he opened the great volume, listening as the metal hinges creaked with the movement.

"It is time you read about your kin. There are indeed others, though not exactly like you. They are the true vampyres. The ones created long before any of us were even born. Long before humans had come into being. A time well before the creation of the world, as we know it."

Scoffing, Mordred looked at Markus to see if the man jested. "Vampyres are creatures of legend. They only exist in the minds of those who tell stories. Are you saying now that they actually belong on this earth?"

"In a manner of speaking, yes. Vampyres were created like any other species. But they proved to be such extraordinary creatures that they could easily have replaced humans as the superior beings. As a result, somewhere, sometime long ago, the vampyre species was halted. Prevented from populating the earth."

"Are you saying they still exist?"

"Aye, that is exactly what I am saying. Look at the next page. The figure there represents an image of the King of the Narangatti. The following pages are the recordings of all we know of the once mighty race.

You will head to Kabil, the king, when the time is right. Until then, it would be wise to put aside your disbelief and read."

The room fell into silence. Mordred pored over the information in the ancient tome, barely able to believe what he was reading. It was impossible. All of this was too incredible to be true. Markus would have him believe vampyres once roamed the earth freely, like any other creature. They were not confined to darkness or thought of as wicked. Vampyres were once simply another species living in this world.

No.

His mind refused to assimilate the information. He denied the words on the paper. Who were these Templars really? Why did they have so much knowledge about vampyres? Suddenly, a wave of distrust formed in Mordred.

Thrusting the text away from him, he rose from his chair.

"This is all a lie. Every bit of it. There are no such things as vampyres, and they sure as hell didn't live alongside man since the beginning of time."

Markus appeared completely unruffled by Mordred's outburst. Instead he calmly retrieved the volume. After tenderly placing it back on the table, inspecting it for damage, he looked at Mordred.

"Believe or don't believe, it really doesn't do anything to change the facts. In time you will be forced to accept what you refuse today. I pray it will not be too late. And as for your statement of 'no vampyres,' what on God's earth would you call yourself, then?"

Still fuming, Mordred glared at Markus menacingly. "I am an abomination!"

Every fiber of his being screamed for him to wrap his hands around the arrogant man's neck. And then he felt the thing within awaken. It slithered close to his heart, constricting. He had the overwhelming desire to rip the man to shreds along with his damnable documents. When he was finished, he would seek out and destroy every stupid knight in the complex. It would be a massive bloodletting, and it would soothe his savage soul.

A strange red film covered his vision. He wiped his hand across his eyes, but still his sight was tainted with crimson. In his ears he heard the seductive sound of a heartbeat, strong and pure. Its steady rhythm sent erotic chills racing across the surface of Mordred's skin.

The love-hate he felt for the man before him was nearly overpowering.

"You would be wise to redirect your anger . . . Now!"

There was an edge to Markus's voice that caused Mordred to heed him. He watched as the giant relaxed his grip on the hilt of a large sword.

"You think to dispatch me so easily? I would think you would need more than your weapon to do so."

Markus returned to a sitting position, so smoothly and quickly Mordred realized he'd never noticed him stand. Frowning, he took a second look at the man. The aloofness was back, Markus affecting an air of indifference. He returned his gaze to another massive book in front of him, but the edge to his voice was unmistakable.

"There is a lot you do not know yet. I would caution you to save your anger for those who truly deserve it. I may be your guardian, but I won't hesitate to kill you if I have to."

Breathing in great gulps, propelling air into his burning lungs, Mordred nodded. He wouldn't expect Markus not to slay him. Especially since he'd almost killed the man with his own hands. The pounding in his head subsided, and his own heartbeat returned to normal. He could no longer hear the blood rushing through his veins.

Yet, while he came back to himself, Mordred was keenly aware the darker side was only resting. It bided its time. It lived within him like an unwanted guest. Quietly, it waited. Silently, it watched from deep inside him. The thing knew, as surely as Mordred's conscious sense of self knew, that there would be another moment of weakness. And when there was, it would spring forth again.

Watching him with veiled eyes, Markus's face remained blank. He, too, waited for Mordred to calm.

"What is the difference between this evil Vlad and the vampyres you claim have existed as long as humankind? Why do you seek to defeat one and not the other?" Mordred asked, peering into the pages of the book before him. He stopped when he came to an artist's drawing of the King of the Narangatti. He could not contain a shiver of apprehension.

"He's a beauty, isn't he?" Markus asked, noting the page Mordred perused. "The difference is quite simple really. Our role is not to exterminate those creatures set on earth by a higher power. We only seek to destroy that which wouldn't exist without the meddling of greedy men."

"I don't understand. Is Vlad a vampyre?"

"In a manner of speaking, yes, he is. He exhibits all the traits we have seen in vampyres in the natural world, but he is not of this world. Men have created him. Fools who thought to discover immortality. They released Vlad into the world, and now it is up to you to stop him.

"Vlad is a bastardized version of a vampyre."

When Mordred would have continued in his line of questioning, Markus raised a hand, and the giant continued, "Man has always been the weakness in this world. Man has always sought the stuff of gods and legends. They have always longed for immortality, power, and glory. Greed for these things tempts the human soul endlessly. Even if it means our own destruction."

Returning his gaze to the book, Mordred looked at the finely written, ancient symbols.

"I can't read this text. How am I to learn about the vampyres if I cannot read the books written about them?"

Markus clenched his jaw. His patience with his student quickly waned, and it was evident in his tone. "Look again."

The torches lining the stone walls flickered. A shift in their movement cast long shadows across the men for a moment. It was enough to hold Mordred's attention. He looked about the room, raising his head. He grimaced, like a dog taking in a scent.

"This is a good sign, Mordred. Perhaps you are not hopeless after all. Already you are becoming aware of Vlad's presence."

Surprised and uneasy, Mordred looked back at the giant.

"You mean he is here? In this very place? I thought Jakob told me I was safe."

"Vlad is everywhere. Evil is everywhere. At the smallest opportunity it manifests itself. Always searching for a weakness. For you, it is even more dangerous. You are the one who got away, another son of his creation, yet you defied him. Now, he will stop at nothing to find you . . . and destroy you.

"You are safe here, yes. Though you feel him in the very air, he cannot enter. He knows, however, that you will leave us eventually, and then he will come."

Mordred squinted into the darkness, half expecting the shadows to come to life in a swirling mass of black. The thing inside him slithered and moved, like a great serpent. For the second time, Mordred felt himself changing. Again his vision clouded with red.

A growl welled up from deep within him, spilling from his lips. The sound boomed as it echoed off the walls of the chamber.

He heard himself speak, though the words came out hoarse and nearly unintelligible. "Get out. Leave!"

Markus apparently determined it would be best to leave his charge alone. He stalked from the room, disgust on his face.

Mordred felt his head turning of its own accord. His neck threatened to snap and searing pain blasted him.

Transformation

The thing inside him squeezed his heart, nearly causing him to faint from the pressure.

He gasped for breath and fell to his knees. Doubling over, Mordred howled as excruciating bolts of heat ripped through his insides, shredding him, ripping and tearing.

He opened his mouth, but was no longer in control of his body. The sound of his own flesh being rent in two filled his ears. His jaws split, unnaturally wide, and he heard the cracking of bone, followed by a blinding light that seared his vision. The pain was unbearable, and Mordred thought surely he would die.

Yet, he remained, paralyzed by the feelings that surged through him, unbidden. Bone split, flesh cracked, lips burst apart. His own blood poured from the wounds and sprayed across the stones of the floor.

Too much blood, it bubbled up from his lungs, flooded his mouth. He tasted the saltiness. His stomach roiled, and Mordred felt the contents of his earlier meal dislodge itself in a gushing pool of vomit and blood.

His eyes burned, blurring from crimson to black. His head throbbed as his brain processed each part of his transformation. He waged a war within his body as his physical being battled the supernatural. It was a battle he was slowly losing.

Choking, Mordred collapsed, writhing in unbearable agony. He was helpless before this part of him, and he prayed it would be over soon.

A voice buzzed in his head, thrumming to be heard above all the other noises. It caressed him like the gentlest of lovers, bringing a soothing calm.

"You are mine. You will come to me, Mordred. You belong to me."

Somewhere, in a place even Mordred did not know he had, his own words burst forth through the haze of pain. They bounced off the stone walls in a hoarse, but unmistakable cry. "Ne-v-er!"

The last he remembered was of his body losing all form and substance. His bones melted, his organs evaporated, and Mordred, outside of himself, in some odd, trance-like state, saw himself as only a large pool of blood staining the floor.

CHAPTER SEVEN

"He wakes."

"Will he remember what he went through?"

"He will feel the pain for many days, but he may not recall the thoughts and feelings during the change."

Mordred felt a hand brush his cheek with something cool. He knew without opening his eyes the touch belonged to Jakob, the Master Templar.

The angry presence of Markus was also palpable within the chamber.

"If he can't remember the details, then how will he learn?"

"Pain is a good motivator when one is forced to confront it on a nearly daily basis. You must trust that Mordred will know to curb his pain, and in doing so, he will learn."

Mordred kept his eyes closed. In reality his lids felt so heavy he feared he could not open them.

"Why do you put so much faith in this one? With all the others you taught them, but always held back. With him you give too much. He could betray us as all the others have."

Cracking an eye, Mordred alerted Markus to his awareness, but it did not deter the man from his tirade.

"I think it is too soon to tell, Jakob. It is foolish to continue his training until we know for sure if he is the One."

There was a sigh from the old man as he rose.

"He is the One. It is what we have all waited for. The others were simply tests, ensuring we would be ready to receive the true Chosen One. And do not forget, he warned you before he underwent his change."

"Not the first time. I had to threaten to kill him to get him to control his bloodlust. I do not like being eyed as if I were no more than his dinner."

Jakob uttered a tsking sound. "The fact remains, he could have killed you without a warning."

"So?"

"So, it proves I gave you a chance to leave," came Mordred's gruff reply from the bed. Both men glanced at him. "I could have killed you and I didn't. Consider yourself lucky."

Markus moved so fast that Mordred felt he'd only blinked before the giant was hovering over his bed. His face was a mask of untamped rage. "You could try, but you'd never succeed. I'll not have my life ended by a soul stealer."

"Markus, be at ease. Mordred speaks the truth." Jakob placed a restraining hand on Markus's arm. The blond man stood back, still glowering at Mordred through slitted blue eyes.

"Jakob, you yourself taught me the ways to stand

against a soul stealer. Now you tell me I could be killed?"

"By not just any vampyre, Markus. Mordred is the Chosen One, and within him lies an enormous pool of power. He has yet to learn to tap into it and control it, but the fact remains he easily could have slaughtered you. Now, put away your wounded pride and help me finish cleaning up the mess."

Silently, Mordred watched Markus adopt the look of a scolded child. He couldn't tell if Markus could be trusted not to kill him. The man overtly rebelled against his forced lot with Mordred. Anger, bordering on hatred, oozed from him.

He shot Mordred a dark look of warning while speaking to Jakob. "I will not fall victim to the likes of him, and if he knows what's good for him, he will not seek to tempt my sword hand."

Pushing himself up to a sitting position, Mordred groaned. Searing pain swept through him. His body shuddered.

"Easy, my boy, you've had a rough time with your first full change. Your body has not yet learned to accept what happens. It is in your best interest to lie back and rest. Let the form of your physical being catch up with your mind."

Mordred sighed and settled back into the softness of the bed. His body ached in so many places, it was hard to tell where the pain originated. He felt battered and bruised, as if he had been in battle for days. Never before had he ever felt so weakened. His jaw felt as if someone had hit him with an axe. Gently, he prodded it with his finger and immediately regretted doing so. He bit back the urge to wince.

"Jakob, will it always be like this when I change?"

Carrying a cloth soaked in red, Jakob glanced at Mordred over his shoulder. He tossed the cloth toward the door where it landed with a wet thud. Mordred stared. There was a small pile of stained cloth bundles.

"Did I do that?" He gestured toward the door.

Jakob smiled and turned to face him. "Yes. But do not fear. That is your blood, my boy. You did not bring harm to any Templars. As for your pain in the change, no, it will not always be so difficult. There will eventually come a time when you hardly notice it.

"When you accept the change, you will hurt less and lose less of yourself in the process." Jakob motioned to the bloody bundle by the door, then he looked at Markus. "Go, begin the day's teachings. There is rumor of war on the horizon, and we must be ready."

Shaking his shaggy blond mane, Markus removed himself from the chamber.

When he was gone, Jakob returned to Mordred's side and lowered himself on a stool, grimacing.

"Age is getting the best of me."

Mordred remained silent. He had the strangest feeling age had nothing to do with what plagued Jakob.

"There are some things even Markus should not know, though I trust him with my life. You will too, in time. His mind just does not easily give itself to our purpose. He is wary and distrustful of you. I cannot blame him, but neither can I involve him to the fullest degree.

"As for controlling your change, I know you have many questions, so I will do what I can to offer answers and help you learn." Jakob handed Mordred a small silver flask.

"Drink," he uttered in a voice that sounded like a command. "It is what your body demanded earlier and what you denied it. Left unsatisfied you will be weak and vulnerable."

"What is it?" Mordred asked, though he was sure he already knew what was contained in the flask.

"It is not human blood, but it is blood. That answers at least part of your question doesn't it? Now, drink."

Mordred brought the container to his lips and let the cool liquid flow past his lips, down his throat, and into his body. He felt it assimilate with every part of his being and immediately the pain subsided. His aches quieted.

"Can I exist on animal blood?"

"No. You are young in your vampyre state, and so you can accept this as a substitute but only for a time. Once you leave us you will need human blood to sustain you. We didn't wish to risk your change by introducing you to human blood while you were here."

Mordred gazed into Jakob's silver eyes. "You mean you feared I wouldn't be able to control myself?"

A smile played on Jakob's lips, but there was an unmistakable underlying sadness. Mordred realized he could sense his teacher's emotions.

He detected a vast and great love directed at him. A love he felt he didn't deserve. It brought back memories of his father, a ghost figure in his life. Would he have been a different man if he had known his father?

The warmth coming from Jakob stemmed the rising tide of dread in him.

"As with all things, the control you seek over the darker part of yourself will come in time. No one can say whether this will come in the next change, or hundreds beyond that. Make no mistake in thinking you are anything less than a vampyre. Though half-born, you will always need human blood. You cannot survive without it."

"So, if I don't drink human blood, I'll die?"

There was a distinct sense of relief in knowing Mordred could bring about an end to his tortured existence.

Jakob held his gaze, as if knowing his thoughts. "You cannot die from denying the hunger, but you will enter a world of madness, much worse than you could ever imagine. You will be helpless. Powerless, and a pawn to Vlad's will. You will become a monster."

"I'm already a monster," Mordred whispered, turning his head from Jakob. So much light emanated from the man, Mordred couldn't stand the sight of him. It reminded him of his fate. Of the challenge that awaited him. Of the sincere faith this man placed in him to succeed.

He felt a hand touch his bare shoulder. A warmth flooded Mordred, stilling his dark thoughts.

"Nay, that is not the truth of it, Mordred."

Jakob rose slowly, brushing invisible wrinkles from his white robe. He paced at the foot of Mordred's bed, a finger resting just below his nose. The room descended into weighty silence.

"You have, for all intents and purposes, merely evolved into another species. As Markus has already instructed you, vampyres are no more or less evil than any other species. They kill only when they need, and they kill as a predator would. They take the weak, the aged, the sick. You must believe this with every fiber of your being. There is a difference between vampyres and Vlad. Only superstitions and man's beliefs have led you to think vampyres are evil."

"But what of Vlad? What makes him different?"

"Vlad is neither a pure vampyre, nor a half-born. He is a creation born of evil. Men brought him to life. They resurrected him with a power that was never mankind's to have."

Jakob stopped his pacing and looked at Mordred.

"You must separate yourself from him. You are not him, nor do you belong to him. In time, with your hunger, you will learn to seek out those who have chosen a path of darkness, and they will become your victims. The human side of you will always feel remorse, as long as you allow it to exist. I will not pretend to think you will not feel a great sadness at your actions. But you will move beyond it, and in time you will rise above it in the knowledge that you are bound for greater things."

Mordred couldn't help asking his next question, "What happens if I fail?"

Jakob met Mordred's gaze. "Then the world will slip into darkness forever, and mankind will cease to exist."

"But why would anyone wish this on civilization? What could be their purpose?"

"It was, as some would call it, an accident of the most heinous kind. Holy men not satisfied with their connection to the heavens sought the key to immortality. They believed that in living forever they would become far more powerful than they are now. Far more worldly and far more wealthy. They would not fear death; they would cheat it.

"They sought the impossible. They sought the true body of their beloved Jesus. They performed a ritual beneath the night sky, among ancient stones. There was a sacrifice and other things that come with the collection of great power. For years these men have blamed us for stealing the treasures beneath the temple mount. However, we did so to prevent another instance of their greed."

Mordred stared, wide-eyed. It was as if he had heard an incredible fable, only it wasn't a tale of magical beings and happy endings. This was a tale that would write the end of the world if Mordred could not defeat the evil that had been unleashed.

"So, they were able to bring someone back to life. I take it this wasn't their holy savior?"

Jakob shook his head. "How could it have been? Jesus was resurrected three days after he was crucified. Bringing his body back to life could serve no purpose. It was a hollow shell, a vessel through which something else came forward. That is what we call Vlad. And he grows ever hungrier and ever mightier as the days and months pass."

Leaning his head back against the pillows of his bed, Mordred sighed. "Jakob, I'm not a religious man.

To become the hope for all mankind isn't something I should be charged with. I have no faith save that which I place in the might of my sword. Why can't you or even Markus take this challenge?"

With a quick movement and a flurry of white robes, Jakob was beside Mordred's bed. He leaned over his charge and whispered, "I am too old and Markus is merely human. You are a vampyre and only you can do this. There is no time for fear or regret. You have faith. You simply do not know it yet. In your weakest moment you will be your strongest. It is the way of all things."

Mordred didn't like riddles. The people in the cave had spoken in riddles too, and he never got any closer to understanding why he had to come back.

A firm grasp on his shoulder brought Mordred back to the present. "They were not wrong about you. The keepers of the Tree of Life were not wrong. They knew you were the Chosen One when they found you. It may take hundreds of years for your skin to accept your path, but it is your path all the same. Do not waste precious time denying that which is undeniable.

"Now rest. You must gather your strength before we begin your official initiation into the ranks of the Templars. After that, your real training will begin."

Jakob smiled, his blue eyes shining. Mordred again felt Jakob's feelings as clearly as if he voiced them. Like sunlight they filtered through him, melting away the ever-present darkness. Forcing the wicked thing within to take cover.

The door closed, and Mordred was alone. He shut

his eyes. There was truth in Jakob's words. He was weak. His body, while no longer suffering from serious aches and pains, still felt as if he'd battled all night. He would lie back and for a moment refuse to think of what awaited him when he opened his eyes again. For now, he would pretend he was somewhere safe.

Pictures formed in his head of a ruined castle. Green rolling hills touched fluffy white clouds that scudded across a blue sky. The smell of heather and peat filled his nostrils. It was as though Mordred had stepped through a doorway into another time. He saw a young boy laughing, swinging a wooden sword. The boy, though still needing years of practice, showed an uncanny grace with the large weapon as he struck out at invisible demons.

He whirled and jumped and spun himself about, never losing his grip on his weapon. Then the boy stopped and turned to look directly at Mordred.

"Hello, who are you?"

Shocked that the boy in his dream could see the one dreaming, Mordred shook his head and opened his eyes. Like a fading mist, the tendrils of his dream drifted slowly away. But not before he realized he had been staring at himself. He was the boy in the field.

Growling, Mordred pushed the sheets away and shoved himself to the edge of the bed. His feet touched the cold stone ground, and he forced himself to stand, waiting for the world to right itself before he moved. Naked, he padded to a large, hammered bowl filled with cool water. He leaned over and splashed it on his face, then he rested his head on his forearms, not caring that his long hair fell into the bowl. He stood for what seemed an eternity. On the edge of some great thing. Simply standing, waiting.

When he found the water did not produce the desired effect, Mordred lifted the bowl and poured the entire contents over his head, reveling in the sudden change in the temperature of his body. A fine steam rose from his skin to mix with the air.

He took stock of his body. From his feet he brought his gaze upward remembering every scar, every break, every bruise. By all the standards he'd been taught, he still looked every bit the warrior now. Every bit human.

Tentatively, he brought his fingers to his lips and opened his mouth. He wasn't sure what to expect having gone through his first change, but his investigation brought nothing. His teeth still felt flat and smooth. No sharp spikes. Maybe they were all wrong. Maybe he had come back from the dead, but maybe only as a human. Maybe he wasn't a monster after all.

† † †

A gentle knocking sounded at the entrance to Mordred's chamber. He didn't need to open the door to know it was Markus. His mind filled with the image of the blond giant, clad in the now familiar white surcoat marked with a red cross. He wore a suit of silver chain mail beneath.

The door creaked open. Markus had not waited to be acknowledged.

"You are to begin your enlightenment now."

It was a simple statement, devoid of emotion, and Mordred found he could sense nothing. He could not feel, see, or hear thoughts coming from his protector.

"You can stop rummaging through my mind, Mordred. As I've said before, I've been around your kind and I am aware of your tricks."

"Tricks?" Mordred feigned innocence, but in truth he was confused.

"Aye, it's not as if I don't know you have the power to search my thoughts. I've learned to block them. Spend your efforts on some other gullible fool."

Meeting Markus's full gaze for the first time since he had entered the room, Mordred queried, "You mean I really do have the power to read minds?"

Markus let out a laugh that sounded more like the low chuffing of a wolf. "In time you will learn how to do it so the other is unaware. At the moment, however, you move through the mind like a bull in a glassblower's shop."

It was strange, but suddenly Mordred thought to apologize. "I'm sorry. I didn't realize I was doing it."

Unexpectedly, Markus's demeanor changed as he moved further into the chamber. He came to a stop before the large wooden trunk at the end of Mordred's bed. Lifting the lid, he pulled something from inside.

"Fear not. We will be together quite some time. We might as well learn from one another. Here. Put these on. I'll wait outside."

After handing Mordred the bundle, Markus moved through the doorway into the hall. He closed the door behind him.

Mordred held out what Markus had given him. It was clothing, similar to what Markus wore only completely black. Even the mail shirt was blackened. There was no red cross emblazoned on the front. In fact there was no symbol whatsoever. When dressed, Mordred realized he would blend completely with the night, or the shadows. It was yet another reminder of the journey he was about to undertake.

Realizing Markus was outside in the hall, Mordred slipped the garments on. Traveling alone much of his life as a mercenary, he had grown accustomed to having to don mail and armor alone. He'd had a special suit made with straps that allowed him to dress without benefit of a squire.

He sat on the bed and pulled on the thick boots. They reached nearly to his knees. The black surcoat met the top edge of the boots. Beneath the surcoat was the mail shirt, and beneath that a black hauberk made of cotton.

Carefully, Mordred slid the fabric cap over his head, keeping his hair beneath the collar of his shirt. At last he pulled on the chain mail *coiffe*. He clasped a heavy black cape around his neck. In the circular ornament he recognized the image of the Green Man.

Gauntlets of black leather, pierced with sharp silver spikes, fit his lower arms just above the wrist. Black gloves conformed to his hands as though they had been made for him.

A thought flashed through his mind, causing his eyebrows to draw together. Looking around the darkened chamber, Mordred realized there was no weapon.

No sword, no axe, no spear, nothing. There was no manner of implement he could use to defend himself. Leave it to the Templars to think he could simply will his enemies into submission he thought, annoyed.

Mordred opened the door. Markus nodded but offered no comment on his attire. Instead he walked down the long corridor. Mordred followed.

As always the complex was eerily quiet despite housing so many men. Torchlight flickered, casting strange shadows across the walls, which in the hallway were carved or painted with fantastical scenes.

The sounds of their booted heels filled the silence. The harsh clicking reverberated across the broad expanse of the corridor. Finally, Markus spoke.

"It fits you well," he grunted.

Mordred replied softly, "As if it had been made for me."

"Perhaps it was."

It was a cryptic response that caused Mordred to slip back beneath the waves of confusion. Everything was a riddle here. Words were twisted to disguise hidden meanings. As he was about to remark, Markus interrupted his thoughts.

"None have worn the black mail as you do now. Not even others of your kind. They were never worthy to wear the champion's garb. Jakob has deemed you deserving."

"I don't understand."

The low, guttural groans of men came to Mordred's ears. At an opening in the passageway, Markus ushered Mordred forward with his hands.

They stood above an enormous oval room similarly decorated with symbols painted in gold and silver. The metal reflected the torches burning below, casting the room in a golden glow. A halo effect rose above the men, and Mordred had to bring a hand to his brow when he peered downward.

Below were at least a hundred men. Each was dressed in silver mail covered with the white surcoat bearing the red cross. These were the Templar knights. The ones who had pledged their lives to God.

As Mordred watched, the men moved in perfect unison, synchronizing their movements. Their swords reflected the light in the room, sending it shooting from their blades like sparks of flame.

No steel made contact. There was only the whooshing sound of the entire group moving. Like dancers they turned and struck out at unseen foes. Then in the blink of an eye, the men spun around facing the opposite direction. Raising their weapons high, they slashed down.

Mordred had never seen men so disciplined. Never had he witnessed an entire legion of men moving in perfect harmony. They stood nearly shoulder to shoulder and still no blades touched, no man reached beyond his own space. So respectful were they of each other, and so deadly they could be in their precision, Mordred thought.

For a fleeting moment he wished he could be a part of it. He wondered what it might be like to melt into something greater. Become insignificant and unseen, yet equally important.

With that thought came the realization that his wish would not bear fruit. He was now destined, or so the Templars claimed, to be the sole savior of the human race. He could not blend, but must stand alone.

All of his natural life he had found comfort in being solitary. Now he wanted to just be normal. To be one of the masses, insignificant and unaware of the dangers this new life offered.

A great thunder resounded in the hall as men now paired off and began striking their weapons against opponents' shields. It was an odd sort of music. Metal slammed against metal. Sparks flew, and still without complaint the men continued their exercises.

It was then that Markus turned to Mordred. "All of them will fight to their death for you. For what you stand for. Not a single man among them will tremble in his final hour. Each goes to his grave knowing he sacrifices for a greater purpose. Now, do you understand the monumentality of your position?

"This mail and this cloth will become the mark of the one who will bring light to a world that will slip into darkness. None before you have worn the armor of the Chosen One. Only you. It will protect you in the years to come. The mail and the armor, you will soon see, will become your skin. Treat it as you would a most precious gift. It will save your life, perhaps more than once."

Mordred glanced down at the sleeve of black mail. It gave the appearance of being like any other mail. Though it had been darkened, and the links were finely meshed together, there was nothing even remotely unusual about the shirt or leggings. It left Mordred wondering just how special it would become.

Markus smiled when Mordred met his gaze. "Yes, it is unlike any other item you have ever worn, but it is not for me to reveal its secrets. Upon the completion of your enlightenment, you will be awarded the sword and shield of the Templars as well as the armor. Only then will its powers be spoken of in a way you will understand. Come, Jakob awaits us in the Temple of the First Degree."

Following Markus, Mordred tried to quell the wave of fear. He could not possibly be the Chosen One. He kept his dark thoughts to himself, quieting his mind lest Markus read it again. In silence they walked to his first test.

† † †

"Ah, you have arrived at last. How are you feeling this day, Mordred?" came Jakob's soft voice.

"I, ah, I'm feeling fine, if a vampyre can be called 'fine.'"

Jakob, clothed in white robes, laughed. He stood at the opposite end of a circular room. On the floor in front of him was the depiction of a giant black raven, wings spread. It had been meticulously painted to look as though it might simply rise off the floor. To Mordred it appeared three-dimensional, not merely flat.

Over his head were similar carvings and moldings of the same birds, and again Mordred felt as though they could become real at a moment's notice. He felt a tremor of excitement race through his veins. Something magical was at work here.

"This is where you will hone your power to sift through others' thoughts. It is very important that you focus and silence the chatter that crowds your mind. Even now, if I were to hear what was in your head, it would be deafening. Beating hearts, blood pumping, boots marching on stone, swords scraping from practice in the hall far away. Even the shifting of the sands above and the whisper of the wind as it seeps through tiny cracks in our walls compete to be heard in your mind.

"All of us hear many things, but you hear everything around you, beneath you, and above you. Yours will be the ability to hear the flutter of a raven's wing, the scratching of a mouse, the creaking of bones. You will hear far more than any human ever could, but in this temple you need to sort through the sounds and attune yourself to that which you most want to hear."

Over the past days, the sounds that jammed Mordred's mind, while still jumbled, had lessened in their roar. It was still hard to detect the direction the individual threads came from. Standing at the entrance to the room, Mordred watched as Jakob motioned him forward.

"Come, step into the temple and begin your awakening. When you wish to read another's mind, you will need to commit to that act. You will learn in time to listen while remaining alert. But in the beginning be wary. When your attention is consumed by the focus of your powers, you will be vulnerable to attack. And not all attacks will be physical."

"Are you saying I will be weak when I read another's thoughts?"

"Weak, no, vulnerable, yes. There is a difference. None will ever call you weak from this moment forward. Understand, it will take centuries for you to grow into what your destiny holds for you. Is it not so that first you must learn to crawl, before you can walk? Your vampyre self is like a child, and in your infancy there is much to cause you harm."

Mordred sighed. As if being a blood-sucking creature of the night were not enough, now he would have to become acclimated to the extra powers that apparently came with it. "If I can read another's mind, is my mind available for the same sifting?"

"Only by those who have a greater power than you do now. Vlad will, and has, already plucked thoughts from your mind. What makes him so deadly is that he can steal into your mind taking thoughts you aren't even aware you have formed yet."

"I don't understand," Mordred replied, confusion crowding the mind he was supposed to clear.

"I'll give you an example. Say, for instance, Vlad and you are in a battle, which will happen. More than once, I might add. It is during the battle that you will be thinking and searching for a way to disarm him, or to gain the advantage. Vlad will already be in your mind, and he will know your thoughts."

"So, if I think to thrust a sword at him, he would steal this from me and I will not act?"

"Correct."

"Can I block Vlad from entering my mind?"

"This too will require energy, and in time you will know how to conserve your strength for the battles with him, but for now you are open to his attacks, just as he brought about your change even this deep beneath the earth. There is a connection between you. He created you, and therefore a part of him resides in you. Like a beacon, that part will show him the way to you. You will need to learn to mask it."

Mordred felt a shiver of fear creep slowly down his spine. It slithered, snake-like around his gut, twitching his insides.

"You speak as if there is no hope. If I have a part of him in me, and he can find me wherever I go, what hope is there of my saving the world?"

"That is not for me to tell you, but for you to learn. As much as we know about the Chosen One, there is much we have never discovered. Only others like you will uncover those mysteries.

"Now, we shall begin."

Before Mordred could utter another word, Markus stepped behind him. A length of black fabric was placed over his eyes. He felt it being tied behind his head. He stood in the temple, blind.

"Be still Mordred. Listen to what is around you. What is in this room? Does a torch still flicker?"

Mordred breathed deeply, smelling the acrid scent of flames, the body odor of men, the dampness of stone. He calmed his mind, forcing it to quiet, until he felt the room around him.

There was no longer torchlight flickering. He heard no faint snapping of the flames or the tiny crackling of sparks.

"The torches have been put out."

"Very good. Now, tell me, who else is in this room?"

Mordred detected the whisper of blood being pumped through human veins. He heard a heartbeat. One. Two . . ."

"There are three here."

"Three? Is that all you hear?"

Mordred forced his mind to ignore the sounds that he previously heard and searched for new threads to give him clues. A thought, not his own, came to his mind. "This had better be the right one," and then "C'mon, Mordred, don't disappoint us." Then he heard another. "Mordred, there is another presence here, can you hear it?"

The last he knew was from Jakob. He masked the thoughts of the others in the room and concentrated on new sounds. There was a light ruffling of something soft. Jakob's robes? No, something just segmented. And there, a heart, but beating much faster. Something small and not human. But what?

"Listen, Mordred, listen with your mind now, not your ears."

Again, he heard movement coming from behind Jakob, slight and swift, but present in the darkness. A scraping sound. And then he knew the creature that shared the space.

"A raven. There is a black bird in this room."

"Very good, Mordred. You are correct."

The sound of men moving filled his head, and Mordred turned to face them. They were coming from directly in front of him, and one behind. The familiar sound of steel scraping against the ring that held a scabbard told Mordred a weapon was being readied.

Before he could strike out with his fists, the coolness of metal was placed at his throat.

"Kneel," came the whisper of Markus's voice.

"Do you, Mordred Soulis, in full command of your abilities, commit to the challenge that faces you? Do you agree to hold this challenge above all others? Do you acknowledge, that by accepting this challenge, the fate of the world will rest upon your shoulders?"

Another voice Mordred did not recognize, spoke out. "Do not be quick to answer, for we will know the truth of your intentions. Should you give a false reply, we shall slay you where you kneel and be done with you."

On bended knee, Mordred gave pause. He should, by rights, be frightened out of his wits. He was defenseless, in a darkened chamber with three men. Apparently two of them were well armed. They very well could kill him now. And yet, while he knew he should be feeling fear twisting his gut, the earlier reluctance had now vanished. In his mind's eye there appeared a bright, pulsating light. It was as if a thousand candles had been lit.

Mordred saw his future laid out in his mind. He watched the images move slowly, then faster. Battles with Vlad. Great and terrible wars. Creatures and people he would know. Blood spilled. Laughter. Anger. Failure. Blood drunk. Power. Places he'd never been, but knew he would go. Strange writing scrawled by unseen hands. Coldness. And always, the blinding light never dimmed. Beneath all of the visions in his mind, the light remained.

He could not turn his back on the path that had been chosen for him, though he might rail against it in the months and years to come. Although he might at times wish otherwise, Mordred could not deny his fate. Something within him called to him to rise up and meet the new challenge. Something urged him to become greater than he had been, to give himself to this purpose and be a part of something so enormously powerful it would be remembered forever.

Still kneeling, Mordred recalled the vow he had once made long ago when he had been knighted. Now he pledged fealty to the Templars, and in doing so pledged himself to something more. Much more.

"I, Mordred Soulis, vow that I will become the Chosen One the Templars claim me to be. I will be the bearer of light, and I will defeat Vlad and all other evils seeking to destroy mankind. With the strength of my sword and the might of my will, until my bones turn to dust, this I pledge."

The cloth was removed from his eyes and though there was still no light in the room, Mordred could easily make out the three male figures. Then, turning his head, he saw more men. They must have slipped in while he was making his vow. He could see a dozen more robed figures lurking in the shadows behind Jakob. And there sat the raven. A silent witness to his pledge.

Mordred rose.

"Very well, you have passed your first test, Mordred. We shall leave you here to continue to experiment with your new ability. In a fortnight I will come to you, and we will begin the Second Degree of Enlightenment."

The sound of robes fluttering and mail jingling filled the silence. A door opened in the back of the room, and for a moment light spilled into the chamber. Then the room was plunged into darkness again. Mordred was left alone with his thoughts.

But this time he felt different. Something inside him had blossomed, and for the first time in his new life he found himself eager to continue the remainder of his training so that he might begin the challenge of becoming the Chosen One.

CHAPTER EIGHT

In the Second Degree of Enlightenment Mordred learned of the power of the Air and how to shift into another form. This proved to be harder than Mordred had imagined.

In another circular chamber the stone floor was grooved where the walls met the floor. The stone gutter, like a large trough, it held water. Several men poured buckets of coldwater into the heated groove, causing an enormous amount of steam to rise and fill the room. The sound of scalding water hitting a solid surface bounced off the walls. Sweat oozed from his pores, dripping slowly down his back, and Mordred shivered.

The air in the room was stifling. Like a solid mass, the steam took up space until Mordred could no longer see Jakob. There was a strangely sweet scent lingering above him masking all other smells.

After he acclimated himself to his new surroundings, Mordred began his instruction.

First Jakob had to teach Mordred to let go of his previous life's notions about what was possible and what was impossible. He had to rid himself of the voices in his mind that fought against this new learning. In his old life, none of this would have been plausible, and Mordred would never have considered believing. In his new life, this life, he had quickly learned not to doubt.

"We shall start with the easiest of forms. You shouldn't try anything too complex until much later. Once you've mastered shifting into elements, you can move on to animals, even humans.

"Let us begin again. Focus, Mordred. Keep your mind free of all doubt. And reserve a part of your mind to remain aware of what is around you. It's like having two minds, one keeping time with the other."

Stilling his mind, quieting the voices he heard from others' thoughts, Mordred concentrated on Jakob's words and the form he was to become.

"You must always remember that while in the shape you shift into, you will be vulnerable to all the things that can happen to that form." Jakob spoke, all the while, running his hands through the steam, causing it to dance and weave within the chamber. The dim light of a torch caused drops of liquid to refract into tiny rainbows. Beams of iridescent light filtered around Mordred.

"I'm not sure I get your meaning, Jakob."

"Try again to become the vapor that floats about this room. Become the very air filling this room, sustaining human life."

Closing his eyes, Mordred focused. He saw the steam moving heavily, slowly to and fro, rising high above him.

He felt the air around him. Hot, heavy, thick with moisture. He saw the droplets of condensate created by the hot water as it made contact with the stone grooves. He saw the vapors come to life. Animated, they stretched higher and higher, until they disappeared into the carved ceiling.

A strange feeling came over him as he concentrated. His bones felt as though they were melting, pooling beneath him. His skin liquefied and puddled, and his very core became hollow. Mordred watched as his hand disappeared, only to reappear as a shimmering stream of vapor.

His legs stretched out beneath him into long columns of cloudy air. He felt himself rising as if he were lying on his stomach. Up and up he went, until he felt the very dome of the chamber. Trapped, he remained.

Jakob's voice spoke softly. "Very good, Mordred. Now keep concentrating and try to move about the room. Allow yourself more control. Sometime in the far distant future you will learn to control the form more easily. For now, simply shifting is enough. It will protect you and keep you safe.

"But again I remind you, whatever can harm the form, can harm you as well."

Clapping his hands, Jakob motioned to the walls of the room where several men stood. They each placed a hand on an indentation in the stones. With one more smooth motion, all of the men leaned into the wall.

A great grinding sound filled the chamber, and with it Mordred felt a sudden cool burst of air coming from above him. In an instant, the steam vanished through vents in the ceiling.

It took Mordred by surprise. He discovered he was falling from a great height, and slammed into the stone floor. A blanket of black snuffed his mind.

"Mordred? Mordred, are you still with us?"

He felt like hell, but his mind was alert. For a moment he couldn't feel any part of his body. Then, as if his bones, organs, and skin arrived at this same moment, he was slammed him back to consciousness. Mordred let out a growl of pain.

"Good. I'm glad to see you survived your test so well. There is hope for you yet."

Mordred chewed his cheek while he tried to quell his rising anger. "Are you trying to kill me?"

Jakob merely shrugged. "Come now, it will take more than a fall from these heights to dispatch the Chosen One. But I never said the training would be easy, for where would there be learning if not from adversity and pain?

"Now, as I was saying, when you shift you will absorb all the weaknesses of the form to which you have shifted. Like the steam you just were. You were safe until the draughts of air from above filled the space with cooler air, causing the vapors to dissipate. If you are fire, then fear water. If you are a bird, fear a larger bird. If you choose to become a stag, be mindful of the wolf; and most important, if you become man, watch carefully for other men. Do you understand?"

Begrudgingly, Mordred agreed.

"Know this, Mordred, Vlad has existed for many

centuries, and he has centuries more knowledge and power than you."

"So, how can I even begin to consider defeating Vlad if I am so new? He is far more than I could ever be," Mordred replied. It was hard not to think he was taking on an impossible mission.

"If you continue to be willing to learn, and explore all your powers, you will continue your training long after those who teach you are finished. Then there will be a greater power for you. Vlad is beyond learning. He has become all he needs to be. He will grow no more in his mind, only in his own evil. Do not be fooled into thinking you will fight Vlad only once and win. You and he, father and son, good and evil, creator and destroyer, will face off many, many times."

Mordred slowly rose, feeling every ounce of the pain from the fall ricocheting through his body. At his full height he faced Jakob.

"I will not win this battle in this time, will I?"

He watched a smile of warmth creep across the old man's face. More crevices and cracks were revealed on the surface of the skin that wasn't covered by his beard.

"You learn well. No vampyre has ever been able to sift through my thoughts. You are the first. It is a great compliment. Nay, the fate of mankind will not be decided in my lifetime. You will live on through time."

Sensing they were alone in the temple, Mordred ventured to ask what was most pressing on his mind. "Jakob, if you die, who will help me defeat Vlad?"

An aura of light flickered around Jakob. Mordred squinted for a moment but failed to see its source. No additional torches were lit, no candles burned; yet the light grew and filled the room, as the steam had done earlier. And then, when Mordred blinked, it was gone.

"I am only here in the beginning. But do not despair. Though I will pass on, my teachings will remain with you always and with them, so will I. My form may no longer be recognizable, but you only have to ask for me and I will come.

"Let your concern for me go no further. I am pleased by your training this day. You are a quick study. I will teach you as much as I can about your race, and when I can offer no more, you will go to the first King of the Vampyres, the race of the Narangatti. There you will continue your training. You will walk through many centuries before your final battle, but in each time there will be lessons to be learned. For me, learn them well. You are my only hope."

Quietly, Mordred shifted into the cooling breeze that still filled the chamber. Invisible, he moved over to his teacher and settled himself about the man, like a vaporous cloak. A childlike happiness, something Mordred had long since forgotten, consumed him with the knowledge that Jakob was pleased with him.

"Enough Mordred, it is time to take you to the Temple of the Third Degree."

† † †

A thousand candles or more filled a triangular room that rose to a point. Torches, held in place by large metal brackets added to the golden light. It spilled from all directions and was magnified by walls painted with strange symbols in gold.

In the center of the floor stood a golden pyramid, burning brightly. The heat from the flames was oppressive when Mordred, escorted by Markus, walked in. As always, Jakob had arrived before him and stood in the center near the fire.

He was in the Temple of the Third Degree, and here he would learn about Fire.

"Call upon the power of the flames when you are threatened by a mortal, Mordred."

"A mortal?" Mordred asked, confused. "How is it a mortal can harm a vampyre?"

"There are others who know of your coming. They fear you. You alone have the power to undo all they have worked centuries for. And in those centuries, they learned about the Chosen One and have sought out his weakness. Do not make the mistake of thinking a mortal cannot hurt you," came Jakob's warning.

As the master moved around the room the flames seemed to follow him. Like a living being, they danced in Jakob's direction. Mordred focused in an effort to discover the source of this strange magic.

"Mordred, you are and will forever be the bearer of the light. Your path is as the destroyer of darkness. Do not think those who worship Vlad will not try to slay you. You will have many mortal enemies, and some from other planes."

Shrugging off an intense feeling of unease, Mordred asked Jakob, "Those from other planes? Besides Vlad? What else is there?"

Laughter filled the room, echoing off the stones. It reverberated through the chamber, surrounding Mordred.

"Oh, Mordred, there is so much you could see if you would only open your eyes. Things are never what they seem. Do you think the world is only filled with beings that you've been taught exist? Because you don't believe in ghosts or spirits, does that make them non-existent? What of vampyres? Once you did not believe in the existence of these beings, and now look."

Flames roared with renewed life, and to Mordred they appeared to take shape and form. Mesmerized, he stared into the burning brightness. The red and orange rose higher, the yellow and gold filled the interior of the flames, the white and blue spun away from the core of the blaze, and tiny sparks of the deepest purple shot into the air.

He saw, without really understanding, a bevy of creatures he could not name. Strange beings, human and not. Horns, wings, beautiful, and ugly. Menacing faces peering out at him through the flames. Eyes filled with hatred. The fire jumped and rose higher in an explosive ball.

"Watch the flames, Mordred. They are showing you the faces of your future. Look upon them and know them well. Not all will be as they first seem. Some ugly or evil in appearance will have the purest of hearts. Others, creatures of divine beauty could be your downfall. Mark them in your mind so when you next meet them, you will recognize them," came Jakob's commanding voice.

The Master Templar continued to stand close to the fire, and Mordred feared his robes might combust. But Jakob took no notice of the flames and didn't move a muscle. With one hand cast out and unmoving, it looked for all the world as though this ancient being was indeed controlling the fire.

Something vast and snakelike coiled amid the burning embers. Without warning it struck in Mordred's direction. Mordred stepped back. The thing disintegrated before his eyes.

"Yes, always be mindful of the flames. They can reveal many secrets to you, yet they can bring to life demons you never knew existed. Open your mind Mordred. Learn to accept that which you do not know. Only then will you gain power over those that seek to destroy you.

"Now, gaze into the flames. It is time for you to control them yourself. They will merge with you, hide you and protect you, provided you always respect them."

Frowning, Mordred moved closer. This time the enormous wave of heat rising from the burning center of the room did not cause Mordred to flinch. His body had grown accustomed to the temperature, and his skin had even cooled.

"Speak to the fire, Mordred. Trust it. Revere it. Give it your utmost attention and call it forth. Command it."

It was difficult for Mordred to believe he was speaking to a nonliving entity. He paused, and at that moment the massive fire shifted. The flames reached toward him once more with a viciousness Mordred could feel. The crackle and popping of the burning tinder became a whispered voice.

"You are not a believer. We will never do your bidding unless you open your mind, Mordred. Of all the elements, we are the strongest. It is time you knew us completely."

Shaking his head to rid himself of the buzzing that filled his skull, Mordred realized he was now totally engulfed in the fire. By rights he should be burning alive. He should be screaming in unbearable pain. The smell of smoldering flesh melting against charred bone should be filling the chamber. Yet Mordred neither felt nor smelled the scent of death.

Instead he quivered at the flames' touch. It warmed him on the inside, until the core of his being was alive with heat. His skin vibrated, and though he watched his flesh bubble, it was not burning, merely shifting.

Jakob's voice broke through the incredulity of his experience. "Become the master, Mordred. It is allowing you to know it, but if you do not command it, it will become your enemy."

Mordred narrowed his mind to concentrate on one tiny thread of thought. He stilled his knowledge of the others in the room. He allowed his senses to continue to monitor his surroundings, but in a detached way. The majority of his thoughts sought the flames. It sought the voices.

Reaching a hand to the flames, Mordred watched as his skin became translucent.

"Yes, oh yes, Mordred, you are the One. Your flesh

is filled with the power and the light," came the strange voices in unison above the crackling of the fire. "We can feed off your power. Look at us Mordred, look at what we can do together."

Mordred, hypnotized by the fire, gazed above him. The flames reached to the ceiling and spread across the room. They were no longer confined to the pyramid of metal in the center of the room. The entire chamber was alive with the burning fire. And Mordred was standing in the center.

His entire being shook with tremors. He felt the power of the fire blending with his energy. While he could still see his surroundings, he now saw from a thousand different vantage points. Wherever there was fire, he could see, feel, and touch. It was as if his entire body were now spread across the flames. He felt weightless and amazingly lightheaded. He felt incredibly potent.

Testing this new part of himself, Mordred concentrated. He pointed in a direction above him and watched as a finger of flame shot forth. He copied the gesture in a different place below and was pleased to see the fire respond accordingly.

His conscious mind was trying desperately to tell him none of this was possible. It warred with another part of him. Something much deeper, much more primal, that remained in control.

Jakob's voice brought Mordred back to himself. "It is time, Mordred, to let go. Release the flames. They have accepted you, and you, them. In the future you only need a spark to gain the measure of power you witnessed here today. You can use the flames as a weapon, or as a way to conceal yourself. But do not stay in the presence of the fire too long, for like any greedy thing it will seek to consume your essence. To feed upon you would make it all powerful, something you cannot allow to happen."

Mordred didn't want to release the flames. The feeling racing through him was euphoric. It washed through him like a drug. The sensations within him could be likened to the most intense arousal he'd ever experienced. It was orgasmic in its proportion.

"Mordred! Separate from the flames. Do not allow them to control you." Jakob's harsh tone broke through Mordred's ecstasy. Without warning Mordred felt himself becoming whole again. He felt the heaviness of his body, of his bones and flesh. The weight of his organs, and the clothing that covered him. Finally, the intense burden of his own thoughts crashed through his being. He fell to his knees. The pain of his fall shot through him, and he groaned.

"Good, Mordred. Never forget, power in any form when it becomes all consuming is a danger."

Mordred remained in his kneeling position. He found himself breathing hard, as if he'd just run a distance, and every part of his body ached. He was thirsty beyond belief.

"Yes, we are done for the time being. You may go rest, or drink your fill."

At Mordred's horrified look, Jakob rephrased his last comment. "Of *water*, Mordred. Your body requires replenishment from its experience. Only water."

✝ ✝ ✝

Jakob had told him he was learning at an incredible rate. To Mordred it was excruciatingly slow.

When he was not in the Temples, learning of his powers, Mordred spent many hours reading. He poured over ancient texts, some from books so old they turned to dust after he touched them. Some with strange symbols and languages he thought he didn't know, but magically the words revealed themselves to him.

He read of cultures other than his own. Legends and lore he had once thought only to be myths and fabrications became truth in the dim light of the torches. Through cracked and torn pages and very old scrolls, Mordred read of a world far removed from the memories of his own upbringing. He educated himself on the people around him, reading of the Templars and their role since the dawn of man. Mordred fed upon the knowledge as he would blood. He absorbed it, storing it for the future.

Although he was privy to things he never before could have comprehended, Mordred still felt no wiser. He felt no more equipped to handle what was to come.

It was while Mordred was feeding his hungry mind that the change overtook him again.

Mordred dreaded the transformation. Even though he knew preventing it was impossible, he did not welcome it. Instead he fought against it. When the first fingers of it touched him, he resisted.

The change would drop him to his knees. It would steal away his senses. Pain would fill his entire being.

It would drive him mad. And yet he knew, even in the knowing, that he would relent. It had power over him. He could only hope to control it sometime in the future. For now he was as helpless as a falling leaf in the wind.

At least this time Mordred recognized the signs. He knew enough to send others away, still fearing he would cause harm to those around him. Isolated, he could battle his private demons.

Like the time before, Mordred's body began to tingle and then tremble uncontrollably. A searing heat pushed beneath his skin. In Mordred's numbed mind he heard the sickening sound of his bones shattering and splitting through skin. The ripping and tearing of his flesh echoed in his head, making his stomach roil and protest the images.

He dropped to the floor as his jaw dislocated, distending grotesquely in an effort to accommodate the deadly sharp canines that were even now piercing through his lower lip. The blood from his new wounds spilled onto the stone floor. It gushed from him, spraying the furniture crimson. Some of the salty liquid slid wickedly down his throat.

The blood awakened the beast. It shook him. Helpless before the hunger, Mordred endured. An animal groan burst from his depths, rattling the chamber with its ferocity.

His need for blood grew so great, his rational mind began to fear for the Templars moving about on the other side of the wall. And just when he thought his change couldn't bring him any lower, he heard the door to his chamber creak open. In came Jakob.

Mordred wanted to hide. He wanted to run. It was as much from the shame of his vampyre-self as it was from the fear he could harm the man he had come to respect.

"You must go," he growled as softly as he was able. His lips tried in vain to form intelligible words.

Jakob glanced casually at Mordred and proceeded to walk toward the table. It was as if there weren't a single thing wrong with Mordred.

"Did you not hear me? Go!" He tried again, forcing his mouth into shape despite the pain of his new teeth slashing his lips.

"Why?" Jakob asked. "I am in no danger, am I?

"Yes. I mean no. I mean, I don't know."

"Yes, Mordred, you do know. You know a great deal, and what hasn't been with you since the day you were born you have learned here, among us."

Mordred cast a glance at Jakob, though he remained on the floor. "I do not trust myself. I am afraid I may not be able to control myself."

Suddenly the room was filled with the scent of blood. To Mordred, it was like a pheromone, something that called to him. It was Jakob's blood. It was lush and sweet and strong, and Mordred wanted nothing more than to taste it.

His darker side slithered ever closer, pushing itself up. It ignored the rational side of Mordred's brain. Instead, the predator within rose to take control. Mordred tried to stand. His booted feet slid in the copious amounts of blood pooling on the floor.

Jakob remained where he was. Then he took a seat

at the desk. It was as if he were watching a kitten and not some slathering, drooling beast covered in blood.

The vampyre in Mordred however smelled a measure of fear mingling with the fluid flooding Jakob's veins.

The Master Templar was not as calm as he appeared. "There will come a day, Mordred, when you must test the strength of your will."

"I do not think now is the time. Not with you."

"Some days you will not have a choice. You are young in your new self. It will take you years to control your change and to dictate when and where you will feed. I think now is the perfect time for you to exert some measure of restraint."

Frustrated, Mordred spun away from Jakob. His great black cape swirled about him like wings, concealing his face and body.

††

Jakob knew he played a dangerous game. He had never underestimated the power of the vampyres and didn't do so now. Yet, he knew he would have to be sure that Mordred was not an immediate threat before he could release him. In good conscience Jakob could not let Mordred go only to kill indiscriminately.

He also needed to be sure he was not placing his faith, once again, in one who would prove unworthy. The Templars had wasted precious time with others before Mordred. In the desperate attempt to find the Chosen One, they had time and again watched as each vampyre slipped away from them, each choosing the darkness, causing the Templars to ultimately destroy their pupil.

Only a vampyre could fight another vampyre, and that in itself was a quandary.

Jakob believed true vampyres were neither good nor evil. They were a creation like any other, put on earth to control the human population. They were predators, like wolves or large cats. The pure vampyres, those who came at the beginning of man, would not seek to destroy the entire race of mortals. To do so would mean the destruction of their own race.

Nay, it was the half-borns and the entity called Vlad that posed the true threat. Mordred, being a half-born, caused concern. It was too early to determine if he would be able to resist the lure of the darkness. Half-borns, because of their tormented souls, seemed to become weak. They wished for an ending, and to that end Vlad gave them what they most desired. Immortality without guilt. Power without pain.

Would Mordred turn? Could he turn? None had yet been able to resist Vlad.

Those on the quest for immortality, those at the highest levels of office within the Church, had tinkered with something dark. In their lust to become ever young, they resurrected a being that should have remained inanimate. There was only one who could truly be resurrected. Vlad was blasphemy.

The Templars faced their own struggle with the Church. Because they knew of the existence of Vlad, they were in danger of persecution. Already there was talk they had splintered from the larger religious faction.

Already there were those seeking to condemn them as heretical.

It did not deter the Templars from their purpose. They were on a quest to save mankind. They knew the risks. Jakob, in moments of deep thought, could almost feel the end in his bones. It would start as a coldness in his limbs and edge its way to his heart. There were nights when no matter how many clothes he wore, or how close he stood to a flame, he could not warm himself.

Vlad was the Ender of All Things. He was not a living being in the way of humanity. He could not be controlled; he thrived on chaos. The Templars had learned that Vlad would feed upon the living, growing ever stronger, until there were no humans left.

This did not dissuade the hidden society within the Church. They continued to believe they were the ones in control and that at some greater time the secrets of life everlasting would be revealed to them. And so they would take on, and take down anyone or anything that stood in their way.

Jakob watched Mordred warily. He might well leave the room. Truth be told there was a small flicker of fear akin to a viper twisting its way up his spine, but he refused to give in. If he showed any measure of this deadly emotion, Mordred would indeed turn from him.

"I will not leave you, Mordred. Not now, not ever. Even when you think I am gone, I will be with you."

He watched as the man trembled and then turned to face him. Long strands of his hair stuck to the blood covering his face. He was a nightmare come to life. Long canines protruded from brilliant red lips. His jaw had been pushed forward and jutted out at an unnatural angle.

Even the bulk of the man was changed. Although he was a big man, built of solid muscle, his body seemed to ripple with even more strength. To Jakob he looked ever larger.

Mordred turned to face Jakob. His fists clenched and unclenched, and Jakob saw the long, sharp talons flashing in the torchlight. He was working to control the power coursing through the room. The very air appeared to come to Mordred, silently, sucking the rest of the room dry and empty.

Still Jakob stayed. He brought his gaze to the only thing he recognized as Mordred's true self. His eyes, brilliant blue orbs dancing with silver fire. Even though the whites of his eyes were filled with red, glowing with menace, Jakob could see the man inside the beast.

"Mordred, I know you can hear me. I know you are fighting a great battle, but still your mind is human. Stop fearing your change, Mordred. Let it wash over you, and then control it. There is nothing to fear, and you will not harm me."

Something clouded the sapphire eyes belonging to the half-born. Though Jakob held his ground, it was becoming difficult. Mordred shifted on his feet and began to move toward Jakob slowly. Jakob felt he was being stalked.

He rose and assumed a standing position. This was the closest he had ever come to the ending of his life. In one swift motion Mordred could kill him.

The speed with which Mordred approached was

astonishing. Jakob couldn't even recall seeing Mordred shift positions, and now he held Jakob's throat in his hands. He was helpless.

A tense moment of silence ensued with only Mordred's labored breathing and unsteady gasps coming from Jakob.

"I could kill you," Mordred hissed in a detached voice. Long sharp talons clicked as nail scraped against nail.

"Aye, that you could. But what then, Mordred? Whom would you turn to for guidance?"

Jakob didn't mention that Mordred would never make it out of the fortress alive. The minute his men found his body, they would seal off the exits and hunt Mordred like the animal they believed him to be.

He had tried to enlighten the men, but their acceptance only went so far. The Templars were more than willing to turn the other cheek in many situations. They would draw a line at helping a soul stealer who had killed their Master.

"You think your men would stand a chance against me?" Mordred demanded, shaking Jakob violently. "I am a vampyre, and I can kill all of you if I will it!"

"No, Mordred. You cannot kill us all. Make no mistake, these men who have sworn to protect you will not hesitate to give their lives in the destruction of yours if their faith proves misguided."

Jakob waited. Mordred's eyes glowed a yellow. His pupils were tiny slits in eyes swimming in a sea of yellow and red. A silent prayer filled the Master Templar. It was not for his own soul he prayed, but for the tortured man before him.

As quickly as Mordred had grabbed him, he was released. It caught him so off guard that Jakob nearly crashed to the floor. He righted himself by grasping the edge of the desk.

Quietly, Jakob gulped several large breaths of air. He watched Mordred stalk the room, pacing like a trapped animal. A current of energy rippled through the air, charging it with a bluish haze.

"You've done well, Mordred. Your control will strengthen each time."

Mordred whirled to face Jakob. "Get out!"

This time Jakob didn't hesitate. It was not wise to push a new student too far.

Chapter Nine

"He what?!" Markus shrieked.

"But he didn't," came Jakob's cool reply. The Master Templar was lying in his large bed, resting. It had taken nearly all of his strength to stand up to the force that was Mordred when he underwent his change. It wasn't even Mordred's physical strength that caused Jakob such weakness. It was his presence, and the presence of something not good.

He tried to keep his faith aimed in the direction of The Templars' higher purpose, but he was shaken. It was like having the light sucked from your soul, Jakob thought as he reflected on those tense moments when Mordred had wrapped his hands about his neck.

Markus brought Jakob a cold cloth and tenderly placed it around his neck. There were ugly bruises in purple and yellow marring his flesh. He would need to wear high collar for the remainder of Mordred's stay, if only to protect him from the fury of the Templars. They would never understand what a great triumph Mordred had experienced in the chamber with Jakob.

He had survived his change. Not only had he survived, but he also had caged the beast. Yes, it still raged and had come perilously close to the surface, but Mordred had held it back. It was the single most important accomplishment so far.

Markus shook his head as he stood looking down at Jakob. The man's love and loyalty shone like a beacon from his blue eyes. It would do Markus well not to be so attached. Even he could not prevent what was to come.

"As I said, he didn't kill me."

"But look at your neck. In a split second, Jakob, he could have snapped you in two. You are not a young man, and you should not be toying with vampyres."

Jakob struggled to sit up. "I am not toying with anything. Might I remind you that we are speaking of the entire human race as we know it? If I do not determine he is indeed the Chosen One, what difference will it make if I live today? I will only be dead tomorrow."

"It still does little to quell my desire to kill him myself."

"You would not succeed."

Horrified at Jakob's lack of faith, Markus continued, "I am the strongest Templar in this fortress or any other. You have trained me in the art of dealing with vampyres. You have given me weapons to defeat them, and I have slain those before. How can you say I cannot kill Mordred? He is the same."

"No!" Jakob began a fit of coughing.

Markus quickly filled a pewter mug with water and held it to Jakob's lips.

Jakob drank gratefully in long, slow swallows, wincing at the pain the effort caused him. Mordred had done more damage than he thought.

"Thank you, Markus. Now, let me explain. Yes, you have served us well as the slayer of vampyres. However, Mordred is different. You have not seen the extent of his power. He rules it with the force of his will. You will not take him down. Nor can you be allowed to. This is the One,"

Jakob grasped the edges of Markus's surcoat. "Do you understand me? He is the One. I am more sure of this than I am that the sun will rise tomorrow. We have found the Chosen One."

Markus laid his hands over Jakob's veined, gnarled hands and slowly pushed him back against the pillows. Jakob released his grip.

"I have always honored your words. I have never faltered in my faith in you, but I do hesitate now. I will not let anyone bring you harm."

Jakob smiled then. "It is not for us to say how we will die, Markus. None of us have that power. And we each, in our own way, understand what is at stake here. My life for the lives of countless others is a small price to pay."

Markus turned, white cape fluttering behind him. He spoke to the chamber as he slammed a gloved hand on a nearby table.

"I will not allow you to die at the hands of a soul stealer!"

"Markus, Markus, it is not up to you. He is the Chosen One. This I know. Leave it at that."

† † †

His head pounded. Mordred kept his hands firmly placed on his temples to prevent his skull from splitting in two.

A day had passed since the incident with Jakob and still Mordred felt no better. He hadn't the courage to face the man. He was afraid he had violated the Master Templar's trust. In truth, if he were cast out from the fortress, he had no idea where he would go. Worse still he had no idea what he would become.

Blood had been brought to Mordred in his chamber, after Jakob had left him. The man assigned to the task had looked none too pleased. Mordred had ignored the man's look of disgust and grabbed the flask. He had slammed the door in the Templar Knight's face with a growl.

It was an elixir. As much as the thought of drinking blood repulsed him, his other being relished it. Sweet nectar. Like a greedy child suckling sustenance from a mother's breast, Mordred drank the contents without pause.

Immediately he felt calm. As if he stood beneath a summer rain, his entire being drifted into a state of satiated happiness. He had never been one to experiment with the strange herbs, plants, and powders that some of the other soldiers used. They claimed it allowed them to leave their cares behind for a while. Mordred felt drinking blood had the same effect on him.

As the power of the blood swept over him, it quieted the beast. He sensed his vampyre-self retreating to some dark corner. It would wait there for the next advantage. The next moment of hunger or weakness.

If the physical nature of the transformations and the pain they brought on didn't send Mordred spinning into oblivion, surely the intense desire for blood would. There were now two very distinct entities existing within him, each grappling for control. Each seeking a way to overthrow the other. It tormented him.

The worst of it was that he still did not trust himself. It mattered not that he let Jakob live. He could just as easily have killed him. He did not believe the next time he would not.

The faint sound of booted heels clicking on the stones came to Mordred's ears. As if he were outside of himself, he saw the corridor beyond his door. It was Markus. Quite possibly the very last person Mordred wanted to see.

Markus did not hide his displeasure with Mordred. In fact, Markus hid few of his true feelings. He was like a snarling dog being held in check by an invisible chain. Mordred had no doubt of Markus's intentions. He did not mask the desire to see Mordred dead.

This at least was in the open. Markus did not seek to play a game. He made it very clear the only reason he came within an arm's reach of Mordred was out of respect for Jakob. It was his loyalty to the Master Templar that kept him from killing Mordred. It mattered not to Mordred what Markus's feelings were. But it didn't mean he couldn't have a little fun. In his morbid state, he thought to lighten his mood at Markus's expense.

Concentrating on the heavy wooden door, Mordred tried to open it at the exact moment that Markus reached for the knob. His hope was that it would catch Markus off balance.

The door didn't budge.

Sighing, Mordred lifted his head from his hands and looked at the door. Perhaps if he gazed on what he wanted to move with his mind, he could make it happen.

Again, nothing.

Instead the door burst open, slamming into the wall. A great resounding thunder shook the room.

Markus did not step into Mordred's chamber. He stood silently for a moment, staring at a point beyond Mordred.

"Save your cheap charlatan's tricks for someone who might be impressed. That is, when you learn how to do them."

His voice was a mere snarl. Contempt dripped, coating him with acid. Though the depth of his thoughts was masked, Mordred inhaled the strong scent of intense dislike. If there was fear, it was hidden beneath layers of something bordering on hatred.

He glanced at Markus's gloved hand and noticed it gripped his sword.

Mordred rose and inclined his head, raising his eyebrows at Markus.

Again the man did not look at him, but merely grunted a reply. "One can never be too careful with a soul stealer around. How can I be sure that all we have taught you might not be used against us? I cannot afford to take that chance."

Of course he would be mad. Clearly, he had seen Jakob.

"How is the Master?"

"It is an insult for me to even hear the title pass your lips. You are not worthy of calling him anything. Of even knowing him. Were it not for him, you would already be dead."

Mordred was far too weary and racked with his own guilt to rise to the fight. "It will make no difference to you, I suppose, but I did ask him to leave. He walked in on me in the middle of the change, and I told him to go. He chose to stay."

Markus shrugged. His chain mail uttered a musical sound altogether out of place in the present mood. "It is time for another step in your enlightenment."

"Will Jakob be there?"

"Nay. Jakob is in his chambers recovering from his incident with you," Markus sneered. "Now come. I've no desire to waste a day, thereby delaying your departure."

Knowing he was not going to break through the shroud of icy contempt that hung about Markus like a cloak, Mordred nodded.

"Fine. Let us proceed."

† † †

"I'm sorry, I'm not sure I understand."

Mordred stared across the wide expanse of a reflecting

pool carved into a white marble floor. He wondered if his universe hadn't just slipped out of his control. The place before him, though vast, looked nothing like the other chambers he had been in.

Here, everything was bathed in white and gold. Light filled every crack and crevice, coming from candles and torchères lining the white stone walls. The room was filled with a palpable purity. Something innocent and devoid of darkness dwelled here.

It was a palace of sorts. A grand shrine to something or someone of high value. Beautiful tapestries hung on every wall. Colorful carpets strewn about the floor created a patchwork pattern of an unformed rainbow. Velvet, silk, and other rich fabrics draped from metal poles or canopies. Pillows in every shade imaginable were thrown carelessly about.

Several large, comfortable looking chairs vied for his attention before his gaze rested on an enormous bed. There against the far wall rose the most magnificent resting place Mordred had ever seen. Surely an entire camp of men would fit comfortably within its beckoning coverings.

Several marble steps would need to be climbed to reach the soft throws of fur and fabric. Nearly transparent curtains and drapery delicately hung around metal rods. Candles glowed from within the darkened interior. Just staring at the bed had Mordred thinking he could easily slumber forever.

Before the bed, with steps leading into it and columns of marble flanking it, was a pool of water. Steam rose slowly into the air. The pool was larger than the one directly in front of Mordred. On the larger pool's surface, Mordred saw flower petals floating.

Like a living thing it spoke to Mordred of sinful delights and wickedness. For the first time since becoming a soul stealer, Mordred found himself burning with lust. How could the mere image of a bed conjure up such intense heat in his loins?

"You will spend the night here," came Markus's voice.

"Why?" Mordred asked, frustrated by the man's seeming need to keep him in the dark as much as possible.

"This is the Temple of Temptation, and here you will learn to resist nearly all things. You will be fed a grand feast. You are also allowed to drink your fill of wine and ale."

"But?" Mordred prodded. He'd learned so far that everything had a price. He had nearly set himself on fire during the last session of his supposed enlightenment.

Something filtered through the air, causing his skin to prickle in anticipation. Deep inside he felt himself awakening. The unmistakable scents of women filled his nostrils.

As if sensing the change in Mordred, Markus said, "The only rule here is that you are not to seduce, or should I make it more clear, bed down, with any of your humble servants."

"I beg your pardon?"

"I said," Markus continued with an exasperated sigh, "you are not to give in to the temptation of the flesh."

Shaking his head, Mordred replied sarcastically, "Why? I never took a vow of chastity in my knighthood, and I don't intend to start now."

With little warning from Mordred's heightened senses, Markus was upon him. He gripped him by the neck of his mail *coiffe*.

"Listen, you fool, there are many kinds of evil. In the future you would do well to remember it. Death can come in the form of the most exquisite beauty. Hold your lust in check."

Mordred gently, yet firmly, peeled Markus's hands from his person.

"I am to spend the entire night without satisfying my baser instincts?"

"Unlike me, Jakob believes you are more man than animal. Let's see how well you can control the 'instincts' you refer to."

Laughing, Mordred asked, "So, when do I begin this grand test?"

"Now." Markus clapped his gloved hands and from previously unseen doors came twelve beautiful women.

Mordred groaned inwardly. They weren't merely pleasing to the eye. They were masterpieces from an artist's canvas come to life. Each could easily rival a goddess of the past.

There was a woman for every preference. Tall and lithe, petite and doll-like, curvaceous and tempting. Blondes, brunettes, redheads, and ebony-haired, they were enough to drive a man to pleasure himself just standing before them.

The predator within assessed each woman with a

sharp eye. Small breasts, rounded buttocks, and slender legs called his attention. Full figures and large breasts to tantalize and tease, had Mordred's cock already straining against his breeches.

Lips that begged to be kissed. Skin aching to be caressed. Hands that desired to touch him. It had been a very long time since Mordred had taken part in the pleasures of the flesh. He had always been careful never to give the impression he was with them for more than one night. A solitary man, a loner such as himself could not afford the trouble a relationship would bring. While other men worried about wives and girlfriends, children and family, Mordred was only concerned with himself. It allowed him to focus solely on the battles at hand. It made his burdens lighter.

Now, however, with the women laid before him like forbidden fruit, he toyed with the idea of making love to each and every one in the room. Clad in diaphanous fabrics of muted blues, greens, golds, and pinks, their clothing did little to cover the most private of their parts. Every curve, every hidden secret was there for Mordred's viewing.

He saw the treasured clefts of their womanhood; some covered with a dark mat of down, while others appeared to bear not a single hair and instead gave him the image of a virgin. His mouth watered at the prospect of delighting in the unique taste of each woman. The air was full of the heady aroma of their musky scents. If he were more beast than man, he'd have begun rutting with them on the spot.

Unfortunately, Mordred found with the increased

awareness of his sight, hearing, and sense of smell, he was not quite sure this was a test he could pass.

He groaned again under his breath and remained rooted to the spot. He wasn't sure exactly if he wanted to proceed, or run. To spend the night with such beauties and not touch them would be a most unpleasant task.

Markus, who had up until that time taken a position behind Mordred, turned to depart. His footfalls echoed on the marble floor, and he called to Mordred as he slipped through the door, "Did I mention these are Temple Virgins? They are sacred. Do not defile them with your 'baser instincts.'"

The last was said in an unmistakable tone of sarcasm. Mordred turned to watch the Templar step into the passageway. He caught the ghost of a smile lighting the man's face, as if he knew what he asked would be impossible.

The women moved forward silently, on bare feet. They looked like pastel clouds of succulent pleasure. When they came to Mordred, they fell to their knees.

In unison, their voices complementing each other, they said, "We are at your service. It is our wish only to please you. Whatever you desire, we are at your command."

Not every desire, Mordred thought sardonically. The most obvious one, taking them all for a tumble, was clearly off limits. He wasn't sure whether to laugh, curse, or thank whatever benevolent powers had seen fit to lock him in a room with women he couldn't have imagined, even in his dreams.

They didn't touch him, and yet the entire surface of his body tingled in anticipation. If he didn't know himself better, he would swear he was drooling. Mordred licked his lips and swallowed around the lump that developed in his throat, just to be sure. While he didn't wish to appear a complete lecher, he knew there was no sense pretending they didn't have a most obvious effect on him. They would, after all, notice soon enough. His breeches were tenting from the strain of his arousal.

One by one the women rose and surrounded him.

"It is time we make you more comfortable," they whispered in husky voices filled with erotic promises.

Virgins. Remember they are virgins, Mordred pleaded with his conscience, but his physical nature was fast taking control.

Two women took his gloved hands and divested them of the leather coverings. Another woman worked to unfasten the clasp of his cloak. It fell to the floor as other women unbuckled the belt around his waist.

Mordred felt his mail *coiffe* being raised gently and then watched as it was pulled over his head and cast away. Next came his surcoat. Then the mail shirt and cotton gambeson.

A brunette with eyes the color of jade motioned for him to sit on a low bench. The only thing Mordred could think of at the moment was her kneeling on the same piece of furniture while he filled her from behind. For a moment he doubted they would even be able to unlace his breeches they were stretched so painfully tight across his heated groin.

In no time he was naked among twelve heavenly

creatures. One of the women held open a soft black robe for Mordred to wrap himself in. Rising, he did just that, but the robe did nothing to hide the erection that by now was as hard as the marble in the chamber.

Thankfully, before things went too far, two women who had apparently exited the chamber during Mordred's disrobing, came through one of the doors. They carried silver trays, which they set on a low table among the many floor cushions. Some of the other women now moved away from him, casting a smile or a sideways glance before departing. They removed themselves from the chamber only to return carrying more trays.

The smells of spices and aromas he couldn't place filled Mordred's nostrils. His stomach growled. Quite unexpectedly Mordred discovered his appetite had magically returned. He felt ready to devour a bull, should they bring one forth.

The remaining women helped him to stand and walked with him to the cushions surrounding the table. They waited until he took a seat before settling themselves quietly around him.

Before he could comprehend what was happening, he watched as several women picked apart the food with their fingers, bringing those same fingers to his lips. Incredible as it was, Mordred was being fed as if he were an infant. And yet he didn't feel childish. Instead, this new activity caused a heavy fullness to settle in his nether regions on his already fully blossomed cock.

It was wicked, this attention, as Mordred tasted both

food and flesh. Fingers slick with fat from the meat and poultry slid across his lips, teasing him. Inadvertently, he found himself licking the juices, sauces, and drippings of the food from their hands. The women giggled with delight. Mordred, too, laughed at the absurdity of the decadence.

A woman with hair the color of flame brought a large hammered goblet to his lips. Tilting his head, he allowed her to pour the sweet liquid down his throat. It was honey wine, and he drank as though dying of thirst. When he drained the first vessel, another was brought, administered by yet another beauty.

Over and over they refilled his goblet. At one point, Mordred moved his arm, spilling frothy liquid over the exposed skin of the woman who held the vessel. Feeling carefree, Mordred pulled the woman onto his lap, leisurely licking the wine right off her skin, delighting in her squeals of pleasure.

He pulled the cloth of her gown lower, until his lips found her breast. Just as he was about to hone in on a pert nipple, the other women prodded him back to awareness. They urged him to stand. In one swift motion he was disrobed.

Mordred had never been one to be overly concerned about his body, or how he appeared when naked. It mattered not to him that all the women could view the evidence of their teasing. His erection rose stiffly.

In the haze of his mind, he tried to search the women's thoughts. He could find nothing. Someone had done a good job instructing them to keep their minds clear. It reminded him of the surface of the nearby pool, where he was being led.

Without preamble, the women pulled him down the steps into the warm water. Within minutes they were all in the pool with him, their gowns floating up around them, exposing what he hadn't already seen.

In sensory overload, Mordred failed to see how any Templar could resist this bevy of expertly trained beauties. While they didn't go too far in their efforts, just seeing them naked was enough to get any young buck to forget his purpose.

Mordred felt someone begin the process of letting his long hair free from the thong that held it back. He was urged to tilt back, and he felt the water soak his hair. Slender fingers adeptly massaged his scalp. Mordred groaned at yet another pleasurable sensation.

Many hands began to caress his body both above the water and beneath it. Mordred could not tell which hands belonged to which woman, and he found he didn't particularly care. He felt breasts and buttocks rub against him as they washed the soap from his hair.

Temptation be damned. Mordred was not a man of the cloth and had never claimed to be. He did not need to pass this test . . .

† † †

Grabbing a woman under each arm, he hauled them out of the water to the massive bed. Like a barbarian, he pushed them into the welcoming folds of fur. He was pleased to discover the others had followed his lead.

Without any talking, each woman found a place in

Temple of Temptation

the bed. Mordred was most definitely living every knight's—hell, every man's—dream. He touched, stroked, and licked the wet flesh surrounding him. Soft moans and sounds of pleasure filled the air.

His hands toyed with heavy breasts. A blonde before him presented herself to him, and when he laved her nipples, her hands caught in his wet hair. She pulled him closer, arching her back in ecstasy.

He felt lips touching his skin, licking the moisture. They were near his neck, his chest, his legs and, oh yes, his groin. Closer they moved until he felt the warm, slick depths of a mouth as it wrapped its succulent flesh around his cock.

Mordred might well be half vampyre, but he was still half man and that meant he had been brought to the brink of losing control so many times this evening that if the woman continued applying her talents on his hard flesh, it would be over for him. He knew he could not let this night end without experiencing the true euphoria promised to him within the depths of their womanhood.

Moving on the bed, he slid a woman beneath him. It was an orgy of the flesh. Hands reached out, moans filled the room, and as Mordred drove his throbbing member into a plump redhead, another woman toyed with his balls. It was pure heaven, a bliss so incomprehensible that Mordred feared he might burst into one enormous pile of oozing spunk.

He plunged himself over and over into slick, wet sheaths. Pumping his cock in and out until it erupted again, and again. Mordred ceased only when his body could do no more. He passed into oblivion with naked bodies sprawled over him, around him, and under him. Surrounded by flesh, Mordred passed happily into a deep slumber, a smile planted firmly upon his face.

CHAPTER TEN

"Sir."

Jakob glanced from his notes to find Markus standing in front of him. He had been so engrossed in his research he had failed to notice the blond giant approach. The man wore a thunderous expression and anger vibrated through him. The air was pungent with Markus's unreleased fury.

"Yes?" Jakob sighed.

"Sir, continuing on this course is madness!"

Jakob noted the tic in the man's cheek. He fidgeted with the hilt of his sword, fists clenching and unclenching. He clearly sought an invitation to speak.

Jakob nodded. "What did he do *this* time?" There was no need to ask who had upset Markus. Jakob was surprised the man hadn't exploded weeks earlier.

If not for Markus's complete loyalty to the cause, he would have feared for the vampyre's life. Markus might not be able to destroy Mordred, but if he acted on his rage, he wouldn't go down without a fight likely to cause lasting damage.

It was Jakob's fervent hope that both Markus and Mordred would have settled their issues with one another, establishing some sort of truce. Each knew what was at stake, and the constant bickering belittled the quest.

The rivalry between them could easily be construed as a brotherly feud for all the hostility each man had for the other. They were constantly throwing verbal barbs, threats, and insults as children did.

Yet, their actions masked something deeper. There was between the two a growing, albeit grudging, respect and conscious diligence to their duty.

It was at that moment a plan formed in Jakob's mind, an idea to bring an end to their animosity. They would be forced to work together. Making them operate as a team would, hopefully, ensure they were on the same side.

Pushing his thoughts aside, Jakob studied the man before him. "Markus? Go ahead."

The man fisted his hands for a few more moments. Jakob recognized the action, and knew Markus was trying to find words to plead his case calmly.

"The man is incorrigible! Evil to the core. At the next opportunity he should be sent to the fires of hell where he belongs. I, for one, will be happy to send him on his way!"

"Easy, Markus, calm down. It doesn't do you any good to become so angry."

Turning, Markus paced the chamber. "You don't understand, Jakob. He has crossed the line this time."

Jakob sat quietly, taking in the sight of his trusted

commander falling to pieces. "Enlighten me. Why has he crossed the line?"

"He . . . he . . . he . . ." Markus sputtered.

"Say it, Markus. What is it that Mordred did to upset you?"

"He defiled the Temple Virgins!"

To punctuate the severity of his words Markus slammed a gloved fist against the desk, sending the parchment scrolls to the floor. The man ignored the papers and glared at a spot beyond Jakob.

Jakob feared he might burst into laughter. He forced his face to remain emotionless and met the knight's heated gaze.

True, defiling the Temple Virgins was a violation of Templar law, but it was just too ridiculous to believe. No one, not even the undead before Mordred had dared break the Templar rules.

Jakob turned slowly to face Markus. "Are you telling me he has," Jakob paused in an effort to find a polite word.

"Fucked," came Markus's helpful reply.

"Yes, right, as you say." Smiling he continued, "He *dabbled* with all of them?"

Jakob watched Markus nod. The man's face and neck were mottled with red splotches. He thought perhaps he didn't get the full impact of Markus's gesture. "All *twelve* of them?"

"Yes."

Shrugging, the Master Templar tapped a finger on his chin. This truly was a quandary. If Mordred had been merely mortal, and the women had been no more than wenches from a nearby village, Jakob would have been slapping the man's back and congratulating him for his apparent inhuman prowess with women. As it was however, the women weren't simple barmaids and Mordred wasn't human.

Markus remained glowering at him, waiting for an answer.

Restitution would be demanded from not only Markus, but also the whole of the Templar Empire. Jakob had to think fast. Of all the tests he'd thought Mordred might fail, this wasn't one of them. Then again, maybe this really was a blessing in disguise. Yes, it was just that. Mordred had failed the test set before him, but all things considered, copulating with twelve women wasn't the worst thing a vampyre could do.

"Markus?"

"Yes," the man grunted.

"Are all the women alive?"

"Yes," Markus replied, "but they aren't virgins anymore."

"I understand. But are you telling me he spent an entire night with the women, and he didn't bite any of them?"

"No, he simply chose to fornicate with, defile, mate, rut, and debase all *twelve* of them. *Twelve!*"

"You've made your point, Markus. Think on this for a moment. Mordred is not a Templar. He will never *be* a Templar. Therefore, perhaps it isn't right that we hold him to the same codes. He can fail this test and still be the one we seek."

As Jakob was beginning to realize, something far

more important had occurred during the hours of night. None of the women had been harmed. Mordred had spent his time experiencing rapture of the flesh, rather than the nirvana a vampyre attained in drinking blood. It meant his human side was still a part of him.

Markus however, didn't appear willing to accept this line of logic. He sent Jakob a look. "Have you gone mad? He's played hide the cock with every woman in that temple. They are no longer pure. The worst part is, now they all fancy themselves in love with a vampyre! He's committed a grave sin against the Templars and . . ."

Although Jakob was sure Markus would continue his tirade, it was getting them nowhere. He raised his gnarled hand and uttered a command for silence. "I will ask you to calm yourself in my presence and obey my words. Mordred is not to be reprimanded in any way. Convey this to the others."

"None know except me."

"I see. Very well then, you will give your word that you will speak no more of this. As I have said, Mordred is not one of us. His failure to contain his lust is of little consequence to me or to the cause. I will not hold him to our laws on this count."

"But . . ."

"Enough," Jakob's voice boomed, filling the chamber. "He has succeeded in far more important tests."

Markus uttered a choking sound but immediately closed his mouth. "Apologies, Jakob, but the man has no self control."

Jakob smiled and waved Markus's last statement off. "Over his loins, no. But over the evil growing within him, yes. All things considered, I'd say the latter is the most important. Wouldn't you agree?"

There was nothing Markus could say to refute the reasoning.

"Come, you must take me to him. He shall be ready to leave at nightfall."

Markus's jaw dropped. "Tonight? He's not ready."

Jakob whirled faster than seemed possible for a man his age. "You will do as I say, and you will not question my authority again, ever. Is that understood?"

Markus hung his head and followed Jakob from the room.

† † †

Mordred leaned back against the soft cushions on his bed. The coverings were bunched around his hips, exposing his upper body to the cool air wafting through the room. He yawned and stretched like a great beast.

The muscles in his body ached in an entirely pleasurable way and reminded him of his recent nocturnal activity. It brought a smile to his face. *Did I really have sex with twelve women at once?*

He reflected on his history with the fair sex. As a knight he'd never been one to abstain from pleasures of the flesh. Most women appeared to want a warrior beneath them, and Mordred was only too happy to oblige. He found the act of lovemaking energizing. It got the blood, among other things, pumping, he mused.

Resting his hands behind his head, Mordred's thoughts drifted to lovemaking and battle. There were men he'd encountered that didn't allow themselves a good fuck prior to a battle. Instead, like temporary monks, they denied themselves the pleasures, thinking it would improve their fighting ability.

Mordred couldn't help shake his head at the ridiculous notion. Dabbling in activities of the flesh actually made him more focused. He'd heard of the legendary Norse Berserkers and their battle madness; how, when they scented blood, they went into a killing frenzy. Mordred likened his sexual behavior to a madness of a different kind. It charged and reinvigorated him.

If making love was a sin, then Mordred was not about to repent. It was one of the few things he enjoyed, if a bit selfishly. Not that he'd had any complaints from his partners, he mused.

Last night was different. It was as if he had been possessed by another entity, something that made him care about the pleasures of the women. And in their releases Mordred discovered his own was made even more powerful.

A feeling of lethargy washed over him. He could lie in this bed for a day or more, recovering from his gluttony.

But his musings were interrupted by the harsh sound of knocking. Immediately his mind revealed the image of Jakob, clad in his flowing white robes, flanked by a dastardly looking Markus.

Mordred made no immediate move to cover his body and watched as Jakob and his giant companion came into the room.

Jakob stopped when he reached the edge of the pool

and cleared his throat. "Mordred, I heard you slept well last night. Would that be the truth of things?"

"I don't recall sleeping much," came the sardonic reply.

Mordred watched as the Master Templar smiled at him. The big oaf behind him, however, looked like he was straining on an invisible chain. It was obvious it took all of Markus's will power to control his rage. Patches of red mottled the man's neck and his face was screwed so tightly, Mordred wondered if it might stay that way.

He knew what had set Markus off, though he was not about to apologize. Earlier, it was Markus who had walked into the Temple. Unfortunately, the timing was off. Mordred was still in the throes of performing what he considered his duty to the bevy of virginal initiates. Pleasure was such a welcome relief to all the darkness that surrounded him these days, he was loath to stop. And he hadn't.

Like a wounded bull, Markus had roared his anger when he had discovered the twelve former virgins, naked and lying with their limbs entwined with Mordred, cooing and cuddling him. The only thing Mordred could do, after extricating himself with reluctance from between the thighs of a particularly tall blonde, was flash the giant a wide grin.

Markus's rage had shaken the walls of the chamber, and the women scattered. They disappeared quickly leaving him alone with the knight, who rushed around the pool and lunged at him, cursing the entire time. He called Mordred so many vile names, he wasn't sure he understood all of them. It was as if Markus were speaking in tongues.

Snapping out of his momentary reverie, Mordred watched Jakob place a restraining hand on Markus's arm.

"Easy, Markus, let your master do the talking this time," Mordred baited.

Jakob raised his hand. "Enough. Mordred, Markus has just cause to be angry. You were after all told not to defile the virgins. Clearly, that went unheeded."

When Mordred started to interrupt, Jakob sent him a warning glance. "I have decided this is a mere infraction and not something irremediable. The fact that you left the women alive and unbitten gives us all hope.

"I had thought that you two would have come to an agreement by this time. That you would have put aside your differences and learned to work together toward the common goal. I can see that isn't going to happen however, and we are out of time. You will begin your journey tonight, one that will take you far from here. You will be forced to get along out of necessity."

Surprised, Mordred was about to rise but he remembered he was naked. He sat up and yanked a sheet around his waist.

Meanwhile, Markus appeared to have had the wind knocked out of him. He stood with his mouth agape. "Master, you cannot be serious. I want nothing more to do with this vampyre."

"And don't think *I* am pleased. I can go about this quest on my own," Mordred snarled.

Suddenly the room filled with a brilliant white light.

Before their eyes, Jakob levitated. Higher and higher he rose, until he looked down upon them both. He pointed and spoke in an otherworldly voice.

"You will go forth from the safety of this stronghold. You will become companions. You will learn to respect what each of you has to offer the other.

"Did you think you would have a choice? There are things far greater than either of you at work here. This is for the good of all. Now, put away your childish insults and prepare for your departure. You leave tonight."

There was no room for argument. At Jakob's final word, he slipped from his lofty position, crumpling to the marble floor in a pool of white cloth. Markus and Mordred immediately knelt at his side, each looking briefly into the other's eyes before they roused the Master Templar.

"Jakob, are you all right?" Mordred asked, gently shaking him by the shoulder. He lifted the man to a sitting position, only now realizing how very frail Jakob was. He felt like a skeleton.

Jakob opened his eyes. For a moment all Mordred could see was a milky white film covering his normally vibrant pupils. Then Jakob blinked and his wise blue gaze returned.

Inside Mordred's head he heard the voice of the Master Templar. *"Do not concern yourself with me. My time is ending and yours is just beginning. Keep this knowledge to yourself. Markus would never leave if he knew I was not well. And he must leave with you. He, too, has a destiny to live up to far beyond these walls."*

Markus reached out for Jakob as well, and saw the look that passed between master and pupil. Mordred quickly masked his thoughts. He had a suspicion that Markus merely played at appearing the big oaf, and he didn't want to give him any hint of what had passed between Jakob and him.

"Jakob, you shouldn't be using your energy on us. While it is true we do not see eye to eye, we will in time."

Mordred raised his eyebrows. This was closest thing Markus had probably ever come to offering an apology. "We should get you to your chambers so you can rest."

"Yes, there is much to do before tonight," Jakob said, his voice trembling.

As Mordred lifted Jakob into his arms, he felt a hand on him. "I would ask you to allow me. I will be leaving soon and have little time left with him." Markus's voice cracked.

Mordred nodded and strode to where his clothes were neatly folded. As he dressed, he watched Markus lift the old man as if he weighed no more than a feather, and carry him out of the chamber.

In Mordred's mind he heard Jakob's voice again, *"Thank you for not revealing all you know to Markus. He is not ready and it would make his departure harder. He may give the appearance of an uncaring warrior to most, but he has a soft heart. I would not seek to cause him any more pain."*

Mordred focused his thoughts for a response. *"I don't know exactly what you mean. I only did as you asked in not telling Markus you are gravely ill. As for grander knowledge, I fear I have failed you."*

Dejected, Mordred sat on the bed, head hanging.

"Do not feel that way, Mordred. You have come farther than any other vampyre. You are more than ready for this quest. You will make us proud. I will always remember my time with you. You gave me a gift I could never have imagined."

The voice was growing faint as Jakob was carried further away from Mordred.

"You speak as though we will never see each other after tonight."

"Only time will tell, Mordred. Only time."

† † †

The room was the largest Mordred had yet seen. He marveled at the secret fortress so far beneath the sands, and found it amazing that so many men had pledged their lives to the Templar cause. Ready to sacrifice their lives, if need be, for the greater good. Apparently, the Templars were devoted to what they believed was the future of the human race.

Standing off to one side of a raised dais, Mordred stopped counting the knights when he reached one hundred. The chamber with its arched, vaulted ceilings and beautifully carved pillars could easily hold thousands.

Each man was clad in the familiar white surcoat with the red cross emblazoned on the front. Their silver mail cast a brilliant light throughout the room, reflecting the glow of the torches.

Mordred pondered the thought that, if one had enough faith in his belief, maybe he could make a difference. If all these people came together for a common goal, perhaps they could change the world. The knights' loyalty to, and love for their cause was awe-inspiring. How could they pledge themselves to something they couldn't be sure existed?

The faith in a higher power, in a God of all gods, brought out both the best and the worst in humankind. Mordred had seen this first hand. The crusades had been launched under the guise of spreading the "right" religion, yet hundreds of thousands had died. Those considered infidels had been slaughtered *en masse*. Women had been raped and murdered, and babies skewered on the tips of swords.

The hills ran red with blood, all in the name of a holy war. Ancient cultures had been tossed aside, beliefs crumbled beneath the crusaders' booted feet. Towns, villages, and religious buildings had been destroyed in the name of God.

The irony was that many of the soldiers committing the atrocities had no more faith in their god than Mordred. They had either been forced to come to the Holy Land, as their liege commanded, or they had come simply to steal their part of a fabled wealth.

With isolated detachment, Mordred had watched as men died, and whole countries fell like sheaves of wheat beneath the fierce machine of war. How could any god condone such behavior? Yes, he was a warrior and killing was his profession, however, he never claimed to be anything else.

Returning to the present, Mordred marveled anew at the men of the Templar order. Each one of them held to a code far older than any could remember. Hearts, minds, bodies, and souls had been freely given. While he couldn't understand it, he at least respected it.

When Jakob entered the hall the room fell into respectful silence. He was a powerful man, yet everything Mordred had witnessed told him Jakob did not wield his power foolishly. And he could see the toll the power had taken on the man.

The holy warriors in the vast chamber fell as one to bended knees. They pulled their swords from their scabbards and laid them reverently on the stones, keeping their heads bent respectfully.

Markus appeared behind Mordred.

"Are you ready?" he asked quietly, without his usual sarcasm.

Mordred cocked an eyebrow and regarded the tall man. Had he turned a new leaf? "I don't think I will ever be ready, Markus."

"You speak the truth, and I do not envy you. We must go to Jakob now."

Markus walked up the steps in front of Mordred to take his place beside the Master Templar. Mordred, clad entirely in black, followed.

Jakob motioned for Mordred to come closer.

"Today, you take the first steps of your journey. Coming here was a prelude to something greater. The path you must now take will be the ultimate test of your will. It will either save humanity, or condemn it."

Jakob glanced at Mordred, and surprisingly for such

a serious occasion, he winked.

"We do not know if you will succeed or fail, for the end of your quest will come far beyond our lifetimes. But while we, the Knights Templar, are still here, you have only to find our hidden symbols to know you will find sanctuary."

Jakob pointed with a gnarled finger to the domed ceiling. "Look for the Green Man and the five pointed star."

Nodding his understanding, Mordred remained uncomfortably silent. He did not like to be the center of attention.

"We have a few other things to give you that will aid you long after the Templars are gone. Like the mail, they have secrets that will take you time to unlock. Secrets that are not for us to divulge. But be assured our gifts will aid you when needed most."

Jakob motioned, and two Templars came up the steps staggering under the weight of a large trunk. The men put it on the floor in front of Jakob and then disappeared into the crowd.

Wrought of silver and decorated with exotic symbols, the trunk itself was a sight to behold. Jewels winked under the light of the torches, and the piece vibrated subtly, as if it were a living thing.

"First we gave you the mail made long ago for the Chosen One. Now we give you armor crafted in a time before mankind. It will protect you from those who seek to do you harm."

Markus and another Templar opened the silver chest and lifted from it a piece of blackened armor. Section

The Green Man and the Templar Star

血を分けた兄弟

The Blood Weapons

after heavy section was removed from the trunk and laid at Mordred's feet. Markus and the Templar began dressing Mordred.

Throughout the entire process, Mordred remained silent, marveling at the incredible suit of armor. He wondered at the strength of enemies that forced him to wear something so powerful. Feeling the weight of the armor, Mordred knew the burden of his path.

Tiny inscriptions, some of the same symbols he had glimpsed on the trunk, appeared on every piece of armor, but he did not understand them.

"In time you will comprehend the message of protection written on this suit of armor. Just as you learn any language, this too will be revealed to you."

He watched Jakob pull something else from the trunk. It was a round shield, blackened to match the armor. Mordred took the gift from Jakob, surprised to find it weighed nearly nothing. Mordred put the shield over his right shoulder, surprised to see his name already etched on it.

"Yes, it belongs to you," was all Jakob offered.

A jeweled scabbard encrusted with rubies as large as a man's fist and inscribed with the same markings on the armor and shield, was revealed next. Though Mordred had yet to see the sheathed blade, he knew it must be a weapon of great worth.

Markus placed it on Mordred's back and fastening it with leather straps, the burden fell into place. It would take some time for Mordred to become accustomed to this new weight, not simply because of the sword's size but also because of where it was positioned.

Mordred had formerly worn a scabbard at his waist.

"And now your sword. You must use this with the greatest of intentions, Mordred. No mortal may die by this blade," Jakob instructed. "This is the Blood Sword, the only one of its kind. It will inflict damage and death to those who follow Vlad, those who are not of this earthly plane.

"It is fitted on your back so you will not draw too quickly. This will give you the time you need to measure your opponent. Go ahead, Mordred, reveal the blade so all may see and bear witness to the gift of the Templars."

Hesitating only briefly, Mordred raised his gloved hands and grasped the elongated hilt. He knew by grasping the pommel that he could use both hands if need be. Thus, he had both a two-handed and a one-handed sword.

Immediately after touching the metal, it felt as if the sword had been made for him; it fit his grasp and molded to his hands. The weight of the weapon, as he pulled it over his head, was nothing less than perfect. Mordred knew that if he placed a finger where the blade met the hilt, the sword would balance like the lightest of burdens. Only a master swordsman would know this. Without a doubt, the Blood Sword was a great blade.

Suddenly the sword began to pulsate, sending a strange sensation through Mordred. It burned in his veins; the metal came alive in his hands.

Mordred gripped the hilt more tightly as the blade moved of its own accord. Silver turned to red and the inscriptions on the blade glowed. Had the sword not melded to his hands, he might have dropped it.

"Steady, Mordred. Let the power flow through you. Do not fight it. Let it become one with you." Jakob's voice sounded inside Mordred's frozen mind. Aloud, he said, "You are the keeper of the blade, Mordred."

"What is happening?" Mordred whispered. "It's as if the thing is alive."

Jakob looked out over the crowd and nodded. "The sword knows its master. It glows crimson because it recognizes you."

What magic lay within the steel, Mordred wondered. It was an honor to carry the Blood Sword.

"You may still carry a sword at your hip, in fact, I would recommend it. You will use a man-made blade against human foes."

Once again Jakob spoke to the throng. Mordred found that he was alone on the dais with the Master Templar. "Behold, Templars, I present to you our shining hope, our light by which victory is near certain. It is with my words and my wisdom that I, Master Templar, declare Mordred Soulis the Chosen One. The destiny of all humankind lies with him."

Jakob stepped back, leaving Mordred alone before the hundreds of holy warriors. A deafening roar sounded in his ears, the noise echoing off the stone walls. The thunder of hundreds of cheering men caused the very walls and floor to tremble.

As one, the knights raised their swords and presented them to Mordred, a field of steel before him as they continued to cheer.

He wished he felt stronger. He wanted to be able to

assure the knights they had placed their faith in the right
man. He couldn't shake a nagging doubt however it
was difficult not to turn and run. With a great effort of
will, Mordred remained frozen, watching the soldiers
who had pledged to give their lives for his.

Sensing his turmoil, Jakob gently pulled Mordred
down off the dais. The cheering subsided.

"It is done." Jakob said, "Now you begin your journey.
You will not fail us, Mordred. I know this in my soul.
You were born to do this."

"Might I remind you I'm dead?"

Jakob smiled. "Then let me correct myself. You
were reborn for this." Jakob winked.

Mordred was saddened. He had to leave Jakob now,
the one man who had sought to bring him to a better
place, a man who had never faltered in his beliefs even
when Mordred had doubted.

Something else twisted in Mordred's gut. He was
afraid him he would never see the old man again.

"You must not concern yourself with me, Mordred.
I am only the vessel from which your fate has flowed. I
have merely been an instrument in the creation of your
higher self. My destiny, my life are not important, only
yours."

"Jakob, you . . ."

The Master Templar held up his hand, stilling
Mordred's voice.

"The walls have ears and you can show no weakness.
Those you care for will be the first targets of evil. You
must harden your soul against feeling the human emotion
of affection, else it be used against you."

It wasn't affection that Mordred felt, but he kept his thoughts to himself as directed.

Jakob turned so he was standing in front of Mordred. He placed both hands on Mordred's shoulders and gazed at him with an expression of determination. "You will prevail. You are the light, and you will bring your grace to the world of humanity. Stay the course, Mordred. In those moments when your courage wanes, think only of the light and of your purpose. Never waver. Never stray from the path you have been set upon."

Jakob removed his hands and backed away. Mordred could not help his human weakness. It demanded he embrace the old man. As quickly as he did so it was over. Neither Jakob nor Mordred spoke again.

As if on cue, Markus materialized from the darkness wearing the traditional garb of the Templars, complete with a cape and sword. He cleared his throat.

"We should be on our way. We must go above ground some of the way and the distance is great."

Mordred turned back to look at Jakob, only to discover he had already vanished. Mordred felt empty.

"Come," Markus said gently, "it is time. You will see Jakob again."

Mordred dropped his head. His long black hair, unbound, fell forward to cover his face. He took a deep breath. There was so much to say and a million reasons why he couldn't utter a single word.

When Markus spoke again, his voice was filled with a compassion Mordred had never heard before.

"You and I have many differences, but it is time to put them aside. Your journey becomes mine, and I accept the new role with honor. Together we will uphold the hope of the Templars. We will succeed."

Markus placed a hand on Mordred's shoulder and met his eyes for the first time in a long time. Wisdom, pain, and strength flowed into Mordred. Together they turned and began the long climb to the desert, and their future.

CHAPTER ELEVEN

The unlikely pair, the Templar and the vampyre, left HarMeggido and made for Egypt. That was as much information as Markus was willing to share when they left the stronghold. He didn't say much except to relay instructions, and these sounded more like orders to Mordred. Since he needed Markus, however, he put up with his condescending manner.

Gone was the compassion Mordred had glimpsed the night they left the Templar fortress. Now Markus was back to his usual gruff and unpleasant self. It took all Mordred's self-control not to level him.

Markus told Mordred that on the long journey ahead, they would pass through Jerusalem, a magical city, but one that had changed hands often. In the event Jerusalem was in enemy hands they swathed themselves in desert robes, one in white and one in black.

They traveled swiftly toward the holy city. Mordred knew he could have made the trip without rest, but he had to keep a slower pace for the knight.

Under cover of night the pair pushed on. They

passed through unnamed villages and towns, some with chapels, some with cathedrals, some with palaces and others with simple shacks. They drew no attention, sought no help and before the sun rose each morning, Markus led them below ground. Their shelter always bore the mark of the Templars, and Mordred became an expert at searching out their hidden symbols. Even in the mosques Mordred found the mark of the Templars.

It was urgent they reached the Narangatti. For, Markus explained, every time they came above ground, it gave Vlad the chance to search out Mordred's presence. Mordred was a beacon for Vlad, and it was only a matter of time before Vlad perceived its light.

The night proved equally challenging; while they were safe from mortals, they were vulnerable to Vlad's minions. The night was ruled by his demons. They lurked in the shadows, watching and waiting for the Chosen One. Mordred felt their presence even when he could not see them. Only in Jerusalem would they be safe from Vlad. It was the only place Mordred could roam freely because, as Markus explained, the entire city was warded by great magic. Three separate religions had found their beginnings in the ancient city, and none but men could enter the gates. Hearing this Mordred feared he might not be allowed to enter, but Markus assured him otherwise. He was human enough yet to gain entrance. But first they had to reach Jerusalem.

Along the way, in an effort to reduce their chances of being discovered, Mordred tried to keep his mind still. He masked his thoughts, envisioning them as the surface of an untouched pool.

"Do you feel them?" Markus asked. They had stopped to drink.

"Yes." Mordred nodded. "I don't know from where or when, but something is coming."

"It is them. Vlad's army of darkness," Markus murmured, and shuddered. He took another swallow and offered the flask to Mordred.

"Save it. I've no need for water any more."

Nodding, Markus restoppered it and slung it back over his shoulder.

"Jerusalem will be the last refuge before we head to the Nile River. Come, we can make it to within a day's journey of the city to a place we can rest for the night. It will throw off those searching for you."

They crested a dune as the late afternoon sun dipped into twilight, painting the landscape blue and purple. They slipped and slid to a plateau of red dirt, baked and cracked by the sun that stretched in front of them. One lonely hut broke the flat horizon. It was the only vertical thing that could be seen in any direction, save the dunes.

Then Mordred saw a large golden shadow moving through the dusk, an animal he had never seen. Long, spindly legs supported an odd shaped body, a hump rising from its back.

Large brown eyes, fringed with long thick lashes, peered at them. As they approached it splayed its legs in a defensive posture and hissed at Mordred. He felt a wad of something wet and sticky hit his face.

Markus laughed. "No, friend, he didn't spit at you because you are a vampyre," he said, reading Mordred's mind. "He would just as soon have spit at me but I know his game. The thing is called a camel, used on the desert for transportation. But camels are ill-tempered beasts."

Side stepping to avoid another spit attack, Mordred watched Markus trying hard to mask his humor. His giggle proved harder to control.

"I'd venture to say it's no more ill-tempered than my companion," he snapped.

Markus sobered. "I see you lost your sense of humor the day you became a vampyre." He stalked away from Mordred toward the hut and looked inside, then spoke in a foreign tongue. A moment later a diminutive man appeared in the doorway. He smiled and nodded as he clasped Markus's shoulder. Then, he turned to Mordred. His smile faded.

Markus motioned Mordred forward and the two entered the hut, bending low to accommodate their height. Something sizzled in a pan over a cooking fire. By the smell Mordred knew it was meat.

The man blew the sand out of two cups and brought them, along with a clay jug, to a small table. He spoke briefly to Markus and exited the hut.

"He says he'll return when we've left. He prefers not to remain inside with an undead."

"Nice to meet you, too, sand bastard," Mordred growled.

"At least he's letting us stay here. It's a place of strong magic, warded as in Jerusalem, against those who seek you."

Markus proceeded to help himself to the meat sizzling over the fire, cursing when his fingers made inadvertent contact with the flames.

"Would you like me to help you?"

"No, it's quite all right. I have it under control." So saying, Markus dropped the morsel into the fire and uttered another string of curses.

"Some control. And you're supposed to be my protector?" Mordred removed his glove and stuck his hand into the flames. After he retrieved the piece of meat, he handed it to Markus. "You may want to let that cool."

"Thanks," Markus acknowledged grudgingly. "Our host left something for you as well in the jug."

Mordred lifted the jug and sniffed at it suspiciously. It was blood, human blood.

"Do I want to know *why* this man has a jug of human blood in his house?"

"You'll find these people have a wide and varied belief system," Markus said. "They keep offerings to a number of deities, even vampyres. It's why the hut is warded."

Mordred sipped the thick, sweet nectar from the jug. He set it back on the table and looked at Markus. "I had always thought your order was formed to help slay the infidels. Yet, infidels are among those who have sheltered us, the very people I might have been told to kill at one time. I'm confused."

Markus cocked his head, shoved a hank of hair out of his eyes, and swiped the grease from his chin with the back of his hand. "It is a paradox, isn't it? But, the enemy isn't someone whose beliefs are different. Our enemy is the one who forsakes good and worships evil. God comes to us in many forms, with many faces and speaks in many languages, but the underlying wisdom is always the same. Live your life by being like that which you worship. Be humble, compassionate, and honest. Refrain from judging others. Aspire to goodness."

Mordred knitted his brows. "There *is* no religion like that."

"You're not alone in your thinking, which is why the Templars remain a secret society. Speaking out against what religious leaders call 'Truth' is inviting trouble. But that doesn't mean an organization can't seek to right the wrongs done here by the crusaders. Our original role here was not to slay unbelievers, but to aid pilgrims seeking out holy places. We were never to pick up a sword against those whose only crime is not believing the same things we do."

Mordred reflected a moment. "So, when I fought in the crusade, I was fighting an enemy that really wasn't my enemy at all?"

Markus nodded solemnly. "Yes," he murmured. "Every time we war with each other we allow those without souls to gain. Fighting among ourselves will be our downfall. It is the Templar hope, indeed our prayer, that focusing on the menace that is Vlad will unite us in a single purpose once again."

"What of the history of the Templars? Is this their only purpose?"

After stoking the small fire, Markus stood, stretched, and then let out a weary sigh. He paced the confines of the hut, peeking through the cracks into the twilight. "That is not easy to answer," he replied at length. "Jakob knows our history. The Templars have been around since the inception of humanity. Since the time of the first vampyres. I wish I knew more. Unfortunately, as Jakob would probably tell you, I'm a slow learner. Hell, I'm still learning."

Mordred laughed softly.

"As much as I'd like to think otherwise," Markus continued, "You and I have much in common. I was a ruthless knight when Jakob found me. I'd been excommunicated from the Church for my refusal to believe in religion. I thought having no faith would be preferable to one I despised."

"You do not have faith?" Mordred asked.

Markus ceased his pacing and stretched out on the floor. "I've always had faith. I just didn't know it. If not for the strength of my faith I would not be here with you now. It is not easy to journey with a vampyre, knowing that a creature of the undead is humankind's last chance for salvation. It makes me feel helpless and insignificant, but that is the way of things. I am who I am because of my faith and, of course, Jakob, who found me and helped me see the light of my faith."

"Are all the Knights Templar those who have been disenchanted by the Church?"

"Basically, yes. I don't know when it happened, but the Church, as we know it, became greedy and adopted an unquenchable thirst for power and glory. This is what the Templars defy, not God, but the distortion of His teachings."

Scratching his head, Mordred set his empty cup on the table. "So, the Templars do, indeed, believe in God?"

Markus laughed. "Yes, of course we do. We believe most devoutly in God in His purest form. Although it is no longer what the Church believes. Even the book that contains all that we know of God has been altered by those in power, for their own purposes. Sometimes what they do aligns with the original purpose, but sometimes it is opposite. It has been going on for centuries. Templars exist in the hope that one day all humankind will be enlightened. But, as Jakob has said, it won't happen for many, many years, if at all."

It was Mordred's turn to stretch his legs. He found the talk vaguely confusing. He was a vampyre who wasn't wholly evil and was needed in a crusade against a growing threat that was difficult to comprehend. "Why me? I was an average man, living an average life. I wasn't particularly holy. I never wanted power or glory. I just wanted to live."

Markus turned to face Mordred. He wore an expression of understanding that erased all the hard lines and scars that marked him as a mighty warrior. "I cannot presume to know why you were chosen. Only Jakob would have an answer and maybe not a complete one at that. In time perhaps what you ask will be revealed to you. Until then, know that things in this world don't always make sense, and it may be that it is an average man that will rise from a complacent existence to prove greatness lies in all of us."

Mordred hung his head, suddenly weary. "I'm afraid I won't succeed, that I'm not worthy. I'm afraid that I will not fail just mankind, but you and Jakob as well."

Markus gripped Mordred's shoulder. "You have my strength and my courage for as long as it is willed. I will do what I can to help you believe, both in the quest and, more importantly, in yourself. You will not fail. The ending hasn't been written, but you will not fail."

Markus had become heavy lidded and within moments he drifted toward sleep. The vampyre, however, remained awake and alert.

The sounds of the night descended on the desert: wind whirling grains of sand against the mud and timber dwelling, the howling of a night hunter, then a sharp yip followed by a long cry echoing across the dunes.

Mordred shifted his gaze to the flames, which had burned low. He focused his mind, creating a blanket, and the fire winked out, snuffed by his thoughts. The hut was plunged into darkness, although with his keen vampyre eyesight Mordred found he could see quite clearly. Through the cracks in the walls of the hut he saw the moon had risen above the plateau, highlighting an empty, otherworldly landscape.

A snake slithered in a curling, arcing pattern, creating strange marks on the sand. The skin it was about to shed scraped dryly across the sand. A desert mouse, nearly dwarfed by its enormous ears, watched the predator warily. Then it hopped into a hole and disappeared.

The air was filled with the scent of wildness and the salt tang of the sea not far away. The desert perfumes wafted to Mordred, and he sifted through them trying to identify each one.

The burning heat of the day had melted away as soon as the sun had sunk below the horizon. The coolness of the moonlit air created a dewy mist that slowly formed above the earth.

And within the cloud something foul formed among the drops of moisture.

Although Markus had told him the hut was warded, Mordred remained alert. Through the crack he watched the vaporous mass spread across the ground. He sensed its wickedness, its malice.

Like a hand with long thin fingers, it stroked the floor of the plateau, searching, probing. Mordred knew it was looking for him and he remained still. He forced his pulse to slow, fought the fear that coiled in his gut. He tried to mask his thoughts and merge with the sand flooring of the hovel. The air shifted, changed, and vibrated with a malevolence that threatened to steal the breath from his lungs.

Mordred watched in horror as Markus turned in his sleep. Fearing the Templar would make a sound that would alert the mist to their presence, Mordred noticed Markus was awake, blue eyes reflecting the moonlight. Markus's expression told Mordred that he too was aware of the thing outside.

Mordred returned his gaze to the crack in the wall. The venomous mist was coming closer and had changed from silver to a putrid yellow even as it doubled in size, spreading out over the desert floor.

Mordred willed himself to become the sand with every fiber of his being. Nothing happened. He remained in human form. Perhaps he was only able to shift into a living thing? But, no, he had become mist once. Why was he unable to use the form of the sand?

Mordred shoved the question into a corner of his mind to be researched later and hurriedly searched for something else in which to change.

Then he spotted the rodent. The mouse was perched just inside the door, sitting quietly as if it too sensed something evil. The demonic cloud continued to grow. Over the wind Mordred heard a great snuffling sound like a large hound picking up a scent.

With unnatural speed having nothing to do with the wind, the mist rushed the tiny hovel, only to be stopped by an invisible force. The presence filled in the area around the walls outside and above the hut but it could not gain entrance.

Thinking to hide his form from the mist Mordred blended with the mouse. Markus's eyes widened as Mordred simply vanished.

Mordred let himself feel the rodent, from its tiny beating heart, to the veins in the membranes of its ears. The sound of the cloud created a deafening noise, terrifying the mouse.

Remembering too late Jakob's warning about becoming hostage to the form he took and the dangers to that form, Mordred found himself running out into the mist.

The heinous cloud came at the rodent from all sides, stirred by the sudden movement, but it was compelled to remain on guard near the hut. After a few tense moments, it ignored the tiny creature, waiting instead for a chance to slip past the wardings.

But the danger to Mordred was not over. The snake too had seen the movement.

The Night Sky Comes to Life

Mordred tried to focus all his energy on the mouse to get the creature to move, to run from the danger. But the rodent remained frozen, staring hypnotized at the snake, as the reptile undulated closer and closer, tongue darting, sensing the warmth of its prey.

And then Mordred heard a great clatter. The mouse jumped and, thankfully, ran toward the shelter of the hut. The snake moved off into the night. As if in answer to a silent prayer, the mist evaporated as if it had never been.

As the rodent raced back inside Mordred saw Markus sheathing his blade. He realized Markus had created the clatter by beating his sword against his shield.

Mordred's last thought while in the form of the mouse was that Markus, for once, had executed perfect timing. The next thing he knew he was lying on the floor of the hut, in his own form, safe for the moment. The floodgates opened.

A stream of foul oaths, epithets, and curses flowed into the night, then absolute stillness. Mordred collapsed by the fire pit, hugging his knees, and for the first time since becoming a vampyre, he prayed for the sun to rise.

"A mouse?" Markus asked, arms akimbo. "What the devil were you thinking shifting into a mouse?"

"It was the only thing I could think of at the moment." Mordred said sheepishly. "I wasn't sure if the warding would hold up against such an onslaught, and I was looking for a place to hide. Did you see the mist?"

"Aye, couldn't miss it. But a mouse, Mordred?"

"There was nothing else in the hut I could find."

Markus reached down and gingerly picked up something dark and shiny. He held it by the tail.

"You didn't think a scorpion would be a little more worthy?"

Markus went to the door and tossed the creature into the night.

Feeling all the more the fool, Mordred muttered something not meant for human ears. "Go to sleep, Templar. Tomorrow we go to the city. I don't want to spend another night like this."

Mordred heard Markus snickering long after both had resettled themselves for the remainder of the night.

CHAPTER TWELVE

The sun had barely risen above the high dunes, its golden glow warming the air, sucking the moisture from it, when Mordred nudged Markus with a booted foot. The man was slow to rise; Mordred pushed him again.

"Come. It is time we go."

Markus rubbed his eyes and groaned as he sat upright. "What on earth are you doing waking me so early? I'm not a vampyre and I need my rest. I feel as though I just fell asleep."

"You've slept long enough. Your snores could have awakened the dead. You are lucky the mist was not hunting you," Mordred snapped.

In truth he was annoyed that Markus had slumbered at all. He, on the other hand, had remained wide-awake. It would do nothing to lessen his stamina, but it irked him all the same. He had not been able to close his eyes for a moment, out of fear the evil would return. What was it?

He wanted to get to the city quickly. He wanted to lose himself in the anonymity of the throngs of peasants, peddlers, and worshippers. And he wanted one night of undisturbed rest, something he hadn't had since leaving the stronghold.

"Are you still angry about your shifting last night?" Markus asked, reaching for his flask of water.

"No. I did what needed to be done."

"And with thoughts like that, I've no doubt you'll be dead long before the final battle. A thank you would suffice."

Mordred stared hard at the knight. "A thank you? For what?"

"I saved your ass last night. If I hadn't gotten the clever idea to come outside, you'd be snake shit by now."

Turning from Markus, Mordred rummaged through his satchel. Finding his long, wickedly curved knife, he turned to face Markus again.

The knight only shrugged and moved past him.

Mordred reached for a flask lying under the nearby table and poured water into a shallow bowl, then he scraped the hair from his face. He refused to look on the outside like the beast he felt on the inside.

He withstood plenty of ribbing from Markus at his morning ritual. As the Templar explained, growing facial hair would ensure his face didn't burn under the sun. Mordred believed sunburn on a vampyre would prove to be something that didn't exist.

"I'll thank you," Mordred growled, "but only if you never bring up the mouse issue again."

"Fine. As soon as you're done, let's move. We have at least half a day's journey before we reach the city walls. And I'm sure you'd like to be inside before the gates close for the evening." Markus stepped through the door and out into the sunlight, stretching and yawning.

A few minutes later, after Mordred had repacked and rearranged his black wrap, they moved on toward the city of Jerusalem. Each was lost in his own thoughts, and although Mordred knew Markus had to be feeling the effects of the heat and the sun, he never once urged them to stop.

They moved until the heat became unbearable, sought shelter in a small rock outcropping, and pushed on when the sun began its descent.

Cresting another hill, Markus halted. A literal river of people moved in the direction of the enormous city that sat perched among the rocks. Hundreds of people, peasants with carts, soldiers on horseback, and families moved through the gates gaining entrance to the great treasures contained within the walls of the city, a great cloud of dust rising into the air above them.

Upon closer inspection Mordred saw there were actually two sets of walls rimming the city: a high curtain wall, where soldiers patrolled, and a lower outside wall. There was a large ditch, serving as a moat just before the lower wall, yet the streams of people traversed the narrow path through the gate without difficulty.

"We will go through the Golden Gate, there." Markus pointed to the right. Fewer people entered through that gate, though there appeared to be more soldiers. "The Templars have a base of operations by that golden dome."

Mordred scanned the view before him and narrowed his eyes as he gazed upon a large, rounded rooftop, gilded and shining brightly under the rays of the sun. It stood like a sentinel, clearly visible from all angles, no matter from which direction one approached the city. Like a beacon it rose above all the other rooftops guiding pilgrims, holy soldiers, and other followers of the three religions that called Jerusalem home.

When they came to the gate, several men appeared, dressed in the familiar white garb of the Templars, but with a much smaller cross positioned over their left shoulder.

Clearly, they recognized Markus as one of their own and immediately converged on him, slapping his back with their gloved hands.

"By all that is holy, Markus, is that really you?" a brown haired warrior questioned.

"We thought the carrion birds had plucked your mangy carcass for sure," another said.

Yet another man came forward, "It's been too long, friend. How is Jakob?"

Smiling and returning the gestures of welcome, Markus replied heartily, "No vultures are going to be picking these bones clean, at least not for a time. Jakob is well and sends his best to you all, as always."

Turning to Mordred, who had until this moment stood in the shadows cast by the large stone gate, Markus reached out, grasped his shoulder and brought him into the circle of six men.

"This, my brethren, is Mordred."

Immediately, several of the men took a step back giving Mordred a wide berth. They knew what he was without asking, Mordred realized. But how?

Markus answered his unspoken question. "It is your dress. They recognize the Blood Sword and the clothes beneath your robes. They also see it in your eyes. Who you are meant to be."

Before Mordred could respond, all the men, in one smooth motion, went down on bended knees, heads bowed. The deference they showed him made him uncomfortable.

"It is not necessary for them to kneel. I know well what they would do for me. As they can see in my eyes who, or rather, what I am, I can see in theirs the full measure of their faith."

And it was nearly blinding to the vampyre, this immediate loyalty to a man they didn't even know. The feeling that Mordred held so many lives in his hands flooded through him again. It was as if he were drowning and floundering to come up for air.

Proving himself always aware of Mordred's moods, Markus said to the Templars, "Come, let us show Mordred the splendor of this city and our quarters."

One of the knights came forward. "How long will you be staying?"

Markus fielded the query. "We will stay the night but then we must press on. It is urgent we reach Egypt."

Another Templar nodded as he fell in step beside Markus. "Yes, we have heard of the strange mist that came over the desert last night. We knew you must be close."

"I fear they will come again tonight. We were able to avoid them last eve, but I am not stupid enough to think they will leave us alone. Whatever it was, it sensed Mordred," Markus said.

Another of the knights took the lead as they wound through narrow streets that twisted and turned, sometimes revealing smaller passageways and larger roads, past tiny shops, larger churches, and places of residence. Markus explained the layout of the city as they traveled. He also shared the bloody history of Jerusalem and how it had been conquered by the crusaders.

At the mention of the soldiers sent to the Holy Land to rid it of infidels, several armed men appeared behind them and Mordred wondered if they were being followed.

The Templars picked up the pace.

"It is not much farther," one offered Mordred.

"That may well be, but I fear we are walking into a trap."

The man's eyebrows shot up at the calm statement coming from Mordred.

"Truly? No evil can stalk these streets. This city is warded by all the faithful."

Mordred gave a sardonic laugh and flexed the fingers of his right hand. Ever so slowly he brought his hand to the hilt of the sword that lay belted at his waist. He had no doubt the people following him were simply men. There was no need to use the Blood Sword.

Glancing at the Templar next to him, Mordred cautioned, "This city may be warded against things that go bump in the night, from ghosts and banshees and otherworldly creatures, but I doubt it will do anything to protect one from the evil of men. If I were you I'd have my hand close to my sword as we are about to make an abrupt stop."

The knight nodded, not questioning Mordred.

Although the sun had not sunk below the horizon, shadows still crept long and dark among the city's myriad buildings. They headed into a deserted quarter, and Mordred turned sharply. He stopped and faced the stalkers, his sword already unsheathed. The Templars followed his example, standing shoulder to shoulder, booted feet splayed in the dirt.

The gang that had been trailing them numbered twelve, a rough looking bunch. Foot soldiers mostly, Mordred surmised, yet one looked strikingly familiar.

"Mordred Soulis!" came a shout from the leader of the pack. "You are wanted for the murder of your fellow soldiers in the attack at Dorylaeum."

Mordred's eyes narrowed to mere slits. His nostrils caught the scent of the men, unwashed and full of pent up energy. They were itching for a fight.

Markus replied first, "And who dares level these charges?"

"King Conrad himself. He claims to have seen the bastard take down as many of his own men as he did Saracens."

"That is a lie," Mordred bit out in something resembling a low growl. "King Conrad ordered me to stop the suffering of the hundreds of men left wounded in Dorylaeum. I only honored his wishes. Now he dares accuse me of murder? He's the murderer who led those men straight to their deaths."

"Take it up with the King, Soulis, but for now you are to come with us. And if you don't come with us of your own free will, we've been authorized to use force." The leader said the last as if he relished the thought.

It was then Mordred realized he did indeed know the man. "Philip."

"Aye, I see you've put the name to the face. It makes no difference. Now, are you going to come with us of your own volition?"

The man was Conrad's weasel, his spy, and one of the few men who had survived the slaughter and doomed trek through the desert. Mordred smiled. He was a man who belonged with the dead. Of course Philip could be counted on to do Conrad's dirty work.

"Come now, Philip, are you afraid you might not be able to complete your king's command?" Mordred taunted.

Markus stepped in front of him at that moment, temporarily blocking his view. "This man is no longer a soldier in the crusades. He is of no concern of yours or your king's."

"And why might that be?" Philip spit a quantity of brown saliva and gripped the hilt of his curved sword. "He's found a higher calling?"

This last was said as an insult to the Templars. While many regular soldiers gave the holy warriors a wide berth, there were others who coveted their power and their position. Philip was only one of many in a sea of men who came to foreign lands to find fame and fortune. Having found neither he was now all the more dangerous.

The Templars stepped forward as one. Now, Mordred stood behind a wall of armed men. He smiled. It was obvious he had made friends none too soon.

"Mordred Soulis belongs to the Templars now and

even your king can do nothing about that. Tell him to petition the Grand Master if he wishes, but for the moment we will be on our way." Markus held a wicked looking falchion in his right hand. It was complete with a few gaps toward the hilt specifically designed to catch an opponent's blade and break it. In his left he had another curved blade, a long, deadly looking knife.

"What's the matter, Mordred? Can't fight your own battles anymore? Have to hide behind the skirts of these God lovers?'

Mordred pushed between two Templars. He stopped scant feet away from the reach of Philip's sword. "Come and get me, if you think you can."

Mayhem descended in the deserted street as Philip's soldiers rushed forward to be met by the wall of Templars. And, as soon as the fighting began in earnest, Philip quickly fled to the back, urging his men on from relative safety.

As if something dark crawled up Mordred's spine, he felt the very marrow of his bones vibrate with an unnatural energy. His nostrils filled with the scent of unspilled blood, and his throat went dry.

In a clash of steel the knights, even outnumbered two to one, proved to be far more ready for combat. A skull was cleaved in two by the stroke of Markus's great blade, while another man yelped in pain as his hand, still attached to his sword, went flying.

A third man felt the bite of steel in his stomach. As he doubled over in the vain attempt to prevent his guts from falling out, another blade slashed through his throat. He fell forward and another took his place.

The fourth man showed at least marginal ability with a sword, but he made the fatal mistake of taking on Mordred. Within the vampyre the beast strained to break free. It wanted to kill, but not with swords or steel. It wanted to rip and tear flesh, to taste the warm blood filling its throat.

In a few short strokes, another man fell before Mordred.

The Templars held the others at bay and when a fifth man was eviscerated where he stood, the remaining soldiers turned and fled, Philip among them.

Five men dead, bodies still twitching in the last throes of life, lay in pools of crimson. The Templars wiped their blades clean on the clothing of the dead and returned their swords to their sheaths. At the end of the street people milled about, some looking at the bodies lying in a heap.

"We must leave quickly," said one of the knights.

Markus glanced at Mordred.

Without comment, Mordred knew Markus was aware of the inner turmoil raging through him. He desperately wanted the men to leave so he could unleash the vampyre and feed. The desire was fast becoming uncontrollable, and he feared he might turn on the knights.

"Give him a minute. Then we will move on."

Mordred expected the men to go but, without words they formed a circle around him, facing outward. Side by side, with their legs splayed, they took up positions and waited.

"Markus? What are they waiting for? Why aren't

they leaving?" Mordred hissed through his clenched teeth.

"They are waiting for you to finish your business. They will guard you. Their job, as well you know, is to see to your safety, and there can be no assurances that Philip will not return with more men. Begin."

"No, I need you all to leave. I am not confident I can control myself."

"Well, you must. At some point, Mordred, you are going to have to discover if you are strong enough, and you can only do so by having your guides and your defenders near you when you change. Now, begin. We haven't much time."

Mordred's next reply was a cross between a curse and a snarl, but he could no longer maintain his composure. The beast was creating havoc within him and the blinding pain in his head was enough to bring him to his knees. He landed next to a dead man.

The cracking sound of his jaw filled the silence. As razor sharp canines protruded through his upper lip, Mordred bent his head. He pierced the tender, exposed flesh of the soldier's neck and drank.

Euphoria drifted over him. His eyes glazed and he drained the body. Rapture, akin to the most intense sexual climax he had ever experienced flooded through him. He felt every part of his body tingling.

He slid from one man to the next, glutting himself. He would have continued, but for Markus's warning which broke through his pleasure-soaked mind.

"We have to leave. There are more men headed this way. Kyle, Rene, dispose of the bodies. There is no crime if there is no evidence, correct?" Markus smiled and touched Mordred's shoulder.

Mordred wiped his mouth on the sleeve of his black robe and waited for his jaw to contract. The vampyre within, satiated, retreated, leaving only a heavy exhaustion. In the blink of an eye Mordred was quite human again. Markus nodded.

The knights broke the circle and rid the scene of the bodies. Three Templars stayed behind while Mordred, Markus, and the three others continued on to the headquarters. It was almost as if nothing out of the ordinary had happened.

"We need to be careful that no one else recognizes you tonight. No doubt Philip will seek to petition the Grand Master, but it will do him no good. Once we get to the temple you will be safe."

"Of all the enemies I must face, I did not consider regular soldiers among them."

Markus offered him a faint smile. "Trust no one."

† † †

The small band of warrior knights and the vampyre moved through the city without further trouble. Arriving at the Temple of Solomon, which served as the Templars' base of operations in Jerusalem, Mordred was shown to a small room.

"You may wish to clean up before we meet the Grand Master," Markus advised. "I'll be down the hall should you need anything."

Just before he closed the door, Markus stuck his head back in. "And Mordred?"

"Yes?"

"You have gained control over your vampyre-self. This is a very good thing."

Mordred didn't comment. He heard the door close and moved to a large basin already filled with cold water, and splashed his face, eager to remove the evidence of his earlier bloodletting. It wasn't until he brought a swath of cloth to wipe the beads of water away that he realized, looking into the bowl, just how much blood there had been.

And yet he had strolled through the halls of this temple, seen many men, and they had not recoiled or even acted as if this were a strange sight. While it was true each of the men bore signs of the skirmish—bloody tunics and mail—none had blood on their faces. None bore the proof of being something other than human.

Patting dry, Mordred glanced at his clothing. It too was covered in dirt and blood. He tore off the robe and suddenly he couldn't stand being confined anymore. Quickly, he pulled off his surcoat and his tunic. It was as though he was shrouded in holy vestments representing the sanctity of his new path, and he felt anything but worthy.

He had killed those men in the street without a second thought, and worse still he had relished their deaths, knowing he could drink their blood in the aftermath. Lust for destruction had risen heavily within him, blotting out reason. While the men had attacked him, he had felt an inhuman, murderous need for violence. He had been swift and lethal.

What had he become? As a mercenary he'd always

been in control. He had never wavered. He was dangerous because he studied how others reacted and then countered rather than fighting blindly. The heat of the battle and the thirst for blood never overcame him.

He was a killing machine, but he had never lost sight of himself. He killed for the life it afforded him and the freedom to drift wherever he pleased. But he had taken no pleasure in the deaths of others until today.

Today he had desired nothing more than to watch his attackers fall beneath the might of his blade. He had soaked himself in their blood, let it spray across his face and body like a fountain. He had reveled in the joy of their deaths, willing them to bleed. He had wanted nothing more than to crush those who sought to control him.

If the Templars had not been there, urging him to move on, Mordred feared he might still be there, glutting himself on the soldiers. Feeding until he could drink no more.

A shiver raced up his spine.

What had he become, he wondered again. But the room gave him no answer, filled as it was with images depicting Christ and the Crucifixion. Wood panels carved with Jesus' deeds covered the walls and ceiling. The carvers had poured their love for the subject into their work, and the finished product shone with their emotion.

While he was not a believer, Mordred knew enough of the story to identify the different scenes depicted, and one panel drew his eye. It showed Jesus healing the blind, the sick, and the infirm. Mordred could make out the image of a leper beneath the hand of Christ, seeking relief for his weary soul. Had he found it?

Would Mordred find it? If there was a god, any god, would He save him now?

He sat on the edge of a small bed, the leather straps holding the mattress creaking under his weight. He hung his head in his hands and remained still. Could he take this path? Could he continue on the journey? For Mordred, the question wasn't about the outcome but about the quest. Would he prove to be made of the stuff others claimed him to be?

He didn't have the answers. He wanted to scream at the walls to take it back. He would rather be dead than alive in this hell. A blood-sucking monster was not someone men should look up to. He didn't deserve the loyalty of thousands, didn't feel worthy of their reverence.

He was just a man. A simple man. A warrior. He never wanted to be the Chosen One . . .

† † †

A short time later with Mordred still half dressed, a soft knock sounded on the door. He lay on the bed, one arm flung over his eyes, the familiar exhaustion from the change settling over him. He made no move to acknowledge the sound or invite the person inside. Instead, he waited, a part of him hoping whoever it was would go away.

In his mind's eye, he saw a boy, a child, standing outside the chamber, covered from head to toe in white robes with the unmistakable red cross on his left shoulder. Under one arm he carried a bundle of black cloth.

Sighing heavily Mordred sat up slowly.

The door opened with a great groaning sound magnified by the stone walls of the temple.

"Excuse me, sir. I was told to help you dress. I was told you might need clean clothing."

The boy padded in quietly on sandal-covered feet. He had skin and eyes so dark they were neither brown nor black, but served to make his pupils look unnaturally large. He looked at Mordred, his face devoid of expression.

There was no fear, no animosity. Nothing but a willingness to serve his charge. Mordred cocked his head.

"Who sent you?"

"No one, sir. I volunteered to come," the boy said softly.

Surprised that anyone would want to come to the dreaded vampyre, Mordred peered at the boy intently while holding his hands out for the bundle.

"You willingly came? Do you know who, or what I am?"

"Yes, sir. You are the Chosen One. And I hope some day to fight beside you as a Templar."

An odd buzzing sounded in Mordred's head as images from some far away place and time gathered at the corners of his consciousness. He saw the boy, now a man, those same brown-black eyes staring at him from the face of someone older and wiser. And he saw the man beside him as they stood among buildings that reached to the sky.

A sharp pain shot through his head, and Mordred returned to the present. The boy stood, a shy smile on his tanned face.

"Not even you can see what the future brings, sir."

The boy had guessed what he was thinking. How could it be?

"Who are you, and how did you know what I was doing?" Mordred asked.

"I am Galeal, and I have the gift of knowing what others know."

"Tell me then, Galeal, why is it you wish to serve me?"

"Because you are the One. The only one to bring salvation to the race of man. It has been written and prophesied for thousands of years, since the beginning of time. You are Mordred Soulis, and you're our one true hope."

Mordred made a sound somewhere between a laugh and a bark of annoyance and began the task of pulling off his boots. Galeal quickly stepped forward and lifted Mordred's right foot. With a tug of strength that seemed impossible for such a small boy, the boot came off. Galeal staggered a few steps back.

"You should fear me instead of wanting to assist me. If you know I am the Chosen One, then you must know, too, what I am," Mordred growled, unsure of how he felt about the boy's desires, like a squire looking to the knight he served. The squire sees only the knight in his polished mail or armor, riding an armor-clad destrier going off to tournament. In the beginning the boy only sees the best of the man, the way women adore the knights, the way kings respect them and the riches the knights bring back from their fantastical journeys. No one tells the boys of the harsh realities of war. The fields of blood. The miserable conditions. The deplorable food and lack of water. None have witnessed the deaths of comrades. None have seen what grown men do to each other in the heat of battle. Or what they do to the enemy's women and children.

Mordred shook his head, shaking away the horrific images of his past.

The boy waited until Mordred fixed him with an intense glare.

"You are undead. A vampyre."

"Why do you have no fear of me?" Mordred asked, finding himself both amazed and appalled by the boy's apparent admiration. He was a fool for being so brave. And that could cost him his life.

"Because you can do nothing to hurt me," came the reply, as Galeal helped Mordred off with his breeches. He handed Mordred a clean pair.

Mordred stood and tugged the clothing over his legs, lacing the area from his groin to his waist. He loomed over the boy and gave the most animalistic growl he could muster.

The boy only laughed. Mordred flopped back down on the bed.

"You cannot scare me either."

"Why is that? Don't you know I prefer the blood of humans, and most especially those of young Templars?" Mordred goaded, feeling a tiny bit foolish for acting like such a buffoon.

"The undead killed my family."

All stilled in the room and the air became heavy with despair. Mordred wisely decided to remain silent and allowed the boy to finish his thought.

"One night the unholy came like shadows to my village. They murdered everyone. We were helpless in the face of such evil. They drained my mother, father, grandmother, cousins, sisters, and brothers of their blood. And then they did the worst thing possible."

"I would think the killing of your family would be the worst."

"Nay, the cruelest thing was that after a time the undead brought them back to life. Some thought it was a miracle. They did not see the unholiness within them. Only I was able to see it. And I was forced to kill them with my own hands and watch them die again."

He saw the family, laughing and sharing a meal as the sun slowly sank behind the hills of their homeland. He heard the evil in the shadows as they moved across the sky. Saw the horror of the men as they tried to raise their weapons. They were only farmers and herders and bore only shovels and pitchforks. They held not the implements of war.

There was screaming and cursing. An old woman in a corner rocked back and forth chanting, praying for divine help that never came.

The images turned red with the family's blood. The smell was everywhere, acrid and bitter. It coated the back of Mordred's throat, and he choked on the taste. Everyone was dead. There was almost total slaughter. Only a single living being remained. Even the children, some only babes, were murdered.

There was nothing Mordred could say. Great waves of pain washed over him. Each was more powerful than the next and nearly brought him to tears. He knew he was drawing the boy's sorrow to himself, making it his own. He wrapped himself in the misery and willed himself to take away the boy's grief.

Finally, Mordred dared to speak.

"How can you not hate me? How can you not see that I am no better than those who killed your family?"

For the first time Galeal's face lit up in a full smile. To Mordred it was as if gazing at someone years beyond his physical age. Warmth glowed from the boy. He reached out and touched Mordred's hand.

"You are nothing like those that took away my family. I wish you could believe that. I am here because you need me."

At the touch of Galeal's hand, Mordred stilled his doubts, cleansed his mind. Before he could speak another knock sounded on the door.

"Mordred, are you ready?" Markus strode into the chamber. "Ah, I see you have met our Grand Master."

CHApTER ThirTEEN

It was with some regret that Mordred left Jerusalem the next morning. He had slept soundly for the first night since his new life had begun. No wicked dreams plagued him. No evil things waited outside his door. He felt more rested than he could remember.

As if sensing his reluctance, Markus said, "Do not fear, Mordred. You will return here one day."

And the pair set off. Markus told him they would head south, passing by the Dead Sea, before turning west. There they would cross a tributary of the Red Sea before coming to the Nile.

"We must be sure to keep clear of any crusader engagements. I spent the better part of last night surveying the battlefields and believe I have taken us on a route that will avoid them all. But I cannot be sure about any skirmishes."

"I can't believe on top of all I have to watch for, I am now wanted by King Conrad," Mordred grumbled. "That bloody bastard left us to die in the desert, and now he wants to pin the death of his troops on me?

I swear if I see him again I'll tear him limb from limb."

Markus smiled.

"You think that's funny?"

The Templar continued walking, wiping sweat from his brow as they traversed another arid landscape. "No, I think it an appropriate statement from a man who has been greatly wronged."

It was Mordred's turn to smile. "What happened to 'turn the other cheek'?"

"In time perhaps, but now it is good to hear you speak so freely. You should always allow the poison to come to the surface. Hate and fear are poison."

"Don't give me any of your sanctimonious shit, Markus. You'd be thinking the same thing if it were you."

"Perhaps, but in this case I should really be thanking King Conrad. You see, he fulfilled a purpose he doesn't even know about. If you had not come on this crusade, you would never have fallen in the desert. And you would never have been bitten, thus starting the first chapter in your new life."

Mordred glanced at Markus, brows drawn together. "I think I might have preferred my journey ending right then and there, thank you very much."

"That wasn't up to you."

"Yes, I'm finally starting to realize that," Mordred spat bitterly. "I am merely a pawn in a much bigger game."

"No, Mordred, you were never a pawn. You chose to do this with every fiber of your being. One day you will know this to be the absolute truth."

"Like hell I chose this. I'm a cross between a human and an animal. You saw me, Markus. I drank a man's blood for God's sake. How can you even stand to be around me?"

Without looking at Mordred, Markus gazed into the distance, shielding his eyes from the glare of the sun. "It wasn't up to me."

Mordred groaned. "Is this what I get for not going to Church all my life? I get to be saddled with a great man of wisdom?"

"Depends on whether you consider what I say wise," came the reply. Changing the subject, he asked, "Did you hear about Damascus?"

"I heard the crusaders attacked the city they had claimed an ally to Jerusalem, which makes no sense to me."

As they continued plodding down one dune and up the next, nothing stirred. The entire area was devoid of even a breeze. Mordred felt the heat pushing down on him and was amazed that Markus seemed not to be similarly burdened. He just kept moving as he continued, "Yes, odd indeed. Apparently, the troops were decimated by the Damascenes. The crusaders weren't even sharp enough to stay within the safety of the orchards outside the town. Instead they chose to pitch their battle on a flat strip of land that offered no cover from archers on the town walls."

"Let me guess, Conrad was at the helm?"

"So it seems."

"That man is truly one of the worst commanders I've ever seen. He's driven by greed, and he does not understand strategy."

"Yes, he has proven himself a rather foolhardy leader," Markus agreed. "He got many of his men slaughtered at Dorylaeum when he refused to wait for the French King, and now he's chosen to attack a city where the people don't pose any threat. It baffles the mind."

"So, what of the crusade now?" Mordred asked.

"It appears it's lost. They suffered such a devastating defeat at Damascus it will be hard to rally men to the cause at this point. I heard just last night that Conrad is pleading ill, and Louis is returning to his homeland."

Mordred shook his head and sighed. "So, men gave their lives for nothing. They came to a foreign land, fought for something they didn't believe in in the first place, and died here . . . For what?"

Markus was silent. What could he say?

† † †

The sun had set, but Markus explained they were now on the most dangerous part of the journey to Egypt. Between here and the Nile there would be very little shelter save a few, long forgotten outposts reclaimed by the desert.

They could not stop knowing they were being hunted. Markus kept on, even when Mordred knew most normal men would have long since succumbed to the heat and exhaustion of walking endlessly. Yet the Templar forged on.

The wind picked up, growing more ferocious by the hour until it created great whirling shadows of sand.

The men covered their mouths and noses with the ends of their head wraps.

Blowing grains stung their eyes, and each man found himself walking at an angle against the wind. It was slow going, and Mordred reached out to touch Markus's shoulder.

"Should we stop, Markus? We could find an out-cropping of rocks or even just lie down with our backs to the wind and let the storm pass." He was, in truth, worried about the blond man.

Markus shouted to be heard over the roar of the wind. "Nay, we cannot stop. Something evil fills the air tonight, and I'll not have it catch us unawares. Best to keep moving."

"Aye," Mordred acknowledged. "I feel it too. I hear a faint thunder on the wind, like the sound of an entire army coming this way."

"Crusaders? Do you think they are hunting you down?"

Mordred shrugged. "I cannot be sure of anything these days but no, I don't think it's soldiers. At least, not in the way I know them. There's something else brewing here."

"More of Vlad's dark magic then."

Markus began to trudge again, and in a few moments was nearly lost from view. If not for the gentle tug on the rope Mordred had insisted they tie between them, he was sure the Templar would be swallowed up in the roaring storm.

Mordred shouted again, "I smell death . . . hundreds. Nearby."

"But there isn't a settlement or city near. There would have been no battles here even if crusaders did march through," came Markus's confused voice.

All the same the stench grew until the wind became the buzzing sound of a thousand flies, a great cloud of insects appearing out of the sandstorm. And the smell; it was enough to make a man retch. Decaying flesh and rotted bone. Dried blood and fetid bodies. It was the essence that filled the air after any great battle, and it was all around them.

At the smell of the corpses, regardless of how horrible it was to his human side, Mordred's vampyre-self awakened. His nostrils flared at the now sweet aroma of death, while his vision tilted and became shaded in red.

"Markus, get away from me. I am changing."

The knight remained, unmoving and clearly undisturbed by Mordred's message.

"Markus, damn you, I cannot be sure I will be in control."

"You were in control in Jerusalem. I thought you handled yourself fairly well for a vampyre. Why should I fear you now?"

"Because I . . ." Mordred's voice broke into an animalistic growl as he fell to the sand on his knees. The sand cushioned his fall and the power of the change coursed through him at unbelievable speed. It snapped his head back as his jaw dislocated. The sound was even louder than the approaching mass of buzzing insects.

He knew just before it arrived that it was unholy. He pushed Markus away as the edge of the horde came forward.

"Run!"

"You know I can't leave you," Markus shouted, unsheathing his great blade.

"This is no time for heroics. If you don't run now, you will die! Go!" Mordred commanded, voice booming over the racket pressing down on them. Markus turned and ran down the dune they had previously crested.

Then all hell broke loose, as the shadows, the flies, and the cloud of death came to life in the ghoulish form of an army of darkness. Appearing as a legion of rotting corpses, soldiers came out of the night, across the dunes, heading for Mordred.

He did not need to think twice to know these men were undead, revenants bent on his destruction, brought back to life by an ancient and malevolent power. Mordred uttered a silent prayer for Markus, and then inhaled.

He pulled the great Blood Sword from behind his head, using both hands. He let the sword feel his grip on the hilt. The symbols and letters etched in the blade glowed crimson, lighting the area before him. His arms vibrated with his vampyre power and the strange force of the sword in his hands.

With a running charge, Mordred came swinging at the putrid decaying masses of rank flesh. The air erupted into an enormous roar, and it took Mordred a moment to realize the sound had fallen from his own lips. His body reacted of its own accord. Unleashed, the beast within took over.

Mordred felt the incredible speed of his reflexes filling his shoulders, legs, and arms as he hacked and slashed

Revenant Horde

with the Blood Sword, forward and back. Splitting corpses in two, rending soldiers into piles of decayed flesh. Innards spilled onto the desert floor in piles of rancid putrification.

A malodorous liquid, not blood, since that had gone away long ago, spewed from the corpses, coating Mordred with sticky, yellow slime. It was nearly enough to make him throw down his sword in disgust and cover his nose and mouth, but he continued fighting.

There were no random actions, only finely calculated movements meant to slay each opponent with one blow. They came at him in twos and threes and sometimes more, sickening hordes with missing eyes, gaping maws, and sometimes former wounds clearly visible. They clawed and attacked him with their bare hands when Mordred disarmed them.

He cut and slashed and hacked his way through the macabre throng. Bloodcurdling howls filled the air as over and over the revenants fell beneath the might of the Blood Sword. Sweat trickled down his face, blinding him as it stung his eyes. It felt as if he'd been fighting for hours, yet strangely the normal exhaustion that accompanied battle was absent. His body ached, but not in the familiar way he knew from years of warfare.

Standing in the midst of at least twenty attackers, Mordred wondered vaguely how long he could keep it up. The legions of undead seemed unending and he a lone man, even a vampyre, eventually would tire.

Suddenly the animated corpses before him fell away like sheaves of wheat beneath a sickle, yet they did not fall from the touch of his blade. A sense of victory settled in Mordred's gut.

But before he could think further on the cause, the wind grew to an incredible force, nearly blowing Mordred from his feet. The sand around him billowed and shifted and he knew, beyond knowing, Vlad was coming.

Clutching his sword, Mordred stared into the darkness.

Concealed by the sandstorm, a tall figure slowly revealed itself, a man clad in the garb of the upper classes. Fine fabrics and lace and jewels twinkled in the darkness.

As the man drew closer, his features became clearer. It was then Mordred knew he was looking at the face of his creator. Vlad had indeed come to him.

The wind stilled. The night became eerily quiet.

"My son," came a cultured voice, "you have impressed me."

With a firm grip on the hilt of his sword, Mordred stood, heels digging into the sand. He kept his knees bent in preparation for a strike and looked for the opportunity. He would show no fear.

The Blood Sword shifted in his grip, coming alive, seeking what it knew it was meant to touch.

"I am not your son. I am not of your body."

A cruel smile split the handsome face. "That may be true, but I have given you something no other could. I gave you the kiss of life and none can claim you except me. Bow before your creator."

Clenching his jaw, Mordred tried to mask his thoughts. Piercing laughter filled his mind.

"You are so young, Mordred. Do you think you have learned so much with the Templars that you can defy me at will? You belong to me. You are mine."

Mordred raised his sword and leveled the tip at the base of Vlad's throat.

"I know not what devil's spawn you are, but I belong to no one. You cannot control me."

Again laughter, but this time it filled the silence, rolling off the dunes in a thunderous roar, nearly felling Mordred. The ground shook beneath him, and suddenly he felt himself leaving the sand.

He levitated into the air while Vlad remained standing just above the dune, looking up at him. His lips curled in a malicious smile.

"Your head has been filled with lies, Mordred. I am the One, the only One, and I rule you. You are with life because of me, and you will do my bidding."

At that Mordred felt himself being spun upside down. Helpless, he tried to remain calm. Vlad waved and Mordred was flung up, buffeted about like a bird caught in a storm.

There was no mistaking the vastness of his powers, but Mordred refused to give in. Somehow within the chaos Vlad unleashed upon him, a familiar voice whispered in his mind. Jakob!

Jakob instructed Mordred to change, to shift into the mists that slowly filled the air. It was as if Jakob floated alongside him. He clearly heard his voice, and he watched Vlad become annoyed and swatted at something near his head.

Calm floated through Mordred, filling him completely.

He concentrated on the vaporous cloud.

Another deafening roar came from Vlad. This time, however, it was not brought on by amusement. Anger thundered across the desert in great, rolling waves.

The ground rushed up at Mordred as he felt himself being thrown back to the sands with a force that would surely immobilize him. Yet at the precise moment when he should have felt the impact, he felt nothing.

His body had melted away. He felt himself floating in a disconnected way, drifting up and around Vlad. He was a mere whisper as he watched the demon twist about, searching for him.

The sound of men approaching reached Mordred as he allowed his mind the freedom to visualize the clear, water-filled droplets that made up the mist.

"Vlad!" Markus boomed when he reached the top of the dune. Behind him Mordred watched knight after knight appear, clad in the familiar white garb of the Templars. He recognized several men he had met in Jerusalem.

"Markus," Vlad purred, smiling dangerously.

For a moment Mordred feared Vlad would crush Markus. But the Templar said, without a trace of fear, "Be gone from here."

"You, Human, will not dictate to me!"

Appearing completely unconcerned, Markus took a step forward. Only the sound of his jingling mail could be heard.

"I have not come unarmed, Vlad." Markus raised an ornately decorated silver container. "Do not force me to use this, for I will without hesitation."

"You will die before your hand reaches the latch, and even if you should open the box, you will kill yourself and your men. You don't have the balls," Vlad goaded.

"Perhaps I will die, but there are a hundred more men, each willing to die along with me. The choice is yours. Though we know we cannot kill you, we can disable you. And it will be long before you can regenerate. Be gone from here."

Moonlight appeared from behind great billowing clouds to shine upon the container, and it glowed with nearly blinding brilliance. The light of a thousand torches could not possibly glow as brightly, Mordred thought as he drifted closer to Markus.

Several knights swatted at the dewy vapor in annoyance. In a different situation, Mordred might have smiled.

He wondered what was in the container. The thought was his undoing; he lost his concentration and reverted to his human form to crash down upon several burly Templars. Amid the commotion Mordred tried to extricate himself from a tangled mass of mail clad limbs.

"You are lucky this night, Markus. When next we meet, I will delight in drinking the blood from the marrow of your bones."

Markus raised the container higher as if it were a light. "Brave words, but when next we meet, I will be the one who shall remove you from the face of this earth."

"We shall see. Mordred, we will meet again."

Untangling himself, Mordred watched with the rest of the troops while Vlad vanished as mysteriously as he had appeared. A great gust of wind picked up the sand, swirling it high into the air, obscuring sight.

Then all was still once more.

† † †

"What made him leave?" Mordred asked. He glanced at the container now being placed inside a silk bag.

Markus gave the bag to one of the Templar knights before motioning Mordred to follow him. He moved some distance away and stopped.

"It is not as important as what happened here. Do you know the men you slew?"

Mordred shook his head. They had all been so decrepit and decayed he didn't think any one of them looked familiar.

"These men are all that remains of the Second Crusade," Markus continued. "Except for the kings, these are the soldiers that attacked Damascus."

"But that is impossible. Damascus is several days away and . . ." Mordred paused, not knowing exactly how to go on. As if his mind were just beginning to process the battle, his former human-self failed to acknowledge what he had just done.

"These men were undead. Brought back to life by Vlad. They failed in their attack and lay about the desert. Vlad simply reanimated them and brought them here. He knew where you were. Mordred, this was only a test. He is baiting you to see how much you have learned and how much he has to fear from you."

"He doesn't fear me," Mordred scoffed. "He would have killed me if you hadn't intervened when you did."

"Mmm, while that might appear to be true, I think he is wary that you were able to shift so easily despite his efforts to keep you off balance. In fact, when I came upon the scene, I think he did not know truly where you had gone. He knew you were still there, just not exactly where."

"Markus, if he has the power to bring the dead back to life, what can I do to destroy him? Those soldiers, every one of them had been killed before, and yet they fought on with as much strength as if their souls had never left their bodies. They fought as one carefully controlled unit, and I've no doubt eventually they would have taken me down."

Mordred, earlier absorbed in the task of battle, now saw the details of their garments. Tattered, torn, and hacked apart, each man bore evidence of fighting elsewhere, mail rings ripped apart by swords, dented armor and bloodied cloth. Yet that was not the worst of it.

It was their faces, gaunt and haunted, still bearing their last expressions before death claimed them. Howling, open-mouthed, screaming in anger, that their lives had been taken.

Markus interrupted his grim thoughts.

"This clearly proves that even the Templars do not know the full extent of Vlad's powers. We never suspected this. Waste no sympathy on your comrades. You did them a favor by sending them to their rightful place with the Blood Sword. They were already dead, just restless. Now they know the way home."

Mordred looked through the shock of black hair that had fallen over his face. His headcloth dropped to his shoulders.

"Where did they come from?"

"They were with us all along. There will be more, until we reach Egypt. They will go as far as the Nile and then turn back. The Templars know the dangers you face, and they are committed to doing their part in keeping the Chosen One alive. Luckily, this time, they brought a holy relic along with them."

"What is in the container?"

"That will wait for another time. For now, we should press on." Markus touched Mordred's shoulder. "Despite what you may be feeling right now, you did well this evening. You were able to withstand an attack of hundreds of revenants under Vlad's control. And when it came down to just you and him, you were quick enough and calm enough in the face of danger to survive. You called upon what you have learned, and you grow stronger everyday. It is a good day."

A sharp pain needled Mordred's head. It filled his mind and he winced. Markus watched him.

"It won't always be this difficult."

"Aye, it will be far worse," Mordred responded morosely, as he surveyed the hills stretching out before them. The landscape created myriad places where unknown treachery and evil might hide.

"You cannot lose faith in yourself. We must get you to your own kind so they can continue to enlighten you.

One day, Mordred, you will redeem your tortured soul."

The last comment caught Mordred by surprise.

"Mayhap you are beginning to warm to me, Markus?"

"I am beginning to understand what is being asked of you, and I do not envy you. I will remain, as always, your faithful protector for as long as it is asked of me. Come, let us continue on our path to the Narangatti."

With that Markus moved to the group of knights, spoke softly to them and came back to Mordred. The knights looked his way, nodded once, and turned, heading in the opposite direction.

"Should we not keep the bag?" Mordred asked.

"Nay, it is as dangerous to us as it is to Vlad. For us to bring it forth would mean our own destruction. I'd rather not have it around."

"Easy for you to say when you are not the one being hunted."

Markus looked at Mordred. "Don't make the mistake of thinking I will not die beside you, if it comes to that."

"But you could stop this madness if you wanted to. You could go home and find a wife and have a family. You could disappear and live on a farm and pretend the whole world is as you knew it, before you came to the Templars."

The shadow of a smile crossed Markus's face. The full moon shone brightly across the sands, lighting their path. They walked through the desert night still wary.

"I can't turn back. Knowing what I know, having seen what I've seen, I could never turn my back. What man could, knowing that by doing so you alter the course of history forever and very likely spell doom for your entire race?"

Mordred thought that in the same position, he might not have much of a problem.

"Nay, Mordred, your thoughts are false if you think you could have done otherwise. You have a choice in this to some degree. You can end the journey, for how would I force you to continue? I am not fool enough to think I could keep you on the path if you choose to stray. You have free will, Mordred. It is up to you."

Halting, Mordred grabbed the sleeve of Markus's tunic. "Wait a minute. I have been told I don't have a choice, and now you are spinning riddles around my head telling me I do? Which is it?"

Markus slowly gripped Mordred's offending hand with a strength that surprised him. So much for thinking the man could be easily bested, he thought. No doubt it would prove one hell of a fight if Mordred decided here and now to stop.

"No one can force you to do that which in your heart you do not will. You came on the crusade because you wanted your own glory. You killed your own soldiers because you knew it was the right thing to do. You have not sought to run from the truth because you know there is no running. You can spend a lifetime hiding from your destiny, but it will always be waiting for you."

They fell into the silence that came with them throughout the long days and months of their travels, each lost in his own visions.

† † †

Markus shifted his gaze back to the vampyre more than once. He studied the firm set of his jaw and the solid bulk that made up the warrior. And while Mordred tried to keep his true feelings hidden, Markus clearly saw them in the depths of his blue eyes.

At first, it was true, he had despised the thing that had come to them what now seemed long ago. He did not want to extend himself for another creature that would prove to be a failure. He did not fear his own death, or the deaths of the Templars, as he knew they had each pledged their lives to the cause. What he feared the most was that he would see the defeat in Jakob's eyes again.

Never had he met a man with such hope. It affected all he did. He exuded emotion from every pore and every step back they took in their own crusade, Jakob saw as a chance to learn and move forward more steadily.

And then came Mordred. Into a world not of his own making. Clearly the man had not sought this new life, but who could predict the twists and turns that life would throw?

Markus figured Mordred was only a few years younger than he was. They had similar disenchanted backgrounds, bringing each of them to a place where they had been offered a chance at redemption. Markus had not taken up with the Templars altogether willingly, just as Mordred had not accepted his new lot in life.

Nay, each had resisted and learned the hard way. It was only because Markus had walked a similar path before, finding the holy order, that he could now begin to understand Mordred's fears.

And it was true that Markus did not envy him. Once he had been jealous. When he had seen the look of admiration and love in Jakob's eyes, when he taught Mordred how to shift, Markus had been angry. He, the knight who had stood by the Master Templar for all the many years, had been replaced. Or so Markus had thought. And he had stalked out of the chambers that day, swearing he would not be a party to another failure.

He'd threatened Mordred on more than one occasion, should he betray the order. How much that really mattered to Mordred remained a mystery. Every time Markus goaded Mordred, he got the same level of it thrown back in his face.

There was pride now in Markus that he had been chosen to act as guardian and protector, for the time being, for the Chosen One. There were hundreds of knights ready to step up to the job, and each one would have carried less animosity. But Jakob had picked Markus. Jakob had known he needed this even as he did not.

Again he looked at the man who was their one true hope. Mordred, lost in his own thoughts, did not acknowledge him. Markus felt a kinship come over him, something he never thought possible. He was actually coming to care for the vampyre. At first the thought disgusted him, but then he realized the only reason he had those feelings was because of the actions of those in the past, the other vampyres.

Nay, within Mordred there lay courage, honor,

nobility, and dedication to the cause. It was dormant at this moment, but there all the same. Like a spring breaking through the icy earth, Mordred's true self would not fail him and would bubble forth when needed most.

Markus smiled. They had come a long way, both in body and spirit. And they still had far to travel.

CHAPTER FOURTEEN

The pair moved as one during the long days and nights that followed, one dressed in white, one in black. One man and one vampyre. Each headed for a single destiny even they did not fully understand.

They trekked to the Dead Sea, where they paused to bathe the dust, grit, grime, and blood from their bodies. There they rested briefly, for Markus's benefit, and ate the provisions from their packs: dried meat, hard bread, and some goat's cheese for one, flasks of blood for the other. Always they were silent and watchful, looking out for another attack.

They avoided all humans as well, fearing word had spread that Mordred still lived. With a bounty on his head there were few they could trust, and they preferred to enter towns at night under cover of darkness.

They traveled through places Mordred had thought of as legends, places such as Masada, a huge complex carved from sandstone, perched atop a mountain. They passed the long lost city of Lachish where only a huge mound remained, covered with grass and flowers.

When they came to Hebron, they made their way past the city walls and spent the night in a burial cave, where Mordred found himself plagued by strange dreams. Images of times long past, times before his birth, filled his mind, and he saw things in visions that he could not comprehend. He heard the voices of the dead.

They passed Hazor, whose high mud-brick walls were blazing red, and Beersheba, where they saw evidence of Roman occupation. They came at last to the great desert of Negev. Now they traveled only at night and by day slept in rock outcroppings, ruined temples, or burial chambers, waiting until the sun began its descent, and the deadly heat withdrew.

Finally they crossed a tributary that led to the Red Sea and came to the Delta. Descending into the lowlands, Mordred saw the lagoons colored in shades of blue deeper than that of the sky. Green in a thousand hues swayed gently beneath a cooling breeze. It seemed like paradise.

Small lakes reached further out from the verdant oases like fingers stretching toward the horizon. Flowers as large as a man's hand danced on tall stalks, lolling beneath the heat of the sun.

"We have reached the ancient city of Tanis," Markus said, once they had reached the delta. "We will stay here tonight and then find a boat to take us down river."

"Is this the Nile?"

Markus laughed, extending his hand in a wide sweeping gesture. "This is only one end. The rivers you see here are only small extensions of the Nile. She is a great and mighty river, capable of bringing life or death to the people who have lived here far longer than you or I can imagine."

Mordred took in the vastness of the land. It seemed to go on forever. Where the delta ended, sand claimed the land once more. Only the sky established the end of the earth. If he kept walking he wondered if he would simply fall off into another world.

The Templar brought them out of the delta to the ruins. As they picked their way carefully through the broken rocks and tumbled earth, Mordred saw enormous and strange statuary. One had a lion's head but the body of a man. Another had the body of a lion and the head of a man wearing an unfamiliar crown. More fallen images linked men and beasts in ungodly unions.

"Who were these people?" Mordred asked, his attention caught by the form of a woman with a cat's head.

"They were the Egyptians, who created a culture very different from the one you know. They worshipped many gods and goddesses. What you see here are the representations of those from whom they sought good will. Come, we will find safety in one of the burial tombs."

Following Markus into what at first appeared to be a small dark square, Mordred ducked his head to fit through the opening. Once inside however, the ceiling rose to a grand height while the floor sloped downward. Clearly most of the building lay below the earth.

Cracks in the roof structure provided light in small bands, and Mordred saw treasures almost too magnificent to absorb hidden beneath the sands. The entire floor space of the tomb was covered in gold, small flakes that stirred with their movements. On either side lay enormous slabs of stone, like boxes with heavy lids, inscribed with elaborate writing. The carvings reminded Mordred of little pictures. He made out flowers, people, and even animals among the foreign symbols.

In a corner of the tomb lay a cache of treasure to make a man rich beyond his wildest imaginings. Mordred touched gold bowls and furniture stacked against the wall, as if the tomb's occupants had merely been in the middle of moving it.

A jeweled box, twinkling under a ray of light, caught Mordred's attention. He touched the lid, opened it, and saw the most spectacular items of jewelry he had ever beheld: intricate necklaces made of pure gold and embedded with strange blue stones; bracelets heavy enough to require strength to lift one's arm when worn, all exquisitely crafted.

In an inner chamber Mordred saw paintings of people and animals, scenes of daily life once upon a time. He marveled at their skill. These people had existed long ago yet had created things the kings of Europe might only dream of. What other wonders did the sands conceal?

Inside the tomb, it was soundless. There were no voices of the dead. Odd, for it was a place of death and burial, and should be filled with conversations of loved ones long gone. Yet it was still.

Markus found an open space and hunkered down on the floor with his back against a wall. His pack thudded to the stones. He closed his eyes and leaned his head back. Exhaustion was visible in the lines on his face, yet he had not uttered a single complaint on the entire journey. Mordred pulled a flask from the pack, unstoppered it, and handed it to Markus.

"Here, drink. It will cool you."

Markus cracked an eye open. "I'd rather bathe in one of the lagoons but they are rife with the most ugly beasts."

Mordred quirked an eyebrow and Markus continued. "Crocodiles, they are called. They'll sneak up on you beneath the water and take you under for a roll until you've drowned. I've watched them make off with full-grown oxen as well as men. Once they have a hold on you there is nothing to do but make peace with your god." The Templar moved slightly to indicate the wall behind them.

"Have a look yourself. Gruesome, I think. The Egyptians made them look remotely nice, but then again they had a god or goddess, can't remember which, that was part crocodile. Or maybe they had a god of crocodiles. It's entirely possible."

Narrowing his eyes, Mordred saw an odd grayish color that seemed to emanate from his companion.

"Markus, are you unwell?"

"Nothing a little sleep won't cure. Don't worry about me, Mordred, I've seen worse . . . Well, actually, I haven't," he rambled, his speech becoming slurred. "This is the most energy I think I've expended in a long time."

Mordred grabbed the flask, this time realizing how

light it was in his hands. He shook it and heard nothing, turned it upside down and watched as one lone drop fell from the opening. He searched Markus's pack and found another flask, only to realize it too was empty.

"Markus? When was the last time you had water?"

Delirious, the knight mumbled unintelligibly.

Removing his glove, Mordred placed a hand on Markus's forehead. It burned.

Markus had fallen into unconsciousness. Goddamn the man for keeping the lack of water to himself, Mordred thought angrily. Served him right if he died in the tomb.

A shiver of fear crept under Mordred's skin. And then what would he do? He had no idea where the Narangatti were, or how far away.

Sighing, Mordred rose and glanced about the crypt. He was surrounded by treasure that would make a man rich beyond compare and it meant nothing to him, he thought ironically.

He took a blanket from the pack and draped it over Markus, curling the edges of his cape around him as well, then glanced toward the opening of the tomb. The sun was past its zenith and night would come swiftly.

He stalked to the doorway and stepped into the afternoon light. The temperature was more moderate here than in the desert, far more bearable. Cursing, he set off although he had no idea where he was headed. He only knew he had to find water.

The sun was sinking quickly now, the air cooling. Mordred heard a thrashing up ahead in a dense cluster of reeds and pulled the sword from the sheath at his hip, fearing he had stepped into a nest of the ugly crocodiles.

He felt instead the presence of humans on both sides. Raising his sword, Mordred whirled.

Several men, stood nearby, having emerged from the rushes nearly soundlessly. One man broke from the group and raised his hands, palms toward Mordred.

"We bear you no harm, Dark One. We have only come to ask if you would like to join us."

"You want me to join you? Who are you?"

"I am Saladin. We are fighting the Caliph of Egypt, and then we will battle the intruding crusaders who seek to take what is not theirs."

Mordred lowered his blade, but kept it unsheathed. "How do you know I am not a crusader?" he asked.

"You were once, but that has changed. We saw you fight against the soldiers in Jerusalem. We think you do not like the crusaders any more than we do."

"I fought the soldiers in the city because they put a price on my head. I don't like the crusaders, but I'm not going to fight them either," Mordred replied.

"But you fought the undead too. We saw you take down hundreds."

"As you said, they were undead and I had little choice."

The man named Saladin glanced at the other men and nodded.

"We would like for you to share a meal with us. We wish to know more about you."

"While I appreciate the hospitality, I . . ."

Mordred's next words were cut off by more rustling from the reeds, and he watched incredulously as the men scattered, running up the gently sloping hillside away from the waterway.

Sensing another presence, Mordred backed away, but not quickly enough. Something shot from the undergrowth and charged straight at him.

The thing moved nearly as fast as a horse but it had no fur. Its legs were small in comparison to its huge midsection, and its face like nothing Mordred had ever seen. It opened its mouth and roared. Mordred turned to flee.

"Come, this way! You can't outrun it."

Mordred turned, gathering speed, and saw Saladin astride a white horse. The man held out his hand. Mordred grasped it. With a strength he found surprising, Saladin dragged him up and with a well-placed leap Mordred was able to land behind him. Riding hard they raced from the delta and across the sands leaving the monster in their wake.

After what seemed like miles Saladin pulled his mount to a halt. He whistled and from out of the dusk came five shadows, four men on horseback with a fifth riderless horse.

"What the devil was that?" Mordred asked, still trying to catch his breath.

Saladin smiled as he dismounted. "It is a hippo. A river horse. It is very protective of its young. We must have disturbed its lair."

Looking back toward the river, Mordred shook his head. Strange land, strange beasts. He didn't really want to know what was next.

"I thank you for coming when you did."

Dangers of the River Nile

"I've no doubt you'd still be running if I hadn't. Now, as a measure of your thanks, please come to our camp."

"I can't. I have a companion, a knight who is very ill. I need to get him water."

Saladin nodded. "We have water and a safe place for your friend to rest. We also have medicine that may help heal him. We will go with you to get him and bring him to the camp."

Mordred stood silent for a moment. He sensed no ill will, only a genuine curiosity.

"All right," he conceded finally.

Saladin nodded. "It is a good thing." He motioned for the man leading the fifth horse to bring it forward. "You will ride with us."

Mordred inclined his head briefly in acknowledgment and mounted. In an instant they were off, only one thought in Mordred's mind . . . Markus.

† † †

Sheer rock walls rose above the desert floor, nearly blotting out the evening sky. Plateaus at various heights served as the bases for myriad encampments of Saladin's followers. One night as the stars twinkled above, Mordred sat with the desert warrior.

"You carry a heavy burden, Dark One," Saladin offered, after giving Markus another healing draft.

Cursing under his breath, Mordred chewed a piece of meat. "Does everyone know who I am?"

"Why do you ask? Anyone with eyes can see you

are a cloud of death. You dress in black for it matches your mood. I call you Dark One because that is what you are—dark. What has made you this way?"

Mordred realized then that perhaps Saladin didn't know the truth. He had seen him take down an army of undead but maybe that could be expected from a knight. For the first time since becoming a vampyre he wondered what it might feel like to have another person treat him simply as a man.

"We are on a long journey and it has taken its toll, as you have seen." He nodded in Markus's direction.

"What do you seek here?" Saladin inquired, dark hair and eyes shining in the moonlight. "You are far from home and far from your own kind."

"Markus is my kind," Mordred replied defensively.

"No, Markus is a holy man. A . . . how do you say . . . a Templar. You are not. You search for something. What? It is not gold or treasure, you did not pillage the tomb. It is not glory, or you would have tried to kill me. What then holds you in its thrall?"

Mordred threw a piece of kindling into the fire and thought about the question. Saladin watched him closely. "I might know the answer," the desert leader continued, "but I won't be able to help you if you don't ask for it."

"Do you know of the Narangatti?" Mordred sighed at length.

"The soul stealer? Yes. He lives in the Great Pyramid."

"There is only one Narangatti?"

The man shook his head. "Yes, the king. When this land was filled with people and the tombs were not dead places, but places filled with souls looking for life ever-lasting, the Narangatti lived among the Egyptians like any other beast. The people were wary of them, but they also needed them."

"Needed them? For what?"

"The pharaohs, the kings, and queens of this valley, believed that they would find new life with the gods after they died. But to do so one had to be mummified."

Mordred cast Saladin a puzzled look.

"In the tomb you saw the resting places of royalty. They were mummified before they were laid to rest. All of their body fluids and organs were removed, and the body was wrapped in cloth."

"So they retain the form they had on earth?"

"Yes, in their heaven," Saladin finished. "So, the funerary cult was created by the Narangatti, and the Egyptians and the vampyres lived together. But over time the Narangatti were reduced to only one. I do not know the reason why only the king still resides within the pyramids. A lonely existence for one who has seen lifetimes pass."

"Your need must be great to go to see that one. Many have sought his wisdom, but none have returned. Even our people give the king a wide berth.

"I wish you luck, Dark One."

Mordred watched Saladin stand, his robes catching in a night breeze. The desert warrior was an interesting combination of formidable combatant and charismatic leader. He was cloaked in an aura of mystery, yet it wasn't hard to see why men chose to follow him.

"We will break camp early in the morning," Saladin

said softly. "Your companion will be ready to travel then. I would leave you horses, but you will need to cross the Nile and the animals cannot accompany you. You must continue your journey on foot. I wish you all good things, Mordred Soulis."

Saladin bent his head in a simple gesture of deference and disappeared silently into the night.

CHAPTER FIFTEEN

True to Saladin's word, Markus was up and about the next morning. Saladin himself was gone.

"If you ever decide not to tell me you are without water again I will make you suffer more from my hand than you would for being thirsty," Mordred stated gruffly, as the two made preparations to leave the caves.

Markus did not miss the undercurrent of compassion in Mordred's voice.

Mordred kept his head down, his hair covering his face. "Do not mistake my warning for concern. It is only that you are as useful to me as a pack animal, and for sheer practicality I'd rather not lose you."

The Templar grunted, noting however, that Mordred stowed a few extra flasks of water in his own packs.

Finding a boat to ferry them to the other side of the Nile did not prove difficult. The boatman asked no questions and demanded only a few coins. Markus paid him and soon they traveled south from a smaller tributary to the main portion of the river.

The vast expanse of blue, fringed with green from the delta, was a spectacular sight. But what attracted Mordred's eye were the strange buildings on the horizon. Mordred stared in wonder at the mammoth monuments. They were the most magnificent structures he had ever seen, enormous triangles of stone, taller than anything he could have conjured in his mind.

"What are those?" he asked, awe stricken.

"They are the pyramids of Egypt, built by the Egyptians long ago as tombs for their great kings and queens. The Egyptians believed that the buildings were actually stairways to the heavens. They worshipped the god of the sun and the sun was the key to life. So, the theory is they built these buildings to keep their sun god happy. Look, there." Markus pointed off the bow of the boat to the left where the largest of the pyramids rose into the sky. "That is where we are headed."

"There are no castles that can compare with these." Mordred said. "No cathedrals."

"Aye, they are well built. When we reach the Great Pyramid, or Beautiful House as it was once called, you will meet the Narangatti."

Mordred recalled his conversation with Saladin. "I've learned there is only one Narangatti left. The king still lives, but no others of his kind."

Markus appeared puzzled. "Do you know why there are no others?" he asked.

"No. Saladin couldn't tell me. He didn't know."

A thrill of nervous energy raced through Mordred's body. His skin puckered. He had never dreamed a world like this existed.

"Does Vlad know where the Narangatti live?" he asked.

"No. He does not believe in their existence. Only the Templars and now, apparently, this Saladin knows of him."

"How is it you know?"

The boat bumped against the shore of the Nile, and the ferryman secured it to a wood piling. He motioned to Mordred and Markus to disembark.

As they began walking the final steps that would bring them to the next lesson in Mordred's education, Markus spoke quietly, offering a grudging respect for the Narangatti.

"Many years ago, when Jakob had just joined the Templars, they were excavating beneath the Holy Sepulcher in Jerusalem. They discovered a series of scrolls in several jars, some on pieces of papyrus that had long since decayed or fallen apart. Piecing the information they gathered together, they learned of the day when a great darkness would come disguised as a man. A malevolent being brought forth from the sins of greed and power."

"Vlad?"

"Yes, but within the scrolls there was also written something of the vampyre race. Where they began and what became of them. They were brought to life, just after man, on the eighth day. But they proved to be so cunning and so adept as predators that something had to be done to dissolve the strength which threatened the human race. When a great flood failed to destroy them, they were cast to the five corners of the earth, as we know it, to live in the harshest environments. It was hoped they would in time die out, since they could not reproduce. And it appears that most did, save the kings. The kings are who we need now."

"What happened to the scrolls?"

"I could only hazard a guess. I have never seen them myself. Jakob is the only one still alive who knows of their existence. It, of course, changes everything we have been taught to believe about the beginning of the world."

The men fell silent as they approached an impossibly large tomb. The side appeared solid, but Markus was undeterred.

"You may wish to know if the scrolls mentioned you. According to Jakob they did, though not by your actual name. It is why we placed such faith in the vampyres before you. We were never sure."

Mordred eyed the Templar. "And how is it you believe I am the right man now?"

"You are if Jakob says you are, and I have witnessed first hand a prelude to your greatness as champion."

The pair moved to the next side, and then a third before Markus began to climb the side of the building. He placed his fingers and toes into the grooves between each large block of golden stone, pulling himself up. Markus pointed to a small patch of black that marked a possible opening. Reluctantly, Mordred hoisted himself up behind him.

"This is the door to the Beautiful House," Markus said.

Entering the pyramid, the men faced a wall of complete darkness.

"You will have to be my eyes," Markus whispered. "I cannot see a thing and we must take care. There are hundreds of traps designed to prevent intruders."

"Who exactly set all the traps?"

"The Egyptians of course. These are palaces constructed for the deceased pharaohs and members of royal houses. The riches here will make you think what you saw in Tanis to be a peasant's coffer.

"And this is the place of the Narangatti, the givers of immortality, or so the faithful believed."

Mordred stepped in front of Markus, who shifted his satchel to his left shoulder before continuing. "The Egyptians believed the soul was immortal and that after death, if it had been judged worthy, it would come back to its body and live again. So the body needed to be prepared for that time."

Comprehension filled Mordred as he realized the extent of the ancient civilization's beliefs. "It is the perfect place for vampyres then. The Egyptians brought their newly dead, still full of blood, and the vampyres fed on them?"

"Exactly. In order to preserve the bodies they needed to be drained. The Narangatti were the perfect creatures to do such a thing. To the Egyptians the vampyres were the closest thing to god-like beings. The Narangatti were thought to be immortal themselves and were revered by queens, kings, priests, and pharaohs. They sat at the thrones of rulers and conferred with the leaders of the nations."

Eyes adjusting to the absence of light, Mordred moved forward slowly. He felt Markus place a hand on his shoulder, and a light scent of fear wafted from him.

"Markus, are you afraid of the dark?" He expected a scoffing rebuttal. Instead he got the truth.

"Yes."

Mordred smiled in the dark.

Markus continued. "The dark and confined places."

"Great. It's a fine time to tell me now."

They stood in a hallway that sloped downward at a steep angle. On either side of the descending passageway were many rooms, now shielded by masses of cobwebs. The scent of dust, rotted corpses, and damp stone filled the air.

"Which way do we go?" Mordred asked when they came to a crossroads, their passage intersecting with several others.

"I've no idea. I was only told the Narangatti live beneath the Great Pyramid."

Mordred decided to continue downward.

"Remember," Markus said, "that though you are immortal, I am not. We need to be careful and move slowly. You will need to use your senses to detect anything unusual. There are rumored to be many devices for the unwary. Not to mention the curse."

Mordred's eyebrows arched. "Curse? Pray tell, what more could befall me?"

"Never ask, Mordred. Just when you think you've reached bottom, life will send you deeper still. Forget the curse for the moment. How about holding my shield in front of you, just in case . . ."

"In case what?" Mordred drawled, unable to imagine what, besides the last remaining Narangatti, could possibly live in the tomb that would be large enough to hurt two fully armed men.

"Um, well, there are also rumors of mummies . . ."

"Jesus, Markus, what else haven't you told me? What the hell are mummies besides the things in the stone boxes in Tanis?"

Markus stopped Mordred again and lowered his voice to a whisper. "They are the corpses of those that have passed on. Restless and unable to accept that they are dead, they wander the night looking for the source of their doom. It has been said they will kill any who come across them."

A slight shiver raced up Mordred's spine. "For the love of god, Markus, keep your ghost stories to yourself. Let's just get moving."

Markus didn't argue. He handed Mordred his shield and they continued.

Mordred stopped suddenly, and Markus slammed into his back.

"You might want to give me warning when you stop, Mordred. I can't see a damn thing."

Sensing trouble, Mordred replied, "Is this the time I tell you to duck?"

Both men immediately hit the ground as the air filled with a high pitched buzzing sound. Mordred watched as hundreds of tiny, sharp missiles flew through the air at man height. A sight up ahead confirmed it.

The skeletons of four men lay strewn about the stone passageway. Spider webs wove between the rotted bones. Rusted armor lay in a heap, tiny projectiles embedded in the skulls.

"What the devil was that?" Markus asked, voice trembling.

"Apparently, we've just encountered our first trap. They were tiny darts and up ahead as we pass them, you'll see evidence that they were deadly. I am amazed at the force with which they came through the walls, and even now it is hard to see where they were housed. The tiny holes have been worked into a large painted surface. Let me check ahead a moment to be sure there are no more of these little surprises."

Mordred tested the space in the passageway, touching the walls and pacing the center of the stone walk. Nothing more came at him.

"Should you even be with me?" he asked.

"What do you mean?" Markus questioned.

"Well, let's see, you've mentioned traps, of which we've stumbled on one. Who knows how many more there are. You've mentioned mummies and we've yet to meet them. Curses too. Although then of course there's the King of the Narangatti. So, I'll ask again. Should you even be here with me?"

"Quite frankly, probably not. But I gave my word to Jakob that I would see you to the king. I'll not be leaving until I know you are safe. Why have we stopped again?"

"There's a problem."

"Another one?"

Mordred heard the anxiety in Markus's voice and he had to admit he, too was growing more apprehensive.

"We've reached a dead end. There doesn't appear to be any way out except back the way we . . ."

An earsplitting sound filled the passageway, and Mordred watched as the stones behind them moved. Within moments, faster than he had time to think, they closed the pair in. "Oh, great, now what the hell do we do?"

He watched as Markus felt the walls around him. "Oh, God, we're trapped. It will only be a matter of time before we run out of air . . ."

"Shit!" Mordred yelled and felt the floor give way beneath him. "Hang on to me, Markus. Just hang on!"

The two descended rapidly, feeling nothing around them but the cold air that whirled past. Mordred tried to peer into the darkness, but even he was unable to make out anything for the long moments they tumbled down. Then he spotted something.

"Close your mouth!" Mordred yelled.

They jostled and jolted against the stones. The passageway closed in on them from all sides, and then ended. They were spit out of the tunnel and into an enormous chamber, but before Mordred could get his bearings they hit water.

He felt Markus land behind him and shoot by. He reached out and using all his strength jerked the man up. They broke the surface together. Markus however, did not appear to be breathing. Mordred held him upright in the water and pounded his back repeatedly.

"What in God's name are you doing, trying to kill me?" Markus sputtered.

"I thought you had left me."

"Not a chance, vampyre. Now where in hell are we?"

Mordred glanced about, his gaze coming to rest on a set of stone stairs rising from the water.

"Well, hell might be a good place to start. Where in hell? I'd have to guess pretty far beneath the earth judging by how far we fell. Come."

As if Markus weighed no more than a child, Mordred hauled him out of the water. They both stood side by side on the steps by the underground lake wondering where they were. And then they heard a noise.

† † †

"Who dares violate the sanctity of the Beautiful House? Who among the living desecrates this place?"

Mordred's head snapped to the right and he saw a figure seated upon a beast of stone. Actually, two stone beasts that together made up a throne. The animals appeared to be lions, yet had the upper torsos and heads of women. Great golden wings created the sides of the massive chair. Two torches flickered to life in the darkness. Mordred heard Markus gasp.

He turned to where the man's gaze was focused and realized, by the dim light of the torches, that every square inch of the place that wasn't water or stone, every nook and cranny, every spare inch of the area was covered with treasures.

Mountains of gold, cups, coins, trunks, chairs, and

jewelry sat in piles rising to impossible heights. Gems twinkled and winked, casting tiny rainbows across the floor and walls of the chamber. Silver, bronze, and a host of other rich materials lay strewn about, like children's toys.

The thing on the throne, angry that no one had yet answered him, spoke again. "There is one among you that is not of the living?" It was a question, asked as if the thing had been caught off guard.

The language was unfamiliar, but as quickly as the sounds reached his ears, Mordred's mind processed the words. He saw them as interesting visions, much like the symbols and drawings surrounding him. Then they broke apart and formed words. And Mordred understood.

"I am Mordred Soulis and . . ."

"You are a half-born." It was said with disgust.

Mordred watched the figure that came to life in the flickering of the torches. First only a shadow, then the thing took form and a nightmare came to life.

It was shorter than he was and wore no clothing. Its body was completely bared to Mordred's view, and it was hard to hold back the revulsion Mordred felt at the sight of the thing. It was furthermore, most definitely male.

A smooth brown skin glistened with a yellow liquid that dripped periodically in great globs, leaving its body in a stream of fluid that reminded Mordred of saliva.

As if the smell of hundreds of dead people wasn't enough to make Mordred want to vomit, a strange odor filled the cavern. Mordred's keen sense of smell found the stench altogether unpleasant, bringing to mind images of rotting flesh and fetid corpses.

Unnaturally large oval eyes stared at him. There was no circle of color surrounding the pupils, or any white, only black filling every part of the eye. They were so oversized, they took up most of the creature's face.

Two tiny holes, mere needle pricks were located where the shape of a nose should have been, causing the entire face to appear distorted. It was as if the thing's face had melted, and this was what was left. The mouth was a huge, gaping orifice filled with pointed teeth. Two enormous canines poked from its thin upper lip and extended nearly to its jawbone. The lips were stretched taut, mere slashes of red against its hairless brown-yellow skin.

It was a thing from a nightmare.

Suddenly, and without any warning, the creature came at them. Huge, reptilian wings, covered in scales, extended in either direction. A rush of hot wind blew past Mordred. Immediately, he moved to stand in front of Markus.

"Stop!"

The creature dived and then rose sharply coming to land upon a ledge above them. It watched them, head cocked.

"We come here seeking the King of the Narangatti," Mordred said boldly. He had no idea if the thing meant them harm. And he had no idea if he had the strength to stop it.

"Who dares to ask the Narangatti for help, and brings one of the living? Or perhaps he is a gift for us?" the creature lisped. A clicking sound reverberated throughout the cavern as it rubbed its hands in anticipation, long sharp fingernails clattering together. The creature licked its lips and spittle dripped from its lower lip in strands of glistening fluid.

"No, this man is my protector. He will not be harmed."

The creature let out a hissing noise. It resounded off the rock walls of the chamber, and like a snake's rattle, it warned of something dangerous.

"What immortal needs a protector? I think you toy with me. I will tell you what you wish to know if you allow me to feed on this being," the thing proposed.

Mordred watched the beast intently, never taking his eyes off the gruesome thing. "And I will say no, again. Markus is a Templar. And I have only found you because of him. You will not dine on him while there is breath in my body."

Another hiss. "So much bluster and bravado for a newborn." The thing rose to a full standing position on the ledge. While its body was shorter than Mordred's, its wings were enormous. It amazed Mordred that the thing could even stand under the weight of the scaly appendages.

An image of a bat fluttered through Mordred's mind. The thing looked very much like the animals he had come across in his own homeland. They had small bodies, but large wings, and would often suspend themselves upside down, wrapped in their wings clinging to the ceiling of caverns.

The thing interrupted his thought and spoke again in a rasping voice.

"The Templars?" The creature spoke as if tasting the words on his tongue. "Ah, yes, the Templars. They sent you to me? Markus is a Templar?"

"Yes." Mordred didn't know if this was going to save Markus or condemn him.

"Then he shall not be harmed." The voice became startlingly authoritative.

A sigh escaped Markus. And Mordred felt a great wave of relief roll off the knight behind him.

"Mordred?" the thing asked.

"Yes?"

"What is it you wish to know?"

Thinking for a moment, Mordred replied, "First, may I have the name by which you are called?"

"Kabil, King of the Narangatti."

Mordred glanced about the chamber half expecting to see more creatures in the shadows. He could only imagine what this place would have been like when filled with these strange vampyre forms.

"Alas, there is only me, the rest are gone, long gone," Kabil replied, clearly picking through Mordred's thoughts as a vulture with a carcass. He swooped down from his perch to find another ledge on the opposite side of the chamber.

Mordred watched as Kabil turned upside down. Yes, Mordred thought, he was a large bat.

Wrapping his great wings around himself, Kabil declared, "Mordred Soulis, the Chosen One. The champion of all mortals."

Again there was a hissing sound. More copious amounts of saliva dripped from its mouth. Mordred couldn't tell from his tone whether Kabil mocked him.

"Welcome to my palace, Mordred Soulis. The tomb of the soulless. I am at your service."

Mordred recognized the sarcasm dripping as heavily from Kabil's lips as the streams of drool.

"What is it you wish to learn, half-born?"

"He is here seeking your help," Markus said suddenly. "We could only teach him what the Templars know, but that is so little compared to your ancient wisdom."

"Ah, so he *is* newly born then? That explains the disgusting odor he exudes."

Mordred sniffed the air. The king himself oozed an underlying scent of putrid rot.

"So, he needs lessons in how to be a vampyre? What has he learned?"

"A lot. Shape-shifting, thought sifting, controlling fire."

Kabil extended an arm and waved his hand as if there were something moving about his face.

"Child's play. Tricks. The stuff of charlatans."

Indignant, Mordred folded his arms across his robe-covered chest. He was expected to believe this disgusting creature was the key to his future survival?

"You may not think much of me in my present form, Mordred Soulis. Yet, if I choose, you will learn such from me that you could rule the world. Do not forget, I once did." Kabil swung his arms wide in a grand gesture meant to punctuate his short speech.

Mordred realized Kabil had just plucked the thoughts from his mind. Clearly, any effort to block his mind from being read wasn't working. He would have to try harder.

This thought brought a round of wicked laugher from Kabil.

"Poor Mordred Soulis. He thought he knew so much. Young whelp. You've plenty to learn if you are to save mankind. And even the learning does not guarantee you will succeed."

"So you'll teach me?" Mordred asked.

Kabil launched himself into the air, returning to the throne. He took a seat, leaving his great wings to hang about him like a scaled cape.

"We shall begin, but first the mortal must leave. No more secrets can be revealed to the Templars."

Chapter Sixteen

Kabil instructed Mordred to guide his protector out of the pyramid. Markus traveled with him in the darkness again, but on a path without traps or pitfalls. Once Mordred saw the giant painted image of the sun that Kabil had described, he knew he had brought the Templar to the place where now they had to part. From here a groove, notched into the stones, would allow Markus to find his way out.

For the second time since becoming a vampyre, Mordred found it difficult to say goodbye. He considered the knight a friend. He would be sad to see him go. Two men, starting from such very different points, yet in the same place now, made Mordred hesitate to say the final words. He didn't know if he would ever see the blond giant again.

Before he could speak, however, Markus stepped forward. In a gesture that both surprised and pleased him, the Templar drew him into a powerful embrace. Then the Templar stepped back to look the vampyre in the eye.

High above was the opening in the stones, where Markus would climb out of the pyramid. Now, as he backed away from Mordred, the man became the shadow of a great warrior outlined against a glowing sky filled with evening stars.

"The journey home, wherever home is, will it be a long one for you?" Mordred asked.

Markus nodded, "Aye, but it is a path I know well enough. The men wait for me in the place we last met Vlad. They will return with me to the stronghold."

Mordred cleared his throat. "Will you be safe?"

He watched a smile break across the knight's usually stern face. Markus replied seriously, "Is there ever a time when we are truly safe? Knowing what you know now, and what you must become for all of us, can we ever really feel safe again?"

It caused Mordred to reflect. For a fleeting moment he saw his youth swim before him, teasing him with the innocent view he once held of the world around him.

It had always been his dream to be a knight. To be a master of his own destiny. He rose above hundreds of thousands of soldiers through his years as a fighter to become highly sought after by kings and nations. His name struck fear into the hearts of the enemies he was paid to dispatch. None could match his skill with a blade.

Yet, now, if he were given the chance to do it all over again, would he still choose the path of the warrior? Or, knowing what he knew now, would he find something gentler? Would he care less about himself and more about the world around him? Would he follow a dream with all his heart instead of making dreams come true for those who could afford his price?

A hollowness filled Mordred, leaving him feeling as though he were now only a tattered remnant of what he once had been. The biting wind of his future howled through the hole where his soul had once existed.

Barely able to conceal his mounting sadness, Mordred turned back toward the tomb, into the darkness. Markus's touch upon his arm stayed him.

"Within you I see the constant struggle you face each day. I know of the battle you wage between what you once were and what you are now. I know you are filled with regret and confusion. You cannot change the past Mordred Soulis, but you alone can change the future. You will spend endless amounts of time, wasted time, reflecting on these things. Some of what happens to us is much larger than we can ever understand.

"Burn bright with the knowledge that the Templars, no matter where, no matter when, will always be ready to aid you. You only need to call upon us. And always you will find sanctuary in buildings wrought by our hands."

Markus turned to gaze skyward, his blond hair lifting gently in the cool breeze. This time it was he who cleared his throat. He set his blue gaze once more on Mordred.

"You will not fail. You've the heart of a lion, the courage of a thousand men, the embrace of the Templars, and a faith you've only begun to understand. Do not despair. You are the Chosen One, and with you lies the glory of that which is greater than all of us."

Markus extended his hand and grasped Mordred's leather bracer at the forearm, above the deadly metal spikes. Mordred returned the knightly gesture, and was pulled once more into an embrace.

No words were spoken for a moment when the two broke apart. Markus nodded and graced Mordred with a melancholy smile.

"I look to the day our paths will cross again, Markus," Mordred said. He turned and slipped back through the entrance that would take him to the depths of the tomb.

† † †

Mordred leaned against the stone wall while Markus strode away, his gloved hand feeling the groove along the wall. The vampyre waited in silence as the Templar made his way out of the building. Then he too climbed to the opening in the stones that led to the outside world. He remained standing there, a mere shadow among the dead, watching Markus's silhouette as it blended with the trees and river far below.

He couldn't help feeling empty. Although their relationship was strained by Mordred's destiny, Markus had become a friend to him. Now, twice, he had parted company with those who had taken him in and guided him. And once again he was left set adrift in a dark and unfamiliar sea.

What now, he wondered as he pushed from the stones and began his descent back to the King of the Narangatti.

Lord of Darkness Kabil

Stepping into the glowing chamber that was Kabil's grand throne room, Mordred heard a low hissing sound. It was Kabil, harrying him again.

"You would do well not to spend so much time in the company of humans, young one."

"It is only right that I do so, since I am half human," he lashed out.

"If you are not careful, it is that part of you that will kill you."

Mordred realized Kabil no longer appeared in his vampyre form. Instead he looked altogether human, garbed in an outfit befitting a true king. An ornately jeweled headdress of gold and black covered his bald skull and fell to his shoulders. A golden snake lay coiled around his forehead, looking so real it might spring to life in a heartbeat.

His face was no longer grotesque to behold.

The king's eyes, though smaller now, were rimmed in strange black makeup, making them look even more penetrating and mysterious, dark voids of nothingness piercing the shadows of the tomb. His eyebrows were thinned and also blackened with makeup. His lips, a brighter red than before, set off the sharp angles of his cheekbones and the now concealed rows of human looking teeth.

A large golden collar studded with blue stones glittered beneath the torchlight. The jewelry gave way to a long, white sleeveless robe, embroidered with fanciful symbols and odd markings. The cloth flowed to the chamber's sand and rock floor, shifting with the king's movements.

Emblazoned on his chest, above his heart was a large golden beetle encrusted with jewels. Beneath the insect, rising like wings, were two half circles, nearly touching. They were made in shining blues, reds, and gold.

Sandals of the finest gold chain encased his feet. His bare arms were adorned with gold bracelets and armbands, tinkling musically when he shifted his position on the throne. Again, the form of the snake shaped the items of jewelry. They wound up and around the length of his upper arms.

In one hand he held a strange looking gold and black striped staff curved into a hook. In the other hand he held a gold staff with several strands of beads hanging from the tip.

"I see you are more pleased with my human appearance. It takes much energy to hold this form when you are as old as I am. Everything takes more strength when you have lived for centuries."

Mordred had to agree he did prefer the human appearance. "You mentioned something about my human side being the part that could kill me, but I am immortal, am I not?"

"Silly fool, there are many ways to die while still living. Being human is a weakness that will be used against you in the future. And when it is, you will truly wish you were dead."

Both confused and irritated with Kabil's condescending presence, Mordred brought his hands to his temples.

"You speak in riddles. I find it tiresome."

Kabil smiled, a great, toothy grin.

Apparently, Mordred realized, not all of Kabil transformed when he became human. His great canines gleamed in the dim light.

"Life and death are the greatest of riddles. You must have patience and understand that which is being given to you. Even if it is in the form of a riddle you must find meaning, for at times that will be all you are given. Now, shall we begin your learning?"

† † †

Kabil reverted back to his vampyre form. It took only moments, and Mordred thought it was rather like watching the skin peeling away from the creature's bones. In the blink of an eye he was back to his grotesque persona. He hung, once again, upside down from a ledge.

While the king of the Narangatti was able to fly to his current perch, Mordred was forced to climb. The entire time Kabil berated him for staying in human form.

"How can you learn to be a vampyre if you will not allow the vampyre out?" The king asked, doing nothing to hide his displeasure.

"I am half vampyre."

"Then you will only be half a champion of the mortals. There is nothing wrong with acknowledging what you have become. The more you resist, the harder it will be for you in the end."

Mordred finally reached the place where Kabil

hung. The king smiled at him, revealing his sharp teeth. "Now, jump."

"What?"

"Jump. Today we learn to fly," Kabil stated matter-of-factly. "Are you afraid you might kill yourself? You are immortal, remember?"

Everything within Mordred, every fiber of his being, every thought in his head, and every cell that made up his human form, revolted. He couldn't do it. To jump from such a height would surely break his neck.

And yet what Kabil said was supposedly true. While in the confines of the Templar stronghold, his human mind had been put to the test. His former belief systems had been ripped apart, forcing him to question everything. What was the truth anymore?

He'd learned he was dead, or undead. He'd learned there existed in this world creatures far darker than he could have imagined. He'd been taught to believe in the impossible as a daily occurrence. He could control fire and was instructed that at some point he would be able to borrow strength from other elements.

Beasts he'd only known in fairy tales actually roamed the earth. Places he couldn't begin to dream had revealed themselves. Corpses reanimated. Evil waged a war against good, and Mordred Soulis was trapped in the very middle of it all.

So, why did he balk at learning how to fly?

He hesitated a moment longer and then approached the edge of the rocky shelf.

"The first step to flying is letting go of the human side that tells you you cannot fly," Kabil said from behind him. "Now, jump!" the king commanded in a booming voice.

Mordred stepped off the ledge. Air rushed past his face. His hair billowed upward. Clad in nothing more than a swath of white cloth Kabil had given him, Mordred continued to fall and the vampyre-self took hold. It reminded him, once again, that he could not die. He could feel pain and debilitation for a time, but eventually he'd recover.

But just when he thought he'd hit the ground and break every bone in his body, Mordred felt Kabil's presence. The king latched on to him stopping the freefall. With inhuman strength Kabil ascended to the highest part of the cavern, and Mordred discovered he now soared through the air with the help of his new teacher.

Though he was indeed being supported, it was an incredible feeling to realize he was gliding like a bird on the air currents, shifting, swooping, diving, then rising again. High among the gilded rafters of the chamber they flew, to dizzying heights that reminded Mordred of the large, jagged rocks far below. Tiny now, insignificant from this distance.

"See how it feels, Mordred? Feel the lightness and the very air around you? It is different this way, in human form, than when you are taking over the form of another creature."

Kabil continued his lecture, flipping over and then under. Upside down and in countless circles, he took Mordred through the air. "When you are in the form of another creature, you are most times hostage to nothing more than instinct. This means if something should disturb the creature while you are in its form, you will be forced to go with it."

"Yes," Mordred acknowledged, "I had that experience recently."

Intrigued, Kabil questioned him. "Truly? And what form did you choose?"

It was embarrassing to admit to the king of the Narangatti, a vampyre that could undoubtedly shift into anything he desired, at any time, his incident as a mouse. Kabil, however, probed his thoughts and began to laugh.

"You shifted into the form of a mouse when you could have chosen a scorpion? Am I wasting my time with you?"

Incensed, Mordred tried to explain. "It was the only presence I could sense."

"Ah," Kabil sighed, "then you didn't engage your senses long enough or hard enough. The best forms for shifting are often those you feel the least. But to fly as a vampyre flies means you are in control of all you do. You do not need to worry about snakes and other creatures. Now, let go."

If stepping off the ledge wasn't hard enough, Mordred realized he was expected to simply let go of the flying king. Again, he warred with the two sides of himself.

"Young pup, you will need to let go of me else you rip what little flesh I have left from my miserably bony body."

Mordred realized he was indeed holding on to Kabil for dear life, clutching at his glistening flesh, clawing at the creature's arms.

Kabil tried again. "Mordred, what is the worst that can happen to you? You will fall down on those rocks. You will feel the pain of a thousand spears as they pierce the flesh of your form. You will bleed, ah, yes, you will bleed, but eventually you will come back as if it had never happened."

"I'd rather not fall."

"That is the problem with a half-born," Kabil sneered, "you think too much. You are immortal, Mordred. Feel that burning through your veins. You cannot die. Believe it. Become it."

Suddenly, without warning, Kabil was gone. He disappeared into the air as if he'd never been. Mordred plummeted once again toward the floor of the cavern.

This time, he fought the panic and silenced the human voice in his brain that could not comprehend what he was about to do. This time, he gave himself over to the vampyre who had nothing to lose in falling to his death.

At that moment, just before the rocks came up to greet him, he began to fly.

"That's it, Mordred Soulis, become the vampyre. Allow no doubt to enter into your mind. Fear cannot rule you here. You must trust the vampyre."

At the sound of Kabil's words, Mordred remembered he didn't want to become a full-fledged vampyre. Afraid if he allowed that part of him to rule for even a moment he would never be free of it, Mordred forced it away from him.

And then he hit the ground. His bones snapped in sickening succession. First his legs, then his hips. His ribs crushed beneath the force of his fall, then his shoulders and finally his skull. His spine cracked loudly.

Once his bones had turned to shards, his internal organs, with no protection, exploded against one another. Spleen, intestines, kidneys, heart, lungs, and brain all became jelly. Mordred tasted himself in his throat.

His impact with the floor of the chamber sent a huge cloud of golden dust up around him. The last thing he saw, before succumbing to the blackness brought on by the pain of his injuries, was Kabil's smiling face. The sound of his laughter filled Mordred's ears.

"You have so much to learn, Mordred Soulis. So much indeed."

† † †

Mordred awoke to a disturbing sound, a slurping noise. Over and over, in long, drawn out notes, the strange din drowned out all other sounds.

It was far too close to him for comfort. As his brain climbed steadily up the ladder of consciousness, he realized whatever was making the noise was right next to him.

He tried to shift and groaned aloud as fragments of pain shot through every part of his body. Oh, God, the pain. It was unbearable.

He couldn't move a muscle, and it felt as if his skin had been flayed from his body. His bones felt like mush, and his head throbbed so badly he could only see shadow out of his right eye. What had he done?

He heard a familiar laughter and realized Kabil was with him.

"So you wake? I thought perhaps there was not enough vampyre in you to bring you back."

The shadow in his right eye moved, and Mordred realized it was the form of the king blocking his view. He was very close, staring at him. Crimson smeared the thin lines of his lips and dripped from his canines.

Kabil moved out of his line of sight, and again Mordred heard the sounds of sucking and swallowing. Mordred tried to move his head, but it was no use. It felt as if the weight of one of the base stones rested on his skull. He stilled himself in an effort to summon more strength.

"You broke your neck. It's no good moving. And there is no need to. I don't think your human side would like to see what I'm doing."

"What are you doing?" asked Mordred tightly. Slurred, the words sounded odd. As if he didn't have enough bones in his jaw or teeth in his mouth to make the words.

"What else? Feeding."

A shockingly disturbing image came to Mordred's mind. He remembered Kabil's strange remark about his blood if he did fall from the air onto the rocks. And then he felt the pressure of something being applied to his skin. What the devil did he mean, feeding?"

"Are you . . ." He couldn't manage to get the rest of his thought past his lips. The man . . . no . . . creature, was drinking his blood!

"It was here. I was hungry. And there is no harm done to you."

The nausea did not dissipate with Kabil's confirmation.

In fact it grew to the point that Mordred felt he was in danger of vomiting, except he wasn't sure he had a stomach anymore.

"Keep the contents of your stomach inside, or you will choke. Another injury that will keep you down even longer, and we've no time." Kabil shook his head as he moved to a point where Mordred could see him clearly. He was still in his grotesque vampyre form, which made the thoughts all the more unpleasant.

"You drank my blood?"

Smiling, Kabil nodded. As if to prove his point, his snake-like tongue darted out to lick his lips, allowing tiny droplets of blood to drip down his chin. He looked like a creature from hell, and Mordred suddenly wasn't sure he should trust this being with his life.

Sighing, Kabil moved away, out of Mordred's line of sight again. "If not me then who, Mordred? Who will teach you what you need to know? You need to trust your vampyre-self and trust me. Besides, you will learn one day that drinking blood is the only way to truly know. Within the blood you can see everything. Lies and deceptions, thoughts and feelings, all can be gleaned by tasting the blood of another. I needed to know if you would be worthy of the knowledge I am imparting to you. After all, you could very well bring about my destruction if you learn too much."

Mordred heard a snickering sound.

Though Mordred had the urge to reach out and strangle Kabil to within an inch of his life, he realized there were two problems with that course of action. The first being that his body was still broken and he was unable to move. The second, and perhaps more important of the two, being that no matter how disgusted, or angered Mordred was by Kabil's actions, Mordred needed the king. It was that thought that leveled the rising fury.

"Do you not have a question for me, Mordred Soulis?"

Mordred thought for a moment, wondering why he would need to voice his query if Kabil could read his mind.

"It is so you may sort out your thoughts that I ask you to voice them. There is much troubling you."

"Really? I'm surprised. I went from a flesh and blood human to a blood sucking vampyre overnight, and now, supposedly I am the savior of the human race. I can't even learn to fly properly. On top of that, the man I've been told will help me has spent the last God knows how long drinking my blood! I can't imagine why I'd be troubled in the least, can you?"

"It is the human side speaking again. Half-borns are too much trouble." Kabil fell silent.

Mordred lay immobile, cold, and in excruciating pain, but there was a small flicker of something lurking within him that gave him strength.

"Kabil?"

"Yes?"

So, he was still in the room. A strange sense of relief crept through Mordred. "Tell me about drinking blood."

"Ah, yes, my favorite subject. Yes, I will tell you all you need to know."

"And some things perhaps I don't," came Mordred's sarcastic reply.

"Are you mimicking me, oh great Chosen One, whose body is in pieces before me?" Kabil asked before continuing. "As I said before, blood is, by its very nature, the liquid of life. And that being the case, when you drink blood, you learn about the being you are draining. It is important to note that at first you will also experience their life."

Still lying on his back, Mordred asked, "I'm not sure I follow."

"When you have lived for centuries as I have," Kabil began again, "you no longer are hostage to the feelings of those whose blood you drink. But when you start out, you see everything in your mind's eye. You perceive victims' hopes and fears, how they lived their lives. Who they loved and hated. If they killed, you will see images of the person or people they did that harm to. You will experience their joys and their pains. It will be an exhausting experience for you."

"But I've already taken blood from soldiers and none of that happened," Mordred offered.

"Because you were under the protection of strong magic. The Templars knew they could not teach you about the rules of blood. That you would have to learn from me. They also knew that if you felt a person's life as you drained them, you might resist your calling even more. So they shielded you. They kept the experience from you. Were you not in the company of the Templars when you drank the blood of these soldiers?"

Thinking back on the time, Mordred recalled his

apprehension in sucking the blood from the bodies of the fallen soldiers. It was Markus who told him the Templars would remain while he did so. He was told it was to protect him, but Mordred had thought it was to prevent outsiders from seeing what he was doing.

Reading his mind, Kabil said, "No, it wasn't that they were worried about others, although it wouldn't help their cause if the world knew they harbored vampyres. It was to create a blanket of nothingness around the bodies so that when you drank, you saw and felt nothing. Only the most basic instinct—you replenishing yourself—was left to you."

Mordred wondered what other magic the Templars had used in an effort to keep him on the right path.

"Their sorcery is basic at best, but they do fill a purpose. Don't fault them for their concerns. After all, they are trying to save the human race." Kabil laughed again.

Annoyed, Mordred asked him to continue.

"When you drink the blood of a human, be aware that what they've experienced, you will experience. You also need to know feeding is your weakest time. This is when you are susceptible to injury. Your senses will be so focused on drinking that you will be unable to discern trouble. Always know where you are, and it helps to know a little about your victim before you taste them."

Mordred remained on the floor of the cavern, feeling his body mend itself slowly. In his mind's eye, he saw his bones piece themselves together and fuse into place.

Even the thought of his body restructuring itself was

enough to make him sick again. Pain was ever present and Mordred felt himself drift in and out, in a state of madness. His thoughts blurred, and at times he feared he had passed out while Kabil still talked.

"Now, we come to the part about good blood and bad blood," Kabil said. If Mordred had missed anything, the king didn't let on.

"I'm sorry, did you say good blood and bad blood? Isn't blood just blood?"

"Not for vampyres. For us, it is the measure of the individual. You will always be able to drink both kinds, but I caution you not to glut yourself on bad blood."

"How do I know it's bad blood?" Mordred asked.

"That's why I instruct you to know your victims before you strike, if possible. If you drink the blood of a murderer, do you think you have tasted bad blood?"

"I suppose so," Mordred replied hesitantly.

"Wrong. Unless you have seen the murder yourself how can you assume the person who killed is bad?"

"Because it is wrong to kill?"

"You kill," Kabil pointed out. "Does that make you bad?"

"I don't know," Mordred answered honestly.

"No, it doesn't, which is why you must be careful. If you drink bad blood because you find it easier to swallow," Kabil said, laughing at his own joke, "do so in small doses. Because the more bad blood you drink, the more bad you will retain. Understand?"

"I think so."

"You cannot think so, Mordred, you must know so. If you drink good or pure blood, its effects will be most positive on you; but drinking pure blood is like a drug and you will become quickly addicted. But be warned, becoming a drinker of pure blood and killing those who possess it will bring you unwanted attention. Humans don't seem to care if a criminal goes missing. But they do care if a saintly priest is found with two pinpricks on his neck.

"My point is, blood is your food, your survival, your aphrodisiac, and your undoing," Kabil finished.

CHAPTER SEVENTEEN

Mordred's body convulsed, wracking him with a new, more vicious pain. It consumed him, devouring everything within. He bit his lip, tasting the blood.

That action left Mordred with another sensation, one of absolute horror. He found he could not stop himself from suckling, feeding greedily upon his small, self-inflicted wound.

Kabil stood above him, staring down curiously.

"Pup, when was the last time you fed?"

Feeling as though his body had just shattered into a million pieces, each piece stabbing his gut, Mordred tried to concentrate.

Unable to move, he remained frozen upon the rocks.

Kabil dabbed at the saliva bubbling from his lips, wiping it away with the sleeve of his white robe, staining it crimson with Mordred's blood.

"You do understand that you cannot regenerate, or heal for that matter, unless you feed? You will simply waste away into nothingness, but you will still live, unable to die. You will go completely mad. It is best you feed."

A look of suspicion crossed Kabil's features as he narrowed his large, black eyes, leaving Mordred with an unsettling feeling.

"Mordred Soulis, you resist feeding? Ah, that explains why you still lay upon the floor. You are young, yes, but even so, your body should be healing, and yet you remain like a wounded lion, filled with courage but helpless."

Memories flooded Mordred. "I do not resist the drinking of human blood. I drank blood while with the Templars. I drank it on my journey. I do not revile the drinking of blood when I am forced into a battle. But, the thought of taking a life, any life unknown to me that has not sought to do me harm, that is what I resist."

A hiss came from Kabil, sounding like a hundred cobras. It echoed off the walls and ceiling of the great tomb. "You must cast out this revulsion. You must feed on humans. There is no way around this."

"No."

Kabil shrugged. "Very well, then you will remain, rotting, but alive, like now. When you have been injured or when you fall ill, the failings of your human side, you will continue to feel every bit of pain. You will be immobilized and helpless for weeks or months, for however long it takes your vampyre self to recover. It will in time heal on its own, but without blood you leave yourself vulnerable to those wishing to harm you. It is not a good path to choose."

He disappeared from view again, and Mordred wondered if he'd left. He was not disappointed when from across the room he heard the sound of wood creaking, then something being dragged across the floor.

Kabil appeared, kneeling this time.

"In tasting your blood, I have learned of the man you will become. You are indeed the champion of mankind, but that is not the reason why I will help you."

"What is the reason?" Mordred asked.

"It's what I tasted within you. Within your being. You are a half-born now, and there is a darkness that should be growing within you from Vlad's kiss, yet you provided me with the most wondrous feeling that I have ever felt drinking another's blood. You are conflicted, Mordred, and that is to be expected, yet within you lurks something greater than even I, King of the Narangatti, and I am intrigued. I wish to see how this story ends."

Frowning, Mordred closed his eyes, attempting to block out the waves of nausea and pain rolling over him like a thick black fog.

"What is it you fear, Mordred?"

"That I will become like you."

"Like me? Am I so horrible a creature that you would fear to be like me? I feed upon human blood just as you feed upon the flesh of other creatures. What is it about this that bothers you? There are humans who feed upon one another. Worse still, humans who kill each other and waste the lives they have been given. Am I worse than they are because I must live like this to survive? Am I evil though I seek to help others cross over to the afterlife?"

Mordred remained quiet as Kabil continued. "I have lived for centuries, Mordred, literally hundreds of thousands of years and I have seen many races come and go. In the time of the pharaohs I was revered as a god because I brought peace to those in death. I embalmed and mummified those brought to me, treating each offering like a king or queen. I brought a measure of comfort to those who loved the dead. Now, I sit here in this tomb, a king of nothing and no one. Yet in my lifetime I never knowingly killed without reason. Never for power or vanity, or even for money."

Kabil's eyes shifted to Mordred once again, and Mordred felt Kabil rampaging in his mind, searching for evidence that his words were ringing true.

"Get out of my head!" Mordred snarled. There was much to the words Kabil spoke. Much he had to admit made perfect sense, but it had simply never been phrased in a way Mordred could understand. It left him in turmoil.

He did not want to become a dark thing, a soul stealer. Yet, if what Kabil said were true, it upset Mordred's delicate measure of right and wrong. Was Kabil guiltier for having sought to live? Was Mordred then not the evil one already for taking lives in the name of wealth and for causes he did not believe in? Mordred groaned.

" 'Tis not so hard to see, Mordred. Even in your vampyre youth you possess a great mind. Do not waste valuable time debating your new lot in life. Vlad will take advantage of your weakness, of your doubts, and your refusal to accept your fate as a half-born. Mordred, you cannot go back to the way things were, as much as you would wish it otherwise."

Mordred heard noises near his head. The sound of flesh tearing and a suckling sound.

"Do not drink from me again!" Mordred commanded, feeling in some way violated by the knowledge that Kabil knew things about him even he had yet to learn.

Laughter mocked him, and for a moment Mordred wished he could move his arms just enough to throttle Kabil.

"I am not drinking from you. Once was enough. Your blood is too powerful to taste more than once. Here, you must feed."

Kabil brought a golden chalice encrusted with multi-colored jewels to Mordred's lips, as he lifted Mordred's head gently with his other hand.

Mordred turned away.

"Mordred, you must drink. Drinking will not turn you into a creature like me. It will only strengthen you and allow you to heal more swiftly. You cannot simply lie here when the future of the world is waiting for your next move."

Wincing, Mordred felt a wave of sadness wash over him. Defeated, he opened his mouth and like a child, swallowed the contents of the goblet.

Immediately warmth spread, taking the pain and pushing it to the far corners of his body.

Mordred heard his heartbeat and a pounding in his ears, his own blood surging and rushing within him like the mighty Nile outside.

A ripple of something soothing started at his toes and worked its way upward. It sounded like water bubbling.

Opening his eyes, he stared back at Kabil, who appeared pleased with his efforts. Kabil smiled, revealing his long, wicked teeth.

It was, for a moment, as if Mordred were drifting high above his own body. He watched as it pulsated, coming back to life. Detached, he floated, his spirit free for a moment from the burden of his future.

It was a euphoria he had never felt. Better than being drunk, better than having sex, better than breathing or being alive. The feeling raced through him, and he was addicted.

Mordred heard a voice that didn't sound as if it had spilled from his lips. A chill raced up his spine, as he slowly comprehended the meaning.

"More."

† † †

In the days that followed, beneath the drifting sands of Egypt, deep within the inner sanctum of the Beautiful House, Mordred learned to drink human blood. It was the beginning of acceptance of his fate. The beginning of accepting what would be asked of him in the days and years to come.

True to Kabil's word, after drinking his fill of the blood his host provided, his body healed quickly. He recovered from his fall as if he had never been injured.

Within the Great Pyramid, Kabil took immense delight in revealing the mysteries of the Funerary Cult of the Pharisees to Mordred. Inside the stone embrace of the enormous tomb were literally hundreds of ornate coffins, or sarcophagi, lining the walls of nearly every room.

Inside each was a perfectly preserved human being

wrapped tightly in linen bandages. Kabil explained the first step in the mummification process was the removal of the bodily fluids, the blood, of course, being what the Narangatti took for themselves.

Then each of the important organs was removed, dried in linen, and placed in richly decorated canopic jars. The Egyptians believed any part of the body could be used against the deceased person in a spell. Therefore, the jars were placed inside the sarcophagus alongside the body.

Intricate, ancient spells were painted or engraved on the sarcophagi, the jars, and even the tombs, to protect the deceased from ill will or evil magic.

"This one here is asking for the goddess Nut to welcome the person into the afterlife. And this one," Kabil pointed to another beautiful coffin, "wishes the moon god Thoth to help the person cross the waters that separate the earth and sky."

Stopping before a tiny gilded sarcophagus, Mordred asked, "Is this for a child?"

Kabil gently lifted the lid, revealing the contents. Wrapped in linen lay a mummy, but it had the head of a cat. "The Egyptians believed their cats were sacred animals. They mummified them just as they did themselves. Not too far from here there is an entire necropolis containing only the tombs of cats."

Standing near the tiny coffin was a large bronze statue of a female form with the head of a cat. Several tiny bronze kittens flanked her feet.

"That is Bastet, the cat goddess. She was the daughter of Ra, the sun god. Many believed she was the mother of kings. And that box over there holds the bodies of four falcons, all mummified."

"Were these their pets then?"

"Most definitely," came Kabil's reply.

They drifted from one large room to another in an endless labyrinth of sandstone chambers. Secret doors and hidden passageways were all revealed. And within each lay a cache, each greater in size than the one before.

Kabil spoke the names of the gods aloud, his voice echoing off the stones. Mordred almost expected the lids of the coffins to rise, and the mummies to come forth at his incantation.

"These are the gods and goddesses you must be aware of. Anubis, Lord of the Necropolis, and Nephthys, protector of the dead. Osiris, god of eternal life after death. Ra, god of the sun and light, and Thoth, Master of Spells. Know these names. Keep them within your soul. They will aid you on your journeys."

Mordred couldn't help but scoff. "How can gods from a belief system that is not my own come to my aid?"

Smiling, Kabil reached out to touch a square pillar painted gold. He stroked it lovingly, looking off into some vast place within his mind. "You are so very young, pup. It doesn't matter that you do not believe in them. They believe in you. They slumber, waiting for the time when you will need them most. Do not make light of the gift I am giving you. You will, when you have learned all I have to teach you, have the power to summon gods."

That silenced Mordred completely.

"Yes, Mordred, know the extent of the power you wield. It is not a plaything, something to be taken lightly. You cannot control the gods, merely summon them. Getting them to do your bidding, whatever that may be, will be up to the strength of your own soul. If you are judged worthy, they will aid you. If not, you will be destroyed and your heart will be fed to the great beast of the underworld, Ammut. And you will never return."

† † †

The lessons continued, until Mordred lost all track of time. He had no idea how many days, or months, he had remained beneath the Great Pyramid, yet he looked forward to his studies with Kabil.

This thing, this creature of the night, was an endless source of wisdom. He was patient, and at times Mordred even felt compassion emanating from the beast.

The king was highly intelligent, which made Mordred look inward again. Had he met this thing at another time and place in his life, he most likely would have sought to destroy it. Yet in his current predicament Mordred was beginning to learn yet another in a long line of lessons: appearances could be most deceiving.

With grudging respect over time, Mordred became an apt pupil. He disputed less and less what was being taught to him and opened his inner mind, welcoming new thoughts, ideas, and feelings.

Each segment of his enlightenment was filled with

some new wonder, reasoning that defied human logic. Yet it remained all the same whether Mordred chose to accept it or not.

The pair wandered throughout the massive complex. They journeyed underground through a series of tunnels, each ornately carved and gilded. The palace of the dead appeared to go on forever.

They passed through rooms with beautifully carved thrones and furniture fit for kings and gods. Halls of limestone were decorated with endless images of daily life, the life after death, and countless other moving scenes, each painting detailed so intricately, though it was ancient, created by a hand long ago, it throbbed with vibrancy and life.

Kabil called the strange symbols hieroglyphics. These were etched neatly in continuous rows upon floors, ceilings, walls, and furniture. Nearly every inch that wasn't covered with a painting held these marks. It was the language of the Egyptians.

Upon the pillars carved to resemble papyri and sweeping palms, Mordred began to learn the secrets of the death culture of the pharaohs.

He let his hands trace the scrolling patterns and designs. Touching a lotus leaf carved into the curved column, Mordred listened as Kabil spoke again, sharing his wisdom of the people he so obviously respected.

"The lotus is a symbol that appears frequently in Egyptian texts. It represents the rebirth of the soul in the afterlife. The ankh is the 'key of life' sign."

Mordred brought his hand to each glyph, touching it as if he might feel the energy in the symbol. As soon as a word was stated, it was committed to memory and when next Kabil tested Mordred in the chamber with a thousand decorated columns, Mordred spoke of what he had learned.

"That is the symbol for protection and that for joy," he offered as Kabil observed. "This is for beauty and this one here," Mordred said, as he touched the carving, "stands for Ra, the sun god."

Standing before the giant pillars of language, a flash of recognition passed through Mordred.

Knowing his thoughts intimately, Kabil nodded. "Yes, yes, you have seen some of these before."

Kabil spoke the truth. Many of the images were also found on the shield, armor, and sword given to him by the Templars.

Time marched slowly forward as Kabil taught Mordred about the lives of the pharaohs and their culture. He learned of their reverence for birth and death, their belief that as above, so below. Dying was not the end of life, but only the next step.

"How is it you still have bodies to feed upon?" Mordred asked, suddenly concerned because the bodies in the sarcophagi were not exactly fresh. Yet, Kabil appeared to have a ready supply of blood.

Again proving himself a puzzle, Mordred learned that Kabil preferred to drink his blood from what he called a magical cup. It was, in fact, a large golden goblet etched with another form of writing that the king told him was called hieratic script, and translated into the Cup of the Undead.

Teacher studied student with fathomless black eyes,

revealing no expression. Most times Kabil appeared indifferent and unreadable.

"There are many who, even today, believe in the ways of old. They bring the bodies of their loved ones to the pyramid. There is an opening above with a steep decline, the same one you and your companion discovered, that they push the deceased through. Then I begin the process of embalming and drain the blood. If there is too long a span between offerings, I seek out those in the nearby towns."

Mordred narrowed his eyes. "You call them offerings?"

"Yes, many believed that I and the other vampyres were the closest thing to gods."

"How long have you existed, Kabil? And what happened to the others?"

"By others do you mean other kings?"

Confused, Mordred asked, "You mean there are more like you?"

"No, there is only one king of the Narangatti and I am he. But there are other kings. Each one the same, but different from me. Each one a vampyre. You, young pup, will need the help of them all to succeed in saving the human race, and not all of them will wish to be as gracious to a half-born.

"I cannot remember a time when I wasn't walking upon this earth. At first, I was with the others and we were of one family. We could travel anywhere and feed whenever we liked. The earth was full of those less than us, but then came a great flood, and we were separated."

Mordred was going to ask another question, but Kabil snatched it from his mind. "How many, you ask?

There are five kings. Each resides in his own kingdom, far from here. I have not seen the others since the time of creation, but every now and again I can sense their presence in the world. They live on, though I wonder if they are alone as I am."

They had come back to the vast chamber with the lake and throne. Mordred sat on the steps leading to the water. Kabil moved to the ornate piece of furniture, settling his small form on the gilded seat.

"What of the other Narangatti?"

An expression that mimicked sadness swept across the vampyre king's face. "They were all my children, but in time they were not strong enough to survive the evils that men do. Each brought about his own destruction by alerting humans to their presence in the outside world. Long after the Egyptians these tombs lay dormant, but then strangers from other lands came and they did not see the value in us that the Egyptians did. I am now all there will ever be of the Narangatti."

Uncomfortable with the way Kabil looked, Mordred changed the subject. "Can Vlad sense you like you sense the others? Can he seek you out?"

The last statement elicited a laugh from Kabil.

"The Evil One has many names. Your Templars and your church people call him Vlad, but we know him by another name. The Egyptians would call him Seth. Vlad is not even a half-born but something far worse. He has no human feelings, and he does not concern himself with existing merely for the purpose for which he was brought forth. As his power grows, so does his lust for conquering the race that conjured him."

"He is not a true vampyre?"

"Not at all. He is not a creature like me, or even the other kings."

"What is he then?"

"The product of man's greed. He is the resurrected soul of one who should have never been brought back to life. You will fight the battle of your life when you fight him."

A heavy weight that had pressed on Mordred seemed to have lightened since he came to spend time with Kabil. It had made him think there was a chance that he could do what was asked of him. Now his thoughts darkened once again.

"How can I possibly win? I have just been turned into a vampyre while Seth, Vlad, whatever you call him, is as old as time."

"Yes, there is the problem of your being a half-born and not a full-blood. But then a full-blood would never champion the cause of mortals," Kabil reminded him.

"I can't defeat him myself, can I?"

"You must learn quickly all the traits and tricks of our race. I am afraid even I do not possess all the knowledge to help you, but perhaps my brothers do. And even with their wisdom, all you learn may not prove to be enough. That is why I have gifted you with the power to summon the gods. You will very likely require their help."

Mordred sat silent, watching the flames of the torches cast long shadows on the gilded walls. A feeling of unrest had begun to nag at him, making him anxious about something he could not comprehend. He couldn't shake the feeling that he needed to continue his journey, but where would he go?

With Kabil's help, perhaps he could find the other kings. Maybe with their help he could defeat Vlad.

"You do not know where the other kings live. How will I be able to find them?"

"You can't, without first seeking *The Book of the Undead*. It was taken from this corner of the world by your friends the Templars, but it no longer resides within this realm."

"Do you know where it is?"

"Back where you came from."

Standing, Mordred brushed the dust from his bare legs. He listened to the scurrying sound of hundreds of scarab beetles as they disappeared from his shadow. While he didn't particularly care for the creatures, he'd learned the Egyptians revered them.

Mordred watched with his keen vision as the tiny black forms covered the darkened corners of the tomb, waiting for the stillness to return.

"You speak in riddles again, Kabil. What do you mean *The Book of the Undead* is back the way I came? It is not at the temple?"

Shaking his bald head, Kabil shifted on the rock he perched on.

"You must go back the way you came. Back to your beginning, before you journeyed here. There is a place in your homeland where the book is hidden from the view of both mortals, and your Vlad."

Dawning settled over Mordred like the rays of a sun he couldn't see. "Do you mean Scotland?"

Kabil shrugged his shoulders. "I can only hear it whispering now and then. It tells me you are to come to it. I have no doubt you will hear it too, when you get closer."

Glancing around the confines of what had become his home, Mordred queried the vampyre king one more time. "What now?"

"Leave here, Mordred Soulis. I have taught you what you need to know for a time. Go forth and find the book."

"Will you not come with me?" Mordred could scarcely believe he was asking a vampyre to accompany him. How dramatically his life had changed.

"Not this time. You will be back for me, and then we shall see if you have learned enough for me to journey with you."

"But there is still so much I need to learn," Mordred pleaded.

"That is the truth of the matter, but the time has come for you to find the book. This is the next step on your quest."

The Atlantic Ocean

Orkney Islands

NORWAY

SWEDEN

SCOTLAND

Edinburgh
(Rosalyn Chapel)

IRELAND

ENGLAND

HOLY

ROMAN

EMPIRE

FRANCE

KINGDOM
OF
ALMORAVIDS

Sicily

NOMADIC
TRIBES

The
Mediterranean
Sea

1147 AD

THE JOURNEY OF
MORORED SOULIS
TOWARD THE
BOOK OF THE DEAD

Chapter Eighteen

Mordred said goodbye to the wise and prophetic Kabil, King of the Narangatti, and began his journey back to Scotland with no clear idea as to how he would get there or where to look for the fabled tome. *The Book of the Undead* could be hidden in a thousand places, and Mordred doubted that without divine intervention he'd be able to determine its location alone. After all, he had failed miserably in learning how to fly. He failed in the drinking of human blood, first by not being able to stomach it then by not being able to control himself when he finally tasted it.

He had never faced a problem with his confidence until now. There had never been any time to question one's skill with a sword, when the sword was what one lived or died by. Yet Mordred began to wonder if indeed he was the right choice. Who claimed him the savior of mankind and by what right? Why hadn't he been consulted in this great and grand scheme?

Anger filled every cell in his body. Tense and frustrated, he railed silently against destiny. What the hell was fate?

In the solemnity of his thoughts came another, even darker one, swooping down on him like a hungry raven. It was a great, black fear, opaque and nearly suffocating, that encircled his heart. It nearly stole the breath from his body in its wickedness. Mordred realized that between Egypt and Scotland he would need to feed. It meant actually taking blood from a human.

Shivers coursed through him as his human-self protested.

There was, of course, no choice, as Kabil had pointed out so clearly beneath the Great Pyramid. If Mordred did not quench the damnable thirst that stained his soul and satiated his never-ending hunger, he would become weaker. He would become an easy target for the creature known as Vlad.

If there was one thing Mordred detested more than his vampyre-self, or the possible failure of his quest, it was Vlad and what he demanded of Mordred.

Kabil had done well to reassure Mordred that vampyres were neither good nor evil. They were merely another species that once inhabited the earth. Vampyres fed upon humans, not with malevolence, but from instinct like any other animal.

Choosing his route carefully, Mordred decided that rather than head back the way he had come, he would cross the Mediterranean Sea by boat. First to Sicily, then on to Italy. From there he planned to head through France. He'd cross the channel and land in England.

If he were lucky, he would be able to avoid being detected while on English soil. There was much animosity between Scotland and England, and it grew by the day. It would not do to be caught alone in enemy territory.

He had no idea how long the journey would take, only that he had no choice but to begin. Once in Scotland, he prayed he could locate *The Book of the Undead*, and with it in hand perhaps glean an indication of what his next course of action should be.

The thought of going home to the decrepit castle he had inherited after all the years of his absence was bittersweet. He would not come back to a warrior's homecoming. Too much had changed. But how would he begin to explain to the people who still lived under the protection of the Soulis clan that he could no longer be their laird? How could he tell them they were better off fearing him? That he could be their greatest adversary? How indeed.

Mordred believed wholeheartedly that he would serve his purpose better if he distanced himself from others. He certainly didn't intend to begin feeding upon his own clan. No, he'd have to search for something else. Perhaps the English? Now there was an oddly pleasing thought.

Given some time, he might actually help his country defeat the dogs who constantly tried to assert their authority over a land that would not bow to English rule. He could use his newfound self to exterminate those who sought to wrench Scotland from its rightful heirs. None would even know what to make of the shadow of destruction that would swoop down in deepest midnight to claim its victims.

Dwelling on his last train of thought, Mordred found his spirits buoyed. A new sense of purpose grew. He adjusted the burden within him so as to not weigh so heavily upon his soul for the time being.

Alone, Mordred left the Great Pyramid and headed down the Nile Delta of Lower Egypt. He stayed on the west shore, but in the distance he could see the ancient city of Tanis. Longing pierced him deeply when he thought of Markus and Jakob. How could he possibly do this alone?

Moving under the cover of night and keeping well out of sight of humans, Mordred became very much a shadow. He remained wary at all times, using his keen senses to guide him away from danger.

He was well aware that Vlad could, at any moment, appear to challenge him and, quite possibly, destroy him. He traveled with a flask of blood Kabil had given him, and sipped from it sparingly, forcing himself to taste only a few drops at a time. It was his inhuman strength that kept him from gorging.

Mordred never rested, though during the daylight and around large populations of people, he hid in caves and beneath the dunes, waiting for the time to resume his travels unnoticed.

It was a daunting task to travel so far and never truly rest. Several times during his journey he thought of shifting his form, but always his fear of allowing his vampyre-self to take full control outweighed his growing desire to get home.

It was a quiet insanity, left alone with his thoughts each day. No advice, no encouragement, just his own spirit sometimes challenging him to continue, sometimes chiding him to end this madness.

And always there remained the constancy of his need for human blood.

† † †

One evening, after leaving a small Templar chapel that had fallen into ruin, Mordred, clad in a simple black tunic, crossed yet another stretch of sand dunes. He knew he was close to the Mediterranean. He could smell the salty air and the temperature became cooler. A moist breeze wafted over the landscape, creating a dewy stillness.

Coming to the top of a particularly high mount, Mordred's ears warned him of something moving below. It was the low growl of a great predator. Then he heard the sound of labored breathing. He had stumbled upon a death dance, the time a predator circled its prey.

With his keen sight he searched the surrounding area and found a small oasis. Several sets of wicked yellow eyes stared back at him, blinking in the darkness.

The moon shone high and full, and though he could not make out the kind of creatures lurking in the greenery, their malevolent stares shocked him in their intensity. Clearly he was not wanted here. The animals were angry at his intrusion.

As the things grew bolder, and with help from the

blazing light of the stars, Mordred made out their shapes. The color of their skin was almost white. Like ghosts they drifted slowly, purposefully, circling.

He heard a low, huffing growl. At first he thought he had stumbled on a pride of lions. But there was something altogether otherworldly about them. Mordred couldn't exactly place it, but the beasts didn't resemble anything he'd ever seen before.

Then he counted four animals and saw their heads and faces. Fierce, with long, sharp, glittering teeth, they hissed at him, warning him to go away.

Mordred realized he could understand their language in his mind.

"Leave us. This is not your fight," came a throaty growl.

"Yes, go away," said another. *"It is not your time for judgment."*

Then a third called out, *"Not yet, not yet."*

Speechless, Mordred noticed another dark thing, larger than the phantom beasts and obviously laboring to stay alert. He saw it was a horse, once a beautiful destrier now abandoned to the whims of the desert.

So far from its own home, it had no hope of survival. The horses that came from the crusaders were huge animals capable of bearing a fully armored knight. While this served them well in the northern climes of England and Scotland, here under the terrible heat and scorching sun, the animals became a liability.

The Saracens rode horses half the size of the warhorses. With smaller, light colored horses, the desert people were able to mount swift and deadly attacks.

The knights, with their mail and armor, were unable to muster an effective response. The only tactic that had worked for the Europeans was to mass together and present a solid wall of towering steel and horseflesh. When they rode shoulder to shoulder as one unit, marching slowly down upon their enemy's foot soldiers, they found themselves often successful. But, soon the enemy learned their maneuver, and before the knights could rally, the Saracens had cut groups from the main body of the army. They were then able to slay their dreaded enemies.

Mordred focused on the horse. He should not care what became of the animal. It was none of his concern, and the strange beings below had given him fair warning to stay out of the fight. Although, there wouldn't be much of a fight.

The animal's black skin had been abraded in places. Large patches of blistered flesh crisscrossed the beast's hide. Its massive head hung low as if resigned to its fate.

Mordred knew the animal would not make it through the night. Perhaps the predators would act as angels of mercy. It might well be the better thing than to have the horse die a miserable death from starvation and thirst.

Again, his thoughts were invaded by the things below. *"If you dare to remain, you shall suffer the consequences."*

In his mind, Mordred replied, *"I am not afraid of you. Who are you that you should tell me what to do?"*

A growl sounded closer than it should have if

The Beast of Burden

Mordred had been alert. *"We are the Ammut, and we have come to take this beast."*

Thinking of all he had been taught while in Kabil's presence, he remembered the Ammut were the creatures that ripped the heart out of those souls who were found untruthful or unrepentant.

"Why would you come for a horse?" Mordred asked, genuinely curious. He'd thought the monsters lurked in the fabled underworld of nightmares. He wasn't prepared to be greeted with them in the flesh. Yet as his human mind worked to deny their existence, his vampyre mind accepted them and wanted to know more. *"Where is the judge, Anubis, or do you now weigh hearts without your keeper?"*

There was a pause. Silence hung in the air.

"Human! What do you know of our world? This is not a horse but a Beast of Burden, and it is ours to do with as we wish."

The ugly things tightened their circle. Great ivory beasts with long yellow teeth that matched their yellow eyes. Mordred heard their growls and huffs as they communicated with one another.

Feeling a kinship with the horse, Mordred made a decision. He had come across another whose only crime was that it had lost its way. Mind made up, Mordred descended the hill.

The horse abruptly changed its behavior. Rearing, it struck out with its forelegs, in a move so swift and with such force the Ammut were knocked backward. Coming back down to four legs, the horse maneuvered and kicked again, this time with its hind legs.

Again hooves connected with the hide of a predator, and a yelp broke over the dunes.

Mordred was stunned to watch the horse. By all appearances, mere moments ago, it had appeared defeated and ready to die. Yet at the last possible moment it had determined to live.

The horse raised its great head proudly and reared once more, uttering a high-pitched whinny. It was challenging all comers. Lashing out again, the horse moved from beast to beast. As each approached, it kicked out first with front legs, then the back ones.

Mordred unsheathed the Blood Sword and held the hilt in both hands. He moved from behind to charge the rear of the Ammut. The hell things backed away from the wild display of hooves, gnashing teeth, and threatening sword. Slinking back into the nearby brush, they invaded Mordred's mind.

"Stupid human. One should never interfere with the business of the undead."

At that Mordred felt himself smile, and for the first time wasn't unhappy with his next choice of words.

"I am undead."

As if they had never been, the Ammut simply vanished.

Mordred approached the beast and whispered soothingly, watching as the animal's ears were first laid back against its neck, then as they swiveled back up in the direction of Mordred's voice.

The horse's head turned to him, one large brown eye focused clearly on him. It did not appear to be frightened of Mordred.

"Well, boy, it looks like you could use a friend, and so could I. Shall we form an alliance?"

Pulling a flask of water from his shoulder pack, Mordred cupped his hand and allowed some of the liquid to fill his hand. He brought it to the horse's muzzle. The horse drank greedily. Mordred had to repeat the process several times.

"Let's be on our way. If you can make the journey, we'll get shelter and food in the next village. Then we head to my homeland."

Mordred didn't care that he was speaking aloud to a horse. It felt good simply to hear his voice, and the animal didn't seem to mind. As Mordred walked away from the tiny oasis in the desert, he listened for a sound to indicate the horse followed him.

He didn't have to wait long. Without a bridle, halter, or even a rope to tie him to Mordred, the horse chose to follow him, and together they walked slowly under the guiding lights of a thousand stars through the desert toward their destiny.

† † †

During their journey Mordred stopped as often as he dared to rest his new companion. With care and feeding the horse quickly returned to its former glory. Its coat was glossy ebony, its mane grew long and full. It was the perfect horse for a warrior, and Mordred was happy he had found the animal.

Riding him, however, proved to be an entirely different matter. Mordred realized only after he'd landed on the ground several times that the animal had not been ridden in quite some time. Perhaps a victim of the First Crusade, it had somehow managed to survive in the inhospitable climate of this land.

Eventually, however, Mordred was able to mount the huge animal and ride without being thrown. He couldn't help feeling the horse had tested him, tried to determine if he was worthy of such a gift.

At some point on their trek, though he wasn't sure exactly when, Mordred earned the right to ride the horse.

Mordred found transport that would carry them across the Mediterranean Sea to the Kingdom of Sicily, then on to Italy. From there they rode north up the west coast, along the sea toward France.

The climate change was a welcome relief from the hot, dry desert and cold, biting wind that had plagued the mountains Mordred left behind. Now the evenings were filled with a salty sea breeze.

It seemed to Mordred to take more than a year to make the journey home. Truth be told he had lost complete track of time from the moment he'd fallen in the desert. It seemed an eternity ago.

But as he drew nearer to Scotland, something twisted and turned in him, urging him not to delay. Anxiety built, gnawing at his gut.

Mordred continued to travel only at night and bypassed populated areas. When he reached England, he took even greater care. While he did not appear to be a Scotsman, having given up his plaid long ago, he wanted to take no chances with the English soldiers.

It became especially important to conceal himself when he approached the border between England and Scotland. A border that for years kept changing, depending upon which side had been victorious in the latest round of battles.

One night as he picked his way carefully around lands belonging to the English, Mordred heard voices entirely too close for comfort, surprised he hadn't heard them before now. Worried, he realized the voices belonged to a battalion of English soldiers on patrol.

He was trapped. A castle lay to the right, and Mordred could not determine if its inhabitants would prove friend or foe. Behind him lay English territory; not an option. He would need to head straight through the men to continue his journey, or double back and go around, which would take days. Even then there was no guarantee he wouldn't run into others.

Cocking his head, Mordred chewed his lower lip. He'd never been afraid of confrontation, and this was not the time for timidity.

Mordred urged his horse forward, and knowing he'd have to fight his way into Scotland, he quickly assessed the terrain. He didn't want to start a battle among the dense trees and undergrowth, as he wouldn't have room to fully execute his maneuvers.

Dismounting, Mordred approached the men. Six stood around the campfire, horses tethered nearby. Though they were only wearing mail, each man was equipped with a short sword. Mordred knew his weapons well and determined the blades had been created for thrusting rather than cutting. It meant that even if he had been wearing his armor instead of just mail, he would still need to be wary. The swords could be forcibly jabbed between plates and rings of mail, puncturing metal and flesh alike.

The swords also gave away the level of expertise of the soldiers. Mordred made a wager with himself that the men were not well trained, and instead were equipped with a weapon that even the most inept swordsman could utilize with deadly result.

The assumption, however, still didn't mean the fight would go in Mordred's favor. There was always a chance that reinforcements would arrive. He would need to be quick.

Charging into the camp with a howl, Mordred used the element of surprise to his advantage. Sword in hand, black robes flying, he imagined he looked quite the specter of death.

The weapon of choice for Mordred was a specially designed sword that did duty as both a slashing and a thrusting weapon. This bastard sword could be wielded using one or both hands and had sharp edges on both sides of the blade. The sword also had a cut in the blade that could trap an attacker's weapon and break it.

The point was deadly and sharpened so that with enough force, it could pierce both armor and mail. Mordred grasped the sword with both hands and began swinging. He watched as each man drew his weapon.

The men circled Mordred, trying to get behind him to attack. They looked for a sign of weakness in the wild man who had just burst through the trees with a howl.

Fluidly, like the most graceful of dancers, Mordred moved among his enemies, slashing and cutting. He conserved energy by measuring each move he made with the effectiveness of one who'd seen countless battles.

It wasn't until Mordred drew first blood that he realized he'd unleashed something wicked in himself. The bloodlust that accompanied a seasoned warrior in those moments of life and death crashed headlong into the vampyre within. They merged into an unmatched storm of steel.

Flesh melted from bone as his blade found its home in the bodies of two of the men. Their compatriots jumped back with the realization that they were out-skilled by this stranger, but there was nowhere to run.

Quicker than the blink of an eye, Mordred rushed them in turn, parrying and thrusting, slashing and cutting, until he found his marks. The agonized sounds of men screaming brought the still night to life.

Mordred heard a death rattle. The first two were gone, but he fought on. With renewed vigor, his attackers came at him, each man bearing injury yet determined to defend their lives. They struck out blindly.

Baiting them, allowing them to get too close, Mordred reached and pierced one man straight through his heart. The spray of crimson was more than he could take. He felt his jaw begin to stretch and grow to accommodate the fangs that even now lengthened to deadly points.

Just as he was about to take the last two men, Mordred heard the pounding of hooves on the ground signaling the arrival of more men. Within seconds he was surrounded by at least twenty more English soldiers. This time those that broke through the clearing were heavily armored and armed.

Mordred took a blow to his left arm, and dropped to his knees. It wasn't the cut of the sword that momentarily caused him to falter, however, but the coming change. The men in front of him took it as a sign he weakened.

"Kill the bastard, now!" came a shout from behind.

"Well, this'll be like sticking a pig, now won't it?" another said.

Overconfident in their numbers, assuming there was no escape for the strangely outfitted intruder, the soldiers crowded him.

One brave soul took no chances to allow Mordred to catch his breath, but instead sheathed his sword in Mordred's mail covered chest. The blade skewered him.

There was a haze of red, and Mordred could not determine whether it was his own blood or that which spilled from others. His nostrils flared at the tangy scent. He fell forward with the sword sticking out of his back, and heard the men jeering and cheering their victory.

It would, of course, be short lived. In a brief moment of blackness, his vampyre-self took protective control.

The men staring down at Mordred watched in horror as his body came alive again with a mighty growl.

"He was dead. I-I-I killed him, I did."

"Well, you didn't because he's obviously not dead."

"Hey, William, there's something wrong, look at his . . . Oh, God! He's a vampyre!"

Mordred reached up and with one hand, sword now lying useless upon the ground, grabbed the front of the man's mail-covered gambeson and yanked him forward. Without ceremony, he bit down on the soldier's neck. He sought the warm liquid that would sooth his tormented soul. Blood spurted from the wound and spilled down Mordred's lips. He threw the dead man away and, like a snake, struck another.

They couldn't run fast enough, or far enough. Mordred flew through the air, great black cape billowing behind him. He captured every man and dispatched him with his fangs.

Ripping and tearing flesh, breaking bones, Mordred was no longer a thinking being. He had become a predator devouring his prey.

Each man tasted slightly different. Mordred drank as much as he could hold from those with bad blood. He found it bitter and distasteful, though sustaining. Images of evil deeds washed over him, making him shudder and twitch.

There was only one among the soldiers whose blood brought Mordred to the heights of ecstasy claimed by Kabil. It was pure, and filled Mordred with a brilliant light, and burning warmth.

He drank his fill. When he had taken the lives of every last Englishman, he slumped against a tree trunk, heady from the sheer exhilaration coursing through him, and he closed his eyes.

There was no feeling on earth like that of stealing souls. In the darkness of the forest, quiet descended. Mordred, bloated with his feed, rested.

Somewhere in the satiated recesses of his mind, he thought he heard the sound of laughter.

CHAPTER NINETEEN

CHAPTER NINETEEN

The first fingers of dawn broke through the forest's heavy overgrowth. The sun's rays filtered down to the moss-covered ground in misty golden light.

Mordred's eyes opened, and for a moment he was confused. Then the memories of the night just past came flooding back. He rose and gazed about him.

The bodies of the soldiers lay haphazardly strewn about the clearing. It was enough to remind Mordred of the destructive force he had wielded, and of the blood on which he had gorged.

A churning began in his stomach. Broken and distorted images raced through his mind. Mordred leaned over and vomited. Again, and again, his stomach protested his last meal until Mordred knelt with the force of his dry heaving.

Wiping his mouth on a black sleeve, Mordred saw the red vomit, evidence that he hadn't dreamed the whole vicious scene. He pushed a gloved hand through the length of his tangled hair, cursing when he encountered the snarls. He must look the very image of a madman.

Amazingly, Mordred bore no sign of having been in a fight to the death. There was only the hole in his mail, which he felt with his hand. His body felt alive, better than it had in a long time.

In fact, as he got back to his feet, Mordred watched a tiny ray of light touch his hand. He removed his glove, anxious to feel the sun's warmth, but felt nothing. A small barb of disappointment buried itself deep in his heart.

Kabil had said that as Mordred fed more often, his body and his vampyre powers would become stronger, while his human senses would lessen.

Putting his glove back on, Mordred shoved away from the tree and turned around. In a few moments he determined he was completely alone, surrounded only by the bodies of the dead English soldiers. Mordred picked up his sword and began the gruesome task of beheading each man. He had been told to do so with every human he bit, ensuring the victim would not return as a revenant.

Both Kabil and Jakob had explained to him the importance of this act. Vlad needed no more troops. Sure he'd covered his tracks, Mordred whistled for his black stallion. He mounted and continued his journey northward toward his home. Keeping deep within the forest he rode hard, as if the very demons from Hell chased him.

† † †

Mordred sailed across the churning waters of the North Sea with his horse as his companion. As he drew closer to Orkney and his home, the anxiety that had plagued him grew stronger. It twisted in his intestines with such intensity he thought for a moment he was physically sick.

As dusk settled over the rolling green hills of his island domain, Mordred's gaze sighted something beyond the next rise. A thick, dark cloud hovered low, nearly obscuring the distant foothills.

A prickling sensation raced down Mordred's spine. The pall being cast over the hills was not from a storm.

Suddenly, and with sinking dread, he realized he was looking at a huge plume of smoke from a burning fire. The flames were coming from the direction of his castle. His home!

Mordred put his spurs to his horse, and they sped toward their final destination. Covering the distance that separated him from his birthright, Castle Soulis, he paid no heed to the breakneck speed or the fallen logs they jumped over. Ducking to avoid low hanging tree limbs, Mordred focused only on the vision growing before him. He took the last hill at a headlong gallop and reined his mount in abruptly.

The entire place was aflame. A massive inferno greedily fed off the castle and the land surrounding it. Mordred couldn't see any part of the fortress that didn't spew streaks of orange and yellow fire.

As if the image of the destruction of his castle wasn't enough to bring him to his knees, Mordred picked up the smell of death lying low and heavy on the air. It settled around him like an invisible fog.

He brought his gaze down and even from this distance

he could see hundreds of bodies littering his lands.

What had happened? Who dared to attack his clan? It couldn't be the English, Mordred knew, for he was too far north for them to care.

But if not the English, then who? The horror of the scene filled him with an overwhelming need for vengeance.

Mordred dismounted and walked closer to his burning castle. Everywhere around him people lay slaughtered like cattle, yet there was no evidence of a fight. There were no weapons, and the scene gave the impression his clan had been struck down where they stood, in total surprise.

It would have required a large army to cause this much damage and an army could not have surprised his people. Futhermore, guards patrolled the nearby shores and hills looking for rival clans and, on the rare chance, English. Surely an alarm would have been raised if an army had been responsible.

Mordred quickly checked off in his mind the neighboring clans. Many were too small to begin to pose the slightest threat. The few that did consider the Soulis clan their enemy could not have mustered the might of an army. Who could have done this?

It wasn't until Mordred nearly tripped over one of the bodies that the answer slammed into his gut. There, under the glow of the burning castle, Mordred made out two neat puncture wounds.

As he stumbled in his grief stricken haze, the scene was repeated again and again. Every body had the same familiar wounds. Some were missing their throats entirely.

Mordred felt his heart grow cold as one name came forth through his pain. Vlad!

† † †

Night passed into day, and back to night again. Still the castle burned like a funeral pyre as Mordred worked. Severing heads from bodies, Mordred would not rest until every single fallen man, woman, and child was assured a final rest.

He could not risk any of his people returning to life. He knew it was exactly what Vlad had intended.

With his father dead long before and Mordred acting as laird from afar, he was relieved to know that although the destruction of his clan was a harsh reality, there had been no loved ones to suffer at the cruel hands of Vlad's terror.

If he had been seeking to wound Mordred more deeply, he had not succeeded, though the fires of vengeance burned bright as he continued the ghastly task of beheading the dead.

He had long since stripped to his breeches, and his skin was covered in blood. It clung to him as a reminder of what it all meant.

Several times while performing his hideous work, Mordred felt himself changing, but he fought it with every ounce of his being. He would not feed on his own people. Never!

As Mordred approached what he hoped was the last of the bodies near the inner bailey, he heard a sound. It was the beating of a heart. Someone was still alive.

Dugald Trapped

Had a revenant come to life? How would he know? He feared to kill an innocent. Yet, how could he allow one of Vlad's creations to live?

Searching the area, Mordred's gaze came to rest on a body beneath the fallen timber of what had been the great hall. It was a man, clad in an unfamiliar garment the color of deer skin.

Mordred approached cautiously, his hand gripping the hilt of his sword tightly. Tense and alert, he remained ready to strike.

Bending, Mordred touched the man on the cheek and stepped back when his eyes flew open. Golden eyes stared at him, imploring him to help.

Surveying the situation, Mordred bent to the timber and with his strength lifted the wooden beam from the man's body. But surely it would be better to put him out of his misery. No one could survive the crushing injury for long. There couldn't possibly be a bone in his body that wasn't broken beyond repair. Even if the man survived the breaks and shatters, there would most certainly be an infection that would kill him.

Returning to look upon the man once more, Mordred noticed he bore no bite marks. Mordred marveled that he had been spared.

Then he saw the gleaming silver cords of metal wrapped around the man's body. He'd been chained to the burning timber like a wild animal, and left to burn to death. Given the circumstances the man was lucky the timber had fallen on him. It had put out the fire when it crashed to the ground.

Golden eyes gazed at him, eyes filled with intelligence.

Mordred rethought his plan to send the man to his maker.

"*Please*, do not kill me."

"I would be doing you a favor," Mordred replied gruffly.

"No. I will heal. I just need time to rest."

The golden eyes closed once more, and this time they did not reopen. At first, Mordred thought perhaps the man had passed on, but the sound of his shallow breathing told him otherwise.

Whoever the man was, he certainly had a warrior's spirit.

Looking around Mordred determined that all but the north tower had been destroyed. Although the stairs were shattered as if from a siege weapon, and the door and rails missing, Mordred surmised the upper apartments would be untouched.

Breaking the chains with his sword, he bent and lifted the man gently in his arms. The injured man did not protest, as Mordred walked through the broken remains of his home to the tower.

Once inside, he discovered he was correct. Several chambers had come through the fire unscathed.

Mordred kicked open the door to one of the rooms with his booted foot and brought the man to the bed. There wasn't anything else he could do for him. He turned, striding to the hearth, and lit a fire. Glancing back at his new charge he shook his head.

† † †

"Are you trying to kill me?" the man asked suddenly. He sat covered in sweat at the edge of the bed.

"Why, are you with fever?" Mordred asked.

"Well, I will be if you don't put out that damned fire. No, I'm not with fever you idiot. I just don't need to be this close to a flame."

Narrowing his eyes, Mordred surveyed the figure on the bed. By all appearances he was human, but he acted strangely. Although he spoke to Mordred in the traditional Scottish brogue, there was something not quite right about his speech.

"Who are you and where are you from?"

The man tried to sit up, wincing at his efforts. He stopped and lay back on the pillows. "My name is Dugald, and I am from a land far from here, but that does not matter at this moment. I came here for you."

"For me? Please explain," Mordred said, seating himself in a large, overstuffed chair near the fire.

"I am supposed to help you, but I came too late."

"Really? From where I stand, it is I who helped *you*."

"Yes, and now I am bound to you until such a time as I can repay the debt."

Mordred couldn't help but laugh at the man's noble words.

"Sorry, but I won't be needing your help. You don't need to trouble yourself about my health and well-being either."

Dugald smiled at Mordred. "You are Mordred Soulis, yes?"

Fisting his hands, Mordred nodded as Dugald continued, "You are a vampyre, well, actually a half-born, but to us it's the same thing. You drink blood and steal souls."

"And you would know this . . . how?" Mordred wasn't sure if he should run the man through with his blade, or let him continue. He certainly didn't appear to pose a threat.

The man had a long, shaggy mane of dark blond hair and a bearded face. He was tall, though not as tall as Mordred, and leaner in frame, more wiry.

"Because I am one of the Wareckyn." At Mordred's look of confusion, Dugald continued, "I am a were-wolf."

"Oh, for the love of God, I've saved the life of a bloody beast?"

Smugly, Dugald nodded his head.

"Well, I don't need your kind of help. If I wanted a pet, I'd take in one of the hounds. You can heal yourself and be on your way."

Mordred pushed himself up and strode toward the door; then looked back at Dugald who surveyed him with strange golden eyes. Mordred had the uncanny feeling Dugald could see right through him, into his soul.

"Well, it seems you and I have a small problem. I can't leave. Our leader would have my head. Besides, now there's a debt I must repay."

Mordred shook his head. "No debt."

"That's not how it works."

"You won't go away?"

"Can't."

Mordred grimaced. "Are you sure? I can be very menacing, and I'd rather not."

Dugald smiled. It was a great beaming smile that lit his entire face. "I'm sure you can be, but then again so can I. So it will be a test of wills."

Mordred paused at the door. "You said you were sent here to help me? How did you know I would need help, and just what can you do?"

"Our leader knows things the rest of the Wareckyn don't. I cannot say exactly why he said to find you, only that I had to. I am to help you find the book you seek to accomplish your task."

The enormity of Dugald's words struck Mordred like the bolt of a crossbow. "*The Book of the Undead*? You know where it is?"

"See, you do need me."

"This is no time for trickery," Mordred threatened, frustrated by Dugald's annoyingly good nature.

"I'm not tricking you. I have a keen sense of smell and have been given the scent."

Mordred couldn't believe his luck. If what Dugald claimed was true, it would save Mordred countless days and months searching for the tome.

"There's one more thing," Dugald went on.

Raising an eyebrow, Mordred sent Dugald a warning glare.

"Could you please do something about this infernal heat? I'm roasting in here."

"Fine, I'll just put the fire out."

"Oh, and do you think you could bring me something to eat? I'm starving."

Both brows shot up at Dugald's last request. "I am not playing nursemaid to a dog."

When he extinguished the flames, Mordred returned to the door and paused. "And what exactly does someone of your kind feed on?"

"Unlike you, human food will do quite nicely."

The entire tower reverberated with the sound of the heavy oak door banging against the frame.

CHAPTER TWENTY

In the days following, Mordred and Dugald struck a truce. Mordred agreed to allow Dugald to help him find *The Book of the Undead*, only if Dugald agreed to leave immediately after the task was accomplished.

Although Dugald agreed, to Mordred it seemed just a wee bit too easy. He remained suspicious of the half-man, half-wolf.

It took Dugald several days to recover. In that time he informed Mordred that it was indeed Vlad, though Dugald did not know the name of the man, who had wreaked havoc upon Mordred's lands and people.

Mordred also learned that Vlad had known immediately what Dugald was. He had been bound to the timber with silver chains, the only thing that could hold a werewolf.

The Wareckyn, he discovered, could at times defeat vampyres, though Mordred had to remind Dugald that according to all he had learned so far about Vlad he wasn't considered a true vampyre.

When Dugald decided he'd spent enough time

recuperating, Mordred and the werewolf sailed back to Scotland. They began their journey heading south and west, to a place where Dugald swore they would find *The Book of the Undead*.

Mordred kept a watchful eye on his surroundings, not wishing to repeat the slaughter of English soldiers, or encounter Vlad.

As they neared Edinburgh, Mordred began to wonder if Dugald really knew where he was going. The Templars had taken the book. They had found it beneath the Temple Mount in Jerusalem, along with other yet-to-be revealed artifacts, and had taken it back to Scotland, or so Kabil had implied.

Jakob never mentioned the book. Mordred wondered if the Master Templar even knew of its existence, or if he'd just chosen to let Mordred learn of it through Kabil. Or, perhaps they did know, and had not wanted Mordred to find it. There were so many questions his head hurt on a continual basis.

Dugald kept to himself during most of the journey and only when they neared the city did he begin to banter with Mordred, speaking of his race and his own lot in life.

It was ironic that another man afflicted with shape-shifting abilities would come to his aid. While Mordred felt he'd been cursed by becoming a vampyre, Dugald seemed to accept his fate without difficulty.

"So, you have met the great Kabil, King of the Narangatti, and lived to tell the tale eh, Mordred?"

Mordred glanced at his companion, unsure what to say. He could not read Dugald's thoughts.

"Yes, I met him. He's the one who told me about the book."

"It's amazing he let you live."

"Why?"

"He's a powerful creature. The others, they come from his blood, his flesh. There are four other kings but each of them owes Kabil. He is the oldest and their beginning."

"How do you know this?"

"Our leader related the story to me. He once met Kabil. We Wareckyn have a strange, sometimes uneasy, relationship with you vampyres. We can understand your simply wanting to exist."

"I never wanted this."

Dugald looked at Mordred with his golden eyes. The empathy was evident.

"And I do not want your pity."

"Mordred, you should stop resisting what has been ordained. You cannot fight this, and you waste not only time, but your soul, lamenting your fate."

"Do you know where we are going?" Mordred asked, effectively changing the subject.

"Yes."

"Are you planning on telling me, or are you just going to let me figure it out on my own?"

Smiling, Dugald studied Mordred.

"I was told not to interfere unless needed. You are to discover the book's whereabouts on your own. I am only to lead you to the general area."

"How am I to find it?"

"Use your senses, Mordred. As the book's rightful

owner, you should feel it singing in your blood. It is calling for you. It wants you to find it."

Mordred stopped in his tracks, sensing the world around him. The creatures of the night were coming back to life after having hidden during daylight hours. The wings of owls and bats, and a host of other predators, swept over him, sounds of scurrying and burrowing as the prey animals found safety for the hours of darkness.

Nothing else came to mind. Mordred tested the air with his nose. Nothing. "I feel nothing. There's nothing speaking to me."

"You didn't try hard enough. Listen, not with your ears, but with your soul."

Once more, silence reigned. Then, Mordred heard something akin to the thrumming of a pulse; it matched the beating of his heart. It was so very faint, even the sound of a nearby stream gurgling and bubbling over rocks nearly drowned out the sound. But once Mordred heard it, his senses made a link.

Dugald remained silent, watching Mordred.

Leaving the woods, Mordred made his way across a hilltop to a place marked by large dolmans and cairns. Ancient standing stones rimmed a flat circle as if standing guard. Protecting something unseen.

The Celts had built a ring of stones upon the hill. Mordred felt the cross-currents of invisible power moving in all four directions. Below him was the stream he'd heard.

The place held a charge of something great, and it raced through Mordred.

The moon was full and high overhead. When Mordred turned to his companion, he was gone, knowing Mordred had found the right spot.

Mordred stilled even his own breathing and listened again for the soft singing of the book. It was as if the spirits of all those before him called out to him. Like tiny silvery fingers of mist, they wove themselves around him in a net of music, compelling him to move forward to one particular stone.

With his bare hands Mordred began to dig beneath the stone. He continued until he felt something hard and made of wood, and pulled a strange box out from its hiding place beneath the stone. Holding his breath, Mordred lifted the lid.

There, glowing eerily in the moonlight, was *The Book of the Undead*. The writing on the front was in the picture words of the Egyptians, and it took Mordred a moment to confirm he had the right book. When he opened the pages, sand and dust scattered.

The pages nearly crumbled under his touch. Mordred took great care turning them, wondering if he'd ever have time to read them all. For now, he merely wanted to know where to find the other vampyre kings. Mordred prayed they could help him defeat Vlad.

† † †

The Book of the Undead revealed the truth Kabil had spoken. He was, as he had claimed to be, the King of the Narangatti. According to the manuscript, it was said he had lived among the pyramids of Egypt.

The second race was the Finalache. Their king, Lir, lived in the north, above Scotland in the icy cold climes of the Norse.

The Wrathderi existed in jungles of another country far from Scotland, a place to the west across the great ocean.

Mordred learned about the Rasadoon, and Raidan the warrior king, who came from a line of fallen Samurai. Raidan lived somewhere far to the east on an island in the sea.

The last race mentioned was the Alinache. Mordred was shocked to learn that Yseult was a queen, not a king. She was, the book claimed, to be found somewhere off the coast of Ireland.

He lost track of time reading, and it wasn't until Dugald came loping up the hill that he realized dawn fast approached.

"I've found shelter nearby in an abandoned cottage if you'd like to be away from the sun," he offered as he neared. "I see you found what you came for."

"Yes. I mean, yes, I wish to go to the shelter though not because of the coming dawn. I don't wish us to be seen here. And, yes, I found the book."

"Now you can find the others?"

"Yes."

Mordred walked back in the direction from which Dugald had come. He didn't need to look back to know the canine-human followed him.

"Mordred?"

"Yes?"

"When do we leave?"

Mordred whirled his cape, which caught the night breeze and billowed out behind him like an enormous shadow. He narrowed his eyes and stared at Dugald. "*We* aren't leaving anywhere together. *I* will head to the north. *You* will go home, wherever that may be."

"Well, we're in luck then, because I'd be traveling in the same direction anyway to go home."

Anger surged in Mordred. He clenched his jaw. "Look, I saved your life by accident. You don't owe me anything. You did your job and led me to the book, and now I can head off on my own. I don't need an overgrown excuse for a lap dog nipping at my heels. Go home."

The last was said as if Mordred were actually speaking to a beast rather than a man, and he realized too late the barb had found its home. Hurt filled his golden eyes.

"Fine. You win. I'll find another way home. I'll be a disgrace to my people for failing in my purpose, but I'll explain that the great blood sucker was in a bad mood the day I offered my life to protect his."

For one moment Mordred felt something close to guilt, but it was quickly replaced by the urgency of finding the kings.

"Away then. Thank you for getting me this far."

Mordred only heard a gruff sound of acknowledgment before turning once more and heading toward the shelter he knew lay somewhere among the ancient trees. Feeling Dugald's spirit drifting further away in the opposite direction, Mordred was satisfied the werewolf and he had officially parted company.

It was better, he told himself, to operate alone. He would not wish to be responsible for anyone more than he already was. It was a burden to know that by his action or inaction he could determine the fate of the entire human race. That in itself was enough to bear.

Mordred spent the remainder of the night walking and convincing himself he'd done the right thing. He passed the shelter Dugald had found and continued. He'd need to find a boat to carry him to the Norse lands and began to think about his next move.

When dawn broke, Mordred did find a haven. Amid a stand of trees he saw the remains of a small chapel. Taking care to be sure it would be safe, Mordred picked out the familiar Green Man symbol and moved inside. It was a dwelling built by the Templars. He would find sanctuary and safety.

Mordred found his solace in the crypt. Among the remains of the dead, he finally allowed himself to rest. There would be time enough to read more of the book. For now he would simply let his mind and body be still.

† † †

It was the laughter buzzing in Mordred's ears like a thousand tiny gnats that woke him. Without taking more than a moment, Mordred knew to whom the voice belonged.

"I see you've found *The Book of the Undead*. Here I thought it was all a silly rumor. Let me see it."

Mordred rubbed his eyes, waiting for the time when his vision would sharpen.

"Give me the book, Mordred."

"No."

Vlad floated just above the ground outside the chapel, beckoning Mordred with an outstretched hand.

His mind crackled with Vlad's intrusion as he felt his thoughts being sifted and sorted, turned and taken. Vlad searched for something.

"If you will not give me the book, I will take its contents from your mind. You cannot hide from me, Mordred. You are me, as I am you. Everything you do, see, feel, read, learn becomes a part of me. As you grow stronger, so do I."

Wicked laughter filled the confines of the small building, shaking the very stones of its foundation.

"Get . . . out . . . of . . . my . . . head!" Mordred roared, pressing his hands to his temples.

The noise was unbearable and drove Mordred to the precipice of madness. He stormed from the protection of the chapel, into the open, not caring that the sun was at its zenith in the cloudless sky.

Anger fueled a storm of hostility in him.

Vlad did not miss the opportunity. "You dare to defy me?" he asked. "You are nothing but a whelp, a vampyre in his infancy. You are nothing. I made you and I can destroy you."

Mordred used his wrath to levitate himself level with Vlad. His feet left the ground, his cape dangling. Mordred undid the clasp and it fell to the moss covered ground. "You can try to destroy me."

"Fool, you think to battle with me? I am the master of darkness. I am the great evil. I am the unholy god!"

A hot wind blew from Vlad's mouth, and the leaves on the trees nearby withered from the heat, shriveling before Mordred's eyes.

Dust whirled around them like a great desert storm. The force of the gale nearly sent Mordred spinning out of control. He grappled with his sanity as he fought to remain a conscious part of his body.

Vlad ravaged his mind and violated his body. He remained, arms crossed, as if destroying Mordred was a trivial matter not worthy of his full attention.

Mordred's body contorted in painful positions, and before he could blink he was upside down.

"What will you do now, pup? If I drop you, you will break your neck and in the time it takes to heal, I will have taken the book from you."

Using every ounce of energy he could summon, Mordred shook his head. The motion vibrated through his entire body.

He spun himself back to an upright position.

"I see you are a quick study," Vlad said in a sinister voice. Raising an arm, he stretched his hand toward Mordred and began to blow.

The yellow and orange flame flickered once before taking hold in his palm.

"In your studies did your teachers explain that the only scars you can bear fully are those inflicted in battles with other vampyres?"

The fire flared in his palm and shot at Mordred. The flames greedily caught hold of Mordred's clothing and hair. In moments, the fire was consuming him. He was burning alive yet he uttered no sound.

Mordred forced his shattered thoughts together and visualized the cool morning mist, heavy with moisture. The fire died and his body disappeared into vapor.

"We can stop this anytime you like, Mordred. You only need to give me the book."

CHAPTER TWENTY-ONE

Mordred was in mist form preparing to retreat when Dugald's voice suddenly broke into his concentration. Returning to human form, he crashed to the ground.

"Mordred!"

"Ah," Vlad sneered, "so your wolf has decided to join us? Mordred, you are far too human. You pick up strays not worthy of a vampyre."

Mordred struggled to stand, watching Dugald shift from human form into that of his animal soul, the wolf.

The great golden beast, the largest Mordred had ever seen, lunged at Vlad. The vampyre changed into a cloud for a split second, then reappeared in human form some distance away.

Dugald snarled, pulling his lips back to reveal enormous canines. His ears flattened against the back of his shaggy head, and he focused on Vlad.

Mordred regained his composure and levitated. "Let's finish this then."

"As you wish, whelp."

But Mordred's attention was distracted a second

time when the Blood Sword floated toward him. Although he hadn't summoned the weapon, the glowing red blade came at him, gleaming tip pointed at his throat.

"What a lovely weapon, Mordred," Vlad purred. "Is this the sword that kills immortals? Let's be done with it."

The weapon shot forward. Mordred kept his eyes on the tip and flew above the danger. The sword halted and turned in his direction again. It sought him, and it was unshakable. Everywhere Mordred levitated, the sword followed, until he was left with no choice but to grab hold of it with his gloved hands. The sharp edge cut cleanly through the material, drawing blood. He ignored it.

Catapulting into the air, he reached behind the sword for the hilt and grabbed the weapon with both hands. It tried to turn back on him. In his head Mordred heard the voices of Jakob and Kabil urging him to fight. They instructed him to use the strength of his vampyre-self.

Concentrating, face contorting with the effort, Mordred forced his will into the weapon. Long teeth shot from his jaw, and he shifted into his vampyre-self with a bone-chilling scream. The sword became his. He flew at Vlad full force intending to skewer the man.

But the vampyre was too swift. He disappeared and reappeared faster than Mordred's senses could register. Laughing, he again laid siege to Mordred's mind. "You will not prevail, Mordred. They have sent you on a fool's errand. Join me and rule at my side."

Battle with Vlad

Focusing, Mordred conjured lightning. It raced through his thoughts and into his body, and his entire being tingled and glowed with magical energy. He watched Vlad jerk away from the force of his control. Mordred smiled, revealing his glistening teeth.

"What's wrong, Father?" Mordred inquired mildly. "Do I grow too strong for you?"

Vlad launched himself at Mordred and caught him by the throat. As pressure built, he lost his grip on the sword. He brought his hand to Vlad's neck. Grappling, each trying to destroy the other, they fell to the ground.

Managing to free one hand, Mordred summoned the Blood Sword and it came to him swiftly. But before he could run Vlad through, the vampyre snatched the blade away and turned it back on Mordred.

He broke his hold on Vlad and levitated, then flipped and turned in an effort to avoid the deadly sword. He had moved too quickly however and lost his concentration. Mordred fell and watched Vlad fly toward him, Blood Sword in hand.

Suddenly a blur of gold leapt across Mordred's field of vision; Dugald, still in wolf form. He caught Vlad's wrists in his mouth and bit down with all the strength of his mighty jaws, and Vlad dropped the blade. With a curse Vlad shook Dugald off and the wolf flew through the air, crashing into the stone chapel. A yelp, then silence.

Though still levitating, Vlad appeared visibly shaken. "You and I will meet again and when we do, if you have not joined me you will be destroyed."

Before Mordred could blink or savor his success,

Vlad's body exploded in a burst of light and disappeared. Wanting to be sure he hadn't been being tricked, Mordred searched the area but Vlad was gone and did not reappear. He turned his attention to Dugald, who hadn't moved since he'd hit the chapel. Bending he touched the beast's fur. One golden eye flickered open, then the other. Mordred watched Dugald transform from a wolf back into a man.

He made an effort to speak.

Mordred chuckled softly. "Why did you come back? I thought you said you were going home."

"I lied."

Mordred rolled his eyes and smiled. "I see that."

"I can't go back, Mordred. I'm an outcast, a wolf without a pack."

Mordred let out an exasperated sigh. "Enough for now. You can explain later. For now, just know that I'll let you remain with me."

Mordred watched Dugald close his eyes, relieved.

Vlad's accusations rang true, Mordred thought ruefully. He did have feelings and if they were the only things that kept him from slipping into darkness every time he let his vampyre-self take control, he'd be damned sure he'd continue to feel them.

But how would he be able to feel human emotions without caring too deeply? Knowing the power Vlad wielded and the destruction he could bring to those who stood with Mordred, how could he keep them safe?

† † †

Once Dugald recovered, they set out on their journey to find the Vampyre Kings. Mordred couldn't decide if the man-wolf was foolish, or courageous, wanting to help defeat Vlad. But it mattered little, he needed every ally.

Plans changed after Mordred read more of *The Book of the Undead,* and Dugald pointed out that it had been unusual for Kabil to take to Mordred so quickly. There was no guarantee the others would as well, and Mordred decided it might be wise to bring Kabil along to meet the other kings. He thought perhaps with one of their own, they might be more willing to cooperate.

"What makes you think these kings will care one wit about humans?" Dugald asked one evening as they headed back to Egypt.

"I can't be sure they will," Mordred replied. "I think we should bring Kabil with us."

"Again, what would he or any of the others gain from helping you? They aren't human. Why would they care?"

"Maybe they will care only to preserve themselves. Vampyres feed upon humans, and if we save the human race, we save the vampyres," Mordred replied.

Dugald cocked his head, reminding Mordred of a curious hound. "Why would Vlad want to exterminate mankind?"

"Who knows why. Your point is?"

Mordred focused on tinder he'd placed in a small dirt rut. Dugald sat on a log while he concentrated and held his hand out toward the twigs and dried grass. A spark shot from his palm and ignited a small fire.

"I still don't see why the vampyres would want to help you," Dugald continued. "They don't strike me as too concerned with anything but their own survival."

"It's exactly that concern that I'm betting on. I've been told I cannot defeat Vlad myself. I need their help." Mordred stood and took the Blood Sword from the scabbard on his back. He walked away from the flames, testing the weight of the sword. Then for several moments, he battled an imaginary foe. He sparred with the air for a while then he returned to the fire and spoke softly, a tone of defeat in his voice. "I do not understand all of what is written in *The Book of the Undead*. I am more confused than ever before. In fact, I need Kabil to help me decipher the meaning and gain the help of the others."

Dugald rested his head in his hands. "And if they won't help?"

"Then regardless of what Kabil and Jakob said, I'll have to find a way to defeat Vlad myself."

"Why do you do it, Mordred?" Dugald asked. "Why do you undertake this quest? You are undead. You aren't human any more, why do you care?"

"Aren't you still human?"

"That's different. I didn't die to become a werewolf, I was born to it."

Mordred nodded his understanding. "That may be, but there are those who would claim your race as evil as mine."

"So, further to my point, why help those who would kill you the first chance they get?"

"Because I have to believe I am still human. I have

to hold onto who I was before I became a vampyre. I'll not turn my back on my humanness," Mordred declared, even as he tried to convince himself it would be so.

"Do you accept your fate, then?"

"I will never accept that I am dead and have come back to life at Vlad's hands. But I will acknowledge that I am the Chosen One. I will do what I must to preserve humankind."

† † †

"I see I can no longer refer to you as a pup since you have brought the wolf here," Kabil hissed.

Mordred glanced at Dugald, who even in human form bore a look akin to a snarl. He was confused. "What is going on?"

A standoff seemed to be occurring between the King of the Narangatti and the shape-shifter.

"Wareckyn do not like vampyres," Dugald offered, his voice a low growl. He kept his eyes on the king, watching him warily.

"Vampyres despise Wareckyn," Kabil hissed.

Crossing his arms, Mordred allowed a smile to creep across his face and shook his head. "Just what I need, more people who hate each other. You two are going to get along. Kabil, meet Dugald the werewolf. Dugald, meet Kabil, King of the Narangatti."

Each nodded at the other stiffly, expressions unchanged.

"For the love of God, will you two quit? Dugald, if

you hate vampyres why did you stay with me?"
Mordred asked.

Dugald shifted, aware of a crackling sound beneath
his feet and quickly realized he stood on a pile of human
remains. He stepped away from the bones and scoffed.
"You have to ask why I don't like vampyres?"

Mordred glanced down and shrugged. He'd seen so
much death in his lifetime the bones failed to move him.

Dugald wandered away, investigating his surroundings, sniffing the air. "Mordred, you are not a full
vampyre, only half-born. You admit to still being human.
That is why I stayed with you," he replied at length.

"But your kind doesn't like humans either,"
Mordred continued.

"True, but we like vampyres even less."

Kabil shifted from human form to vampyre, flying
with his great scaled wings to a lofty perch. He peered
down at Mordred and Dugald with huge, black eyes.

"Oh, yes, the hypocritical Wareckyn," he said.
"They do not like the company of the soul stealers, but
they are no better. They are predators like us, though
they might pretend otherwise."

Mordred watched Dugald's eyes widen in horror at
seeing Kabil's true form. "You trust this being? This
Blood Drinker?"

"What choice do I have? I'm to battle the greatest
vampyre of all. I'll take any help I can get."

A tsking sounded on the dry air. Both Dugald and
Mordred glanced up to see Kabil shaking a bony finger
at Mordred. "Have you learned nothing so far? Vlad is
not a vampyre. He is worse."

"As if there could be anything worse," Dugald muttered.

"Hush. What do you mean, Kabil?"

Mordred felt a familiar blanket of confusion settling over him. Like the shadows in the tomb, it threatened to block all coherent thought from his mind.

Kabil took his time, delighting in the fact that he had the attention of both men. He rubbed his clawed hands together and spoke so softly Dugald and Mordred had to lean forward to hear him. "I am not a dead thing. I did not have a life and then lose it. I was not resurrected. I am a creature of the night, true, but no more no less than the lions in the desert or the falcon that flies in the sun. I am not undead. I have existed since the dawn of time alongside every other creature on this planet. I was brought to life by the Creators."

"And the difference between you and Vlad would be . . . ?" Dugald's brows were twin question marks.

Kabil left his perch and flew to another, sending a gust of sour air swirling through the chamber. "Vlad was brought back to life by man. He existed long ago in the time of the prophet, another savior, who died then, too, as he should have. Man resurrected him. In a quest for immortality, those in the highest orders of the Roman Catholic faith performed an ancient ceremony to bring him to life. They meant only to have him as a teacher and guide, in the hope that Vlad could bring them great power. But instead he fed off them, and their wickedness was in their blood. Now he is no longer controlled by them, but they do not realize it."

"Vlad is a dead man, a corpse reanimated? Then what am I?" Mordred questioned.

"You are a half-born," Kabil said derogatorily. "And the only hope humans have of salvation. Although you drink blood, you are not like Vlad. I tasted the goodness in you."

Dugald's jaw dropped in shock. "You let him drink from you? And you wonder why I think vampyres are disgusting?"

Mordred shot Dugald a black look. "Don't speak about things you've no knowledge of . . ."

Kabil interrupted, "Yes, I drank his blood to determine if he was the One. There have been too many false champions. I could not risk making a mistake."

"Vampyres are evil," came Dugald's snarl, "plain and simple."

"Nothing is simple, wolf!" Kabil roared and landed at Dugald's feet. He appeared much larger than he had moments before.

"Vampyres are not inherently evil because we feed on humans. Like any species there are bad ones however, those who violate the laws of their order, like you."

Dugald took an involuntary step backward, shocked by Kabil's apparent knowledge of his past.

"Vlad is evil," the king continued. "Mordred was bitten by Vlad, resurrected, and so he has Vlad's blood in him. But Mordred was a good soul once, before the kiss of life. He can fight the evil within him by turning to the good."

Rubbing his eyes, Mordred regained awareness of the exhaustion that had plagued him since finding *The Book of the Undead*.

Kabil smiled. "You must sleep, young one. You are in your infancy. The rest will bring you strength."

"There is no time to rest," Mordred mumbled, his words slurring.

"What's wrong with him?" Dugald asked, concerned.

"It is the vampyre way. He must rest."

Mordred fought against the desire to sleep, but his eyelids were growing heavier by the second, and it was a struggle to keep them open.

"When will he wake?" Dugald asked, watching Mordred slump to the ground.

Kabil approached Mordred, keeping an eye on Dugald and gently lifted him from the ground. Carrying him through the chamber to a great, gilded sarcophagus, lined in gold silk, Kabil laid the vampyre inside.

"He will sleep for years. We can only remain by his side and wait. Do not fear wolf, he will be stronger when he comes back to us. Stronger, and more able to battle Vlad."

"What of the other kings, and the quest? What about us? How long must we wait?"

Kabil laughed and walked to his own sarcophagus.

"We are immortal. We can wait forever, if that is how long it takes."

AUTHOR'S NOTE

This book is first and foremost a work of fiction. Among the pages you will find historical references to real places, people, events, and organizations. However I would like to make it clear that I have used these details for the benefit of the overall fantastical story, changing, embellishing, and recreating things as needed. This book has one purpose, and that is to provide entertainment.

Coming October 2005

THE RUTHLESS

BOOK TWO IN
THE LORDS OF DARKNESS
SERIES

BY L.G. BURBANK

PROLOGUE

Acrid smoke filled Mordred's nostrils as he edged closer to the enormous wall of flame. He should be burning being this close to the inferno. But while he could feel the fierce heat, he was in no danger from it. He was a vampyre.

A blanket of black smoke hovered, clinging to him, filling his eyes with darkness and shadow. The scent of death surrounded him, and nausea threatened when he recognized the smell of burning flesh. He inhaled and then coughed.

381

Mordred shivered. Something bad had happened.

Peering through the flames that looked as though they might touch the sky, he saw wooden posts rising from the ground. A huge pile of kindling had been set around the base of the posts, kindling that now provided fuel for the leaping flames. There was not a living thing in sight.

Then he heard the familiar voice. "Mordred," it called to him, the sound almost lost in the great roaring of the inferno.

Mordred looked around to be sure he was alone then focused his mind on the flames. He commanded the fire to part, allowing him to see what it was hiding from him in its brilliance.

Ever so slowly the flames subsided, allowing Mordred to see into them. But the sight that met his eyes was so gruesome and so horrific, he broke his concentration and lost control of the flame. The inferno blazed anew, and in the center of this terrible conflagration, Jakob stood lashed to a pole. The flesh of his face and body had peeled away from the bone. His skull was a charred mass fused to his body by the ropes that bound him. Yet his voice entered Mordred's mind.

Mordred closed his eyes to the image, denying it, as if by doing so he might be able to turn back time and avert the tragedy.

He swallowed hard. He could not lose control of the fire now. He must create a pathway. He forced his breathing to slow and again commanded the flames to part. He Then walked to Jakob's side.

His mentor's eyes were open, but Jakob was dead. He had been burned alive with several others. Mordred took in the hideous sight, recognizing the charred but still visible marking of the Templars on one unfortunate victim. The man who had taught him so much about what was to come, had been burned alive, along with the others of his order. But why? And if he was dead, how, had Mordred heard him?

"Seek your heritage, Mordred, and uncover your past. All is not as you have been told." Jakob's voice again. Confused, Mordred looked back at the burning figure, the fire coming ever closer to him.

"Do not mourn for me, Mordred. I am gone from this place. The quest is up to you alone now. You must not fail."

"Jakob, how can I hear you?"

"I leave this earthly plane, but my spirit will be with you when you need me. Go now, Mordred, you are in grave danger and must awaken."

"I don't understand? Who did this to you, and why?" Mordred wanted answers. He wanted to know who to kill.

But there was no response, only the crackling of the flames and the stench of burning flesh. Unsure as what to do, Mordred remained gazing on the remains of the man who'd been like a father to him. Anguish filled him and Mordred fell to his knees. Something welled from deep within him, and he released it in an agonized moan.

And so Mordred keened for the dead man, letting his grief and anger explode in a discordant symphony of sounds. It wasn't until he felt his own skin begin to bubble that Mordred realized he'd lost control of the flames, and he fled at last.

His vision went dark, and Mordred was left with only the image of Jakob burning alive. It branded itself in his mind and on his heart, and he vowed vengeance on those who had committed the atrocity. Hell would visit those who had destroyed the Templars, and its name was Mordred Soulis.

The Dream Thief

by Helen A. Rosburg

Fiction
ISBN# 1-932815-20-1
www.helenrosburg.com

Someone is killing young women in fifteenth century Venice. Someone who steals into their dreams and seduces them . . . to death.

Coming in 2005

Coming in 2005

DANIEL'S VEIL
R. H. STAVIS

IF YOU FOUND A BRIDGE TO THE OTHER SIDE, WOULD YOU CROSS IT?

Daniel O'Brady is a burned out cop. When he sees a child blown away by her own father, he's seen one murder too many. Grief stricken and questioning the validity and purpose of his life, he takes off for a drive in the countryside. Daniel's bad day is only beginning.

Regaining consciousness after the single car accident, an injured Daniel sets out to find help. What he finds is a quaint little village full of people who are more than happy to help him. He's given medical aid, food, clothing and shelter...and no one will take a dime from him. If that's not strange enough, after a few days in the tranquil town he discovers an odd house surrounded by streaks of an odd blue light. He decides to investigate.

Dr. Michael Hudson is a scientist bent on proving the existence of supernatural phenomena. His life is consumed with passion to prove his theory, to the exclusion of all else. When his research leads him to a house outside a small village in Northern California, he packs up his team and his equipment and sets out to document and prove his long-held belief in another dimension.

What both men discover will change their lives, and alter their souls, forever.

Paranormal
ISBN# 0-9743639-6-0
www.rhstavis.com

DISCONNECTION

by Erin Samiloglu

Horror
ISBN# 1-932815-24-4

There are no clues to the identity of a serial killer in New Orleans, until a young woman finds a stranger's cell phone. When it rings she answers, and finds herself connected to the killer's latest victim.

Coming in 2005

SIREN'S CALL

by MARY ANN MITCHELL

Fiction
ISBN# 1-932815-16-3

Sirena, a gorgeous exotic dancer, has an unusual hobby she practices in her free time. The guys who go home with her think they're about to get lucky. Actually, their luck has just run out.

Coming in 2005

THE CARDINAL'S HEIR

JAKI DEMAREST

Cardinal Richelieu is dead, a victim of poison. The throne of France, which he has long protected, is once more unstable as rival factions vie for power. But the Cardinal has appointed two heirs; one to his religious position, and one to head the elite spy ring that has maintained France's fragile political balance. Francoise Marguerite de Palis, the Cardinal's lovely but low born niece, is devastated by her uncle's murder, and vows revenge, which she sets out after immediately.

Though the task is daunting, she at least has some formidable tools at her command. Not only is she now the head of the Cardinal's Eyes, but is arguably the most powerful Sorciere in all France. Shapeshifting into her character Baccarrat, notorious swordsman, she sets out to find her uncle's murderer. But with an unexpected ally. Handsome and dashing Jean de Treville, head of the King's Musketeers, is saddened to learn of the Cardinal's death, though both headed groups not generally fond of one another. Sadness turns to stunned amazement, however, when he learns who has been appointed to lead the Cardinal's spy ring...and who is also, in fact, the swordsman who has bested him on numerous occasions.

Not to mention the beautiful, and untouchable, wife of Court favorite, Antoine de Palis. But just as there is more, much more, to the enchanting Francoise, so is there more than simple murder afoot. Side by side, Francoise and Jean descend into a maelstrom of magic as they battle another powerful Sorcier, and enter a bloody race to obtain a fabulous jewel. And the throne of France hangs in the balance, supported only by the magic and mastery of...

The Cardinal's Heir

Historical Fantasy
ISBN#1-932815-10-4

MEMORIES
OF
EMPIRE

by Django Wexler

Fantasy
ISBN# 1-932815-14-7

Amid rumors that the Ebon Death, an invincible warrior, has returned to plague the Empire, sorcerers and spirits battle for control of an ancient artifact.

Coming in 2005

Dark Planet
Charles W. Sasser

Kadar San, a human-Zentadon crossbreed distrusted by both humans and Zentadon, is dispatched with a Deep Reconnaissance Team (DRT) to the Dark Planet of Aldenia. His mission is to use his telepathic powers to sniff out a Blob assault-base preparing to attack the Galaxia Republic. Dominated by amazing insect and reptile forms and by an evil and mysterious Presence, Aldenia was once a base for the warlike Indowy who used their superior technology to enslave the Zentadon and turn them into super warriors deployed against humans.

The DRT comes under attack not only from savage denizens of the Dark Planet but also from the mysterious Presence, which turns team member against team member and all against Kadar San. The Presence promises untold wealth and power to the one among the team unscrupulous enough to unleash the contents of a Pandora's box-like remnant of Indowy technology. The possessor of the box poses a greater threat than the entire Blob nation, for he is capable of releasing untold horrors upon the galaxy.

Kadar San finds himself pitted one-on-one against a human killer, an expert sniper, in a desperate struggle to save the Republic and the human female with whom he has fallen in love. Like all Zentadon, however, Kadar San cannot kill without facing destruction himself in the process—and he has no choice but to kill. In order to save the galaxy from the dreaded box, Kadar San must face the truth that none will leave the Dark Planet.

Science Fiction
ISBN#1-932815-13-9
Coming in 2005

MEN OF
BRONZE
by Scott Oden

Historical Fiction/Hardcover
ISBN# 1-932815-18-X

Leading the fight to preserve the soul of Egypt is Hasdrabal Barca, Pharaoh's deadliest killer. When Greek mercenary, Phanes, defects to the Persians, it triggers a savage war that will tax Barca's skills, and his humanity, to the limit.

Coming in 2005